"THE CAGE is a that keeps you reading on and on: because you care about the characters in it and because the action/tension keeps building and building to a final, very satisfactory explosion. The physical cage that Megan hauls about both exemplifies and mocks the mind cage both she and Habiku are locked into; where she gradually manages to wear away her bars and escape, each twist and turn and deliberate cruelty strengthens his and there is an interesting counterplay between these two processes. What pleases me most (as a matter of personal taste) is the sense of community evoked—not only the complex and vividly realized societies depicted, but that among the much smaller group of focus characters. Megan and Shkai'ra are strong individuals but neither dominates the other or the story; it is the combination that triumphs—not the easiest thing in the world to pull off."

—*Jo Clayton*

THE CAGE

S.M. Stirling and Shirley Meier

THE CAGE

This is a work of fiction. All the characters and events portrayed in this book are fictional, and any resemblance to real people or incidents is purely coincidental.

A Baen Books Original

Baen Publishing Enterprises
260 Fifth Avenue
New York, N.Y. 10001

ISBN: 0-671-69836-2

Cover art by Larry Elmore

First printing, August 1989

Distributed by
SIMON & SCHUSTER
1230 Avenue of the Americas
New York, N.Y. 10020

Printed in the United States of America

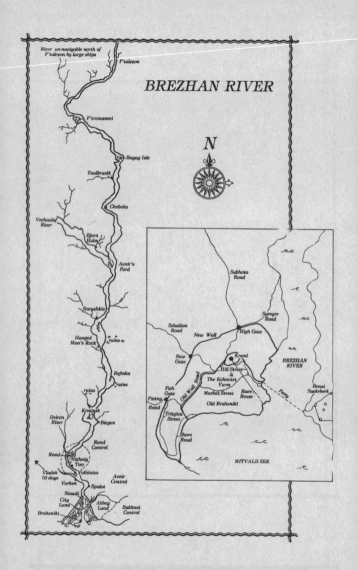

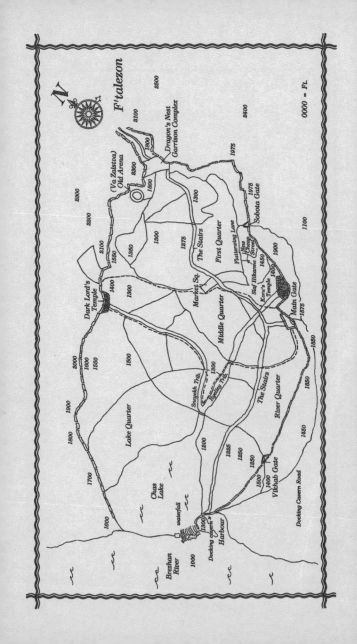

F'talezon

To Jo Clayton, for her kindness. To Shirley's Significant Other, for putting up with us while we wrote it. To Dave Kirby, for lending us the cottage. Most of all, to Jan.

Prologue

Habiku, you son of two brothers, I'm coming home. It's taken me two damned years. Three shipwrecks, outrunning pirates . . . You sold me off so far away you never thought I'd escape or make it back. I hope you're alive so I can kill you. Habiku Smoothtongue. Your flowery speeches aren't going to save you this time. Nothing will.

Chapter 1

THE SLAF HIKARME COUNTING HOUSE
BRAHVNIKI: DELTA OF THE BREZHAN RIVER
SVARTZEE, NORTH SHORE
TENTH IRON CYCLE, THIRD DAY, YEAR OF THE
  STEEL MOUSE
(*Late autumn*, 4973 A.D.)

The clerk looked up from scattering sand on the page and ostentatiously returned his attention to the ledger, trimming his pen with a deft *scrit-scrit* against the razor fastened in the mouth of the inkwell. One had to show this sort of poor trash that the Slaf Hikarme was a respectable House. He looked down his nose at the two women.

"I'm sorry, Teik," he said. "The Head Clerk is a very busy man. Do you have an appointment?" There was a vast difference between his side of the oak counter and theirs; a mercantile house in a trading city dealt with many questionable types, of necessity. Still, he was the guardian of the inner rooms, of respectability, property, order, especially against unseemliness like this—this ragamuffin.

The clientele were watching with interest, nine in a hall meant for twenty. A pity the House had fallen into such financial difficulty. The other two clerks kept their heads industriously bent over their ledgers, but he could feel their attention as well. He cleared his throat.

2

Oddly, the Zak woman who stood across the long wooden divider that split the outer chamber seemed neither daunted nor angry. Purebreed, he estimated, with a covert glance up from under his lids. Disturbingly familiar, though he couldn't think where he would have met such riffraff. Scarcely four feet tall, skin pale under its weathered tan, eyes and hair raven-black; none of the swagger you saw in a tavern bravo, but there were well-used knives in her belt, two more in her boots and a stiletto hilt peeking out from one sleeve. Plain dark grey tunic and trousers and cloak, stained with salt spray.

Off a ship in from the Mitvald, then, even if her accent was F'talezonian and that mother city of her race was far upriver. Nothing unusual in Brahvniki.

The Zak sighed and crooked a finger. "The pen you've just sharpened will do nicely." The clerk found himself handing it to her. She snagged a scrap of paper out of the stack by his elbow, ignoring his yip of, "That's expensive!", and wrote. She turned the page around and pushed it across the desk so he could read the words "Megan Whitlock, F'talezon, Owner Slaf Hikarme."

The collar of his mercantile robe seemed a bit tight, the room too warm, even though he hadn't put a fresh scoopful of blackrock on the stove in an hour. He took a deep breath. "Teik," he said, drawing strength from his position. "You must understand that anyone could fake a signature. I'm sorry, Head Clerk Vhsant is busy. I'm just doing my job." There hadn't been someone claiming to be Whitlock for more than a year. The owner was presumed, though not officially declared, dead.

The Zak looked back at her companion. "Even after he's seen my signature, this officious *person* is telling me I can't walk into my own office, Shkai'ra."

Now the one leaning against the lacquered inner door, *that* one was unusual. Tall and fair-haired; well, a Thane or Aenir might be so . . . but no folk he knew had quite that cast of feature, slanted grey eyes over high cheeks, scimitar blade of nose with a tiny gold ring through one nostril, pointed chin and wide, thin-lipped mouth; and she was smiling at him.

Teeth and eyes pale against dark-tanned skin; not much more than the mid-twenties of her Zak companion. Worn horse-hide jacket and chamois pants, worn bone plaques on the long hilt of her saber. One hand rested on the brass eagle-head pommel of the sword, the other hooked a thumb through her belt; thick-wristed hands, long fingers, thin white scars on the backs. She was smiling and resting completely re-laxed, ignoring the two guards with their weighted staffs.

The blonde woman spoke. "You do him, Megan, or I?" Guttural accent, staccato. Brahvniki was not a well-policed city, and the Watch might be a while in arriving.

The Zak leaned forward and tapped on the wood with a clawed finger. "You probably don't remember working for me, Teik—Yareslav? You were only an underclerk then, but you might recognize me if you think very hard. Don't make stupid decisions on your own. I suggest that you call Vhsant Cormarenc." She was using the Head Clerk's old use-name, before the owner's proxy, Habiku, had elevated him to the position. She knew names. Maybe . . . *Great Bear, the Zak does look uncannily like* . . . No. The owner was dead. The two guards, Bhodan and Anjevitch, watched with bovine patience from their bench. Otherwise the stone chamber was as it always was, bare, growing slightly seedy over these last two years of fading prosperity. The others waiting their turn . . . Two glanced at each other, stood, left in a casual stroll that grew hurried at the door. Yareslav hoped they were going for the Watch. Svorbodin the slaver glanced up from his laptop abacus, away, snapped his glance back. A hurried whisper to his second, and *they* left, sidling along the wall. The other five sought corners and leaned back to watch.

His eyes fell. The Zak woman was digging her claws impa-tiently into the hard oak of the counter, beside the lectern that held his accountbook. Steel nails, not strapped on but growing from the flesh: razor edged, hard steel, on small strong hands with shackle-scars around the wrists. That was an expensive operation; you needed an expert such as could only be found in F'talezon, the Zak capital, and it had its drawbacks; the iron was drawn from your blood, somehow. It took a certain type of mind to *want* that sort of operation.

Very expensive, very rare. The nails went *shriiink* into the wood, along his nerves, the hard wood splintering and fraying . . . *My counter*, he thought.

Megan Whitlock had bought that peculiar sorcery. She had been *dead* these past two years, he repeated to himself, Habiku had said so. This woman couldn't be . . . Trembling, his hand went under the counter, tugged at a hidden string. She was close enough, across the counter, close enough for him to scent the woodsmoke and salt in the cloak, like any poor client of the House bringing their smells in among books and ink and counting-beads.

"Teik—" he stammered.

The door behind him opened with a gust of warm stale air. A voice boomed. Vhsant, the office supervisor. *Oh, Sacred Bear, Honey-Giving One, thank you, thank you*, Yareslav thought.

The Zak was looking beyond him. "Well, Vhsant, you petit larceny piss-ant, are *you* going to recognize me?" The junior clerk eased himself thankfully off the stool and moved carefully aside.

The Head Clerk sat down, almost smoothly. He was a heavy man but not fat, bearded. He waited a moment, meeting the Zak's eyes before speaking; his voice was soft, the pale scribe's face calm, but Yareslav knew he had recognized the founder of the House. *Whitlock. It is*. Yareslav started edging away. When she found out what had happened while she was gone . . . Under the edge of the counter, where she couldn't see it, Vhsant's hand slowly clenched. Yareslav saw a slight sheen of sweat at his hairline.

He's shaken, the underclerk thought. *I've never seen him this, ah, flustered before*.

"Woman," the Head Clerk told the Zak, without waiting for her to say any more. "You have some superficial resemblance to the unfortunately deceased owner of the House of the Sleeping Dragon. If you think you can take advantage of a slight resemblance to Megan Whitlock, and take over a thriving business, you are mistaken. Guards, expel them."

Bhodan and Anjevitch rose and stepped forward; they were brother and sister, peasants expelled from the Benai—the

Abbey's—lands for brawling. They were as tall as the blonde
foreigner who stood between them and Megan Whitlock,
more massive, with arms and shoulders that had rolled logs,
wrestled young bulls, cleared rocks from fields. They had the
instincts of professionals; they spread, wasting no time on
words, coming in on the foreigner from either side with staffs
swinging, ready for their opponent to break the peace-bond
seal on her saber. Yareslav watched, fascinated.

Clack. The sister's staff struck the scabbarded blade the
blonde stranger had drawn, sheath and all, from her belt-
loops. *Tack*, the foreign woman touched down again from the
leap that had taken her over the metal-shod ashwood Bhodan
swung at her knees. She turned, pivoted on the balls of her
feet toward the brother, moving with a smooth leopard grace
that made the siblings look heavy, slow. The brass pommel of
the saber snaked out behind her, struck the top of Anjevitch's
kneecap with the sound of a butcher's mallet breaking bone.
She wailed, doubled, her face coming down to meet a booted
heel striking backward and up. There was a crackling like
small twigs thrown on a hot fire and the peasant sank to her
knees, one hand pressed to her face. She reached a trembling
hand to the floor, slid down and lay still, moaning.

A few hardy spectators remained, backing out of the blonde
woman's way as Bhodan roared, advancing with blow after
blow that would have splintered oak. Somehow the staff
never quite seemed to reach the figure that backed before
him. She spun, holding the sheathed sword in both hands. It
snaked out in deflection-parries against the wood staff that
would have snapped it with a square blow. A moment, and
the remaining guard thrust his weapon in a move that should
have pinned her against the wall behind. Instead, it pinned
him, as the steel tip clanked immovably against the wall for a
single crucial instant.

The saber hilt punched up two-handed, struck his nose; he
felt something crumble in the forepart of his head, and the
room blurred. A looping foot coming at him, impossible
angle, impact like an explosion on the side of his head. He
sagged, as the world slipped sideways. He fell to lie next to
his sister.

Yareslav, backed against one of the locked cabinets, heard a choked-off sound from his superior. Vhsant was still sitting at the stool, but Megan was sitting as well. On the counter, with her fingertips resting on the middle-aged clerk's bull throat, fingers and thumb along the line of the arteries and dimpling the soft flesh without quite cutting it. Or . . . As he watched, a slow red trickle started out from beneath the little finger.

Megan looked at it in annoyance. "Nicked. Have to file it out." She glanced over her shoulder. Bhodan was still conscious, after a fashion; the blonde woman stood over him, saber in one hand, a boot on his neck below the Adam's apple; she was still wearing the same slight smile, and gradually increasing the pressure.

"Shkai'ra!"

She glanced up.

"That is, in a manner of speaking, my employee." Megan's face was an angry mask, her tone dry, and her hand flexed slightly, harmlessly, bringing a sudden explosive gasp from Vhsant as he felt the outer layer of skin nick and part under the razor edges.

"Killjoy," Shkai'ra replied, with a disappointed shrug. She lifted the boot.

The Zak woman slid forward. Vhsant gagged and somehow got off the stool; Megan eased forward just enough and her hand never moved from his throat. The other two clerks had backed against the wall, and one made a small sound of protest. Megan ignored him and stared into the Head Clerk's eyes.

"You," she said. "As I understand it from rumors I heard on board ship and in the city, and the evidence of my own eyes, have been dealing with slavers." Vhsant tried to shake his head, and stopped, very quickly. "You have been using my name and seals to do some—shall we say, less than moral things. It might be that this was all Habiku's idea, so I might give you the benefit of the doubt. *My* doorkeeper dead? Two hired strong-arms needed *inside*? Barely enough business to support *three* clerks instead of a half-dozen? Vhsant, I won't fire you yet, not until I know more about what's going on, but

I think I should have a very good look at what you've been doing." He tried to speak, stopped again as she *tsked* and shook her head. "Slavers, Vhsant. You know that I hated slavers before. That hatred's gone a bit deeper. Maybe you should see what it is to be a slave?" She raised her free hand in front of his face. A red glow built around her fingers, reflected in his eyes.

"You've never been on a tight-pack slave ship, have you, Vhsant?" Megan's voice was as pale as her face. "You don't know what you've been selling people into. I think you should." He paled, started to sweat, made a convulsive movement. "I spent three days in a middle rank, before we were exercised," Megan said conversationally, though she was breathing hard, white lines of tension around her eyes. "I had a corpse on one side, a child with dysentery above . . ."

He was swallowing, his skin turning a pale greyish-green, his eyes locked on something only he could see reflected in the glow of her hand. Then he crumpled, closing his eyes, flinging a hand up to block what he saw, crying, "No, make it go away! Please, Teik Megan, Zar Whitlock—"

"*Yareslav!*"

Her voice cracked out, and the underclerk felt her attention shift for a moment. "Fetch my seals. NOW!" The clerk scrabbled at the officer-supervisor's belt, grabbed the key and scurried into the office. From the open door Megan could hear the rattle and creak as the strongbox was unlocked, the hurried scuffle as he searched for the seals, the slam as the lid came down again. He almost ran across the room and put the House seal and her personal seal on the counter beside her.

"Very prompt," she said and dropped her hands. "I'm glad you recognized me, Vhsant. I'm also glad you've kept my personal seal. Green jade is expensive." He raised his head out of shaking hands. She slid down from the counter.

"Until I know more, you're on leave from any work in my House. Get this mess cleaned up, then get out, until I call you back, *if* I call you back. Yareslav, I saw the healer's sign still up on the corner; I think the two Shkai'ra downed will need him."

The junior clerk bowed. Megan looked up, one corner of

her mouth quirked into a smile; Shkai'ra had transferred her foot to Bhodan's chest. "You can let him up now, Shkai'ra. He's finally realizing that he really does work for me!" The Kommanza grinned back at her.

The blonde hung her sheathed sword back on her belt and rose, giving her wrists and arms a brief, businesslike shake. "If this is the quality of the opposition, it'll be easier than you thought," she said.

"I wouldn't judge by this and get too superior," the Zak said. "It won't all be this easy." Megan strode toward the office at the back, then stopped. "I'm closing this office for the rest of the day," she said, looking at the two remaining clients in the outer office, who were still watching as Shkai'ra walked away from the moaning guard. "Accept my apologies, teikas. All transactions are suspended until I clean House."

Megan and Shkai'ra paused under the carved blackwood sign outside, after the Zak locked the door and stuck the keys in her belt, waiting for the street to be cleared. In front of the Slaf Hikarme's counting house the drivers of two oxcarts, one piled high with round cheeses, the other bulging with bales of wool, stood and waved their goads and yelled insults over which of them had right of way. Around them the street bustled; wool-capped sailors jostled on the narrow, split-log way that kept everyone up out of the delta mud; buildings of timber and rubble and brick leaned out to almost meet overhead. A juggler in bright robes balanced improbable things thrown him by his audience at one corner of the ex-whorehouse. A squad of the Watch trailed by, bored shopkeepers and artisans in rusty kettle-helmets and leather corselets, their polearms canted every which way; one carelessly snagged the backhook of her halberd in a line of washing and yanked, dumping the laundry in the mud. Curses and a flung chamberpot followed.

Shkai'ra noticed the Rand first for his robe; it was ankle-length, of blue silk and embroidered with dragons in thread of gold and silver, with garnets and lapis for eyes and scales. *Wouldn't mind having that myself*, she mused. Too short for her, the man's head only came to her eye-level, but it could be

made over into a nice coat. *Quick thump on the head and
. . . No, not here.* The man wasn't bad-looking either, supple
saffron-skinned handsomeness, with a cat on his shoulder . . .

Not a cat. Cat *looking*, with Siamese points, but the tail
. . . the tail was like a monkey's, loosely curled around the
man's throat. At first she thought it was wrapped in a toast-
brown fur; then it unfurled one three-foot wing and fanned
the air, knocking off a sailor's hat and receiving a resentful
glare. Bat-style wing, with a claw on the leading edge and the
skin webbing between elongated finger bones. The Rand
reached up and tickled it under the chin; the eyes slitted and
it purred for a moment, then crouched with its wings stretched
back. The man let his hand fall, and the cat-thing sprang into
the air, dropped, caught itself with a thunderclap wingbeat,
thrashed its way aloft through the narrow ways of the rooftops
and soared with late afternoon sunlight on its wings, a plain-
tive *meeorrow* trailing behind.

"What *is* that thing?"

"Hmm? What? Oh, that. It's a flitter or wingcat." Megan
shrugged. "Expensive this far south. You can pay a hunter a
month's wage for a flitterkitten. Luxury item."

Shkai'ra stood looking up at the soaring feline musingly.
"Hell on pigeons."

THE KCHNOTET VURM, BRAHVNIKI
EVENING

Megan leaned on the window of their room and looked out
at Brahvniki, down at the grey slate and brown thatched roofs
fading into shadow patterns in the long shadows of autumn
twilight. The towers of The Kreml on the highest point were
like teeth against the cloudy sky, onion domes, patterned tile
and gilding. The street beneath, bustling with Bravnikians
hurrying home, was cobbled with worn round stones from
the river. Faintly she could hear the wooden flute of a street
musician over the rumble of hooves and boots and the shrill
groaning of an oxcart's ungreased wheels. A working port, full
of smells of sea and the silty odors of the great river. She

craned her neck to see the white dome of the outermost spire of the Benai across the river.

Behind her, Shkai'ra Mek Kermak's-kin put hands to hips and pivoted a slow circle on one heel. "Best room?" she asked. All the furnishings were old but sound, like the inn itself. There were deep troughs in the oak doorsill, foot-worn. The Kchnotet Vurm wasn't the best in the city but it certainly wasn't the worst; what had Megan said—ah yes, the "noisiest." Around her feet a battered black tomcat wound, blinked, seemed to stretch out in an arc that landed on the bed; there he sat like a small idol, eyes slitted, forefeet kneading happily into the softness.

"*Dah.*" Megan came in and closed the shutter so the candleflame steadied.

"We've had better," the Kommanza continued. Although they had known what she meant when she asked for an armor stand; no matter how carefully you packed a suit, it was better for the lacings if you stood it upright. She stood back to admire hers standing in the corner, the liquid shine of the black-lacquered surfaces and scarlet trim. Then she gave the fiberglass backings a quick inspection; they could come loose from the bullhide if the glue went moldy, and all the gods knew it had been trouble enough dragging it from the other side of the Lannic. The watertight chest had saved their lives once though, keeping them afloat through a shipwreck.

"And worse," Megan said. "At least we're not head to heels with seventeen other travellers." Megan was unpacking *her* personal chest; books, scrolls, curios, a collection of knives ranging from tiny things that could be bent into a beltbuckle or held concealed in a palm to miniature shortswords. Last of all, a needlesword with a bell guard. She considered it almost distastefully, then leaned it against the wall by the bed. "Much worse, if—" She stopped and clapped a hand to her forehead as Shkai'ra set up a small six-armed joss on the windowledge. "Oh, no, no more sacrifices in our bedroom!"

The tall woman shrugged. "Glitch can have his sheep outside."

"Thank you Koru, Goddess. Much worse places, if you

remember that fisher shack we were stuck in all last winter on that damned island—"

"Not so bad, once the smell faded," Shkai'ra said, bouncing experimentally on the bed. "If there'd been any place to *go*, we wouldn't have ended up so near murdering each other." A grin. "Not that we didn't find *some* things to occupy our time, eh? Mind you, you're near as bad on shipboard, when you can't have a cabin to yourself; and you a riverboat captain! Half the time up the mast, especially those last few days."

Megan laid down the bag of clothing and locked eyes with her companion. "This . . ." She moistened her lips. "I've been two years away, kh'eeredo." She paused, remembering. "I've never told you *that* story, have I?"

Shkai'ra unlatched the walrus-ivory buckles on her boots and braced heel against instep to pull them off. "No," she said, turning on one side and lying propped up on an elbow. "Not the details, just that Habiku was your second and betrayed you." She reached out a hand, a brief light touch. "Got the impression he was . . . hmmm, likeable but suspicious. Hard to distrust someone likeable; which is why we Kommanza try so hard to dislike everybody." The blonde woman smiled, a quiet, almost shy expression, unlike her usual raffish grin. "Make an exception for you, kh'eeredo."

Megan smiled back, sat down on the bed. "Thanks; after more than a year of sleeping together, it's nice to know." She poked Shkai'ra in the ribs with her bare toe. "Up on the mast I'd think about him, too," she said, going very quiet, very still. "The night he betrayed me he came in after his swim, carrying an expensive bottle of wine—" *A Yeoli wine. A Terahan 1541 by their reckoning, year of the Ash Gryphon.*

"I had been watching him like a cat at a mousehole because I suspected everyone then. I thought he'd been the start of a couple of abortive attempts against me but I had no proof. Oh, he was so careful. He never pushed me. Never mocked me. Never threatened my—my stability, you might say. He was a good sailor, knew the river like he knew the inside of his eyelids. So good. So patient with my quirks." She smiled bitterly. "And it was all lies, of course."

"I can tell you word for word what happened. 'Captain,' he

says in that soft voice of his. 'I . . . we thought it appropriate
to bring you this.' I should have known. I should have realized, but I never thought he'd do something so obvious as to
offer me a gift. He told me it was a combination name day
and birthday gift from the crew." *He grinned at me, eyes
twinkling.* "He had some story about how little I paid them
so they could only afford one gift."

Megan's hand tightened on the wooden rail of the foot-
board. "I was stupid enough to believe him. It flustered me.
I even thanked him." *I stammered and blushed like an idiot.
He even got a smile out of me. Even Shyll didn't make me
sputter like that.* "He even pretended to drink a glass with
me." Megan let the coils of her braids down and scrubbed at
her temples; the silverwhite streak in her hair caught at the
light of the flame.

"I still remember locking the door behind him; thinking
that his smile was a bit strange. Then I remember the dizzi-
ness. I had enough time to stagger over to my chair, wondering why the ship was rocking like that, and I heard the leather
hinges as he opened my door. '*I'm sorry that you trusted me,*'
is what he said. 'I'm sorry you trusted me!' The fishgutted
bastard had dosed me with God'sTears. The last I recall
before I woke up aboard the slave ship is him wrapping me in
a cloak and lifting me. I still haven't figured out why he didn't
just drop me overboard. I suppose he had a grudge and
thought I'd hurt more if he sold me safely far away. Stupid of
him."

"*Ia,*" Shkai'ra said, in her own tongue. For a moment teeth
showed between thinned lips, and the skull beneath her fair
skin glanced out through her face. "Very foolish . . ."

Megan stretched, shook the memory out of her head as she
combed out her hair with her fingers, scratched Ten-Knife-
Foot under his chin; he was getting grey there like a jowly
old man. A purr rewarded her as she watched Shkai'ra get up
to make a minor adjustment to the incense sticks in front of
the idol. "Don't you think that the little godlet of fuck-ups
might ignore us more if you didn't keep dinning your presence into his ears?"

"Hai!" Shkai'ra snorted. "He'd be mortally offended if I

ignored him. After all, if it hadn't been for him, Fehinna would have been *much* worse." She sighed: her memories of that kingdom of peculiar savageries were happy, mostly. It was where Megan and she had met, after all; Megan come west-over-sea across the Lannic, she herself wandering down from the interior of Almerkun, from the prairies.

"Imagine the things that could have gone wrong on top of what *did* happen." she continued.

Ten-Knife-Foot stretched and stalked regally across the bed and out the open window. Shkai'ra's mood darkened; the cat walked a little more stiffly than he had. The *Zinghut Muth'a*, the Black Crone, had her hand on him, as on all that lived.

What hasn't gone wrong for me, one time or another? she thought. Exile—well, that had been her own choice. Bitter memory arose: Stonefort, in the Komman of Granfor. The draughty halls of the keep and smoking fires and the roaring clamor of the Salute rising to the morning sun from a tower. Riding the spring steppe, through a foam of flowers, a sweetness so strong it made you drunk like lifewater or cloudberry mead; the bow in her hands and the coughing grunt of the tiger about to charge. Feasting, dancers wild with dreamsmoke leaping the firetrench; the pride of bearing the godborn Mek Kermak blood, offering to the Mighty Ones; victory, glory . . .

And winter bivouacs, her mind prompted. Riding picket against nomad raiders, sacked villages and children roasted and eaten over the embers of their homes. Fleas and filth and cruelty, the endless intrigues of power, knives in the dark, poison in the cup, arrows out of the sloughgrass thickets. Each season a repetition of the last, fighting to hold the wild folk at bay long enough to bring in the harvest. The bottomless black pits of a shaman's eyes, windows into a soul rotted empty with drugs and sacrifice and magic . . .

Long years after that. Drifting southward from the valley of the Red River, selling the skills with horse and lance and bow that were all a Kommanz aristocrat knew. A mercenary's life, a war without purpose or end; squalid siege camps and the dread of fever, loot that always somehow dribbled through your fingers and left you with less than you had before. One campaign after another, fly-blown bodies under southern suns, peasants staring at you with sick brutalized eyes as you rode by the swollen-bellied village children, a comrade's scream as the pikepoint went into her belly, climbing a storming-ladder as the flamethrower nozzles turned their blackened snouts toward her . . .

Until I reached the shores of the Lannic and met you, she thought, looking up from her musings to Megan. *Since then it's all seemed . . . fresher, somehow. Or is it only that you had a purpose, and a goal?*

"Fehinna was . . ." She paused. "Fun."

Megan snorted. "If you define *fun* as nearly being eaten alive in the sewers by the crawlers, tortured, chased by the Sniffers . . ."

Shkai'ra lay back on the bed and linked her hands behind her head. "Fun rescuing you, kh'eeredo," she amplified. "And just think, Baiwun hammer me flat and Jaiwun strike me barren, if I hadn't decided to rescue you one more time on the docks, I wouldn't have been chased on board ship and you wouldn't have had someone to look after you all these weary years—"

"*Rescue?*" Megan whirled and pounced, landing with knees astride Shkai'ra's chest, grabbed a red-blonde braid in each hand. "If I had to list all the times a certain loud, clumsy, often drunken, large, over-sexed—" She interrupted herself to pull Shkai'ra's head up to kiss her. "—barbarian had to be *rescued*! How about the beams of a certain sweet factory? Or a plank floating on the open ocean? Or a ledge in—" Shkai'ra reached up and shut her up by kissing her, grabbed her in a hug around her back and rolled on top of her. Megan went with it, relaxed, wrapped her legs around and squeezed.

The Kommanza smiled, gasped and wheezed, "hhEnough! You'll squeeze the breath out of me!" With one hand she reached up and began tickling Megan under the short ribs and they rolled over on the bed, wrestling. Then the Kommanza had her pinned, used her weight—

"Shkai'ra. Let. Go." Megan's voice was flat. She lay still under Shkai'ra, her good-natured struggles gone in the snap of a finger. Shkai'ra heard the panic in her voice and stopped, let go. This had happened before. Somehow the old fear would well up in the Zak woman, a fear that Sarngeld, who had owned her when she was a child, had carefully cultivated. *The one asshole's making her vulnerable to the second*, Shkai'ra thought. Megan lay still, clenched her fists so she wouldn't claw her lover, and shivered.

"I'm sorry, *akribhan*. I try. I try so hard sometimes but when you just hold me down, I look up and it doesn't matter that I love you, that I know you, that you'd never hurt me . . ."

"Shush, I know. It's all right, *kh'eeredo*." Shkai'ra grinned, a bit forcedly, and tickled Megan's chin with one of her braids. "I know it isn't me you're afraid of." She hugged, warm and careful. More careful than anyone outside this room would have believed. She raised herself on one elbow and traced Megan's mouth as the Zak lay in the crook of her arm, looking troubled. "It's getting better. I should know."

Megan turned and pressed her face into Shkai'ra's shoulder. "I'm just tired of being afraid."

"I know." Over the Zak's dark head, Shkai'ra's face darkened as she thought of Sarngeld, but he was dead and out of reach. Ten-Knife jumped up on the bed, looking proud of himself, and dropped a large dead rat on them; his first kill on a new territory. Megan laughed at Shkai'ra's shout of outrage.

"Out! OUT, you rabid night-stalker! Oh, *sheepshit*, Megan, he's gone under the bed with it. Stop laughing! It isn't funny at all!"

Chapter 2

MANOR OF THE SLEEPING DRAGON
F'TALEZON, UPPER BREZHAN RIVER
NEW CHEAPSTREET, NEAR THE LADY SHRINE
TENTH IRON CYCLE, SIXTH DAY

Habiku threw himself down by the lapdesk under the east
window, smiling.

He was a small man, though tall for one with Zak blood,
with fine-chiseled features, somewhat gone to good living, as
if a sculptor had taken a statue of a strongly muscled athlete
and coated it with an inch of yellow tallow that had sagged
with heat. His eyes were a clear amber color, and the curly
brown hair still refused to be tamed by a comb, dropping one
lock down over his right eye. His cream-colored tunic was
immaculate, with white lace at the throat as well as the
wrists.

"Master." Lixa, his debt-slave, handed him his goblet. Her
voice was soft and pleasing. "There is word from the south."
The rain was turning to light, slushy snow. He looked at her
and was annoyed by her quietness. He had worked hard to
get it, but had bought the woman for her wildness as well as
her resemblance to the dead . . . He leaned back into the
office cushions. Windows ringed them all around save where
the door led to the stairwell; it had been *her* office, as *she*
had furnished it. The cushions, the teakwood lapdesk and hangings were from all along the Brezhan, even an abstract piece

17

from the teRyadn steppe to the east. Of course, *he* no longer had to defer to her love of barrenness; there were Raku spirit-poles between the windows now, carved scarlet satin-wood inlaid with mother-of-pearl. On a bronze stand was a Hriis prayer-box, fantastically ornate with gold and scroll-work. Idly, he wondered how the Karibal river pirates had come by it. Luckily they had no eye for fine things; bright-ness and gaud caught their eye, like magpies, and they charged accordingly. *Although they've acquired a shrewd sense of what gold means to us,* he mused; it was odd, considering that they were scarcely even human, now. Schotter had picked it out for him, down in Brahvniki; the Thane merchant had a talent for finding jewels among trash. He raised an immacu-late eyebrow at Lixa.

"Well?"

"There is word from Teik Schotter Valders'sen. Things are going well in Brahvniki, but there was a fight at the counting house. He sent a letter with details. It's on the desk."

"Hmm. Well, I'll read it later. I'm sure they handled it." His eyes focused on her and he smiled, a baring of teeth that had nothing to do with affection. She was one of the reasons he was glad his mother's rooms were far away. Lixa was a tiny woman, just over four feet tall, with clear white skin and ebony black hair, classically Zak. She was staring at her bare feet so that her eyes were hidden but he knew the color matched her hair. "You're a lovely piece, Lixa." He was disappointed that she didn't react. She used to. She stood, silent and tense, until he beckoned with his ringless hand. "Come, come, my dear. We wouldn't want your parents to hear of your dumb-beast insolence, now, would we?"

She stepped into his reach, passive. He ran a proprietary hand down her hip, feeling her quiver, feeling her want to move away. He left his hand on her, waiting to see if she'd fight him.

"No, master," she said, eyes downcast, hiding the hate he knew was there. He smiled silkenly.

"Remember, darling. I own you and all of your kin. Your parents are too old to take your beatings. You want to please me, don't you?"

"Vilist, Teik."

"Well, that's good. I will be dining with my mother. You will come to my room this evening."

"Yes, Teik."

He watched her as she walked to the inlaid wooden door of his sanctum, bare feet soundless on the plush green rug, then scraping faintly on the grey stone, irritated by the subdued tilt of her shoulders under her wool shift. The light oak of the slave-links hanging from neck to one wrist clicked as she moved. It had taken so much to get quiet answers from her. It had been so enjoyable. It was no coincidence that she was small, and dark, and had been wild. He *owned* Lixa and Lixa looked like *her* . . . but Whitlock was gone, dead. Vhsant had killed her. The slave would look better if he had her bleach the colour from the lock of hair at the temple.

Life is good, he thought.

EARLY EVENING
BALCONY AROUND THE ATRIUM
OF THE SLAF HIKARME

Habiku strolled down the third floor corridor toward his mother's quarters.

Arches to his right opened onto the central courtyard. The milky white glow through the steel-bound alabaster roof was faint and the lanterns hanging from the metal girders were giving off their glow and a faint scent of heated canola oil.

He drew a deep breath of it, along with the eternal F'talezonian scents of wool rugs and slightly damp stone, the wealth-smells of polished wood and wax and incense. Windows to his left were sizable panes of rare imported Arkan plate glass trimmed to fit the pointed arches. Snow tapped faintly against the glass and melted, streaking the view of the narrow strip of brown lawn about the house; *that* was an arrogant boast of power, within the walls of the City, where space was always precious.

The streaked glass blurred his view west, down to the river, but memory painted the details. F'talezon was a mountain city, built up a sloping, V-shaped valley with its broad end facing the water and a long stream dividing it; there was a lake between the city and the Brezhan, and water tumbled into the greater stream over a natural cliff and moving floodgates of metal that were one of the wonders of the northern world. Down there was the Lake Quarter, where the untouchable corpse-handlers and poor foreigners and vagrants dwelt in hovels built among three thousand years of ruins.

A long climb. He had lived there once, a tall blond half-foreign child in this witch city whose folk were small and dark and despised all outsiders. The more so if their poverty left them nothing but their Zak blood to take pride in.

F'talezon was like that: a grey, aged pile that had seen the days of its glory come, and go, and come again, until the layers and the legends ran together as the crumbling buildings did . . . A long climb up the valley, there were ancient, obscene jokes of how each class drank the piss of the one above. Tumbled, steep-pitched roofs of dark slate over buildings of plain dark stone, the fringing cliffs on either side tunneled like maggot-ridden cheese with old mines and quarries, still worked or abandoned or made over into teeming warrens for the poor, back into darkness where only rumor went.

The Upper City; the town houses of nobles built on the rents of their estates, homes of merchant princes and shipowners wealthy from the river traffic; shrines to the Lady and the Dark Lord, and the DragonLord's palace, the Dragon's-Nest, blocking the narrow way into the crater at the mountain's summit.

A long climb, and he meant to go further yet. He was owner, head of House and household; he let the feeling sweep over him again. This had been *her* house, before she . . . died. *Two years,* he thought. The disposal, neat and clean and impossible to trace: but then, Megan Whitlock had been nothing but the child of weavers, self-made, her parents dead and no kin but a few dockside riffraff. It had been profitable to dispose of her; his secret backers had been glad to see the end of the troublesome Whitlock with her habit of carelessly slashing threads of intrigue as she passed.

In the mean streets, on icy decks, when his mother tried to make him take the last bowl of amaranth gruel and pretend she had eaten earlier, the manor of the Sleeping Dragon was what he had dreamed all the long years: safe, secret, enclosed.

The door to her chambers. Inside, he could hear the slave reading to her: it was one of the old Enchian chronicles, the epic of the first Curlion. Absurdly, it made him feel nervous again. As it had when he was a child, summoned to his lessons in the "women's quarters." His mouth quirked. That had been two rooms at the rear of the apartment, his mother's isolation self-imposed. His father had not cared; a Zak ClawPrince might keep a foreign mistress, but the heritage of ancient Enchian nobility and their customs meant little inside the walls of the Zak city.

Mother never forgot what she was, he thought grimly. Pirates, auction block or no, she was Latialia. The *Amam* Latialia. Tor Ench counted itself true heir and descendant of Iyesi, the first empire humankind had made after the Earned Fire; across the millennia, they remembered.

His father had had little time for him; a foreign bastard, with naZak looks and no hint of inner power. Habiku's eyes narrowed. Zak law did not allow any child to be completely disinherited. Mother had always been there; there was always the two of them, when the Zak children chased him home with jeers and rocks and tricks that he was too young to ignore. But Mother had told him of his heritage, beside which F'talezon was nothing but a backwoods pile of stone. The Zak might have been here since the Earned Fire, but what had they ever done to equal Tor Ench? He had his mother to thank that he knew civilized ways.

Now she has a real manor, he thought with satisfaction and rare happiness. *Everything she needs.* He raised a hand and scratched formally at the door.

"One would enter," he said carefully in her own language.

The slave's voice trailed off; he heard the girl moving to the door.

"The *Amam* says that her son, the strength of her age, need ask for nothing." The door swung open.

The rooms within were spacious; they had been Megan's,

the best the manor had to offer. They were conveniently far from his own, since there was much of his life it was necessary to keep from his mother.

Latialia had furnished them in the classic Tor Enchian style; it was the first time she had been able to, in her life in F'talezon, and Habiku did not much like it. The outer halls were still decorated as Meg . . . she had liked them, warm colors but spare, depending on the purity of line in a single chair or picture to fill the space exactly rather than cluttering with many things. Inside . . . the costly rugs were well enough; bright, abstract patterns on wool soft as maiden's hair. Tapestries covered the walls, of Latialia's own embroidering; most were scenes from The Vengeance of Curlion on the Rebels, an odd subject for someone he had rarely even heard raise her voice in anger. On the hammered brass table rested a pipe, a fantasy of spun purple glass and gently bubbling waters, its mouthpiece carved of ivory. It had been filling the air with the burnt sweetness of poppy resin. He scowled at it; the pipe was new, but the scent familiar, a companion of his youth.

She's lonely, he thought. There was no one in F'talezon she could really talk to; the noble families received her reluctantly, even if they had to, now, and in any case they had no conversation the cloistered Enchian noblewoman would understand. But he wished that she would use the poppy less now that he could buy her the things that would make her happy. *At least it isn't dreamdust.* That killed in a year, less for naZak.

She lifted a graceful hand from the tapestry frame and he took it, going to one knee in the Enchian court style. "*Amam,* the sight of your beauty and good health is cherished." He pressed his cheek to her hand and she touched his hair.

"My son. Come, stand up and tell me how your life goes." She spoke the formal court tongue and in her quiet way insisted that he speak a civilized tongue in these rooms.

He brushed the knees of his pants and she rose to precede him to the fire, raising a forefinger to the slave to bring chai. "Wine for me, Mar," he said, and settled back in the rose and cream brocade of the heavy chair.

She clicked her tongue at him but said nothing. The firelight was kinder to her than the candles, smoothing away the wrinkles and burnishing the remaining mahogany in her silvering hair. The lace corners of her mantilla brushed her cheeks as she turned her head; for all her age she was still beautiful, the fine bones of her face carrying her years with grace.

"I am ready, my son." She accepted the cup and sipped, watching him as he thought of what he should say.

"The court is quiet, though the DragonLord is growing bored with his refurbished arena. Teik Avritha asked after your health and wished you well. She is holding a gathering in an iron cycle and sends both a formal and this—informal—invitation to attend."

One of her hands fluttered up to cover her mouth. "How kind," she whispered. "I must write and thank her for it."

He frowned inside. She would not go. Not after all the times before, when merchant ClawPrinces had invited her and made their every glance a sneer at her naZak status. Now that he had wealth and power enough to be dangerous to offend, he could not convince her that Avritha, the DragonLord's consort, honestly wished her well. She'd been hurt too many times by the petty ClawPrinces and their kin. Oh, they had been subtle, more subtle than their children had been to him . . . "And your poor mother . . . How is she? Still alive in those four, or is it five, rooms?"

They knew that he hated them. Once he had been too insignificant for them to notice, even to despise, but now they hated him. He smiled and played their games better than they could and threw his wealth, and Avritha's favor, in their faces.

Zingas Avritha, so easy to please. *All I had to do was tell her I loved her and she believed me.* That was a problem with those reared to trust nobody and see lies everywhere; disbelieving in truth, they became unable to recognize it. As vulnerable as yokels to the right approach; you had to have really *felt* an emotion to counterfeit it properly, or to know pretence from reality. He had her ear and *she* had the DragonLord . . . who was quite biddable as long as she kept him happy . . . although growing dangerously unpredictable in his whims—He forced his mind away from business matters.

"Of course, Mar," he said. He leaned forward and patted her hand. "You write and tell them what you think of the invitation." He leaned back and raised his goblet to her. "To your beauty, Mar."

She blushed and lowered her head. "You flatter me, my son."

"On the contrary. Perhaps I should buy you some new lace? To complement you? Or would you like some company, perhaps? A kitten, or a new slave to train?"

"Only if you can afford it, my son." The comment was strange on her lips, put there by years of living as they had. Father had died and the family had seized his inheritance in trust until Habiku came of age, he being naZak. His mother had had to sell her embroidery to eke out the miserable pittance that their Zak law-kin dribbled out, until he could earn for both of them.

He smiled fondly and squeezed her hand, raising it to his lips. "We don't have to worry any more. The DragonLord has ruled in my favor in the matter of the House of the Sleeping Dragon. I have complete authority to spend the capital now, as well as the income."

Which was just as well, considering what he had been . . . arranging, for the company. Great losses, tremendous losses, so unfortunate: for the books that the tax-assessors would see, at least, if not for the secret ledgers. The funds from the Karibal were becoming very helpful, there.

She nodded, lines of worry smoothing out on her brow. It was . . . declassé to be concerned with money. One instructed the steward, or the head of the household saw to it and varied the allowance for the women's quarters; that was the way of Tor Ench.

"You take much care for your mar," she said, laying a gentle hand on his head. "Many young lords just come into their estate would forget to do so; you have a good heart, my son." She frowned. "It was very wise of . . . "—she made a moue; her one meeting with the founder of the House of the Sleeping Dragon had been a strained exercise in mutual incomprehension—"that woman, Megan, to consign all this to you rather than to her cousin. A woman should not concern herself with such matters whatever these Zak think." Another smile. "Unfortunate that she should meet with an accident; still, what can be expected when those of my sex venture into the harsh world beyond the protecting walls of their quarters?"

Habiku blinked. Could she suspect? No, the hazel eyes were calmly innocent. Better that things remain so, for her. She could never understand what he had done to get his hands on the capital of the Sleeping Dragon, or what he had begun in the early years to protect her from her stinking habit. He hated the odor of poppy resin that permeated her clothing. The Brotherhood ensured that she could only get a limited amount, the drug being fiercely addictive; a maintenance dosage, but though not enough to harm. At the beginning it had been their hold on him. As long as he did what they wanted they limited her supply. Now he was rising in power there as well, and soon she would be free of it. As soon as he was strong enough. He left his mother once more engrossed in her tapestry and climbed the stairs to his chambers where Lixa waited.

SLAF HIKARME, HABIKU'S ROOMS

She lay under him, unresponsive, face dull and dead. He slapped her and when he failed to get a response again he took her anyway, thrusting heavily until, with a small, muffled sound, he arced and spasmed, still thrusting deep. And she lay there. He collapsed on top of her, seeing the long black hair twisted in his relaxing fists; he imagined a startlingly bright strand in it, like Whitlock's. He'd only had *her* once, and she'd been unconscious, drugged, and he *needed* her, had to have her. He pulled Lixa's head around and tried to imagine she was Whitlock.

He ignored the tolling of the bell by the door; the servants would deal with it.

Sweat trickled down his neck and fell on Lixa's cheek as he

raised his head and looked down at her, hate in his eyes. Threaten, punish, flog, nothing could make her respond anymore. "You aren't her," he whispered. His fists tightened, pulling on the mass of hair, forcing her head back and forth. "Show something, damn you," he whispered, then louder, "You're not *her*, but you're *mine!*"

He pulled out of her and sat up, semen dribbling into the hair on his leg as he shuddered again, slightly. And she lay there.

"Bitch," he said, then pulled her up, hanging limp from his hands. A backhanded slap flung her into the heaped pillows of the bed. "*Bitch!*"

He scrambled for his robes as his door opened. Who—

A DragonGuard from the Nest, walking past a valet torn between fear and an almost irresistable urge to protest.

Pure Zak face and build, tunic leather covered in steel plates lacquered black, rippling liquidly in the lamplight. Belt of jet circlets, long knives on each hip; a ceremonial helm of black steel tucked under one arm with the ruler's five-headed dragon symbol. A squire in grey carried his weapons, a quiver of short heavy darts and their throwing-stick of carved ivory; and a twofang, a double-headed spear. It was an insult to come carrying weapons, contempt on top of insult to have them carried by another. A parody of Zak court etiquette, a statement. *You are a stranger, an alien, whose word is of no account: therefore I send a specialist in violence to deal with you. But only one, because you are of no account.*

One of Ranion's own Guard, even the common soldiers well-born. Habiku frantically tried to think of some reason the DragonLord would suddenly take a personal interest in his life. Whom had he offended? Avritha was still purring from last time.

"Smoothtongue, you are summoned," the guard said in a bored voice. He strolled to the quilted mattress, his soft chamois boots silent, turned Lixa's bruised face to the light with one disinterested toe. Idly, he toyed with the long black braid of his hair; the squire stood motionless, a trained half-pace to the guard's left where he could stretch out his hand to take a weapon. A faint lift of brows above eyes the color of blackrock, commanding: *Make yourself decent, naZak.*

Ranion's jokes, Habiku thought as he wiped himself down sketchily before throwing on a robe offered by his valet. He could imagine the titters behind hands and fans if he arrived smelling of sex; Avritha would not be pleased, no. *Ranion's jokes.* The DragonLord held all their lives in his hands; now it pleased him to order his guard to be as insolent as possible. It was just to see what happened, the impulse of a nasty child who kicked open an ants' nest to see the tiny creatures scurry.

The little bastard has to push, and he can get away with it, Habiku thought, as he pushed his feet into wooden-soled street shoes. *His father was a killer, but he killed as a snake does, for food or when threatened. This one is like a weasel; mad, and kills for the joy of it.* Ranion's need for killing was coming on him more and more often, as if there was some secret frustration eating at the taproot of his soul. *If only I could convince Avritha to bear a child off someone else for the sterile little bastard.*

The half-Zak merchant prince cleared his throat. "To which court am I summoned, sir Guard?" he asked politely.

"Court, sir Merchant?" the guard said, turning and examining the fingers of his metal gauntlets. He closed the hand, the movement rippling like water across the cunningly jointed plates; F'talezonian metalwork was unmatched anywhere. "The mindspeaker at the Nest has a message; the DragonLord bids you there, to go about your business." He smiled, a patient, understanding expression. "It *is* a rare honor for one outside the Nest or the noble Houses to use the mindspeaker's talents, sir Merchant, ah, no, my small error, *ClawPrince.*" The Claw was the F'talezonian unit of currency, but the ancient houses preferred to take their share from rents, property, land, rather than active commerce.

Koru, Habiku swore in a relief that was half rage. His own return bow was a masterpiece of understated courtesy. *The DragonLord hasn't bothered to ask about the messages in iron cycles, not since the spring.*

THE ABBEY OF SAEKRBERK
BRAHVNIKI, EASTERN SHORE
TENTH IRON CYCLE, FOURTH DAY

"Zar Benaiat," Megan said, with the shadow of a bow.

The breezeway flanked one wall of a courtyard garden, near the heart of the Benai. Warmth radiated from the bluish-gray stone walls, keeping greenness here after the outer fields had turned sear with frost. *Fraosra* moved between the long beds in red robes, readying them for winter.

"Captain. Megan, Honey-Giver be thanked that the rumors of your death were false," the Benaiat replied; his tone was businesslike and brisk, but the look he bent on Megan was warm. The light-brown eyes that perched over his beaked nose were shrewd; Shkai'ra was reminded of the curious gaze of a raven or fox. He was not a tall man, midway between the two women in height, very thin but not cadaverously so.

He dropped the trowel he carried into the basket of the Vra attending him, a dry rustle from the papery bulbs dug for the winter rising, and accepted a cloth to wipe his earthstained hands. Then he dropped some of his formality and reached out his hand to Megan.

"Thank you, my friend," she said and took his hand in both of hers, smiling, missing his startled look. Smiles were an expression Megan had seldom worn, before. Sixteen when she killed Sarngeld and took his ship, five short years to build the House of the Sleeping Dragon into a force to be reckoned with along the Brezhan, in all that time seldom more than an ironic twist of the lips; and she touched others even less, only when courtesy demanded and that with reluctance.

Shkai'ra saw the quickly hidden flash of surprise, and grinned to herself. *She* had had time to see the change in Megan, like the slow unfolding of a plant as winter relaxed its grip; all these old friends were seeing it suddenly, the changes of two years matched on the template of unaltered memories. They were making heavy weather of it.

"Vra Walatri," the Benaiat addressed the Vra still holding

the basket. "Since the Captain and her friend have graciously come to visit, I will not sup with the Siblings." He turned to his guests. 'You will accept a meal, I hope," he continued, letting go Megan's hand and turning to lead them under the stone arches toward his private chambers.

"Thank you, Ivahn," Megan said.

"For three then, Vra: in my rooms."

"Benaiat," the Monk bowed, before padding away on silent bare feet, without the whispery scuff of sandals.

"I am glad that your pride doesn't forbid a accepting a little hospitality," Ivahn said.

The Zak could feel his appraisal of their ragged clothes and weather-beaten skins. Shkai'ra hitched at the small wooden chest slung beneath her shoulder, a corner flashing through a rent in the soft brown wool of her cloak.

"Your charity honors the recipient." Megan spread her hand at her companion. "Ivahn, may I present Shkai'ra Mek Kermak's-kin shchi Akribhan."

The Benaiat's brows rose toward his hairline as he inclined his head to the tall red-blonde barbarian. *Akribhan* was a word of complex meanings in the high-Zakos tongue they had been speaking: "acknowledged lover" was only the first of them, with connotations of absolute trust, as close a commitment as could be, short of marriage; Megan had the reputation of a solitary, and this one was not even a Zak. Her plain tunic and breeches of wool and horsehide were commonplace enough, but the cast of the aquiline features was not of any tribe he knew. That saber . . . a little like the Yeoli *kraila*, but different. Careful eyes noted the way she held it, left hand tilting the scabbard for the draw-and-strike.

A reaver, he thought. Her pale grey eyes were scanning his Benai with the automatic looter's appraisal of one born to raid and foray. *One of the many I've spoken with, lately.* These were troubled times, along the river and in the great world beyond. *An age is coming to an end*, the abbot mused. *An age of peace and prosperity, when wars were scuffles between neighbors and we thought the years would go on forever in their accustomed path.* A new era dawned for the peoples about the Mitvald, and whether the change was for the better or the worse, its birth would be bloody.

Unless an old man mistakes the creaking of his bones for earthquakes, he thought wryly. Then, aloud: "What magic did you use, Teik, to befriend this one who is as comfortable as a night-siren?"

"Oh, almost got her killed in various gruesome fashions. After that we were firm friends," Shkai'ra said lightly, with a flash of white teeth. Her Zak was fluent but careful, sprinkled with terms from the trade-pidgin; a F'talezonian accent, obviously learned from Megan. "Not a day's peace since we met, a true gift for trouble."

"Trouble, hah." Megan snorted. "Ivahn, it follows her shadow," the Zak said, as they passed the polished wood of the door to the Abbot's study. It was plain, but the grain shone with a swirling grace that spoke of hours with cloth and wax.

"You will pardon me while I change my robe," the monk said, motioning toward the seats. They were of a piece with the rest of the corner room: simply made. For the rest there was a high desk, cluttered with papers; one wall held books, locked and hung from pegs in cases of oiled leather; on the other a tall, slender mandala was painted in bright colors against white stucco, crowned with the ever-present onion arch. South and east were pointed windows, open to the cooling air.

Shkai'ra went to one, looking down over sloping land. Growing over slow centuries, the Benai had sprawled over the promontory that gave it birth; blue walls, white stone domes, slender minarets reached toward a sky darkening into night. The river and the city that had grown up under this building's protection were at her back; ahead, land sloped downward more gently than the cliff they had climbed from the ferry. Along the horizon loomed the wildwood and swamp of the Brezhan delta.

She shifted her gaze southward. The sea was still the dark Svartzee blue-black she had found so curious, breaking froth-white on the small bay. A cluster of weathered buildings grouped around a wharf, fishing boats beached among spread nets. Trotting up from the wharf came a squad of horsemen, red light bright on their lanceheads and scale mail.

Rich, she thought. *Metal armor for common soldiers . . . no, guard-monks, Megan said.* On the wall below, a monk swung a padded beam hung in slings against a bell taller than herself. The sound hung in hazy air, bronze and mellow and lovely.

Megan came up behind her and drew in deep lungfuls of air, watching the lone monk, highlighted by the setting sun, the moon already showing coin-round. "Smells like home."

"This priest," Shkai'ra said quietly. "How far can you trust him?" Megan smiled, eyes hooded, watching the land through the open window.

"When I left," she said slowly, "he was one of the two *frehmat*, not blood-kin, whom I would have trusted with my knives."

Shkai'ra's lips puckered in a silent whistle, *trust indeed*. "Before we give anything away . . ." Megan shook herself and turned away.

"Now who are you trying to teach?" She cocked a head toward the door. "He's coming. With one other."

The door opened again, readmitting the Benaiat, earthstained robe gone, replaced with one of red linen. The monk who followed looked for somewhere to set the large tray. The only place was the unsteady, sliding surface of papers on the desk. He placed it on the bench. "A moment, Zar," he said.

It was only a while before he returned with a light table, and at the abbot's nod, withdrew.

"Megan. Two years is a long time to search for a son." The bittersweet scent of kahfe filled the room as he poured three small cups, liquid thick and darker than earth. "You found him?"

"My son? Is that the story Habiku spread?"

"Either that or that you were dead. I chose to believe the former." Megan looked at him, shrugged as if she didn't care and turned away so he couldn't see that it affected her. That he cared . . .

"Ivahn . . . the kahfe grows cold. Today, I stand on courtesy and talk does not go with food."

"As you wish." The Benaiat pursed his lips thoughtfully.

The meal was quickly over, eaten in silence. Megan carefully picked up the tiny saltcellar and offered it to Ivahn, who looked at her, then accepted it and put down his cup. "You were not away, then, on a quest of your own. I suspected as much when the papers of agency were withdrawn."

The old man's sharp as a Warmaster's grace-knife, Shkai'ra thought. Megan ran a finger around the rim of her cup, the syrupy sweet flavor still on her lips. It was the one indulgence the Benaiat allowed himself. "No, Ivahn. Had I sought my son, he would be with me." She raised her eyes to him. "As you see, he isn't. I haven't changed *that* much, that I'd give up or abandon kin. I was wondering about the papers when we cleaned up the counting house yesterday. Vhsant is gone and certain important books with him."

Shkai'ra reached over and took Megan's arm, raising it so that her cuff fell away from one wrist. The manacle scars were two years old now; thickened white tissue showed in twin bands around tendons of the Zak's wrists.

The Benaiat pursed his lips. "Habiku?" he said. "And Vhsant, obviously." He shook his head. "There was little I could do, even when Vhsant began engaging in . . . questionable activities." At her look he shrugged. "Large-scale slaving; from Thanish sources upriver, mostly outward bound to Laka, Tor Ench, even the Empire. Legal, quite legal, but as you know, the Benai has always refused participation; it was somewhat of a relief when Habiku revoked our agency." Brahvnikian trade-law required a local sponsor who would stand good for any unpaid and uncollectable debt of a firm based out of the city.

"Then . . . I've had suspicions, shall we say, of the origin of some of the goods Vhsant has been dealing with. Not through Brahvniki, but parcels acquired upriver; the *Fraosra* of the Guard suspect they originated on missing ships. That *would* be illegal, of course." The cities of the river valley lived by trade, but the river was long and much of it was wild, thousands of leagues of forest, marsh and hill; the basin it drained was *mostly* wild, and there were many navigable tributaries. Suspicion and hatred prevented the joint patrols that would be the only way to stamp out the river pirates once and for all, but the law-merchant everywhere forbade dealing in stolen cargo. The problem was enforcement.

Megan nodded. "There was nothing you could do, Ivahn," she said grimly.

"Nothing," the priest agreed. "Brahvniki's trade-treaty with F'talezon is quite specific as to whose domestic law covers ownership of single-capital firms based there; I could not violate that without permission of the Praetanu and would not if I could. Too many livelihoods depend on the metal trade. But now, one hopes, matters will be different. But . . . friendship compels me to be blunt, Megan. Here in Brahvniki there is no problem; you are owner of record, your identity can be sworn to by myself among others, we have received no communication revoking it. Elsewhere, you will need resources to reestablish yourself. Habiku has had the use and direction of your ships and business for some time now; even with the losses, there is still wealth enough to buy knives and shut mouths. Were your headquarters in Brahvniki . . . As you said, the Benai doesn't even have papers for your holdings here."

Megan took a deep breath. "I thought something like that when I couldn't find half of what I needed. Thank you for that information, my friend. Do you know who has them if Vhsant didn't just steal them?" she asked, deadly quiet. The company had taken five years of work and effort, a thing built from ruins and pain, her only hope for ever buying her son back . . .

"Schotter Valders'sen."

"A *Thane*?" Megan asked. Her right hand began a slow, unconscious rubbing at the scars on her left wrist.

"Late resident of Aenir'sford. Expelled for commercial fraud, as I recall."

Megan felt an anger take hold of her she had never thought to feel again, not after Sarngeld died. *I listened to him scream, drove the knife into him again, blind rage, stop, stop moving, stop squealing, not human, die, I hate you but please die.* I knifed him in the back. He tried to be my father so it would suit his Arkan soul that he use me any way he saw fit. He pulled my son, my Lixand, away from me though he clung to my chains with two-year-old hands and I screamed and cried and begged to keep him. Sarngeld chained me that day, to do that. *Hamstrung, knifed in the back, the blade going in with the sticky resistance of kitchen knife into raw chicken, grating on bones.* I hated him for what he did to me, then hated him for not dying fast enough. *Bleeding everywhere. I hated him and everything.* The old anger deep and black and full of rot. What warmth she had in her eyes cooled and her face set.

"I remember. I was on the coalition of merchants that spoke to the court there." She glanced Shkai'ra's way, looking past her, then her eyes snapped into focus as she looked at the Kommanza. "Quicker to kill one's enemies," she said quietly.

"So I've always said, kh'eeredo."

Megan turned back to Ivahn. "Ivahn, would you take the agency back? Is there anything left to take back? Do you know?"

"Yes and yes and yes. Of course, all I know is hearsay." He got up, lifted a book free of the wall and unlocked it. "I can't afford to take sides, but somehow you happened to spy all of last year's revenues, before the papers were wrested from the Benai by the Zak courts, lying open on my desk." He handed the book to Megan. "I didn't see you." He turned his eyes to Shkai'ra. "I fear that your akribhan will need some assistance in repairing her state. It is good that heavier steel stands at her back."

Silence hung heavy for a hand of minutes, until Megan shut the book with a snap that would have been violent if it were not so carefully controlled. She closed her eyes a moment, and white lines of tension stood out around her mouth as she controlled herself. The anger disappeared.

"Ivahn, thank you. Habiku has sold the warehouse and is renting at twice the price. The timber trade is dealing in lumber for scrap, and the Laua, the weavers, no longer trade with us."

"Megan, it seems that the Benai is going to have a slight surplus of revenues this season cycle." The abbot tapped his lower lip with an index finger. "If necessary, a rather small loan could be arranged . . ."

Megan turned to Shkai'ra, her attempt at levity brittle. "A small loan, he says. To Ivahn, small means giving me the Benai." She considered a moment. "Show him."

Shkai'ra shrugged and set the wooden box on the bench. It was Fehinnan, from the other shore of the Lannic, plain black wood with a fiber-ceramic combination lock. She covered the tiny dial with her palm and twisted four times.

"It is not entirely empty-handed we come," she said. "We have a *small* deposit for your establishment." The lid tipped back; Shkai'ra folded open the rack of trays within. "We traded the gains for high value and small weight."

Abbot Ivahn had steered the affairs of his cloister for many years; it was not poor, and levied a toll of trade between the sea and the Brezhan, which drained half a continent. His breath hissed between his teeth at the sight before him. There was a tray of cabochon-cut rubies, deep crimson sparkle in the light of the lantern and the setting sun. Rose-cut diamonds. A ring of sapphires, set in lapis lazuli, come six thousand miles west from the mines of Ph'astan, near the roof of the world, and more . . .

He scanned their hard-worn clothes again, looked at the grime worn into the knuckles of their hands, hair faded by sun and salt spray. "Wise," he said. "Very wise. In Brahvniki, I know personally of only four I would trust with this; I am one, you another, Teik Shkai'ra—" He nodded to her. "I'll trust Megan's judgment on the matter."

"Ivahn," Megan said. "Take my company back. I'm the owner. No court is going to stop me from cleaning house, and no court has jurisdiction because I am not deceased. You can get your monks to prepare the parchments of Agency." After a moment: "Standard deposit interest, with letters of credit for upriver?"

"We'll be taking time and ready money to get a ship," Shkai'ra said. "A riverboat: small, fast, sound but not new. All found, Megan would know the details."

"And a crew, of course," Megan added.

Ivahn nodded, thoughtful. "All this will take some time,"

he said. "We have extensive banking business, but this will add a third to our loan capital. We must confer with other . . . No matter, your affairs may proceed at once. As for a crew, you will find hiring easy. Especially with so many of your former shipfolk looking for berths."

"*Former* shipfolk?" Megan began, then cut herself off. "Enough. Tomorrow. Oh, Habiku," she continued softly, "how I *long* for the sight of your face."

MINDSPEAKER'S CHAMBERS
DRAGON'SNEST, F'TALEZON
TENTH IRON CYCLE, SIXTH DAY

The mindspeaker dribbled and whined, face twitching, soft, baby features strange coupled with a man's body. Then it settled into a dough-impassive mask, and the lips moved.

"Communication," they said. The accent was slurred, but had a crisp south-coast tone. That was the key word, implanted in the damaged brains of the relay speakers. This one's twin was in Brahvniki, hearing the words spoken by the keeper there.

"From: Benaiat Ivahn of Saekrberk."

"To: Habiku Smoothtongue of F'talezon."

The idiot savant talent of the mindspeaker gave an eerie mimicry of the voice that was dictating the message to his brother, two thousand kilometers to the south.

"Greetings. Let this message constitute formal notice that the Benai Saekrberk, on instruction of the proprietor, Megan Whitlock, has resumed Agency for the Sleeping Dragon trading company in the Free City of Brahvniki and its environs."

"Further note that we are instructed to ignore all further communications from Company headquarters in F'talezon until the proprietor has resumed residence therein."

"End of message. Costs reversed. Communication ends."

The small stone cubicle echoed with the last words of the mindspeaker. The room was cold, having none of the normal tapestries or hangings to muffle the sharp corners and stone. The only heat in the room came from a grate in the wall by the floor, where a carefully shielded brazier stood. His keeper hurried to touch and reassure the mindspeaker who was reaching out, clutching at air like a baby in search of contact, a whimper already rising. She threw a look over her shoulder at Habiku, who gripped the arms of the folding chair until they creaked, close to breaking. He was pale and sweating, hair matted around his face as he stared at the two, keeper and mindspeaker, ignoring the disinterested guard by the door. He was rumpled, disheveled, unshaven and unwashed. His lips moved, slightly, his voice a strangled whisper.

"That's im . . ." He swallowed. "Impossible. Impossible!" His voice rose. "No! I refuse . . ."

"Teik." The keeper cut him off, her voice low and soothing for the telepath she tended, but her glare was icy. "Teik. Last time Jahn here had one of his fits he almost killed someone. He did set fire to the DragonLord's audience hall because we were forced to go there, and the tapestries and cloths torn down and shredded were invaluable. If you don't want me to let him have you, *keep your voice down!*"

Habiku would have paled further if that were possible. He had no power, no inner eye, not even to the slight degree that an ordinary Zak did; the manrauq frightened him. It was sorcery, terror from the world beyond. *Liar, liar, witch*, his mind screamed, only his will keeping tongue and throat from echoing it; easy to see, to feel the reason for the pogroms against the Zak elsewhere. He wanted to smash, to pound his fists like mallets into the keeper's smug face that stared at him as if he were a blind man, a deaf beggar . . .

Instead he closed his mouth and rose, bowed jerkily to the keeper, ignoring the smirk on the guard's face. He avoided looking at the vacant, empty stare of the idiot savant; a baby had more knowingness in its look. *An obscenity*, he thought, and shivered.

Outside, he leaned against a wall a moment, breathing heavily. She was alive. Vhsant had sworn he had killed her. Sweet DragonLord's favor! He felt at his middle, at the roll of fat gathered there over the last two years. She had stretched him, always too clever, always too quick, always a half-step ahead until that last time . . . *Why didn't I kill her myself, after I used her?* Habiku felt the question slide over his consciousness; the answer was there, but his mind refused to look at it.

Run, something prompted him. Take the cash and the banker's drafts, hire a few guides and *run.* North, up the white-water stretches of the river where only canoes could go, up past the salt mines. Into the trackless forests, where the fur traders went to deal with the woodsrunning tribes, then west. West to the Schvait cities, then south into the Empire; he could buy his way in where she would be barred by Arkan law and custom, a woman and dark—

No, he would meet her here, in the center of his power. Oh, not here; she could die, die in the far south. *Slowly. Slowly,* he told himself. He was not her second officer now; he was a man of wealth, of power. He had agents, hirelings; eyes were for sale in the river cities, and knives. And here in F'talezon he had the favor of the Court, Avritha, as well as the power of wealth. *She'll die, or be mine again. Mine forever.*

Once outside the Nest he did break into a run, confounding his escort. *Where did I send her arms-master? The salt mines?* Already his breath was wheezing out between clenched teeth, the smooth pavement of the Upper City suddenly feeling rough and uneven—*like when I was a child*—as he ran; the sling-litter following behind their master, running.

THE TRAINING CIRCLE
SLAF HIKARME
TENTH IRON CYCLE, ELEVENTH DAY

Thud. The blunt tip of the wooden practice sword caught Habiku under the ribs. Breath hissed out between clenched teeth as he backed and parried, oak clacking on oak; the arms-master followed, striking with smooth precision. Habiku forced muscles and lungs to function with a fierce effort of his will, tasting blood where he had bitten his cheek, detesting every moment of the discomfort. But there was no value to a combat skill you could not practice through pain and weariness.

A voice interrupted his focus. Uen; supposedly his representative at the DragonLord's court. Actually the DragonLord's watch on him, of course. The Zak spoke:

"A ship was purchased in Brahvniki, in Whitlock's name. An arrow-ship; she left the city at dawning, yesterday; light cargo only, but a full crew. She is coming home, Smoothtongue."

Habiku strode to the rack beside the courtyard entrance and replaced the sword, seized a towel and began drying the sweat-slick skin of his torso, moving with controlled violence. The arms-master sank back on her haunches, shoulder to the smooth cool stone of the wall, sword across her knees. Uen reflected that only real need could have driven the merchant to use a female instructor. Habiku notoriously disliked women, although oddly he rarely slept with men. But Anahe was the best he could afford; or rather more. *I wonder where the gold is coming from*, Uen thought. *We aren't paying him that much*.

The tall merchant halted before the news bringer, looking down from his double handspan of height. Uen was very much the Zak noble, small, slight, sharp-featured, black of hair and eye. The other's stature did not trouble him; he drew conscious superiority about him as closely as the dark F'talezonian cloak. Absently, he noted that Habiku had shed considerable weight these past two weeks; the skin hung loose over the revealed muscle, not having had time enough to tighten. His sweat had a sour smell; no wine or dreamweed, the Zak guessed, and his system was purging itself.

The fairer man bent. "I don't need to hear that," he hissed suddenly.

Unconsciously, the Zak took a firmer grip on the dagger in his sleeve. A terrified man was a dangerous man, and for all his naZak mother this one had been physically formidable once. Freed of self-indulgence, he could be again. But he'd never *dare* lay a hand on a Zak noble.

"Of course, ClawPrince," the smaller man said, hating to flatter this commonborn, a ClawPrince's half-breed, with the title. He did not know why the Dragon wished to continue using Habiku, but it was best to pry only so far into the young ruler's plots. If you went too far . . . He recalled the last one who had known too much, who had lasted days in the lion pit. His face had been licked off by the defanged lions and wet, bubbling noises had been the only sound he could make.

I will not make that mistake, he thought. *I will be useful, and inconspicuous, and I will wait. Ranion's power is rotting out from under him, and when he and those who rose to the heights just under him are gone, I will still be here.*

Habiku watched the Zak's impassive face, wanting to throw the towel into it. This one bent with every breeze like a reed in the river marshes, and thought his pliability was strength. *The Sheep-herders will be glad of your services when F'talezon falls,* he thought. *If I decide to tell them to let you live.* He tossed the towel over the rack, stretching until joints cracked.

"Uen," he said, signing for Anahe to leave. "We could speak in more comfort within." His breathing was smoothing and the cold air of near winter touched him not at all.

"Of course, Zingas. It must take much gold to maintain such genteel surroundings in the Upper City." The smile on Habiku's face froze even more.

"Uen, my friend, your eye was ever sharp. Tell me, how does the gentle lady Avritha?"

The Zak noble almost stopped in shock. *The Viper is giving him gold?* Habiku was her current favorite? A powerful ally, if she was smitten enough to give rather than take. *Dark One guard me from such favor,* he thought. *May you have joy of her, naZak.* His eyes dropped, hooded.

"The Woyvodaana is as beautiful as ever." *And whoring as always,* he thought. He pushed the thought back, into the guarded keep in the back of his mind. She was the only one Ranion listened to any more, and even she could persuade him less and less.

Lixa met them at the door holding a tray with steaming cups and a tunic folded carefully over one arm.

"Still have the pretty one, Habiku? You always did have good taste in slaves." Human chattel were growing less rare in F'talezon than they had been.

"Thank you, Uen." He shrugged into the tunic and took up the remaining cup. "Attend," he said to her.

"It grieves me that I outbid your steward for her," he said to the Zak noble. A wide, rueful smile, one man to another. "But there are some things in which there's no friendship, not so, my Lord?"

"True as the Lady's mercy," The Zak noble laughed, seating himself on the long couch in the alabaster-roofed atrium. *I know an adept who could heat your bones from within. That could last for many days.* "Perhaps a loan of her services, in my household? To teach a new one of mine, of course." Uen watched the girl stiffen for an instant, sensed her fear. She knew he could see with the inner eye, of course; that made certain . . . diversions possible that the naZak could never know.

"I fear I will need her skills here," Habiku said. The warm tone that had earned him his use-name slipped for an instant as he watched the Zak draw a finger down her cheek. "She *is* mine."

The Zak looked up sharply, aware of the strange note of hate and lust in the blond man's voice. *You hate her and she you: why so jealous, sir naZak?* He turned his gaze back to the slave girl, searched his mind's eye for a picture of Megan Whitlock. *Ah . . .*

Habiku smoothed his hands over his face. "It is possible, I understand, that the . . . former owner of the Slaf Hikarme will attempt to return to F'talezon." A laugh. "Unfortunate, that she . . . well, perhaps it was understandable that she should feign her own death; as you may know—" he made a palms-up gesture "—when the stewardship fell into my hands, grave debts were discovered. Grave debts, yes, and despite all my efforts—" *the company is still solvent and I cannot liquidate it in bankruptcy and buy the assets for a pittance when the debt-notes held by my proxies are brought before the court,* he continued silently as his palms opened in a gesture of helplessness. *Not without too many questions. Not yet.*

"For example," he said, "I find we owe more than 50,000 Dragonclaws for, umm, ship repairs in Rand. Old debts, from Whitlock's day; she *would* not pay attention to the accounts, and she was always too extravagant with repairs and wages, I warned her but . . ." He shrugged. "What can one expect, from one of hand-labour blood? Still, how unfortunate if she were to reach Rand itself, and find the creditors demanding the debt. With interest. They might even do her violence; the Rand are . . . intolerant of outsiders who neglect their debts." He put on an expression of grim concern. "I myself would be willing to spend as much to see that all went smoothly there. You understand me?"

Uen pursed his lips. "That is sad news. I grieve for your anxiety, however unworthy your former benefactor. Rand. Ah. My lord Ranion must send his respects to Rand. They do much bridge repair there and someone not home for several years would unfortunately not know the unsafe ones . . . The rival king's heir met with an unfortunate accident on one of those spans, did he not?"

Habiku mulled over the noble's counteroffer. An accident might be more plausible to arrange, for *her*, one disappearance with a lame cover story and hints of suicide was about all credibility would stand. And the DragonLord would sanction this. So unfortunate that the Rand King's heir died. For them. And the Zak wanted Lixa. He clenched his fist on the table he sat by and remembered the flicker of reaction when Uen touched her. The Zak was known for his tastes and a few days of that might make her more enjoyable, for him.

"Yes, poor man. Unfortunate." *Unfortunate that he announced an anti-Thane policy before his accession; the Sheepherders only needed to whisper in certain ears close to the King's second child.*

"It is difficult," Habiku continued, "to deal diplomatically with the Rand; the mores are so different, their bureaucracy so unforgiving of a lapse in protocol. Lixa has studied their methods quite intensively. With my compliments, lord Uen, take her for a few days and see if her . . . ah, *scriptorial* skills are of assistance."

"My friend, you are too generous. I cannot accept such a gift; please, allow payment, if only for my honor's sake."

"Oh no. Your good friendship is more than enough. Would you care for a glass of wine rather than chai, Uen? I have a seven-years pressing just in. But I fear that wine is much too self-indulgent for me, in recent days."

"One glass would do you no harm, and me either. Thank you."

"Lixa." Habiku called her to bring the wine, flicking the lock of hair out of his eyes. Uen leaned back comfortably, watching the naZak's eyes follow his slave. *He must burn, to have to lend her. Almost as if she were the one he truly desires, and loves and hates. How amusing; I must leave a few unmistakable marks for him to find.* Habiku turned back to the Zak courtier, a smile stretched across his face, and Uen felt the slightest stab of alarm; a fainter version of the fear a summons into the DragonLord's presence brought. *Then again, perhaps not.* It was a strain to sit and chat and drink with the naZak. He cut it as short as possible without seeming to rush.

"Farewell, my Lord," he said at last, rising and bowing. For an instant Uen felt weary, with a mortal, moral tiredness seeping out from his bones; a desire to escape. *Nonsense, F'talezon is the world,* he thought. "Leave the message to Rand to me; you must have many matters to occupy your time."

"As many matters of *that* type as I can arrange, all the way upriver from Bravhniki," he said. They bowed and parted, in perfect understanding and utter hatred.

You are mine, or dead, Megan, Habiku thought as Uen left. *You are.* A soft whisper: "You just haven't gotten the news, yet."

Chapter 3

THREE WEEKS NORTH OF BRAHVNIKI
BREZHAN, WEST BANK
OUTSIDE THE WALLS OF THE VILLAGE OF
  NARYSHKIV
NINTH IRON CYCLE, TWELFTH DAY

Dammit, Shyll, Rilla Shadows'Shade thought, *keep that overgrown monster of yours down!*

There was a muffled thump some distance away in the thicket of scrub cedar, a drum-sound like some large animal being struck on the ribs, and a subdued whine. Then a faint rustling, and the blond teRyadn nomad slithered in beside her, bringing the smell of horse, dog, sweat and leather along with a crushed cedar smell like the linen-chests of home so long ago, when the summer clothes were laid away with fragrant branches and packed away . . .

"Inu's hungry," Shyll whispered, and reached for Rilla's telescope: Arkan, and hideously expensive as all imports from the Empire. She surrendered it grudgingly, went back to a wide-angle sweep of the scene before them. There were other sounds in the thick brush: a clink of weapons, a muffled curse in Zak or Aeniri or Dark-Lord-knew-what as harness caught on twigs or insects bit and burrowed. Her crew were river sailors, not woodsrunners, nineteen off the *Zingas Vryka*, the *Lady Grey Wolf*.

The west bank of the Brezhan was higher than the floodplain and steppe to the east, scattered with rolling loess plains and gully-scarred hills like the one they were on. The town squatted to the southeast, on the bluff where the Oestschpaz flowed east to meet the Brezhan.

Lucky I don't have to attack it, Rilla thought. Megan was the one known as Siegebreaker. Hmmm, four large sails at the docks, she could see the masts over the bank. Doubtless barges and poleboats from up the Oestschpaz; it was shallow draught at the best of times and the summer had been a dry one. The trademart outside the walls was breaking up, wagons and muletrains fanning out along the dry dirt roads leading west, or down to the docks. Dust smoked into the gold-hued autumn air, borne away northward in a hazy plume by the prevailing wind. Mare's-tail clouds in the sky. Rain tonight.

"Our informant was right," Shyll whispered beside her, handing back the telescope. "Habiku's man is taking them overland. Gotten a fear of sending them further upriver with the *Vryka* hunting about."

She felt herself flush. *I'll ruin his slave trade for him, take back what is lawfully mine*. Rilla Shadows'Shade, father's sister's child to Megan Whitlock; a close tie by Zak law. Heir to the House of the Sleeping Dragon, if there were any justice in the DragonLord's courts. *If Megan were dead. The half-breed naZak son-of-two-brothers says so, and that's enough to make it a lie.* Now he controlled the House, and put it to what use? Slave trading with *Thanes.*

She forced the rage-trembling out of her hands and put the tube to her eye, pushed and pulled to focus. A long coffle was threading its way from the mart, out between the reed booths and the merchants striking their tents. *Careful, careful*, she thought. Lives depended on her decisions, and she was a merchant skipper by trade, not a land bandit.

"His manager isn't going to keep them overnight in town," she said softly. "Probably no facilities, and the governor wouldn't want to have so many within the walls, damage bond or no, and they'll have the strongbox with them." Closer now; files bound neck and neck with forked wooden poles, their hands behind their backs, children running beside their mothers. A few guards on horseback; a dozen or more trudging on foot, and five muledrawn wagons bringing up the rear. That would be the supplies.

"So they'll camp inland," Shyll said, chuckling. "All nice and safe from the *Zingas Vryka*." The *Vryka* was actually anchored fifty *chiliois* upstream, well hidden in a branch-channel of the east-bank swamps with a skeleton crew. "Or so they think."

"Most of those slaves are Moryavska," Rilla whispered. "If we have a chance . . ." Shyll grinned at her. "I know just the crew who'd love a chance to let them go," he said.

"Once into the woods Habiku's men will never catch them." She nodded, decisively. "Right. Pass the word to keep well back until they camp . . . And *you* keep a tight hand on that overgrown puppy of yours."

INLAND
BEFORE MOONRISE

The slavers' campfire was a thick bed of coals under the half-cooked pig; the ruddy light picked out faces, hands, the blackened outer surface of the beast. The fat dripped, bringing spurts of yellow-bright light against the dull glow of the hardwood embers. Scent flowed downwind to the hidden raiders, a mixture of the savor of roasting pork and the filth and fear of two hundred slaves. The guards talked among themselves, laughing and passing a goatskin flask around the fire; one used a stick to scrabble a clay-covered potato out of the fire and broke it open, juggling the hot food from hand to hand, blowing and cursing.

One of the sentries turned his back on the dark, a short wiry man in horsehide, barbaric trimmings of wolves' teeth woven into his black braids.

"*Na*, Dietr," he called, in harshly accented Thanish, waving a short horn-backed bow. "Stick to the wine, it's safer. And when're you going to bring out the women?"

The man with the scalded palms stood, and took a swig. "Shut up, Imre," he called back. "Keep your eyes on the woods; we'll have the girls after the meat is done, you rutting

Mogh-iur bastards have no sense of occasion." He laughed and waved the goatskin again. "But red wine with both meat courses!"

The sentry shrugged and turned to the woods again, as a roar of laughter ran about the fire.

Still an hour to moonrise, Rilla thought. *Shamballah's light isn't enough to cut the dark. We outnumber them only by three, and the dog.*

She could hear the crewfolk nearest her, but that was because she was listening; soon she would have to order them into combat, and win or lose there would be hurt and dead. They knew it, had accepted it when they had signed on for this private privateer voyage that everyone else would call piracy. Many had their own private feuds with Smoothtongue; the man bred enemies the way Shyll's damned hound bred fleas . . . That would not make the deaths any less real, or lessen her responsibility.

There. The slaves were in a crudely made lean-to of sapling trees bent over in place and lashed together, some shelter from the rain that was on the wind. The picket line for the horses was to one side, the wagons and the leader's tent pitched beside them. *Shyll and Iczak should be in place by now, by the horses and mules*, she thought. *Inu has to be downwind so he doesn't spook them with his smell. Now, nobody do anything stup—*

Arrrroouff! A sound halfway between a bellow and a bark, cracking thunder-loud across the clearing, and a dog leaped out of the darkness toward the fire. A white hound, sharp-eared and feather-tailed, tongue lolling between sharp white teeth; a teRyadn greathound, four feet at the shoulder, thick legs pounding nine hundred pounds of weight forward as fast as a galloping horse, armor turning a dog into a demon creature.

"*Inu!*" Shyll's voice, commanding. The greathound's tail tucked between his legs, his ears flattened; a look of haunted guilt narrowed his eyes as he slammed through the ring of shouting, bewildered guards and seized the roasting pig, lips curled back from the hot flesh, and galloped into the surrounding darkness. Crashing sounds followed him into the woods.

"Grey Wolf! Grey Wolf!" The crew of the *Zingas Vryka* rose and threw themselves forward with a roar, and the throwing-darts of their first volley sleeted down out of the dark, humming like a swarm of meter-long bees.

"Shiiiit!" Rilla screamed as she leaped to her own feet, snapping out an overarm cast at the mailed figure of the Slavemaster; he whirled, and the dart plunged past him to kill a guard rolling screaming in the coals where he had been knocked by the dog's passage. Then the throwing-stick went back over her shoulder into the quiver, and she was at handstrokes.

Blood, always so much, always a surprise. There were warm slow drops running down her face; she shook her head, clearing her eyes. *Shit. Shit. I'm supposed to be commanding this mess . . .*

She heard the whistling *crack* as one of her Aenir's swing-stone lassoes wrapped around a slaver. *All I'm doing . . .* She leaped over the corpse, blocked a Lakan's short sword with the haft of the twofang; the hard wood turned the edge. The fire was flaring up, it shone on the greased black hair; she stepped to one side and swivelled the fang to slice across his blue-black hawk face, slashing across his throat. Blood glistened on his hairless chest like sweat. . . . *is fighting.*

The stink of burning blood was thick, her ears were full of clang, batter, thump, an uncontrollable pain-shriek and the mingled fear and rage from the slaves, or the odd battle cry:

"Hai! Hai!" A slaver, a fair-skinned Schvait with a two-handed sword; it cut through her bosun's spearhaft and half through his neck.

"Grey Wolf!" A crewwoman behind him drove her twofang with both hands; it poked through the mountain man's leather corselet and tented it out in front. He dropped the sword and sank to his knees pawing at the inch of steel poking red through the bullhide.

The Slavemaster held a clear space around him, swinging a bloodied mace. His chain coat was close-linked and strong and hung past his knees; blades slithered from it, and the serrated iron head of his weapon punched into a skull with a wet *tock*. Rilla dodged around another fight, saw Danake closing in with a knife flickering in each hand; a moment, and her hand could strip a dart and throwing-stick out of her quiver. The thumb-thick wood clacked into the groove of the stick; the dart point flickered in the firelight and sprouted from the Slavemaster's arm. He dropped the mace and Shyll had him, the thin, stiff smallsword bursting through his mail.

Shyll yelled, eyes wide with alarm; Rilla ducked, spun around to block one of the Mogh-iur's scimitars. The one in his other hand struck—*no pain, no time*—drove one fang at his foot. He leaped chest-high, fast as a Zak, kicked, struck her twofang; she tumbled out of his reach, back-rolling. There were *Zingas Vryka* fighters all around him but he moved like a blur, shrieking as he fought. A deckhand stumbled back, clutching his belly, and there was a sudden pause.

"Surrender," Rilla said, her voice a croak that left her astonished. "We offer quarter." He smiled, teeth white below a drooping black mustache.

"A bloody horse cock up the ass of your quarter," he called, turned and drove for the horses, whistling. A spotted stallion reared and tore its checkrein free from the line, striking with its forefeet; the Mogh-iur seemed to flow to the stallion's back. The animal wheeled, the great muscles of its haunches bunching. Beside her Rilla heard more than saw a dart slip into its groove, the thrower's grunt of effort; the short javelin struck the fleeing Mogh-iur below one shoulder and hung, bouncing, as he fell forward to clasp his arms about the horse's neck. Hoofbeats vanished in the darkness.

Inu crashed back into the clearing, head held high, the spit dragging out of the pig he still held, his barks and growling muffled by his full mouth. A Thane, with Enchian rapier and parry-dagger, had Shyll pinned at the fire pit. The greathound dropped the pig and lunged, snarling. His jaws closed on the Thane's shoulder, crushing half his chest. The man had time to scream once before the dog shook him.

The horses and mules were milling as far as their lines would allow, one down and tangled, screaming, injured. The crew of the Grey Wolf, stopped, slowed, realizing there was no one left to fight, the slavers dead or surrendered. A crewman stepped to the shrieking horse and the noise drowned in a gurgle.

Rilla looked around at the mess she could more smell than see in the dark, the fire steaming, almost out, heard the dog's panting, someone moaning, and the tense silence of two hundred people caught between fear and the faint beginnings of hope.

The night isn't really black, she thought distractedly, *it's grey. I'm going into shock.* "Sound off, who's hurt? Danake, pick two, get the strongbox. There should be about five thousand Claws' worth there."

"Aye, Captain." With real enthusiasm; that was more than they needed to meet back wages, and to have the *Zingas Vryka* hauled out in the slipway for a refit. Their last few raids had brought more loss to Habiku than profit to them.

She pressed her arm against her ribs, sticking the cloth under the corselet to her wound, and walked over to the lean-to. *Five thousand*, she thought. Sailcloth, new rudder ropes, cordage, tallow, beans, bacon, arrows . . . Boryis had lit a torch from the glowing ember-bed of the slavers' fire; she raised it carefully as she ducked into the lean-to, mindful of the dry twig-wood above. The tree trunk coffle was keeping them together, still. Round faces turned up to look at her, fire-washed, pale as moons, the remains of their brightly embroidered clothing ragged and muddy. They stank, the slavers evidently relying on a morning dip in the river to cure the lack of hygiene in the night. Children tugged at their mothers and were hushed; some of the adults were still ready to fight if given a chance, others were broken, staring at the dirt and grass between their feet.

"Anyone here speak Zak?" she asked, without much hope. Silence, someone in the back sneezed. Rilla sighed and tried Enchian. It had been over a millenium and a half since the fall of Iyesi. Enchian was a living tongue only in the remnant kingdom of Tor Ench, but it was still the tongue of scholars, diplomats and traders.

"Paral-doi' laEnchais?" she said, slowly and distinctly.

A man in the rear rank stirred and half-rose, then sank under the weight of his bonds.

"*Peutre 'npeu*," he said: perhaps a little. She leaned on her twofang and studied him: stocky, middle-aged, with a few bedraggled feathers and shells still clinging to the remnants of his vest.

"*I hight Yoz'f*," he said, also with care. "Would'st thou, noble *soldu*, speak concerning the fate of these my folk?" He spoke in an archaic dialect, remarkably close to the ancient High Speech of Iyesi. Level blue eyes in the weathered face were uncowed; lash marks on his back, from those still raw red through yellow and blue bruises to half-healed lumps of scar.

"*Genhomm'*," she said, the address of respect. "Your people are free, but there is a town of enemies only three hours march to the east. We must move quickly and silently; can you keep your people from straggling? The children will find it hard. I cannot offer you safe passage anywhere on my ship and she is far upriver."

He translated to his people in a low voice. The Moryavska tongue was close enough to Zak that she could almost understand. *Probably because I know already what he's saying.* A babble of voices rose, tears, anger and suspicion, hope, things one needed no language to understand; a few barked words brought silence. Yoz'f turned to her again. His eyes were wet, and she squirmed inwardly as he rose awkwardly to his knees.

'Yea, it shall be so, *Zingas*. Our land be blessed with many a bosky den, the hunter's path no stranger to us." Ochen, the ship's carpenter, came up and laid out his tools, took a chisel, set it against the wooden rod across the mouth of a Y-forked holding pole, looked at her. Rilla nodded at him and he had the first rod broken in three strokes. The old man rose to his feet, touched his neck in wonder, then threw his arms aloft and prayed.

"*Zingas*," he said, coughed to clear his throat, and continued. "To Boghdu and Iasos and Perkn, the Lion and the Twins, I call blessings ever on your name, your house and seed. All hope had been riven from us, ere thou came'st. At a wedding feast were we, when the Mogh-iur fell upon us"—several of the freed slaves paused to spit at the mention of the name—"and we were as babes, for at feast do the Moryavska love to drink deep. For this gift of life, what boon may we give? Ask, and if it is ours, it is thine."

She shrugged, and winced slightly as the motion tugged at the wound on her side, where the quilted padding beneath the leather armor was blood-bonded to the lips of the gash. "*Genhomm*' Yoz'f, you owe me nothing; the man who sent the Mogh-iur against you is my enemy."

An oversimplification, the Mogh-iur kingdoms south of the Karpati Mountains were tributaries of Arko, and the Empire's tax was heavy. Slave raiding in the barbarian lands to the north, among people less trained in war, was one way of meeting the demands and staving off outright annexation; Habiku had merely given them another outlet, easier to reach than the traditional southern route to the Mitvald Sea. She continued:

"My crew is looking to their supplies. See to your people, then come talk to me, please."

The tribesman drew himself up, held out a palm to stay her for a moment, spoke quickly with his people. Or a core of them that had gathered about him, young and still healthy. None of the broken ones, she noted, and some of the women were staring out at the corpses of the slavers with a disturbing intensity.

"I, Yoz'f son of Mar'ya and Broz'f, Lawman and godspeaker of Spisska'ves, say that the honor of my people accepteth not this gift of freedom without a gift in return." He made a gesture, and ten of the younger Moryavska stepped forward. "Thine enemy is ours, and a debt of blood is owed. These youths and maidens are strong and willing to learn, good hunters and fighters, with much to avenge. Thou shall be their lord."

Rilla blinked, opened her mouth and closed it again as the young Moryavska filed up to her. Yoz'f whispered in her ear, "Bread, salt and iron, Lady."

She nodded, cleared her throat, gave orders. The freed slaves bowed, tasted the hastily-scrounged flatbread and coarse salt, touched a blade of her twofang. When they began to recite their deeds, and their parentage and their *parents'* deeds, she cut the ceremony short.

"*Danake!*" The supercargo hurried up, hands bristling with lists. "These are ten new recruits. They don't speak any known language and they've never seen a ship except the hold of a slaver." The woman's mouth opened and closed. *Did I look that silly?* Rilla thought. *Probably . . .* "They can all hunt deer and farm, so they ought to make good crew . . . See to it!" She didn't let the sarcasm color her tone.

She nodded to Yoz'f and ducked outside, leaving the torch behind. The darkness was blessed relief. She leaned against a tree, the rough bark under her cheek. *Koru, I'm tired. Megan, did you get this tired? How did you deal with all these people? Dear Goddess, you shielded me from this but now I know it in bitter measure.* There was a call from the crew rifling the supplies, the Slavemaster's personal hoard—Arkan money-chains, in silver. *The joy of revenge is always so fleeting, why is it so flat in my mouth already?* The wind whipped across the camp carrying the stench with it, bringing the heat of the day. She felt tears catch in the back of her throat, choked them back, then let them flow. Megan was—*is* always the one to control herself. *As long as I don't sob, that'd hurt.*

Lost some . . . too many. Too many friends. She felt a trickle work its way down past her belt. *Koru grant that it's sweat.* She sat down by the tree, feeling the burning thread its way all along her ribs. *I wish I could just—pick a direction and leave all this mess behind. Koru, grant me rest.* "Shyll," she called.

"Rilla?" His voice came from the horse lines.

"I'm on the sick list too. The Mogh-iur scratched me." He was suddenly beside her out of the dark. She slapped irritably at his solicitous hands.

" 'S'all right, Rilla. Iczak! Get over here!" he shouted.

"Oh, go do something useful. I'm just nicked, not dying. Get moving before I bounce your ass all the way to Aenir'sford." She couldn't see his grin in the dark. But he didn't go away, staying to unlace her corselet instead. *At least he didn't say "Megan'd want me to take care of you,"* she thought.

Iczak brought his kit to begin dressing the slash. Rilla tried to pull off her shirt, stopped as cloth caught and pulled, sending pain lacing through her chest. He tssked at her and used boiled water from his canteen to soften the dried blood.

Inu crawled up to her, muzzle in the dirt, still dragging his pig. She winced as Iczak pressed a cloth to her ribs and leaned back against the bone and leather of his armored side, tugging on one of the dog's pointed white ears. "Bad dog," she said, trying to keep her mind off the twinges, listening to her crew, and Inu whined through a mouthful of pork.

AN ISLAND IN THE BREZHAN
NORTH OF NARYSHKIV
NEXT EVENING

"Well," Rilla Shadows'Shade said sourly, poking at the fire. It was small, smokeless, hidden by the roots of the toppled oak; stray droplets of sleet pelted down through the forest canopy and hissed on the coals. "We've made some gains, managed to be a bigger thorn in Habiku's foot, gained ten more on my side, even if they don't speak the language yet, and the *Vryka* is on her way to fetch us. Things could be worse . . . I don't really care if another Thanish town has a price on my head, but I hate to have my options shrinking like this." A sigh. "Things could be worse."

"Yes. It could be winter," Shyll said, and smiled into her scowl, shadowed under the brown wool cowl of her cloak. She was tall for a Zak, three inches over four feet; even at twenty an ageless look was settling about her face, tracks of worry and strain replacing the laughter lines. Glossy, dark brown hair spilled against the cloth, a contrast to his sunbleached tow. She set chin to knees and poked again with her stick, testing the leaf-wrapped roots cooking in the embers. The rain had come on the wind by the time the Moryavska had faded into the dark; bare branches rattled and sighed in the autumn forest, and the susurrus of the river held a promise of ice from the northern mountains.

We've made it back to the river, he thought. *We even found a fishing boat to get us out here.* He glanced into the dark, over to the other fire where the wounded huddled in their bandages. Faster to have the fit trek back to the ship and then pick them all up. *She's just worrying to worry.*

It was no wonder though; the *Zingas Vryka* should have put in for them before sunset.

It hadn't been an easy two years since Megan disappeared. *The wandering life was well and good, until I met the two, Megan and Rilla. I wanted to settle a bit. Megan . . . she could never see that snake's twistings, no matter how I warned her. You could see it in his eyes, something bent out of shape inside his head. Shit, she's not dead. She can't be. Stop thinking about her in the past tense.* If she had been slain, Habiku would have shown the body or real proof, somehow.

Rilla was Zak to the core; F'talezon-born like her cousin. The Sleeping Dragon had been more than a trading company; it was to be the foundation of Megan's House, a shelter for the blood she and Rilla shared, and their descendants; and provide the wealth and power Megan would need to find the son sold away from her when she was a child herself, still bonded to that pervert Sarngeld. Kin and House were everything to a Zak; their lives were rooted in stone, however far they wandered. Watching what Habiku had made of that inheritance was a clawing bitterness to Rilla, despite all they did to reave parts of it back again.

The blond man leaned back comfortably against Inu, who still wore a slightly guilty air. He smiled again, knowing what was behind the washcloth-sized tongue that slurped over his ear, the thumping tail; *I'm a good dog, boss, really, I was just so hungry . . .*

"We can always go into the town in disguise if we need to," he said, grinning. He had played this role with Megan also, a lightness in a spirit brooding and dour by nature.

"Disguise?" Rilla snorted. "With that shambling mountain of puppy forever at your heels?" She raked a 'maranth tuber out of the fire and the greathound's ear pricked. "Inu! No! You had a whole pig just yesterday!"

The dog sighed with sad-eyed resignation and laid his head back on his paws. Unwillingly, Rilla smiled; her eyes met Shyll's and that grew into a chuckle.

"You've got to admit, he *was* useful," Shyll said.

"Yes, but we didn't *plan* for him to attack their cookpit," Rilla said, then shook with silent laughter, until the bandaged slash along her ribs stopped her with a warning twinge. "I hope that the Moryavska get home without too much trouble."

"They're woodspeople, I doubt any Thane could catch them. They're probably on their way straight back to the raids and border skirmishes with the Mogh-iur that got them caught in the first place. And," he continued slyly, "Thanish law holds the owner responsible for any damage they might do. Technically, they all belong to Habiku." It was unlikely that a Thane merchant court would be very sympathetic to the man; half-Zak was wholly damned, in their eyes, and no loophole in the law would help him with that.

"We don't have that many more places to run on the river," Rilla mused. "If he keeps pushing this hard we'll have to retreat up the Vechaslaf where it joins the Brezhan, which is too Thanish for my taste, or sell the ship and stick to land-reaving. I want to stab that bastard where it hurts!" The greathound lurched to his feet, head turned toward the river.

Shyll had just cracked open his tuber, blowing on it, nodding his agreement, when Inu's sudden movement jolted him forward. "What? Inu, down." Rilla had doused the fire by kicking dirt on it, and the walking wounded followed suit without needing to be told. Then, from the river, a hooded lamp shone and flickered. Once. Twice.

"That's the *Vryka*! Come on." Rilla stuffed the rest of the root in her mouth and whistled for the rest of her crew.

"But, but . . . Oh, damn! Why is dinner always interrupted! I didn't even get *one* bite." Shyll scrambled after.

"Mmph, youm." Rilla swallowed and tried again. "You can eat on board. Besides, get the coin changed and stashed away in Aenir-Seitch a couple of days from now and I don't have to think of selling my *Vryka*. Haul your beautiful behind down here!" Inu whuffed and plunged into the river, heading for the ship he knew, splashing them with icy water.

"Shit, dog . . . Why thank you, Rilla. The one woman in the world unaffected by my beauty . . ."

"Oh, hush. We are still in the midst of a tightening net, Shyll."

"You'll think of something. It's your job. Or Megan will handle it when she gets back." They both ignored the silence after he said that. When Megan gets back; not if. Never if. "Yes. When she gets back," Rilla said as she stepped into the jollyboat, touching her helmsman on the shoulder.

BRAHVNIKI, TAPROOM OF THE KCHNOTET VURM
TENTH IRON CYCLE, THIRD DAY, EVENING

Megan smiled. The man was a newcomer to the Vurm, and wavering between standing and using one of the newly built benches; finally he decided to risk pine tar on his clothing. *That* was a common hazard here; the Vurm went through a lot of furniture, and it did not pay to buy expensive seasoned wood for the customers to hit each other with. She and Shkai'ra sat on well-worn chairs in the warm corner of the taproom behind the angle of the main tile stove; there were advantages to being a regular, even if you had been away two years. She closed her eyes and inhaled deeply of the smell of home, ignoring the unwashed bodies and noticing instead the scent of new-laid fire, wood, mulled ale, the musty-earth odor of the brick the Vurm was built of and felt the smooth-worn wood under her hands.

"I still say *my* knives killed the spearbill before you put an arrow through its eye," she said amiably, taking a swig from her tankard. Brahvnikian beer, again. Barley brewed, with hops and fennel. Famous all along the Brezhan, and the cost increased with every mile upriver; in F'talezon at the head of navigation the *prefetatla* drank it, the elite. Megan looked into her mug and narrowed her lids in a smile that warmed the eyes without touching the lips. Brahvnikian merchants drank wine; beer was for the poor, the Vurm's fine brown-foam for the middle classes . . . and for export.

"*Zoweitzum* with that! You'd have been digging at its neck until the Gods came to eat the world!" Shkai'ra snorted and stretched her legs out in front of her. "All this just to come

home! Huhn! We should have stayed in Illizbuah. Not nearly
so much trouble as you getting your revenge on what's his
name."

"Habiku—"

"*Ia.*"

"—And I'm sure you'd have looked lovely behind the bars
of the priest's cage, spell-twisted into a Sniffer. You've been
doing nothing but complain all the way from the mid-Lannic
islands," Megan said.

"Complain? Me?"

"*Dah.* Oh, stop it." Megan stopped Shkai'ra's hand from
roaming under the table. She looked down at the table.

"Why in Halya did that bastard sell me, instead of killing
me outright?" She shook her head. "Habiku knew me, didn't
he think I'd be back? Still wanted as much space as possible
between me and him when I woke up with the dog-sucking
headache that Gods'Tears gives you."

*And the ache between my legs. The bastard used me while
I was unconscious, or someone did.*

"That customs clerk called you 'Fleet'sbane'. Was he just
flattering you or what?" Shkai'ra stretched one arm over her
head as she asked, carefully casual, changing the subject.
Megan looked embarrassed. "I didn't think anyone would
remember after two and a half years." She drew a few circles
in the spilled ale on the table. "During Enkar's war. The
Thanish fleet was barricading Aenir'sford—that's about halfway to F'talezon—and my old *River Lady* . . . Well, we had a
few things they needed . . . so we broke the siege, my crew
and I." *Just like that,* Shkai'ra thought, and raised an eyebrow at what Megan wasn't saying. "Enkar was a fool and lost
most of his force; retreated down through Rand and held one
of their Princes as hostage for passage through the Gates.

"They ended up here and beat themselves against Brahvniki's
walls and were finished here." She sighed. "I guess the name
just stuck and a lot of people blame me for what happened
. . . Thanes."

She pushed herself to her feet. "Time I returned the
borrowed beer." She walked to the back past the empty
raised platform for performers, with the steady care of someone slightly drunk and knowing it.

Shkai'ra watched as Megan disappeared through the curtained door to the jakes. *Great change of topic, make her think of all the blood feuds she's got on her ass . . .* A whirl of chill air fluttered the brightly colored strips of woven linen as the outside door opened, losing itself in the smoky dimness of the taproom. The smaller dinner hearth crackled to her left, joining the larger glow from across the room to throw ruddy light on benches and trestle tables.

The outline was one with a dozen, dozen taverns she had seen in the years of exile; in spirit, at least. On this side of the Lannic, in the northeast corner of the Mitvald Sea, the details were utterly strange. There were sandy-robed Hriis who mingled only with Ieus clansmen, sipping wine and refusing to eat in the presence of unbelievers; dark, slight folk from the southern deserts, caravaneers and merchants who only the very strong or very foolish attacked. Blond Arkans primly hiding their gloved hands, and dark-skinned Lakans with hair earrings; Yeolis gesticulating wildly, their steel wristlets flashing; Sinapland priests with square-cut beards or a strip shaven from brow to nape; Aenir, bright in baggy felt pantaloons, sashes, curl-toed riding boots.

Shkai'ra grinned and tilted the tarred leather of her stein. Black shadow oozing, Ten-Knife crept from beneath the table, stalking the sliced meat that swam invitingly in its pink juices on a trestle an arm's length away. The blonde woman's hand snaked out to encircle the cat's throat.

"*Nia,*" she said in her own tongue. "You've eaten enough today, imp of darkness." The stroking motion of her right hand led it naturally to the long bone grip of her curved sword. Someone had been watching, and now he was making up his mind to approach; the sensation was too familiar to doubt.

The man she had sensed halted a confidential pace from her seat, which gave them a little privacy; the jutting whitewashed sidewall of the fireplace screened them from as much of the room as the man's back did not cover. *A . . . Thane,* Shkai'ra decided from Megan's description. Violently prejudiced against Zak. His hands were ritually scarred, and the last joint of his smaller fingers were missing. *Stupidity,* she mused. Her own folk knew better than to weaken a warrior's grip, and their training left the scars where they belonged; on the back, and in the mind.

"A vriendly warning to straenger," he said in the pidgin-Zak trade dialect, with a heavy accent, thick and guttural as if his native tongue was full with glottal stops and unvoiced vowels. Apparently, while drunk, his hatred of Zak overcame his prejudice against foreigners. *I suppose I look more like a Thane than anything else*, Shkai'ra thought.

"Do you know das your friend is one of the vitch folk?" he continued, leaning closer. Firelight flickered over his heavy craggy features, picked out detail: oil-sheen on light-brown hair and pitted skin, broken blood vessels beneath one eye. His hair was long, gathered into a topknot at one side of his head.

"They can turn on you," he snapped his fingers. "Just like das. Is better das they be all given to the fire, or river."

Shkai'ra leaned over and laid a confidential hand on the Thane's arm.

"Thanks, friend," she said with a smile. Her hand kneaded his forearm slightly; thick and blocky, but the muscle was softening. He had that build, ox-strong in youth but falling into sagging fat in middle age for lack of exercise. Shkai'ra's fingers tightened, and she touched the tip of her tongue lingeringly to her lower lip. "But it's so hard to find any who'll company us cannibals for long. You seem a fine, healthy sort. Firm fleshed, *yes* . . ." Her eyes glittered suddenly in the shadowed corner.

His eyes widened. *A thin, papery voice whispering, 'Old Father gives us food.'* He tore himself free, stumbling backward. "Ah, don't *go*," Shkai'ra crooned.

The Thane turned and almost ran for the door; the frozen stares of half the Vurm's patrons were on them. A cold draft around her ankles told the Kommanza that Megan was back. She abandoned the pretense and laughed, the shrill, high-pitched mocking giggle of her folk. The Thane's pasty color gave way to a bright flush that started with his cheeks and spread to neck and ears. Still laughing, she pulled out a leather strap, wrapped it around her knuckles and began stropping her dagger on it. After a moment of silence the Aeniri at the central table led a bellow of mirth that spread until the inn's commonroom rocked with it, foreigners leaning to ask their companions what the joke was; the far corners joined in for the laughter's sake.

The Thane swung around, his hands making grasping motions; yellow teeth bared unconsciously. Megan slipped up beside the Kommanza and laid a hand on her shoulder; the tall woman bent her head to rub her cheek on the knuckles. Puzzled, the Zak smoothed the white lock at her temple. "Don't I know . . ." she began.

The Thane paled even more. "You're—" he began to blurt, clenched his teeth with an effort. He wheeled and plunged into the darkness beyond the main door.

"What's the joke?" Megan looked after the departed Thane. "He knew me." Shkai'ra leaned close and whispered in her ear. Megan's face lit with a smile and she laughed. "Na . . . A Thane, too! Lots of eating taboos, Thanes; not as bad as Hriis, but nearly. Dog-sucking sheepherders deserve all they get." She leaned against Shkai'ra and sobered. "We'd best hope that Ivahn has the answers that Vhsant ran off with. If I'd had half a brain I'd have realized he'd take off with half of the books and the strongbox."

Shkai'ra yawned. "I'm for bed."

"Aren't you always? I'll come and tuck you in."

STAADT
ONE DAY'S JOURNEY NORTH OF BRAHVNIKI
TENTH IRON CYCLE, MID-AFTERNOON

Piatr hadn't thought it was possible to hate a child of twelve so thoroughly.

"Clown," she said. "Goatfoot. Make me laugh, limper." She was close to him, her body close enough for him to feel its heat in the late autumn air of the garden. Feel it through the short girl-child tunic she wore; unsuitable for one her age, by Thane standards, but her mother refused to acknowledge the passing years, and her father was above giving thought to a mere female not yet marriageable. She stared at him, wondering why she felt so miserable.

I can make him do anything I want. He doesn't like me. I don't like him, either. I can't make him like me. He's a Zak. Nobody likes them. I'm glad he doesn't like me; nobody . . . I'm Schotter's daughter. They better like me. I won't yell at them because they make me angry. Mother says a lady never has to raise her voice. People follow her commands to the letter—but she slaps 'Talia all the time. And calls her names. She picked Pishka up from the path where he was lying, ignoring his whine, and sat down on the garden bench, cuddling the lapdog.

She frowned, swinging her feet. It was just so *hard*, sometimes. Trying to be good; they kept saying that she shouldn't be lazy, but every time she tried to *do* anything somebody yelled at her. Sulky, she cast a glower at her brother from the corner of her eye. *Francosz* didn't have any problems; Pa was always doing things with *him*. *He* never got told to sit still or not swing his arms or climb trees, and Pa had said that after he braided his hair he could take a trip upriver on the trading boat, or even overseas to Selina.

It's like the stories, she thought. *They all say it's such a big thing to be a lady, but all the ladies get to do is wait while someone goes off and rescues them or something. I'm always waiting, why do I always feel tired?* she thought.

My mother's a lady though, even if that nasty Adelfrau said she wasn't. She was right to be mad and throw the teapot, Pa shouldn't have yelled and made her cry. I'm going to make her proud of me. I'm going to be so good that she likes me. She'll see—I wish . . . She loves me—she says so all the time.

Her gaze returned to the clown. Pa had given him to her. *Pa gives me lots of nice things.*

That was the only time Pa noticed her. Sometimes she broke things, because then he'd . . . *see* her again. He just pretended to be angry, then gave her something else, and said she'd be a fine Lord's Lady someday. That made Mother angry, though . . .

But she had to be careful not to break things too soon. Her eyes sharpened on the Zak clown.

Fortunate, the thought ghosted through Piatr's mind as he capered, trying to make her smile, *that she's so young*. *Otherwise they'd have me cut*. Not that she would have tempted him, pretty as she was, even if his taste ran to children. He winced at the thought. *Lady of Life, I'd rather couple with one of the DragonLord's shirrush-lau*.

Springing nimbly in the air, he vaulted onto his hands. His feet wove in the air, the left his own, the right a cloven hair hoof strapped onto a stump that ended a handsbreadth above the ankle. It fitted badly, chafing; not like the one the Captain had had made for him.

"Ah, great one," he said, deliberately exaggerating his Zak accent. Groveling in the tones of their rivals always pleased a Thane, even Thane children. Prancing, he could see the faces of the others grouped around him; the two children of the house, a cousin from a distant branch of the family, their companions, slaves. Francosz, the heir of the house, peacocking in the tunic, breeches and daggerbelt of a Thanish adult. *Fourteenth birthday*, Piatr thought. It bore remembering; Schotter's son would be eager to prove his manhood.

"See how I leap to my feet in joy beauty of Greatesty Lady," he burbled, the clown's makeup mixing and running on his face and lean body. "Feet? Hands?" He pretended to study them, lifting one palm, then the other, then both; fell on his face, bounced to his feet, miming panic as the goathoof flew out in an exaggerated curve and he crashed down on his backside, widening his eyes and rubbing his head with one palm.

"Awe of Greatesty Beauty turns poor Zak clumsy!" The patter and the act were wearing thin, after a year. A year since Habiku had stranded him in Staadt, leaving a debt that Thanish law would levy against any of the *Zingas Teik*'s crew.

He picked up a handful of the gravel path stones beneath him and began to juggle them with his feet, kicking them higher and higher. "See, even stones dance for joy at chance to serve!"

The girl yawned and settled back on the bench, feeding the dog sweets. It yipped and snatched the pastries, fawning on her, snuffling through its flattened nose.

Francosz watched for a moment, then began pitching fruit rinds to break the clown's concentration.

This is boring, the young Thane thought sullenly. *I shouldn't have to play with Sova any more; she's just a baby, and a girl. Pa should remember that I'm a man now, or nearly.* He flexed an arm complacently, feeling the buildup of muscle from sword practice.

But Pa had told him to "go and play", as if he weren't old enough to go on the trip to Selina next season. He bit his lip. *Sometimes Pa . . . forgot things he'd promised.* A memory forced its way into his mind: leaving Aenir'sford after his father had been convicted by the merchant's court. *The household winding through the muddy streets to the docks, past faces indifferent or jeering; his mother had taken a thrown cowflop on the side of her head and had hysterics. Pa had slapped her right there in the street, and told him to get back with the children when he tried to ride beside him and help. The Thane manor-lord had put them up, but when Pa went down to dinner he'd been told by the butler that the master was not receiving that day and Pa had hit Mother again. That was all right, Pa had said she was only a woman, but I wish he wouldn't hit her, but he's my father.*

Pa's enemies have been after him, all his life, Francosz thought, and smiled. *Now that I'm a man, he'll have someone he can trust, not like those others that have always betrayed him, and we'll show them now. But I hope he remembers about the trip to Selina.* His eyes returned to the clown and he threw another piece of fruit rind.

Piatr caught the tough skin in his mouth and chewed with noisy relish, singing nonsense songs around it. *The lapdog is fed better,* he thought, *far better.* There had been little food lately, and less sleep.

A youth spent as a wandering tumbler, years in the rigging of a riverboat, had given him wells of endurance surprising for his slight build. They were nearing exhaustion now, and he saw the gracious swaying of the garden trees through a haze; trees taller than the metal-tipped walls of the courtyard. Easy to climb, but how far could a one-footed slave in clown's motley run?

If he were lucky they would only cut off his other foot.

"You bore me, clown." Schotter's son stood by him. The boy reached out and batted the pebbles away. "As a toy, you disappoint me." His mouth puckered and he pulled at the hair that was not quite long enough to be gathered into the scalpknot of a man. "Perhaps it would be more fun to drown you in the pool."

The clown's one of those; one of the Zak that threw us out. I don't care if it was an Aeniri council, it was the Zaks' fault. I'll make him pay for that.

Piatr bounced to his knees in exaggerated supplication but his breath caught. There was a vicious, curious note to the question this time, as if the boy were considering it. He was too tired to concentrate his small Gift to influence harm away from himself, too tired to do anything but talk.

"Lord, you only wish is my life. Shall I drown myself?" He paused. "But then who would my gracious Lord have to play with?" Francosz smiled, turning away. It made him feel better when the clown grovelled.

"I'll think about it," he said, and lashed out viciously with one foot. Piatr dropped flat under it, then—*oh sweet Lady of Winter, the last time I didn't take one of his blows—I don't think I could stand a beating.*

"Children." The mistress of the house swept through the hedge gate, followed by her tiring slave. "Come, come, dears. Send your nasty fool away and come talk to me." Her voice was warm and honeyed but none of this reached her eyes.

Piatr bowed deeply and limped off. Perhaps he could find a few moments' sleep.

Chapter 4

BRAHVNIKI, A THANISH MANOR JUST NORTH
OF THE WALLS
TENTH IRON CYCLE, FIFTH DAY, MORNING

Schotter Valders'sen settled comfortably into the heavy
horsehide chair behind his desk and let his eyes rove around
the chamber he had made his office. The furniture was Thane,
massive, the fumed oak frames thickly covered in carving.
The cushions were bulging-tight horsehair. Cupboards on the
walls bore accountbooks and a lifetime's collection of knick-
knacks. Pride of place went to an elaborate curlicued beer
mug with a hinged, peaked top; family legend said that the
ancestors had borne it in the migration out of the west that had
brought the Thanes to the banks of the Brezhan.
Like most manors along the river, his house was stone-
built, centering around a courtyard and presenting blank
outer walls to blizzards and summer sun alike. He scowled at
the gravel paths, topiaries and flowerbanks of the garden, a
legacy from the Brahvniki merchant he had bought it from;
likewise native were the inner walls of whiteglaze terracotta,
unornamented save for edging of indigo blue. *Was that her,
last night? The city is buzzing with rumours. Vhsant had
disappeared and Yareslav hadn't sent word of anything else
amiss at the counting house. No. I sold the little bitch myself
for Vhsant, to another slaver going to the Lannic coast,
outside the Mitvald. Guaranteed. I'm worrying for nothing.*

66

All those Zak look alike anyway. It took three discreet taps on his door to rouse him.

"Vat?" he rasped, looking up from an account for fine Yeoli stoneware. It would be higher priced once Arko moved east and tried to incorporate Yeola-e into the Empire, with its tariff policy; which was likely since the mountain people's king, Fourth Whatever-his-name-was (he could never pronounce those slithering names, even the famous ones) was missing and presumed dead. They ought to have taken better care of someone they needed so much. More than worth the capital tied up in storage . . . Another knock brought him back from speculation.

"A messenger from the Benaiat, master," his counting-clerk replied, bowing.

"Two hours past sunrise?" he asked in surprise. "Hmmm, let him wait a while. Vat could that heathen pig want vid me?"

"Perhaps to congratulate you, master," the clerk said. His thin face kept its expressionless melancholy, but the Adam's apple bobbed in his throat. At the merchant's puzzled look he continued: "On your safe . . . escape . . . from the Knotted Worm last night, master."

The clerk bowed and closed the door with a soft sighing of heavy, close-fitting wood. That was possible because sheer incomprehension froze Schotter to his chair for the time it would have taken to count thirty. Then the heavy face purpled; he rose, the chair crashing to the flags behind him, starting around the desk with his mouth opening for a roar. A roar that never came; he turned and, overly careful, righted the chair and sank into it with a thump as he realized just what last night had cost him.

Zight, he thought heavily. *Face.* It was a Zak word, a concept that had spread downriver with the metal trade from that ingrown city of peculiar customs. He had been gulled and terrified, and in public; the loss of *zight* was tremendous. Unbearable, if a clerk of his, eating from his table, could say it to his face.

His teeth ground together audibly, remembering the blonde woman's laughter, the fingers like slender metal bars digging into his arm. He had put it from his mind; what consequence what tavern scum did? Now he realized his mistake; sweat began to gather on his forehead under the topknot of his hair, and he felt it clammy on his flanks. This was not Thane territory; his people were not liked here, particularly not since the disastrous finale of Enkar's War three years ago.

Or the *Wrath of Megan Thane'sdoom*; that was what the Aeniri bards were calling it. *At least we—I. I—rid us of that Zak bitch*, he mused with a moment's satisfaction. The defeat at Aenir'sford had been her doing, and that failure had lead directly to the abortive attack on Brahvniki.

Doubtless she was scrubbing dishes in Farakistan, hoeing beans in Nubuah this very moment, or doing something even less pleasant even further away.

He pushed the pleasant thought aside. He had no personal popularity to compensate for a loss of face like last night's. "*Zight*," he sighed aloud. The tale would be all over town by now. Outfaced by a *woman; the* thought was bitter as seawater on an open sore. If *that* tale ever reached upriver to his homeland . . . But first matters first; he could not operate as a merchant anywhere on the river without face. Who would take him seriously? He thought of laughter behind palms, and began to sweat anew.

Ah, but there was another Zak custom; he could challenge. Brahvniki courts accepted the validity of challenge. Not personally, of course; not to combat. He had fought, in the wars, and against bandits as any merchant must. But . . . there were those Schvait mercenaries, they owed him a favour . . .

He had begun to smile when the second knock came. "*H'rei*," he called. "Enter." The messenger from the Benai was one of the lay brothers, a small neat man with quiet mannerisms.

"Teik Valders'sen," he said, bowing his head slightly. The Thane purpled again. The bow was only barely respectful enough between equals; any less and it would have implied greater *zight* to lesser. "Vra," Schotter gritted, striving to control his temper. To show his upset would cost him greater face. "How can this humble person aid your munificent establishment?" He exaggerated his humbleness to show his displeasure.

The Vra raised a hand in a noncommital gesture. He refused to be insulted by the Thane's rudeness in not offering him a seat, not that any of the chairs in this overpowering room would be comfortable. "In a very simple way, my son. The price and papers for the agency of the Sleeping Dragon Company, have I here, with instructions to buy."

"But, but the owner . . ."

"On the owner's instructions, Teik."

The Thane's mouth was opening and closing like a gaffed fish, soundless. *How could Habiku do this to him?* "But the owner, Habiku Smoothtongue, he . . ."

"No, no, my son," the monk cut in. "Not the proxy, the *owner*, Megan Whitlock." A ghost of a smile flitted over his impassive face. "Fleet'sbane."

Two facts rose to the surface of the Thane's mind, like dead rats in a well. Without the expected profits from the Sleeping Dragon agency, he could not meet his notes—in Brahvniki, the last major port open to him on the Brezhan. It *had* been Megan Whitlock in the tavern with the barbarian, and not just a drunken memory. *Megan Fleet'sbane, Megan Thane's-doom.* A rictus of a smile appeared on his face. *Ruined,* he thought. *I'm ruined, unless . . .*

"I'm sure the papers are in order, Vra." He coughed behind his hand. "My clerk will see to the details." After the Zak bitch was dead, the agency would be his again, in time to meet his debts. As the monk was shown out of the room, the Thane began to rummage in his desk. The mercenaries wouldn't know till too late that he was going to pay to have them lose *zight,* and kill the Zak. *If they hang for murder I'll be able to say I had nothing to do with it. I'll make up my oversight in selling her, even though she did bring me a very good price along with the young Aenir and the Ungishman in that deal.*

His smile, this time, was genuine. Perhaps the family should come into the city to see his triumph. Yes, his heir would learn well by example.

BRAHVNIKI
TENTH IRON CYCLE, FIFTH DAY, LATE
  ## AFTERNOON

A muffled thump, then another rang from under the hull and Megan crawled out from beneath the vessel in drydock, dusting herself off. "There's dry rot in some of the belly-boards," she said, and sneezed. Wood dust from the ship being built in the next slip over drifted on the breeze, powdering everything with light-brown particles. "Other than that, Teik, she's sound."

"Dry rot! Never! Almost new she is! Seized not one season gone from Rithian sea-raiders and rebuilt for Rejinka patrol!" The shipwright leaned over and spat into the water. "Sea-god hear me if I lie."

Megan grinned. "He does. Yulai, if the thing were rotten to the water line and leaking from sixteen sprung seams, you'd swear by the Sea-god's testicles that she'd been built yesterday!" The shipwright grinned and leaned on his adze.

"You know me too well, Megan. Still, for the price this one's good . . . if you need an arrowboat." *Which not many merchant houses did,* lay unspoken between them. Most river craft were built for freight, broad and beamy and worked by sail. This hull would carry seventy oar-pullers as well as the dozen crew needed to work the rigging; a complement that size ate profit and left scant room for cargo. But it left speed and fighting strength in plenty.

Megan turned again and ran a practiced eye up the length of the ship, making a decision.

"For that, yes. Replace the boards, repaint her . . . she'll do." Her belt pouch held a careful assortment of mixed coinage from around the coast. Copper from Yaressal, bright six-sided steel coins from home, finger-length bars of silver from Parha, ankaryal of all metals . . . what any adventurer with relatively good fortune would have. The bulk of their fortune would be dealt out through the Benai, through hands unlikely to cut throats for it.

"To pardon ask, Teikas." The new voice made them look around. A tall, thin Schvait stood there, his dark-green knee-breeches buckled over heavy wool socks, the black shirt showing his status as mercenary and a mountaineer's rope and pitons clipped to his belt. In his hand he held a scroll of parchment. "Is finding of Teik Megan, one Whitlock, possible is?" His blue eyes scanned the two of them. "To me is she not known, but was told to find her shipyard, with."

"I am Megan Whitlock."

He handed her the scroll. "Is challenge opfor . . . pardon . . . offered. Can get read if Teik cannot, before acceptance of scroll is acceptance of challenge."

"I see. Yes, I can read. A moment please." The challenge was from the Thane. *Ridiculous*, she thought. A race over rooftops of the city, in his condition . . .? Ah. The archery involved was to be her downfall. He knew she was no archer. But Shkai'ra was. *If I can drag her into this. Hmmm.*

"This challenge, is it personal or by proxy?" she asked the mercenary.

He gestured. "Not great understanding I have, but my brothers, three, will race."

The people out of Schvait were known as some of the best climbers in this area of the world, rivalling the Yeolis in skill. She squinted up at the sun. *Shkai'ra should still be at the black smith's . . . before I do this,* she thought, *I'll have to ask her.*

"Provision for non-immediate acceptance," she said. "Yulai, witness. My word on returning within two hours before challenge is automatically accepted."

"Teik Whitlock, I hear."

"In two hours," she said, and was gone.

A BLACKSMITH'S SHOP
AGAINST THE KREML WALL

The smithy pressed hard against the inner wall of the city, that had once been the wall of The Kreml itself. Shkai'ra ducked her head under the lintel and paused to allow her eyes to adjust to the smoky gloom. The surface beneath her feet was crushed rock—ancient concrete from the look and feel; it might date from before the Godwar. The hearth of the forge was pressed against the stone of the fortress wall itself, a sensible precaution in this city of tarred timber.

Never had much luck with smiths, Shkai'ra thought with a grimace; for a moment she remembered another place, snow and the smell of blood. Shrugging, she unslung the shield from her shoulder where it had lain hidden by her new cloak.

The smith paused in his work and stared at the outlander. *Cormorenc-feather cloak*, he thought. The fabric was unmistakable; green-grey in ordinary light, almost black in darkness, lightweight.

"You must be off the *Pride of Shoupir*," he said. "Fast work, to have the down feathers woven up so soon."

Unsurprised, Shkai'ra flipped a palm. "Traded four times the weight of raw feathers for it," she said. From what Megan said, a spearbill kill by a merchantman was not common, and news spread fast.

"Yah, you'd have to. Now, what can I do for you, Zingas Forus?" One of Shkai'ra's eyebrows rose.

She pulled the smooth curve of scabbard out of her belt and raised an eyebrow at him.

"I'll rebond the peace wire, Zingas." She nodded and broke the wire, laying the blade on the cleaning silk as she pointed to the hilt. "That," she said. The dimpled bone handle was split along most of its length in two places. "It comes off now, rather than in the middle of a fight." At her nod, the smith took up the sword and probed at it.

"Yah, it's loose already. Now I'm no boneworker, nor in ivory. You could go to the leather merchant and have it bound in sharkskin, special order it from Anya, the ivory carver . . . or I could replace the whole thing with brass?"

She shook her head. "*Nia*, the metal would be slippery when the hand sweats."

"Or when blood runs over it, but braided wire allows grip."

She nodded. "And lasts longer. Also, I can afford it now: do it."

He blinked surprise. "Price?" he asked.

The blonde woman shrugged. "Name one, if it's fair I'll pay."

The blacksmith began rummaging in a drawer for wire. "Two Dragonclaws," he said, preparing to haggle.

"Good enough," Shkai'ra said indifferently; she had not been raised a merchant. Among the Keep-holding kinfasts of the Zekz Kommanz you gave freely or, more commonly, killed and took. "Also, I need a new shield; about the size and weight of this, steel rim and boss."

She toed the shield beside her. It was a disc a meter across, rimmed and bossed with iron. The frame was moulded fiberglass, the surface tough layered bullhide.

The blacksmith picked it up and turned it between huge horn-palmed hands. It had been a good shield, he saw; now the frame was cracked, the rim broken or hacked through in six places, and the boss loose. That was unsurprising: a good sword might be a heirloom for generations, but a shield rarely lasted more than one afternoon of strong warriors and heavy blows.

"I can duplicate it, I have the armorframe and glasscloth . . . that will cost you dearly: most about here use birch plywood."

"No matter, I'll—ha, kh'eeredo." She paused, and looked at the careful lack of expression on Megan's face. "Trouble." That was a statement, not a question.

One corner of Megan's mouth twitched. "That's becoming another of my use-names," she said. Shkai'ra swung a leg over the heavy anvil and flung, "Do the shield, I think I'll need it," over her shoulder. As she turned back to Megan she noticed the closed-in expression on her face, the one that she hadn't worn very often since they'd met; the expression that held everyone at arms' length.

Megan tapped the scroll on the curled-in nails of one hand.

"Challenge scroll?" The smith asked, curious. Megan looked at him in the old way, from the time before she knew how to smile easily, and he abruptly became engrossed in his work.

Can I drag Shkai'ra into this? she thought. *Even after all we've been through and she is my celik kiskardas, my steel sister.* Even the slight flicker of emotion on her face was enough to tell Shkai'ra what she was thinking.

"Kh'eeredo, you're forgetting. There is steel between us, and blood as well." She nodded at the scroll in Megan's hand. "Another charming local custom?"

Chapter 5

BRAHVNIKI
TENTH IRON CYCLE, EIGHTH DAY

Three days later, half of Brahvniki assembled near the Harbour Gate; much of the remainder were strung out along a route that ran in a straight line across the roofs of the city, to the gate of The Kreml itself. Most challenges were far less exotic than this, a roll of dice, the outcome of a spider-fight or some game of skill such as cniffta, and it was rare for a ClawPrince to agree to such public terms, in these days when most preferred courts of arbitration.

It was bright. A chill autumn wind whipped at hair and cloaks, tossed the manes of horses, blew white froth from the tops of choppy waves in the rivermouth behind them. There was an irregular square, here behind the row of tall warehouses that did double duty as an outer wall facing the water; five thousand boots rustled and clicked across the cobblestones. The crowd's clothes were a mass of color and dun wadmal against which faces showed pale as they stared toward the cloth-draped wooden dais where the gentlefolk and officials stood.

There was murmuring, but less than there might have been at a Nardimoot, the public assembly of the Praetanu. Pie sellers and mulled-wine vendors moved through the crowd, pickpockets were busy; token-vendors hawked bits of feathers from the cormorenc killed by the outlander and Megan

74

Fleet'sbane. Betting was lively, the odds changing from minute to minute.

There was more decorum on the dais. Merchants, officials, some of the younger ClawPrinces of the Praetanu and officers of the civic militia sat in blue-fingered dignity. Schotter Valders'sen sat there in the tight trousers, high boots, ruffled shirt and embroidered cutaway overrobe of Thane formality. Wife and children stood behind, the women decently covered from head to toe, their faces hidden by veils hanging from broad hats piled with flowers and feathers. Behind them stood their servants, ever attentive; to his people, they were an essential mark of status.

Megan perched below on a coil of rope. Her face was calm, looking younger than her years, with her hair laced back in a braided coronal. Her feet were bare, for the task to come; a wool cloak held tight against the wind hid leather breeches and roll-necked knitted jerkin. Her slim hands flexed unconsciously, the razor edges of grey claws cutting slits in the dense weave of her cloak.

Shkai'ra stood behind her, braids looped and strapped beneath a headband, flexing and swinging her arms to be sure that the leather armguards did not hinder her. Otherwise her thin shirt covered only the tight bindings about her breasts; this would be work needing all the agility she had. Her feet bore soft kidskin buskins rather than the riding boots she preferred. Her skin showed milk-pale and gooseflesh in the cold, or tan where sun and wind had burned, and the raw copper of her hair blazed in the bright morning sunlight. A wooden chest rested beneath one foot.

"I call thee forth!" The judge's voice boomed out in trained carrying tones as he mounted the block. The loose robe fell away from his arms as he raised hands in the spreading gesture of the ritual. "I call thee forth! I call thee forth!"

At the traditional third repetition the crowd fell silent by segments. At the other side of the dais three black-shirted Schvait stood, two tall, grave-faced men and a woman alike enough to be close kin, holding their crossbows in folded arms. Their climbing ropes were across their shoulders, slung like bandoliers; pitons and hammers hung at their waists.

"Hear the terms of challenge. To redress offense, a race across the city is set from harbor point to the gate of The Kreml."

Hah, Shkai'ra thought. *Offense. The idiot asked for it. I'm never going to get away from running around on rooftops, it seems to go with being around Megan.*

The judge raised one hand, was answered by a flash of mirrors from points staggered on opposite sides of the course approximately one hundred yards from the route. "Targets are arranged along the way for the archery," he continued. "Two forfeits are demanded of Megan Whitlock should she lose. Should she be last to the gate, she is to bond herself to Schotter Valders'sen for one year. Should she be beaten in the archery, the bonding is to be indefinite." He turned to the Thane as a murmur spread through the crowd. This was not mere challenge for loss of face, this was a forfeit demanded of blood feud. "Valders'sen, is this correct?"

"It is." The Thane's voice was thin, whipped to shreds by the wind.

"Whitlock. As challenged you have not named your forfeits."

Megan rose, her eyes scanning across the dais. "The challenge I answer. Since three run against me as proxy for the Thane, I demand a second of my choosing; and that if three run, then all three must beat us to the gate." She smiled. "As forfeit when I win . . . I will demand," she paused. "A favor."

"Whitlock," the judge said. "This is all?"

"All? I will ask one thing of the Thane and he will be bound to do it, should it be in the realms of possibility." Her voice was mocking.

"And for your condition." The judge paused to look at the Thane who nodded. "Agreed. Your second?"

"Shkai'ra Mek Kermak's-kin of the Zekz Kommanz, the one who stands by me, celik kiskardas, my kin in all sight next only to my cousin Rilla."

There was a rising murmur; Megan had been well known along the trade routes of the Brezhan, and was said to be clannish even for a Zak.

"Shkai'ra Mek Kermak's-kin," the judge said, stumbling

over the unfamiliar gutturals of the name. "You agree to share challenge and forfeit?"

Shkai'ra grinned like a wolf, caught and held the Thane's eye. "Ia," she said, toeing open the chest. It was her armor case from the Kchnotet Vurm. She bent, and straightened with a bow in her hands, a bow unknown on this side of the Lannic. No longer than the length of her leg, with thick limbs springing from a central block of hardwood. At the ends of the stave were offset bronze wheels, the string secured to eyelets just below each U-fork running down, over the grooved rim of the opposite wheel, up the back of the bow, and over the other wheel.

The Schvait stiffened with sudden interest, and one whistled softly; the pulley principle was well understood in their homeland, which had many factories run on waterpower. On the left side of the grip was a rack holding five long eagle-fletched arrows with narrow pile heads; armorpiercers.

The Thane glared at her. The tall woman's lip curled back further, and her eyes stayed locked on his as the thumb of her right hand curled around the string; there was a bone ring on it.

She moved swiftly, yet without haste. Arms and body turned; there was a *click* as the jeweled bearings in the wheelbow's pulleys turned, and a *scritch* as the thumb-ring locked under a shaft that appeared on the string. The bow swung up and the arrow vanished, simply a flicker of flight feathers and head, too fast for the human eye to see. Above, a gull halted in mid-air as if rammed into an invisible wall, fell to land at Schotter's feet. A few stray feathers landed on the hats of his womenfolk. Seconds later the arrow followed, sinking a handspan into the timber at the edge of the dais; the bird had not slowed the pile-headed shaft, not even deflected it.

"Wait and sweat, pig-face," she sneered. "You'll never *guess* my favor." She licked her lips.

His wife fainted, her head landing with a hollow *thock* on the boards of the dais. A servant in clown's motley and facepaint made an abortive clutch at her; his truest attention was focused on Megan.

* * *

Koru, Lady of Life! Piatr thought. *She's alive. Alive, damn all your rotten attempts to kill her.*

He caught the glance that passed between the shorter of the two Schvait men and the Thane, and suddenly his heart constricted. He knew that look, had heard enough of the other slaves' rumors. Treachery; no court would listen to his accusation, but he could give warning. He wheeled on his one foot and froze.

Francosz's knife point touched his face.

"You missed my mother, clown. I should take your eyes for that," the boy hissed. Behind him, his sister giggled. The judge glared over his shoulder at the whispered interruption. Piatr watched the knife point now hovering near his face. *Warning,* he thought. *How do I warn her? She wins; I could escape. Escape before they finally cut my throat.* Yesterday the little bastard had actually tried to kill him, cheered on by his sister. The line wasn't working any longer and they *would* kill him now, or very soon.

Lady, show this son of sheepeaters true challenge and I hope to see you win. He sank to the platform before the boy, miming panic, his mind not in it, his eyes fixed on Megan and the tall outlander. When the time came he'd warn them, cost him his life or no, and run. He owed her more than that. He didn't mind that she had not recognized him through the fool's paint. Her face was still and she had looked through him and all the others, her mind already on the race. He'd last seen that look when the Thane's siege was broken. The Captain would win. He knew she'd win, he hoped.

"Ready yourselves, then." The judge sat down next to the sandkeeper with a small hourglass before her on the dais. "One glass," he called.

Megan got up and threw her cloak over Shkai'ra's box, stretching, warming up. From a position of front splits, as she worked the tension out of her tendons, she stared up the course. "I explained that you didn't have to accept forfeit."

"What, and miss seeing the woman keel over?" Shkai'ra chuckled. "Too bad those three are stuck working for a pig."

She nodded at the Schvait. Megan nodded, distantly. The Thane's slave clown, there had been something familiar about him . . .

"Time!"

Megan bounced to her feet and stood beside Shkai'ra, next to the black-shirts. Ahead, city militia kept a path free through the crowd with the shafts of pikes and halberds, a lane of cobblestones littered with horsedung and fruit rinds ending at the first building of the route. That was laid out with poles, bright red ribbands to the left and yellow to the right, the width of a building apart. It stretched, over roof and lane, cutting a raven-straight path over the crooked, twisting streets and tangled roofs. Looming over the sharp-peaked tangle of the lower town, the towers of The Kreml stood against a hard blue sky, streaked with ragged filaments of torn cloud.

Taller poles marked the four archery targets, each set a hundred meters from the path, separated from each other at irregular intervals; those would be paper figures on a backing of planks. Thick clots of spectators furred the rooflines; this would be a challenge to entertain their children's children with, sipping mulled ale before a midwinter fire. The sound of their voices was a susurrus louder than the wind.

The judge raised his hand, and everything else faded from their minds; anything but the challenge suddenly became unreal, unimportant. What was real was the feel of the cobbles on bare feet, the stretch of lungs breathing a slight fog into cold air, the spot of white held in the judge's hand. That fell, the cloth drifted ten paces in the strong breeze, and touched.

They ran, bodies low, legs pumping. Longer limbs brought Shkai'ra and the Schvait mercenaries to the wall first; the Schvait in the lead had swung a grapnel as he ran. Its tines clattered into an eaves gutter; the mountaineers swarmed up the rope, scarcely slowing. The Kommanza halted at the base of the wall, braced her hands against it; her companion ran the last few steps, jumped once from broad shoulders and *sprang*, hands outstretched.

Palms grated on ornament, nails on brick and half-timbering. She reached the roof first, slamming over the edge, got a

glimpse of the Schvait tugging at their grapnel. She threw a
loop of thin, spider-strong line over a carved head, dropping
it back to Shkai'ra, then skittered over the roofridge, diago-
nally down the slanting surface. No time to descend; she left
the edge in a soaring leap that ended with her grip slapping
onto the stone railing of a garden atop the building opposite.
Pavement flew by beneath her; ignore it, swing over, legs
twisting in midair to drop her soles onto the flat, winter-bare
surface.

Shkai'ra crouched, jumped, caught the line a body's length
above her head and went up it hand over hand, toes scrabbling. Child of distant plains, she still moved with bleak
efficiency. Breath rasped, timed to aid exertion, deep from
her stomach to pump oxygen into muscles being pushed to
their limits.

"Down the center, up the left!" came Megan's voice.

The Zak had scouted the route last night and had a better
eye for urban terrain; could travel more swiftly in any case.
Shkai'ra went down the inland side of the first building in a
controlled fall; it was a story shorter than the downslope
facing. Across the street, up a drainpipe on one corner of the
next house. From the low-pitched roof of the warehouse she
could see the first target, an eagle clutching an olive spray
and a bundle of arrows in its claws, with a shield across its
chest. A devil figure in the local mythology.

The target was five hundred meters ahead of her, flat on to
the course . . . but from the street or rooftops closer, it
would be hidden by intervening buildings.

Tricky, she thought, even as she moved. Long legs flashed,
driving her along the ridge of the roof; she leaped to the
house of the garden, sacrificing time for a better angle. Her
boots struck the railing. She was pulled back, unbalanced by
the weight of the bowcase on her shoulder. *Fifteen meters
onto stone* went through her, as she crouched and punched
her hands forward to shift her weight. Shins knocked into the
railing; she landed on forearms among dead herbs that crushed
with a dry smell, spices and decay. She rolled and was up,
sneezing as she ran.

The uphill course was clear. *Any closer, and that roof*

ridge will hide the eagle, she thought, running forward to the upper right corner of the roof; furthest away from the target, but the closer to a side-on angle.

Extreme range, she thought. Four hundred meters, north and west. The bow rose; her mind blanked, stilling like a pool of calm water. *Feel the lines of force to the target*. The remembered words of the Warmaster flowed through and over her, finding nothing, not even ego to catch upon. Her motion was graceful and smooth and fluid as the arc of a dolphin leaping into sunlight. The pull of the bow dropped off as the fletching came to the angle of her jaw, her grey eyes unfocused, blank as mist. The arrow loosed, flicker-thought.

A sigh rippled across the spectators. Bird-high above, there was a single harsh glitter of sun on metal as the long shaft slowed, tipped, and began its descent. Silence, then clear through it the sound of steel sinking into wood, as the eagle's shield split.

The sound carried through the unquiet air, to where the Schvait had halted. They had continued to another roof; two stood to make a shooting-rest for the third, six feet above the rooftree. He was aware of her shot arcing overhead but his crossbow rose to his shoulder as smoothly as before. If he hesitated it did not show despite the impossible range Shkai'ra's arrow came from. Impossible for any local bow.

Shkai'ra was already moving.

The Schvait loosed. Megan barely noticed. *They're off center to the route*, she thought. They would have to descend to street level, cross to the building before them, then turn left to the odd three-cornered one where the next aimpoint was. Gods! Her own descent would be shorter.

The mercenaries had other plans. Their next building was a merchant's warehouse; like many such it had a projecting timber balk braced below the eaves, a hoist for merchandise. The mountaineer unlimbered his grapnel again; the tines bit, with three pairs of strong arms pulling. An end of the line was braced about a chimney, and the three ran across it lizard-agile, a story higher than Megan's head. She wasted no time on stunned amazement, and only an instant for a grudging admiration.

The Zak drove claws into the half-timbered wall of the building and swung around a corner. Yes, there *was* a direct route to the wedge-shaped roof. A clothesline, an old staysail line from a fishing boat from the looks, stretched between the buildings and solidly anchored to brick. But slack, slack.

There were powdery fragments of brick dust in her eyes, between her teeth. Descending to the line, she lost the grip of one hand and her claws squealed on the stone. Then the rough hemp prickled on the cold bare skin of her feet. It swayed, and she half-ran down it to the midpoint, half slid, balance and a madman's luck keeping her centered until she reached a point where her body weight pulled the rope taut without throwing her forward. There it cradled her like a giant swing; she began shifting her weight to set it swinging, in increasing arcs, and felt a frozen swirl of exhilaration lying with the lightness under her breastbone at the upswing . . .

Leaped . . . And was flung like a sling bullet by the impetus, out, up, roof rushing toward her, *impact*.

The crowd roared, that portion of it that could see. A ripple ran across the rooftops, as those closer relayed the news to their neighbors, heads and shoulders bowing and swaying like grain in the wind. Megan traveled through the sound, in a chill circle of isolation fenced by need. The gap between the triangular building and the next was an easy stride; below, the target flashed white.

"Shkai'ra! Target!" She yelled in Fehinnan, which no one here would understand save the Kommanza.

The Kommanza reached the strung line, dropped and went along it hand over hand, swinging like a pendulum at the anchoring end to push herself into a position to grab the roofline. *Some advantage to standing a hundred and seventy-odd centimeters*, she thought grimly, forcing her breathing to regularity. Glancing to her left; saw the odd little building like a wedge of pie, with Megan gesturing down between it and the next in line, then leaping easily across a narrow gap. To her right; the mercenaries swarming along the roofline toward her.

In through the nose. Breathe to the pit of the stomach. Out through the mouth. This was burning energy, drawing on reserves of oxygen faster than even heart and lungs trained by a lifetime's effort could replenish them. *Don't gasp. Control.*

Across to the triangular roof, a jarring thud in her bootsoles. *Tired . . . run lightly, on the balls of the feet . . .*

The target was a gar, a lifesized rendering of the giant Brezhan riverpike. Below her in the bed of a wagon, all of nine meters long, the aiming mark around one little eye. She looked at it and knew at once that there was no way to get a shot except to straddle the two rooftops. She braced one foot, let the other fall out. Just wide enough, and the tendons in her groin stretched and protested.

The target below her; her arrow sliding through the center-line cutout whose groove kept it steady even straight down. *Don't envy those crossbows,* she thought, even as the shaft slashed down, through the painted eye and the boards beneath to stand ringing between two cobblestones. *His bolt will wobble in the aiming slot at this angle. Selfbows they use around here would have been even worse.*

Down on the dais, Schotter watched the five swarm up the first building, his clenched fist pounding on the arm of his chair.

Good, good! he thought. *No one can beat the Schvait, no one has and no one ever . . .* And in the first jumble of roofs, Megan's form showed first, cutting off his surge of relief. Over the uneven roofs it was difficult to tell who led; running figures, a signal from one of the judge's seconds, flicker and schrassh of arrows splitting targets, the echoing of a call distorted by walls and wind. His hands clenched on the chair, knuckles beginning to show white with tension as first one group, then the other was seen to lead. *If I could make the tiles skid under your feet, woman, I would. Falter, slide, you slut, fall.*

To his back, before the cluster of people reviving the Thane's wife, Piatr crouched, his hands also clenched, unconsciously echoing the inarticulate noises that Schotter made as the race progressed, but for different reasons. He strained to see where Megan was, his motley twisting in his grip. *Goddess! Gods! Grant she win!* he thought. He glanced over at the woman, recovering from her faint, voice peevish and harsh; the boy, knife limp in his hand, attention fixed on the race. How he hated them all. He squeezed his eyes shut. *Sweet Gods!*

". . . *not reclaiming your token,*" Megan had said to Piatr, when the surgeons were finished with him. "Since when does losing a foot in my service ensure that your mind was damaged?" It was his first lucid moment after the accident—the red-shot black agony as the boom had trapped and ground his foot into a pulpy unhealable mass against the mast—he still could not understand that he was alive. Most captains would have released the boom and allowed him to smash his head open on the deck far below; there were too many others ready to fill his place.

"But . . . who will hire a one-foot sailor?" Piatr stammered, still not thinking.

"Who else?" she said, looking across him at his net-mate, Reghina. "See that he heals fast. I can use him." Her voice held the harsh note of command; he hung for moments in bewilderment, the sense of what she said warring with the tone. An attempt at thanks was cut off by a gesture, and a face harder than iron.

Strange, he had thought, muzzy with drugs. *Never seen kindliness behind a mask of harshness before. The other way round often enough . . .*

Memory trailed off at a sudden gasp from the watching crowd and his mind avalanched back to the unbearable tension of the present as he craned to see. *I will take that Thane's throat in my hands, for her, if his treachery . . .*

There was a cleared space before the citadel wall, littered with masons' tools; the marked path lay straight across it, to a sortie ladder fixed to the new wall in brackets, a mobile ladder, pinned for easy removal. To one side was the last of the archery targets, another devil-figure. This time a human figure, an evilly senile man, white-bearded, in a starred jacket and odd cylindrical hat. But before the paper figure was a construction barricade of planks.

Megan ignored the Schvait halted ten paces to her left, aiming; she plunged forward. Shkai'ra would handle the archery. Her mouth was dry, and she tried to swallow the phlegm stuck gummily to the back of her throat, retching instead. Down the side of the last building. Difficult, slick stone without carving; new work. Across the littered surface, feet moving as surely as they had minutes ago, as the power of trained will overrode fatigue. The ladder was ahead of her; for once a ladder. Once over the wall, and the gate of The Kreml would be a hundred paces upslope, a straight, clear line. She laid a hand on the bottom rung.

Shkai'ra also raced past the Schvait archers. They responded, with a welcome second's amazed distraction. The last three body lengths of her descent were a fall; she twisted in the air to land on spread limbs, but there was still a ringing blackness in her head, and color-patterns swirling before her sight. *Up, you useless cow* went through her mind. Stonefort; her childhood; the voice of the Warmaster to a child on her hands and knees, sobbing and vomiting with exhaustion. A boot in her ribs. Rage awoke; she rose.

At the midpoint of the barricade she paused, took stance. There was the knot she had selected as an aiming point. The last shaft; fight weariness out of arm muscles that had held and lifted her all that morning. *Push* the shaking away, as she pushed the bowstave. Hold; correct; hold. Loose.

It was a pile head, an armorpuncher, four-sided, tapering to an edge, not a point; an edge like a miniature cold chisel. Designed to pierce armor of lacquered bison hide and fiberglass worn by the cataphracts of her homeland. The half-inch of soft pine boards scarcely slowed it, but it was the roar from the crowd, the crowd who could see over the planks, see that this her last shaft had not been deflected, *that* enabled her to turn and run for the ladder.

As Megan's hand closed around the rung, a shrill, piercing whistle from the harbor reached her ears, then a two-tone falling note that cut off abruptly. She hesitated only a second, abandoned the ladder and scaled the wall directly, unmortered

cracks barely sufficient to hold her claws at speed; metal
screech on stone as a hand slipped once, scramble of toes and
she drew her torso over the edge of the wall, swinging a leg
to sit astraddle. Shkai'ra reached the bottom of the ladder as
Megan grasped the top of the ladder and braced it, throwing
the weight of her body back to hold the ladder in place.
The top pins . . . She held as Shkai'ra swarmed up the
ladder.

"Go for the gate . . . I come," she panted.

Shkai'ra glanced at her then nodded, a quick, incomplete
jerk of the head, and continued.

Megan waited, swallowed a bit of skin pulled off her lips
with her teeth, face impassive as the Shvait gaped up at her,
then climbed. Her eyes narrowed at the one who hesitated.
She held one hand to the leader of the three.

"Cheat. Oathless!" she said in faltering Schvaitisch, and
dragged her hand across the top pins of the ladder, scraping
away the wax and metal filings that filled and hid the sawn-
through metal. Any weight near the top of the ladder would
have peeled it away from the wall to kill or badly injure the
person on it. The two Schvait nearest her, holding to the
wall, turned to the third who had scouted the route the night
before. He paled and stepped back a pace; none of the three
noticed that Megan was gone.

She hit the dirt running, hurtled over the embanked earth
onto the Citadel road and drove the claws of her hands deep
into the wood of the Great Gate.

"Fulfilled," she said to the judge at the gate and to Shkai'ra,
who was resting one hand lightly on the oak. The judge
nodded and she pulled her hands free of the marks in the
gate that men would see there for a hundred years.

The Kommanza reached out a hand and brushed the knuckles lightly on the Zak's cheek. "Not finished," she said. "Worth
it. Go!"

The crowd murmured as the three Schvait halted on the
ladder. Too much unrestful air lay between the knot on The
Kreml wall and the nearest spectators for sound to carry;
there was a buzz from the watchers as the mercenaries let the

Zak go forward without them; that turned to a roar as two of the Schvait loosened the third from the rungs with a few economical kicks. He fell, mouth open in a soundless O of scream, turning to strike the hard pavement fifteen meters below, and was still. Surf-like, the noise continued, growing as Megan swarmed back over the wall; it followed her back down the course, growing at what the mob thought was the bravado of her headlong plunge.

But the Zak had seen what was happening down by the dock. The clown was running from Schotter's son, who was lunging after him with a knife. Dodging around the judge, through the clutter on the dais, hurtling over the prostrate form of the Thane's wife, over the edge of the man-high dais.

Megan could hear nothing of the crowd noise. She moved in the peculiar silence that speed and concentration spark, hearing only the sigh of the wind and the occasional grating of her claws on slate, and her own breathing; eyes fixed on the dais. She knew who had warned her and faintly she heard the judge bellow, "Cease this! I command . . ." as the clown half toppled, falling like a clockwork toy running down. How many other one-footed men knew the *Zingas Teik's* whistle code? How many had been among the *River Lady's* crew?

She was almost close enough to see his eyes turned to her as the young Thane grabbed his hair. Silence fell as the watchers sensed the driving intentness of her plunge; almost falling down the side of the last building, racing across the littered cobbles between walls of staring eyes and the crossed pikeshafts of the Guard. A knife flickered into her hand, held by the blade tip with three fingers and a thumb.

Francosz did not know what the fool's whistle had meant. But it was a signal of some sort, that was plain enough. A signal that would harm his father! It was inconceivable insolence in a house serf; and besides, he had been meaning to kill the man anyway. Now that was doubly urgent, as this might be the last chance he had. He jerked the clown's head back to bare his throat for the cut, wrinkling his nose at the smell of greasepaint and sweat.

Piatr slumped. Not a large man even by Zak reckoning, he would normally have found it easy enough to break the boy's

grip. But it had been nearly a week since he slept for more
than a stolen moment, the children had been too watchful,
and some of *them* were always awake.

He was not tired, this was beyond that; sound buzzed
behind his eyes like fever, a glass wall between him and the
world. He could see the honed blue glint of the knife above
him, but the terror was distant, as if his body had lost all
capacity to feel. And the darkness beckoned; the Captain was
back, and had won; that duty had taken the last of his will. To
sleep . . .

Francosz saw a sudden flicker of light, a painful tugging at
the new-piled topknot that still made his head feel unbalanced. There was a bump painful enough to bring involuntary
tears to his eyes as the back of his head rapped the timbers of
the dais, and a deep *thunk* as Megan's knife drove through
the piled hair and into the oak. Reaching up, he yanked
savagely at the hilt, his fourteen-year-old hand fitting it neatly.

The clown looked up to see Megan's follow-through; as
clearly as a shout her eyes snapped the command to *move*.
With drugged slowness he staggered to his knees and crawled
out of arm's reach of the boy. *I'm going to live*, he thought. It
didn't seem that important. The cobbles were wet-slippery
and cool beneath his palms.

The young Thane grinned tautly and raised the two knives,
beginning the step that would take him near enough to drive
them into the clown's back. That had suddenly become very
important; if this thing that had defeated his father were to
die, perhaps the defeat would die. The logic of it seemed
compelling; he grinned at the approaching figure of the Zak
and began to raise . . .

*Her eyes. Her eyes were brown, very dark, almost black.
They grew. Words whispered in his mind, alien words. Somehow, without looking, he was aware of slim taloned fingers
tying a knot in air, and his hands were caught.* There were
no physical bonds, but beads of sweat broke out on his
forehead as he strained.

"Release him, Zak." The judge's voice was cold; the Zaki
were not much disliked in Brahvniki; they had founded the
city, back in the mists of legend, and most born there bore

some of their blood. Their arts were not illegal, because so seldom seen. But few outsiders cared to be reminded of a skill they could not understand or match, and there had been riot and pogrom in other towns for less than this.

Panting with exertion she halted before the young Thane, considering him and Piatr's plodding crawl, the goat-foot artificial limb clacking against the pavement. Briefly, her lips tightened, and her hands: Francosz winced. Then the hands snapped apart, and his arms fell to his side.

The boy staggered, and backed so rapidly that his head cracked once more against the edge of the dais. He sat abruptly; to the crowd, it appeared he had been faced down and recoiled in terror. There was a snicker of laughter, breaking tension; Thanes were not liked in Brahvniki, and this added straw on the mountain of Schotter's woes tickled their fancy.

Megan ignored him, the crowd, the world, as she stared up at the judge. Shkai'ra was at her back now, panting; as from a great distance Megan could hear the flat *plunk* as she idly twanged her bowstring, smell the familiar musk of her sweat. Her gaze stayed locked on the judge's, keeping her silence until the man shifted uneasily, until the crowd grew straining-quiet to hear the forfeit she would claim. Schotter stood rock-still, but dark stains grew under the arms of his silk blouse and vest. Her own consciousness stayed focused, but the chill of cooling sweat suddenly struck her, and she shivered.

A movement at the corner of her eye. Her hand snatched out, and the roasted apple smacked into it; she caught the irrepressible street-urchin grin of the seller in a glance.

She warmed her icy fingers on the hot fruit, tossing it from hand to hand. "My favor, Most Honorable?" she asked.

"Whatever you would claim," he replied, looking up to the city. Winking mirrors confirmed that the challenge had been fulfilled according to the approved forms. "As you would, Whitlock. And your companion, Farshot," he added.

Schotter Valders'sen was white around his lips, but his face was steady, and the stance he braced against his chair. Despair perfect enough can be as heartening as hope; total ruin faced him, even if the Zak did not demand all he owned, or the sale of himself and his kin as bondservants. Out in the crowd his creditors waited, like vultures circling a dying camel or heirs at a rich man's deathbed. His hand had been heavy while he had the power, and it would be remembered.

What zight *I have is mine still,* he thought. *I will not cringe.* The Zak woman would barely have come to his breastbone, but she loomed before him.

"Thane," she said.

"Zak, ask your favor," he said, thickly. " 'Tis your time. But one day, a Thane will be your death. We remember."

Megan studied his face. Then she stretched out one finger, elegantly clawed in grey steel. "That one," she said, pointing to the clown. "Give him to me."

Schotter sagged in temporary relief, then jerked as if stung. He was fated to lose all he had, but this . . . She was showing her contempt for his wealth and standing for all the world to see, showing that his possessions were worthless in her eyes.

"Given," he choked. "Challenge at an—"

"Not so quickly," Shkai'ra broke in. She sauntered forward, dropping the bow back into the case on her back and thrusting her hands through her swordbelt, looking him up and down. Schotter turned slightly to watch her, hands picking aimlessly at the cloth of his jacket. There was nothing worse that could happen, after all . . . he had a vision of mutilation. Insanely, a jape drifted through his mind: *Perhaps my wife will regret her dead-fish coldness in our bed now. At least, she'll have no more need of it.*

"Name your price, barbarian."

She smiled. "Barbarian? That doubles my price." She reached out and took his son by the wrist, twisting, jerking her other thumb at the boy's sister, on the dais. "That one too. We'll see if ugliness and bad manners mean they're untrainable."

He stilled, his eyes flicking over his children, then to his second son. "You take my blood for slave—" he began, then rasped, "Given."

Shkai'ra studied his face with the cool pleasure of satisfied cruelty. Her birth-tongue used variants of the same term for "murder" and "joy"; the most common word for torture could also be rendered as "relaxation." Some of the ways of the

Zekz Kommanz she had abandoned in the days of her wanderings, but the deep, sensual enjoyment of triumph over a hated opponent was still keen. This man had tried to kill her, and worse, her companion; now he was down and it was time for the boot and knife.

"Fater, *no!*" The girl fell to her knees and grasped Schotter's legs, pleading. "Fater, please . . ." Her words trembled into silence as he ignored her, except for the slight swaying her impact brought. His eyes were fixed below the dais, where Shkai'ra had gripped Francosz by the collar, occasionally delivering a ringing cuff with one sword-callused hand when he struggled too strongly.

Shkai'ra pulled out her knife and made to begin shaving the boy's head. In Fehinnan, Megan said, "No, Shkai'ra, don't do that. Shaving his head means he's a slave." The Kommanza looked at her a moment, puzzled; among her people, children went shaven-skulled until adulthood. "I won't have anything to do with taking slaves," the Zak continued tightly. "Especially children. Even Thanes." Shkai'ra stared hard at her a moment, shrugged and put the knife away.

"Standard indentures of apprenticeship," Megan said to the official on the dais. "Seven years or until the twenty-first birthday, instruction and lodging and a parent's powers."

The Thane freed himself from his daughter's clutch and thrust her staggering to the edge of the dais.

"So I have spoken. My seed I may do with as I wish." He turned to the judge, who concealed his satisfaction under a mask of detachment. The Thane could read the amusement there. From behind there was a squawking scream as Sova was dragged over the edge of the platform by one ankle.

"Given, and challenge fulfilled," the judge said, and turned to the two remaining Schvait, who stood to one side, having also descended from The Kreml. His expression was cold; the mercenaries had come within a hair's breath of treaty violation. That, they had avoided by killing their brother, but Schvait would be at a discount for some time; merchants rich enough to pay good wages demanded trustworthy guards, and no free-company captain would swear blades that might be bribed to violate an oath. Their mountainous homeland lived by its exports, and fighters were not the least among them.

"As losing proxy, we have no claim on you," the judge said, the words clipped short. "Go."

The two Schvait looked at him impassively, then the woman leaned to her companion, whispering something. He stepped forward and spoke.

"No claim you say. We have claim. Betrayment is not good . . . and from doing this we have our brother saved. Taking coin from one who treacherous is . . . not. Hear us. Here price is." They, as one, held out the small pouches that traditionally marked their fee, dropped them on the ground and spat on them, turning to stalk into the crowd.

The judge surveyed the scene, a cool smile appearing on his face; the situation suited his sense of justice. "Challenge fulfilled!" he cried, throwing up his hands, the crowd at last began to cheer.

Piatr leaned his head back against the dais, leaning on one elbow, watching the Schotters' children, held fast by the Captain's companion.

A dream? he wondered. Dark Lord knew he had dreamed of it often enough, these last few days. The Captain back, the Thane destroyed. He jerked his head back as his body tried to fall asleep, tears of fatigue gathering and being blinked away as he fought to stay awake. She was back.

Slowly the world returned to Megan, the strange, muffled single-mindedness fading as she bit into the apple, tasting its cinnamony sweetness, watching the last of the Valders'sen entourage leave the dais. The scrapes and bruises from the race were just beginning to throb.

"You'll have to keep close watch on those two," she said to Shkai'ra. Nodded at the kneeling girl, who glared at her, the boy sullen and afraid at once. "And children?" Seizing children, taking them from their homes . . .

"I didn't need money."

Megan tossed the apple-core into the harbor, hearing it sink with a splash. "I see." *We'll talk about this back at the*

Vurm, she thought. She walked over to the cloth-hung plat-form and tore off a section. Piatr looked up from where he still sat on the ground as she dropped the cloth into his lap. She took in the number of old whip and burn scars. Her head swivelled to the two young Thanes and she took a step back towards them, controlling herself with an effort.

A lock of Piatr's hair matted with the streaked paint on his face, the black around his eyes running tear-like down his cheeks into the white.

"Piatr, wipe that garbage off." She paused a long moment, then whispered, more to herself than him. "I know. Habiku. I should have known before letting him do this to us." Her eyes settled on the goat foot.

"Their idea of a joke, Captain."

At her wordless sign, he unbuckled the straps and handed it to her. Megan took it and looked at the old brown stains where the ill-fitting thing had chafed raw and her hands tightened, leather and wood creaking under her grip. A muf-fled yelp came from behind her and she saw Piatr smile. Whirling, she threw the thing into the water with a violence belying her calm face, watching it arc out over the water, sinking with a splash.

"Not the smartest thing I've ever done," she said. "But . . ." Megan turned back to Piatr and startled him with a smile. "You'll have to use my shoulder to get back to the Vurm." Out of the corner of her eyes, she caught a glimpse of Shkai'ra giving the boy a hefty boot in the backside for trying to hit back, missing the wide-eyed look of puzzlement on Piatr's face. "I think Shkai'ra will be awhile."

Shkai'ra watched her companion helping the one-footed man away and shrugged, realizing that Megan would rather be private for a while. This voyage was opening old wounds; she hoped the final revenge would be satisfying enough to soothe them.

Hands on her hips, she surveyed her prizes. *Not much of a catch*, she thought wryly. The girl was flabby and out of condition; the boy a little better, but soft-handed. And no Kommanz youngster would have lived long with such a glare

of open hatred on his face; not that they did not hate their
elders, the Warmaster whose pupils did not hate was a failure, but control was part of the training. *What possessed me
to ask for these two? These whims will be the death of me yet*.

Wide-eyed, the Thane children stared back at her. They
had been pampered, as befitted the offspring of wealth; and
they were Thanes, scions of a people who held women of
little account beyond childbearing.

"Strip!" she barked. The boy complied; the girl required a
slapping cuff and stood shrinking and covering herself with
her hands. Shkai'ra snorted with the impatient contempt of a
people without a nudity taboo and leered at the two.

"Not to worry, girly; you're too young, and he isn't my
type." The leer grew. "You two have been *very* unlucky:
you've awoken my maternal instincts. I'm going to show you
some proper child-raising, the way my people do it. Get the
softness out of you, make you of some use. Or kill you." She
removed a belt and stood for a moment running the length of
supple leather between her fingers. "About time I got some
of my own back," she mused in a tongue neither of them
knew, thick with clicking gutturals, softly. Then her face
contorted in a snarl, followed by a scream. "*Now, to the
Kchnotet Vurm. Run! Run!*"

She followed, whirling the strap in carefully controlled,
stinging blows.

Megan paced the room with angry grace, one hand gripping the other behind her back to prevent the nails from
slashing the palms of clenched fists.

"Shkai'ra. I hold no slaves." She stopped with her back to
the bed, her face closed in, her posture controlled as a spring
wound just a hair too tight. "Especially not children. No. You
aren't going to do this to me or to them. I should have
stopped you at the dais."

The Kommanza looked up from her cross-legged position
on the bed, raised the fletchings of an arrow to the light of
the window. "Good, no damage . . . Kh'eeredo, I'm not doing
anything to you. As for the sprats, where I come from we'd
have tossed them onto our lancepoints. They're the kin of an

enemy, why the concern?" She grinned. "Besides, think for a moment. That crowd, they were spitting and throwing dung on the Schotter's-kin before we were out of the square: *ia*, and running to sack their house, and I didn't see the Watch objecting. Their sire, he's got no gold nor . . . face, honor, *zight*, now—nor money. What do you think a port city crowd would do to two little honey-pastries like those?"

"You're trying to justify it. Don't give me the bullshit! You've made them slaves. You've taken them in such a way that their father won't take them back, in public. To everyone in sight, to them, they're *your* slaves." Her voice sank almost to a whisper. "I was sold when I was twelve. I. Will. Not. Have. ANYTHING. To do with this!"

The Kommanza leaned back and propped herself on her elbows. "Kh'eeredo, I've no intention of selling them to anybody, *nia*? It was an impulse; always kick an enemy when he's down, as the saying goes. Now, if you really want me to boot them out, I will, it's no great matter to me. Then what? Their family is going to starve; this Schotter seems to have made himself unwelcome everywhere on the Brezhan, from your saying; even his own kindred upriver won't take him back, and he has no gold or skills. These two, Jaiwun bless, they haven't got the sense the gods gave rabbits. Don't know how to squat to shit without a servant to help; and they're the get of a Thane, a Thane the whole city hates. Be lucky to get work emptying slop-pots in a whorehouse, here. *Somebody* has to feed them and teach them something . . . You've told me about the kidpacks in F'talezon, how long do you think these two would live on the street?"

She shrugged. "Anyway, your choice. Say the word, and I'll go tell them to lose themselves."

Megan hunched her shoulders. *She's right. But so am I. It's still slavery and it's still a stupid thing to have done . . . impulse she says. We have to do something with them. She took them. I can't tell her to kick them out. That would be killing them.*

"I won't condone it. The only way I'll tolerate it is if you ask them what they want. If they say they want out, *you* are going to have to find a way to apprentice them, if they want it, somewhere upriver."

Shkai'ra blinked, shaking her head in puzzlement. "Ahi-a, all these years together and you still surprise me. *Ask* a child about what's to be done?" Another shrug. "As you say." She sighed.

"I'll get them," Megan said, turning her back on the Kommanza. "They'll need a bath."

The Zak closed the door behind herself bewildered. *Doesn't she remember being a child no one would ask? Doesn't she remember?*

Francosz put his head on his knees and listened to Sova cry. The walled yard of the Vurm was dark, the lamp by the door blown out by the wind. It was cold, the wind blowing grit over them. The privy stank. *Where could we run?* he thought. *Sova's just a baby. I've got to think. I've got to look after her.* He felt tears choke in his throat and gritted his teeth. *I won't cry. I can't.*

The door creaked open and one of the servants came out, to the well. He was whistling through his teeth as he passed them, stopping to hawk and spit. The blob of phlegm spattered on the boy's hand and he flinched, started to get up, glaring. The man laughed. "Poor slavey."

"We're not slaves," Francosz retorted. The servant laughed again and fetched the water.

When the door thudded closed behind him, Sova sniffled. He put his arm around her, awkwardly, and patted her shoulder.

"Francosz, what are we going to do? What can we do?"

"Pa and Ma are probl'y already gone. South, I guess. Maybe to Tor Ench. Try and start again. But I don't know. And *he gave us away*. Sovy, he didn't want us!"

She started crying harder and hugged him. "They—they didn't." *Pa pushed me away. He didn't care, as long as that woman didn't ask him for money.* She clung to her big brother. He didn't push her away like he always had; he didn't call her a baby, just a girl. He hugged her.

Pa pushed me away. He pulled my hands off his legs like

they were dirty. He wouldn't look at me. She shivered. *We're slaves.*

"Francosz, I want to go home!" Her voice was a thin wail. "I want to go home!"

"We can't." His voice cracked. "There's no home." He patted her shoulder stiffly.

The door opened again, letting out the sound of singing from the taproom. The Zak, Whitlock, looked around the moonlit yard. Francosz pulled Sova under his arm, afraid. What did the witch want?

She saw them and beckoned, the lamplight inside glinting on her hair. "Come inside before you freeze to death. We have to talk to you and you need to get cleaned up." She waited until Francosz pulled Sova up and came in, dragging his feet. Sova tried to keep him between her and Megan.

"You—you aren't going to eat us, are you?" the Thane girl whispered. "Please—"

Megan stopped as if the bottom step were a wall. "*Eat* you?" she exclaimed. Sova whimpered. "I'm not a cannibal," she said more quietly. "I don't eat people." She sighed. "No matter what Thanes think of Zak. Come on."

". . . so that's your choice," Shkai'ra concluded. Francosz and Sova huddled at the end of the bed, his arm around her shoulder. "*I* don't give much of a damn. The best you're likely to get is scutwork somewhere. Stay with us, you'll have a berth and enough to eat, and you'll learn something useful." She grinned. "How to survive, even if I have to kill you to teach you. Put all this kindness down to me going soft in my old age." *And . . . perhaps I need something to do*, she thought.

Megan looked at her. It was better than nothing, but the tall, red-blonde woman obviously didn't understand.

"Your answers now aren't final," the Zak added. "You aren't slaves." The boy looked at her, fearful, hating. The girl hid her face. At last he stammered, "All—all right."

He doesn't believe me, Megan thought. *He's still scared shitless of both of us.* "Right. Nikolakiaj has arranged a bath and you two have the room next door. The water's getting

cold. We'll see about outfitting the two of you tomorrow."
The boy, Francosz, he'll be a while hating us, Megan thought,
watching them go. *And Sova's too scared to spit. But I
thought I saw some hope there. Is that why Kat helped me?
Because she couldn't stand to see hopelessness in my eyes?*

Shkai'ra reached for her swordbelt. "I'm going down for a
game of dice and a drink, coming?"

Megan shook her head. "No. I need to think a bit more."
In the dark, Shkai'ra thought.

As the door closed behind the Kommanza, Megan blew out
the lamp. *It's done,* she thought. *I can't blame Shkai'ra for
not understanding. But I wish she could.*

Chapter 6

The newly-launched *Zingas Vetri* swung at her anchor in
the fitting-out basin of Brahvniki. The sun had set, but the
roofs and towers of the city to the west were still outlined,
black against rose, darkening to umber above. They had
closed the sterncastle windows of the Captain's cabin. Wood
creaked, and the air was full of the warm smell of new
seasoned wood and clean cordage; even the bilges had been
dried, holystoned and sanded.

The little cabin was lit by a single lantern, casting warm
yellow tones over table, chairs, chests and the broad bunk
that filled the incurving rear of the room, picking out the
bright zigzag patterns woven into the wool of its blankets.
Shkai'ra checked the newly installed rack at the base of the
transom window that held her knife, bow and saber, then
shook out her braids and began running a wide-toothed ivory
comb through her red-blonde hair.

"First night on board," she said, after a moment, bouncing
experimentally on the bunk. The straw tick beneath rustled.
"Better than some we've had, *nia*? Remember that cod-boat
we crossed from the Fire Isles on?"

Megan did not look up from her feral pacing. A crackling
tension radiated from her, bouncing from the wood and filling
the air. Her face was shuttered, impassive, the mouth a

99

drawn straight line beneath eyes coldly dark. Clasped behind her, her taloned fingers flexed and uncurled in ferocious, unconscious impatience.

Shkai'ra sighed and began to undress. "Wet dam' river, isn't it?" she enquired, pulling off her boots. There was no reply; she threw her clothes over a chest and slipped beneath the coverlet. Stretching, she enjoyed the smooth feel of the brown linen, the cool heaviness of the blankets that was a promise of warmth. It was something to make a pleasure out of the memory of winter bivouacs crouched wet against a muddy saddle.

Minutes stretched, and the Kommanza lay on her side, one hand propping her chin. Heavy, fine and straight, the hair lay against the milk-white skin of her breasts, where the sun had not reached. Muscle played lightly under the taunt surface of her arm; that was browned, the hairs faded white against it.

"Megan." There was no reply. "Megan!" Shkai'ra paused, pursed her lips, and shouted.

"Habiku's here!"

Megan whirled, half-lunged, her fingers curling up ready to tear. For a moment rage looked into the Kommanza's grin.

"Kh'eeredo, you've been a fighter long enough to know the waiting wears harder than bladeplay. Your guts can digest themselves, if you let them. We'll go upriver, we'll kill him or he'll kill us, as luck will have it. In the meantime, come to *bed* for the sake of each and every god." She held the blankets open. "You're going to need your rest."

Megan looked at the inviting warmth of the bed and her shaking hands, raising them to scrub across her face, pulling her hair loose. "I . . . will come," she husked, looking around the cabin, not seeing the furnishings she'd placed just the day or so ago. "So many ships . . ." She sat down slowly and pulled off her boots and breeches, shucking her clothing as if it suddenly restricted her. "I still have to remind myself it's *my* ship." Her hands curled tightly shut and Shkai'ra frowned when she did not flinch at what her claws must be doing to her palms. Megan opened one hand and ran it down the old scar on her lower abdomen. "What you say is true . . . but hate and fear are such good friends of mine—the smell of even *my* ship brings them back." She crossed to the bunk and slid under the blankets, her skin icy against Shkai'ra's; muscles quivering with the need to move, she stared at the ceiling and one hand sought out Shkai'ra's. Grasping the fingers hard, she shuddered as she forced relaxation on herself and turned to bury her face against Shkai'ra's warmth, lying very still.

The tall woman ran a hand over her back and shoulders. "Tense as iron," she muttered, and began kneading with impersonal skill. "Megan, try to relax a little." After a moment: "Coming back here . . . it's like the end of a holiday, in a way, isn't it?"

"Iron is needed here," Megan said quietly and gasped as the Kommanza's thumbs dug into a knot in the shoulder muscle. "I was a fool to think I could come home, just take up the old ways." She flipped around suddenly and grasped Shkai'ra's wrists lightly. "I'm sorry." She rubbed her hands along the red-blonde woman's forearms, and reached up to touch her face.

There was a sudden *thump* on the blanket between them. The black tomcat stretched, his tail high in the air, yawned pinkly and walked across Megan's face to reach the windowledge, settling into a pool of furred midnight and purring.

Shkai'ra inclined her face into the stroking hand. "No need for apologies," she said, shrugging. "I'm no more an exile here than I was in Illizbuah, across the Lannic." She closed her eyes, for a moment smelling wildflowers on the spring steppe and watching geese rising thousand-winged from the prairie marshes. "It's just . . . in Fehinna, you were a stranger too. Here, old hates, old loves: a web of them, and I'm the new thread that stands out."

She bit the other's hand gently, on the fleshy part just below the thumb, and worked her way down the arm to her mouth. They kissed with the comfortable familiarity of long experience; after a minute Shkai'ra drew back and continued:

"As for your old ways, you're not the same person, really. I've watched you change. Just one thing; when we met, I doubt if you smiled from week to week . . . These folk here, they've had only their memories of you for near three years. More startling for them, I'd think."

"Hm." Megan buried her face in the other's shoulder, drawing a deep breath. "I, I don't know how I feel anymore. I want . . ." One hand grasped for something in the air and her eyes clenched shut as old memories blew through her mind. "I keep swearing not to let any of it touch me . . . why do I feel like howling like a child?" She could feel tears hovering, hot behind her eyes, and suppressed them. "My vision of what I am and what the world is, has changed . . ."

"You move through the world, your point-of-seeing changes; the world changes, everything you knew looks different." Shkai'ra paused. "Harder to do things twice, to have to go back. You came up from nothing, killed the ones who'd hurt you, made yourself a power here on the river where you'd been a slave. Now you have to do it all again, with a new enemy. It makes something in your mind feel . . . put back in the prison you thought you were out of." Shkai'ra cupped a hand under her chin and brought her face up.

"But you're stronger now; wiser, more skilled. And I'm here," she whispered.

Megan gazed at her, unblinking. "Truth. But fear does strange things." She tapped one finger on her lip, chewing at the edge of one of her nails. "Three years ago . . . this," the words came hard and falteringly, "this closeness would have driven me into a killing frenzy to escape." She closed her eyes and listened to the purring cat. "And to admit to anyone . . . that I was afraid . . ." Shkai'ra opened her mouth, then closed it as the Zak continued in a whisper. "Had I ever, ever hinted that I was afraid, I would have died, no quicker than that monk trapped on the snow ledge in the Hal'en range last year, the one we couldn't reach . . . Slow—or perhaps if I was lucky, I would have died quickly, but I would have died." She twisted closer to Shkai'ra. "But as you say, you are at my back. I don't have to watch so hard." She smiled, her head down, where the Kommanz could not see her face. "I'm glad that trust is an emotion that can be learned."

The blonde woman ran her fingers through the other's hair, lifting the heavy mass of it. "You never explained exactly how Habiku got close enough to betray you."

"From the first . . . I thought he was a plant. From the Red Brotherhood, the ones my *beloved aunt*," her voice grew ironic, "brewed her poisons for. Like a fool I thought that if I knew, then I could play with fire. He was good at what he did. A ship was his third arm. For a year or so I kept him, telling myself I'd kill him next time he plotted against me. But I'd end up killing or flogging the poor dupes he'd talked into rebellion, they didn't call him 'Smoothtongue' for nothing, he'd give me that damned smile of his . . . he, he was the first male that I could stand near me."

She stopped for a second, and her voice took on a bitter self-accusation. "Too complacent. 'Ah, Lady. Habiku brewing another plot I have to crush.' Then I woke up chained in the slaver's hold." *Why didn't he kill me? He wanted me so much. It was almost as if he were courting me.* "I still don't know why he didn't just cut my throat. He always was greedy." She spoke dispassionately, but Shkai'ra could feel the muscles of her back beginning to tense up again. "Sheer, unutterable stupidity, on my part," the dark woman continued. "Inexcusable and . . . unforgivable."

"Well, I forgive you," Shkai'ra said, stroking her back. "Someday I'll tell you how I nearly got fed to a forest demon because I was too trusting . . . In the meantime, enough of memories. We're here, we're now . . . and how does this feel? And this?"

"Good, very good." Megan ran her hands down Shkai'ra's body, feeling satin-smooth skin under her hands; she tried to let the sensations drown the voice in the back of her mind. *You forgive me, but can I forgive myself?* She responded to Shkai'ra's hands and lips with desperate urgency.

Late that night, in the cabin that was close with body heat and the smell of new things, Shkai'ra woke to feel the space beside her empty and heard the soft pad of bare feet on the deck above . . . back and forth, back and forth; knowing new

aloneness, staring up at the wooden ceiling that carried the
sound of the quiet footfalls so clearly.

A groan went up from the dockside challenge-ring as the
Aenir woman went down on her face for the second time.
She raised herself to hands and knees, shaking a face rubbed
raw on one side against the rough planks of the pier. Looking
up, she saw faces, amused, eager, some sorrowful as they
paid over their bets.

Megan circled into her sight. *But she is so small*, the
would-be crewmember thought dazedly.

"You want to continue?" the Zak asked politely. The other
woman shook her head, and reached for the helping that the
Captain extended. That let her gather her feet beneath her;
she tightened her grip and jerked backward, locking the arm
and pivoting the smaller figure around and down; her foot
lashed out for the armpit to stun and hold.

As her foot came off the ground the Zak twisted in her
grasp, foot slamming through to connect with the supporting
knee. The Aenir woman tried to let go, regain balance, felt
herself falling, held fast by the hand she no longer wanted;
and found herself on her back, staring unfocused at the
rough, red knuckles just touching the bridge of her nose.

"Done!" Megan said and shifted her weight off the other
woman's chest. The Aenir clambered to her feet and headed
for the edge of the sparring circle. "No, stay," the Captain
called to her, as she accepted a towel from the one-foot
sitting on one of the bales of fodder stacked for shipment.

Megan motioned to him and threw the second towel at the
Aenir who, startled, caught it against her chest.

"But . . . you beat me."

"So. I want a crew that can fight, not competition! Wipe
your face, you're bleeding on yourself. Name?"

"Ilge," the woman said, dabbing at her chin and wincing.

"Go stand over there, we'll dicker price later, Ilge." Megan
turned to Shkai'ra. "You want to take the next one?"

"Teik," Piatr cut in, looking down the list in his lap.
"We've got the lot." He looked up at the Kommanz,
expressionless.

She returned the look blandly, then away, at Megan. "Well, that makes seventy. They all know which end of a blade to pick up, they all have two . . . hands, and they were all alive yesterday sunset."

She didn't look over at the snort that came from the bales on one side. Megan looked at Piatr, then at Shkai'ra, and thought, *Sshaa, the damn fools, not talking to each other. Have to thrash it out between them.* Her grin answered Shkai'ra.

"*Now* do you feel like a game of cniffta? We're both warmed up. Only four knives?"

"Ale," the Kommanz replied, looking at the ship, where the lascars were trundling the last of the cargo aboard. The *Zingas Vetri* was fifteen meters at the waterline and four at her maximum breadth, fifteen oars to a side and a single raked mast slightly forward of amidships. That had been lanteen-rigged, now converted to a jibsail; the fore-and-aft rig would enable her to point higher to the wind, and the two booms would let a crew of ten handle her in all weathers. Bundles of five-meter ashwood oars were going aboard, with barrels of salt pork, fish and hard biscuit. Even the timber and stone anchor swinging beneath the bows and the ship's boat trailing from the square-transom were new.

She looked lean and fast and dangerous, a hull built for things other than running cargo. A pirate's ship, or a blockade runner's, with enough keel and carrying enough sail to make speed, yet with the oars and bottom for inshore work or a darting swiftness in a calm. *Not as good as a horse*, Shkai'ra thought. *But for a ship, she'll do.* Although the rest of the crew would be crowded, as was inevitable on an oared ship.

"All right, why don't you see to the ale you want and your cat, he'll be making Piatr's life hell enough once we're under way. I've got a few things to look up if we want to leave tomorrow."

"*Ia.* When . . ."

"You fishgutted, ham-handed idiot!" Megan leaned over the railing and her voice, surprisingly strong, froze one of the dock-handlers in his tracks. "Any fool can see that barrel isn't secure on the left side! Lift that with the tackle and I'll have

salt port and brine all over *my* deck! Do it right, or I'll
complain to your guild, if I don't take the mess out of your
hide!"

Shkai'ra heard Piatr mutter, "That's the old Captain all
right. Touch her ship wrong and she'd gut you," under his
breath.

She gazed past his head at Megan who was swinging down
to supervise the last of the stowing, when he swivelled his
head around sharply, checking to see if she'd heard him. She
shook a hand that someone earlier in the day had bruised, to
loosen the muscle.

It was just dawn and frost glittered on the cobbles, only a
few people out in the cold. All of Brahvniki had been talking
of the Zak Rivercaptain rumored to be Megan Fleet'sbane,
Whitlock, Shadow'sdaughter, for the last week, but Mateus
hadn't given them credence. Over the last year he had
hoped, had looked for the Captain at every rumor, trying to
repay guildprice that Habiku had said he owed. With no
guild, he'd found nothing but day labor, and little enough of
that. Then, at last, all he could do was beg. He no longer
believed the rumors. He sat at his corner in the lower market, idly running his fingers over his ribs, trying to warm his
hands; he wasn't a good beggar. He caught a flea and cracked
it between his thumbnails, wondering greyly how much longer
it would take him to starve to death. What use was it all
anyway, all he could do well was sail and that was denied
him. Under verminous rags his hands clenched with hate.
Habiku. For his loyalty to the Captain, who had kept him on
even after he had rebelled against her under Habiku's
goading—he remembered that flogging—the man had paid
him by beggaring him.

He didn't bother looking up as someone walked up the
street toward him; didn't even bother with the rasping whine
of the professional beggar. He pressed his hands into his
armpits to warm them, shivering.

"Mateus," a familiar voice said. "Sitting around on street
corners when there's work to be done!" His guild papers hit

the ground in front of him, raising a tiny puff of frosty dust, his eyes tracked up to lock with Megan's.

"Ship sails tomorrow," she said in the flat tone he remembered. "You've got a lot to do till then." She turned and walked back towards the harbor. He gaped after her, then scrambled to clutch the papers and the precious bone plaque and follow, leaving the empty begging bowl in the dust behind him.

BRAHVNIKI
TENTH IRON CYCLE, TENTH DAY

The *Lady Winter* spider-walked out of Brahvniki harbor on a morning black with cloud. Even with her mast bare, she heeled sharply as a gust of cold air struck at her; Megan ignored that, and the first scattering of raindrops, standing beside the wheel wrapped in her dark cloak and mood. Mateus cursed under his breath and wrestled with the spoked circle, bringing the sharp head back into the waves.

Damned newfangled things, he thought absently. Most riverboats still used tillers on the Brezhan. From below came the steady *thump-thump-thump* of the oarmasters's mallets on a hardwood log; the oarlocks creaked, and the thirty blades went *shissst* as they struck the choppy surface of the estuary in unison. Or almost; the rowers were experienced but not with each other, and it was a rough day for their first serious work. The narrow hull pitched; the waves on the broad estuary were enough to hide the low line of the opposite shore.

"Captain—" he said.

"No," she said. "They'll learn quickly or not at all." *I've delayed here long enough. Habiku. I'm coming after you at last.*

He took a deep breath and let it out slowly. "Captain, when you hired me on, years ago, you said 'Don't listen to foolishness, even if I say it. Tell me then, not when disaster's struck,' and I swore to it. This is harbor weather, until the crew settles." She wheeled to face him.

"Mateus, are you rebelling on me again?" she snarled at him, saw his face change. A pause, and calm settled on her with visible effort. "Use that onshore wind." She turned away, pulling the cloak closer against the cold autumn wind, her mind again focusing north, barely hearing Mateus's aggrieved sigh, "Aye, Captain."

She caught a faint, scattered shout from up forward. Shkai'ra was standing, hands on hips, staring up at the two children in the stays.

"Quick! *Move, move*, keep moving. Stop and you'll row another hundred strokes!" Her shout carried well.

Four meters above the deck, Sova whimpered as the harsh fibers of the forestay bit into palms rasped raw by the loom of an oar; she and her brother had been paired on one, and even together they'd lasted a scant half-hour. Tears ran down her face, mingled with sweat to sting her bitten lip; she struggled to swing her hand forward, but the fingers wouldn't unclench. Weights seemed to be dragging her downwards, she couldn't breathe; lights shimmered before her eyes, against the black of thunderclouds and dark water. She fell.

Shkai'ra snapped forward from her relaxed pose against the railing and caught the slight shape, knees and arms flexing to absorb the impact. Blue eyes stared into grey in a blind shock of relief. The Kommanza held the girl out at arm's length and dropped her to the deck, bending over with her fists on her hips and shaking her head in disgust.

"How can I teach someone to be a warrior if they'd rather die than feel a little pain?" she said. "Don't you have any will to survive at all?"

Sova lay on the heaving planks, unable to tell the spinning in her head from the motion of the ship, debated being seasick and decided she was too exhausted and . . . no, not bruised, she *was* a bruise, a large one. Fighting for air, she forced herself to draw breath down to the pit of her stomach the way the barbarian had taught her, resenting the source of the knowledge but needing it.

"I'm . . . I'm not a warrior, I'm just a girl. I don't want to fight!" she wheezed indignantly.

"Keep this up, and you'll be a girl all your life." Sova watched the lean grin on the older woman's face with helpless anger. "As for fighting, you're fighting now, fighting me, and losing."

She bent and examined one of the girl's hands, grunting; then probed at her shoulder muscles with a finger, ignoring winces and whispers. "Enough for now, more would damage, not build. Go draw some salve for these, then work on the stretching exercises for half an hour. Then three hours sleep, no more. Go!"

She scurried off, hunched; her brother landed on the deck a moment later. Shkai'ra turned and chucked him under the chin; he clenched his hands, then relaxed them hastily as nails bit into burst blisters. His glare was as blue as his sister's, but filled with a steady, unconcealed resentment.

"Better," Shkai'ra said. "You're not quite so flabby." Her smile spread. "Now for reward—do it again!"

The ship ran before the storm until an unseen noon. Megan stood beneath the sluicing water, feeling it gradually seeping through the tight-woven feathers of her cloak; most of the crew stripped to loincloths as they wrestled with flailing lines and taut canvas, above a hull that shuddered and bucked, driving deep and rising with a heaving roll to throw gullbanners of spray from her prow. The river had narrowed to half a *chiliois,* and by midmorning they were out of the cultivated lands that acknowledged Brahvniki law. Wildwood replaced pasture and orchard, crowding to the water's edge on both banks: pine on the higher, sandier ground of bluffs; patches of sere brown grass and leafless bush—once the snaggletoothed bulk of a ruined castle.

Bandits or charcoal burners, she thought once as they passed a fugitive gleam of firelight seen through the trees. Or hunters, perhaps; woods elves, if you believed the stories . . .

Mateus shouted an order through his speaking-trumpet, and a crewwoman moved along the spar to reef sail, nearly lost her footing, and stood for an instant gripping wood and canvas. Megan couldn't see her face from the afterdeck.

"If we kept this pace, we'd be in Staadt by the day after

next," she said, adding to herself: *With half the crew dead and most of the rest deserting.* Thunder cracked, the light throwing tossing branches stark against an upcoming bluff; the river curved about it, swinging right. *"What was that, Captain?"* Mateus shouted, over the wind and water. *"I said, strike sail and tie up in the lee of that rise ahead,"* she replied, throwing back her hood. *"We'll wait it out."*

The first mate grunted with relief and bellowed orders, reassured; that was more like the old Captain. Although he himself was anxious enough to meet Habiku again . . . The thin wooden cone of the trumpet cracked under his hand, and he recalled his attention to the tricky maneuver, conscious of Megan's eyes on him. She wasn't one to keep a first mate for old time's sake, unless he'd kept the skills. The ship drove north into the shelter of the ridge, slackening as the sail fluttered and boomed down; heeled broadside to the bank as his hands swung the wheel and lay, pitching, until grapnels were tossed into the woods and strong arms pulled her under the shadow of the twenty-meter oaks.

"Good," Megan said, and astonished him with a smile. Brief, but still a smile. "Where's Shkai'ra?"

"Still below somewhere, with those Thane brats," he said. "I could almost pity them, Captain."

Megan snorted. "Talk to Piatr," she said. "I'll be below. Keep a tight watch, it's a good spot for river pirates."

She kicked the door of the cabin shut behind her and hung her cloak beside the lantern, spread out to dry on a wooden stretcher; the smell of damp wool mingled with silty water and the whale-oil flame. She rubbed her hands together, started to pace, barked her shins on a stool and forced herself to sit at the table. Her mouth was dry, but she ignored the hanging canteen.

Careful hands lifted a book from the wallrack. *Not the Lannic rutter*, she thought. *The old one, from Illizbuah.* That was still carefully packed in its buckled case of oiled leather, and wax-coated paper within. Opening it brought a sharp smell of musty linen-rag paper, and a scent of Fehinna, spices and heat. Remembering: the musky Illizbuah wine, that first night she had met Shkai'ra in the City; there had been a thunderstorm then, too. The manacle scars had been fresher on her wrists and ankles, as well. *Habiku*.

No, she thought, and jerked a sheet of paper towards her, forcing her fingers to steadiness as she sharpened a quill on one razor-edged thumbnail.

Should get one of those reservoir pens from Arko, she made herself muse. The hard mental discipline of translation from the complexities of the archaic Fehinnan into Zak would be calming. Besides, she did not even *hate* Habiku that much. Hate was warm, and she was cold, colder than a star . . . Lightning flashed through the rain-blurred glass of the aft windows; thunder cracked after it: she jumped. The door opened in time to prevent her from throwing the inkwell at the wall and Shkai'ra ducked through, dripping.

Putting on a lighter face, Megan looked up from where she had very gently set the inkwell down, saying, "Done chasing the Thane brats around the deck?"

"No, I was checking the lookouts," Shkai'ra said, stripping and toweling herself down with a rough length of cotton cloth. "Francosz and Sova are asleep. I took them off the oar and sat with them awhile."

"Doing what?"

"Oh, telling stories."

Megan lifted an eyebrow. *Change*, she thought. *Not two years ago she would have thought a whip a better teacher.* "Stories!" She smiled. "I can better see you feeding them to river gar rather than tucking them in with bedtime stories . . . Are they still complaining about the pallets outside our door?

"Not likely," Shkai'ra said. "My Warmaster used to tell me stories, too . . ." She cast a glance over her own shoulder, at the faded whipscars. "Don't know why I'm doing this, really; it started as a joke, but now . . ." She shrugged. " 'Sides, I'm not giving them the full treatment; leaving out most of the beatings, rape and general abuse. Beatings only when they need it, and as for the rape," she shrugged, "I never went in for it. Well, sometimes, but not children. Anyway, they're already *mean* enough, it's the tough they need to work on. A challenge."

She slid into the bunk and began a series of isometric exercises, tensing the muscles against each other on their foundation of strong bones. "This boat-travelling, you could get soft, if you don't have to haul on ropes." She paused, looking out through the diamond-paned windows, to where a vent let out a torrent of water from the scuppers. "Makes me wonder, a little, where that get of mine is, this night." She counted mentally, moving her lips. "He'd be ten, now. Second grade instruction; hmmmm, this time of year, home to his kinfast for the harvest. Hard work, but a good time." She sighed and stretched, then halted.

"What the *fuck*—" she said, throwing back the covers. Something had touched her foot, something bony, hairy and wet. The coverlet flew aside and revealed a rat: huge, mangey and very dead, lying in a broad stain of its own blood.

Megan leaned back, tipping her head to one side, snorted with supressed laughter. "Ten-Knife. He likes us." She caught a smug thought from the cat, somewhere in the room, "*small hairynastytastecrunch*."

"Glitch take it, the thing's crawling with fleas!" Shkai'ra shouted, and grabbed it by the tail. She opened the window and blinked as the cold rain sleeted onto her face and breasts, then flicked the animal out of the rear window into the blowing chill. Crossing the cabin in a single long stride she jerked the door open.

"Clean sheets and a straw tick!" she snapped at the Thane children. She whirled, grabbed: the spitting black form of Ten-Knife appeared at the end of one arm, held by the scruff of the neck, legs splayed and claws out. A dangerous rumbling *merrreoww* was coming through his open jaws, and deep grievance had laid his ears back. "And take this abandoned beast and feed him! Feed him so full he loses all interest in rats; give him cream, give him fish, *and keep him out of here.*" The small, solid weight of the tomcat sailed the length of the corridor with a flick of her wrist, landing with a soft *thud* at the base of the ladder to the poopdeck.

Shkai'ra slammed the door shut on Francosz's blinking

bewilderment and Sova's nervous, "Here, kitty, kitty," and stamped back to strip the bed, mumbling under her breath.

Megan looked steadfastly over Shkai'ra's shoulder out at the darkness of the storm, trying to keep from laughing at the look on the Kommanza's face as she joined in removing the soiled bedding. Yowls came faintly through the door: an indignant, "He *bit* me!" in Sova's voice, and Francosz's: "Throw a blanket, you silly *ouch*." Still, the subdued knock came quickly; Megan moved to take the pile of fresh linen and ticking.

"Children," she sighed, once the door was closed. "Mine— would be seven seasons now—and until I find him, I will never know what he does or did as a child. Whether he's alive, well or badly treated . . ." She sighed. "I have nightmares about it. He's a young boy in Arko somewhere."

Shkai'ra grunted and lifted one corner of the mattress to tuck the brown linen sheet more securely. "Always planned to have a few more myself, did I ever have a home and the time," she said. "Seven, hmm. What were *you* doing at seven?"

Megan looked a bit startled. "Seven. I haven't thought about it much. I was running with a River Quarter pack, learning how to steal jewelled buttons and buckles to sell, or fruit out of the stalls." *Mama didn't like me doing it, but we needed the food sometimes.* "Learning how to throw and catch wooden knives. Learning to swim in the river in high summer. Sliding on the lake in winter with bone blades. Dreaming and talking about what kind of power we'd have when we got old enough with the rest of the pack. Listening to my Papa tell stories. And you?"

Shkai'ra shrugged. "Riding herd with the home farm flocks on a pony. Learning to scout. Sword and bow-drill; picking out tent pegs with a little lance. Swinging the exercise bars with a Warmaster behind me with a switch. Hunting rabbits and duck with blunt arrows; night-survival exercises in winter. Getting whipped a lot; I talked back. Running away to the river on summer days, or shield-sledding in snow season." Seeing Megan's look, she explained, "You stand on a shield, and someone tows you behind a horse with a lariat." A grin. "If you fall, they drag you. Sneaking into the Hall to listen to the bards." *And finding places to hide when a warrior was drunk or* ahrappan *or just looking for a child to abuse.*

"It makes me feel old, having a son that old." Megan said, peering through the rain streaming down the window. "Look there, on the south bank—see the blue flicker? A night-siren, just one or two or we'd hear them over the wind."

Shkai'ra looked over her shoulder, saw the faint blue spark arcing across to ground and river. "Your friend Ivahn mentioned them. I thought they were a tale of some sort."

"They are, so to speak. The folk down here that only see one or two say they are the souls of lost children barred from Halya, until someone released their name to the wind. Further north, where they grow thicker, they say that they mark where war was fought. They keen in the wind when they spread their petals. No one goes near them, really; a big one can kill a man. The blue spark jumps through him to the ground and he dies. During the day, though, they fold up and are usually safe."

She paused. "They'd make a good system of defense if you could plant them, but most people fear them too much to ever try. Our people . . ." She closed her eyes a moment thinking. "Our people tell a story of a man who loved a woman he could not marry, in the days when the Armahi ruled us and tried to decree and control who we married. They met despite the law and were discovered. When they took them to try and separate them, shame them before the people, they broke free and joined hands. From them a blue spark sprang and killed those who would have taken them; power, the manrauq rose and the glow spread, seeking out only Armahi who held the land, grinding their taxes out of our blood and our sweat.

"It is said that they drove the Armahi away, never to return, but when the manrauq faded they were changed. Their feet fused into the ground, spread hands always spreading power. Black petals in the night and, unable to become human again, they cry for joy that they are always together, for loss of humankind, warning to those who would take us or our land again, one of these. Or all." Her voice had taken on the rhythmic cadence of the market storyteller, her face taking on the blank look of someone seeing what she told, then shook back to awareness. "We rather like them. My Papa told that story many, many times."

The tension had faded from the muscles of the Zak's neck and shoulders. Shkai'ra smiled inwardly and turned on the coverlet, her back to the flare-lit darkness of the river, grey froth under iron sky. She unfolded a chess set from the ledge above and began placing the carved ivory pieces.

"Spot you a knight?" she said.

The cat hid under the ladder stairs, glowering, his eyes yellow spots in the gloom, focused on the children in an unwavering stare. A rumble warned them as they pushed the dishes of milk and river gar closer with a stick; then a silence, lapping and crunching noises.

"Stupid cat *bit* me," Sova said again, rubbing the bandage Piatr had put on her hand after washing it with boiled water and the stinging purple medicine the Brahvnikians made from boiled seaweed. *He sort of grinned when I yelped. He's mean too.*

"Bit you?" Francosz said sullenly. "He climbed right *up* me and danced on my head with his claws out when I tried to put the blanket on him."

Sova pouted, her lower lip jutting. It was chilly in the corridor; she returned to the tick and pulled the quilt about her. It was sound but old, sewn from rag-linen and wool and stuffed with raw cotton. *Servants' beds*, she thought resentfully. A bag full of straw to lie on, cheap, machine-loomed wool blankets from Staadt, and the musty-smelling quilt. Her muscles ached, and her hands hurt and her head nodded lower despite herself.

"She's mean," she mumbled.

Francosz touched his head and winced. "And the cat was just trying to *give* her something," he said.

"Ugh, *rats*," Sova shivered. "Ships always have rats." She winced. "Oh, Francosz, what if it puts one in *my* bed?"

"Don't be such a . . . such a *girl*," he said contemptuously. "He doesn't like us enough. Besides, a cat only catches a few rats if it isn't hungry, and . . ." He grinned slowly, despite the pain from his scalp. "Sova! If we saved some of our cheese, I could make a noose and . . ." He leaned close to whisper in her ear. "We *can* get into the cabin when they're not there, and . . ."

"No! I'm not going to *touch*—" She paused at his dismissive shrug; he would get to have all the fun if she backed down now. *Papa wouldn't like me to go catching rats*, she thought. *It isn't clean*.

Her brother blinked to see her lips firm. "I want to get back at her too," Sova declared firmly. "We'll start tomorrow."

Chapter 7

BAYAG ISLE
FOUR WEEKS NORTH OF BRAHVNIKI
TENTH IRON CYCLE, FIFTEENTH DAY

"Sail ho!"

Rilla looked up sharply. The *Zingas Vryka* lay at anchor on the eastern shore of the island, in a creek amid sere winter rushes growing higher than her deck, four feet above the waterline. Painted blue-grey, her twin masts wouldn't show against the sky on this bright autumnal morning; the hull was the same color all along its nine-meter length. Invisible to watchers on the river north of the Witch's Isle, her two triangular sails were lowered and lashed to their booms, the long thigh-thick pine poles swinging idly against the masts at chest-height over the deck.

"Habiku's ship; she's flying the Sleeping Dragon." The lookout rose from the crossbar at the masthead and squirreled halfway down a ratline to speak more softly. "It's the *Kettle Belly*." That was one of the firm's older ships, a big, bluff-bowed river freighter built in the traditional style, nearly round. A single square mast, rudder-and-tiller steering, crew of fifteen on her normal occasions.

"Regular run out of F'talezon," Rilla said to Shyll as he came up beside her. "Bulk cargoes; blackrock, timber, baled hides, rough ornamental stones and steel tool-blanks, for Rand."

The teRyadn shrugged; he was not a merchant, for all the drilling Megan and then Rilla had put him through. He inhaled the set silt smell of the river, looked up at a flight of wild geese honking their way south in a V of grace. It was no worse a day to die than any other; and he didn't intend to die.

Rilla looked at him, then away. *I know you loved—love my cousin. She's been gone two years. You still love her, I can see it in your eyes when you think of her.*

"Do we fight?" he asked. Across the deck, Inu raised his massive head and whined sharply at the tone. The two Moryavska, Shenka and Jakov, who had been brushing his coat, paused too; that was one of the Zak words they had already picked up.

Rilla paused. "It's soon for another raid," she mused. "On the other hand, that's what we're here for . . . Might not be worth the risk, for that sort of cargo, but the Moryavska need blooding." She nodded. "Sound battle quarters."

A yip from Inu, who gathered his paws beneath him and lolled his tongue, but did not get up. He knew better than to move rapidly on a ship. Danake stuck her head in the hatch and whistled softly, the crew scrambling from their quarters below or from their tasks on deck. The quartermaster already had the arms locker open and was handing out weapons. The ten Moryavska each had a Zak partner who directed them with gesticulating hands; they understood what being handed a weapon meant, and they'd learned Habiku's name. Crew filed by, each taking their weapon of choice and such protection as they could afford. The Moryavska had been equipped to their taste in the month since the raid on the slave caravan with bows of horn and elm, broad-bladed axes and stabbing-spears.

One, a squat giant six feet tall and nearly as broad, had taken a smith's forging hammer for his weapon. Moshulu grinned at Rilla, waved the massive weapon and called something cheerfully incomprehensible as his Zak partner/instructor fussed him into the boiled sharkskin jacket and bone-strapped leather helmet, hopping up to make sure the buckles were properly fastened.

"Iczak, got all you need? I hope we can do this without much killing, unless Habiku is still hiring scum." The *Zingas Vryka* carried a crew of forty, far more than most riverboats her size, to provide prize crews.

"Aye, Captain. Though I could wish for a Haian." The healer looked up from his bottles and bandages, preparing to go below to the lazarette where the wounded would be treated. He kept the bone-saws and long needles used for amputations wrapped up; it would be bad for morale to let them show.

"Boryis, take the glass. If you drop it, I'll kick you in the behind with a pointed shoe so it sticks, got that?"

"Aye, Captain." He grinned at her and swarmed up a ratline with her precious spyglass. A moment later he hissed down, "She's tacking west as far around the Isle as she can."

"Temuchin!" Rilla called in a low voice to her new bosun. "She thinks she can outrun us if we happen to be here."

The crew were at their posts. The bosun nodded and whistled; he was old for his post, had been a captain with a quarter-share in his vessel before he objected to the Sleeping Dragon's involvement in shipping dreamdust south. The mushrooms it was derived from grew only in the old mines about F'talezon, Habiku had seen a potential market downstream . . . and had not thought it reasonable for one of his skippers to object. Temuchin had lost a daughter to the drug.

The bosun had learned to smile again, after the *Zingas Vryka* stole her first shipment and dumped it into the Brezhan.

Long-short. Crew ran to unlash the bindings that held the sails to the booms; the bosun whistled again, and two teams of ten broke free the halyards. They bent, gripped the rough flax cables, heaved in rhythm, bend *snatch* heave *back*, their bare feet slapping on the deck as the block and tackle at the masthead squealed in protest. They chanted as they worked, an old tune with fresh-minted words:

> "*Make* the pulleys scream—*oh*
> All together—*ai-oh!*
> *Habiku*'s balls are river mud—*oh* . . .

The long triangles of canvas rose in quick jerks and short

pauses, the swooping curves of the cables that edged them straining and hauling at the weight of cloth; it bellied and fluttered in the light breeze that came over the island's spine, and the hull stirred with anticipation.

Short-long-long. An empty cask went overside, holding the anchor cable for retrieval, no time to waste winching it up. *Short-short-short* and the deck crew broke out the long sweeps to spider-walk the ship out into open water, six strokes and the poles were run inboard and the northing wind caught at the jibsails, luffing, thunder-cracks of rippling canvas.

Rilla stood by the wheel, one hand resting on its knurled teak; the *Zingas Vryka* had started her life as a ClawPrince's toy, a pleasure yacht, and had not a few touches of that sort. But she had a good turn of speed, too, and could point further into the wind than most. Megan had got her cheap at an estate sale, cheap enough to be worth the conversion costs.

The wheel jerked as steerage way came on the ship and the rudder bit into moving water. *Ahh*, Rilla thought. *She's alive.* Shyll came up and clapped her steel cap on her head, hung the twofang and darts from their clips ready to hand.

"Will we catch them?" he said. A frown; their vessel was cutting toward the east bank, while the *Kettle Belly* tacked for the western shore at a flatter angle.

Rilla turned, her face tight with the excitement of the chase and the feel of the long surges as the bow caught the river swell and knifed, throwing up plumes of spray.

"Two points to port," she said to the helmswoman. To Shyll: "You've got a drylander's bones, my friend. We take our port tack to the shallows, then turn and do a long run southwest on the starboard tack. That lumbering ox isn't called the *Kettle Belly* for nothing, and she's square-rigged. Can't take the wind on more than a quarter, we can do twice that. We'll overhaul them inside two *chiliois* with the wind from the south like this." That was the prevailing breeze, three-quarters of the year, and the foundation of Brezhan commerce. South with the current, north with the wind; a fore-and-aft rig was like a full complement of oars, really only helpful to a warcraft, and a recent innovation on the northern stretches of the river.

They cleared the lee of Bayag Isle, and the wind caught them. The ship heeled sharply and put her port rail down, shipping spray over the deck as the wind fought the leverage of her keel. Rilla shouted as the view opened about them, the low rocky humpback of the island dropping astern, the two *chiliois'* breadth of the river opening out to the south like a plain of dark blue-green. Marsh lay ahead and to port on the eastern shore; bluffs and trees over on the western bank, and the chip-shape of the *Kettle Belly* making sail away, her square of canvas dirty yellow-brown. The captain of the *Zingas Vryka* looked up at the proud swell of maroon-red above her, with the outline of a running wolf on both sails in silver-grey.

"*Vryka! Vryka!*" she shouted again, and the crew took it up from their stations at the ropes or crouching on the deck. Inu threw back his head and howled deafeningly, a mournful, sobbing sound that would carry clear to the western shore; some of the crew joined him, the Moryavska more tunefully than most. Rilla glanced left; the reedbeds of the eastern shore were nearing with almost frightening speed. The depth of the river was unpredictable here, with shifting banks and snags, and the *Zingas Vryka* lay deeper in the water than most. It wouldn't do to hang her up on a bank after all this.

"On the other hand," she muttered to herself, "the longer our port tack, the better angle we get to starboard." A shout to Boryis in the rigging:

"What color ahead?"

"Shelving to brown, Captain!"

She nodded. "Prepare to come about," she said to the second mate. Annike nodded and pushed up the wire visor of her helmet.

"*'Ware boom.*" The call crashed out through her megaphone, and even the Moryavska knew enough to duck; the boom was shoulder-high to a Zak.

Rilla slapped the wheel. "Come about, helm," she said. "Five points to starboard."

The two crewfolk heaved and the man-high wheel turned, slowly at first and then with a blur as the bow swung away from the shore; the old illusion seized her, that the ship was still and the land turned, the blue line of the western hills coming up to starboard. And the *Kettle Belly* . . . The ship slowed as her bow came into the wind, swinging back level like a giant pendulum, her mast tops making circles against the blue sky and racking iron-grey clouds. Then the wind caught the sails again and joined the wheel to point the bow starboard in a gathering rush, canvas cracked and the booms swung across the deck to hang off the starboard quarter.

Zingas Vryka took the wind again and heeled; Rilla spoke: "In three on the sheetlines."

The second mate and bosun relayed the order, and the ropes that secured the freeswinging ends of the booms were hauled in a meter.

"Point her one to port," Rilla said, and the helm swung back a tenth-turn toward the south, into the wind. The second mate looked up sharply.

"She'll luff, that's too close to the wind."

Rilla glanced at the sails; they were taunt, only a hint of fluttering along the unsecured outer edge. She shook her head.

"Not quite . . . *yes!*" The ship heeled more sharply, the right rail almost submerged, and riverwater boiled into the scuppers; the Moryavska, Usakil, slid to the edge of the deck, amid obscene complaints about where his spearpoint was directed. The deck heaved and swooped as speed built, and curving sheets of spray planed up from the hollow bows, droplets scattering as far as the stern. Barracuda-swift, the *Zingas Vryka* was cutting south down the reach of the river at an angle to the wind the *Kettle Belly* could not hope to match.

Rilla grinned tautly, judging distance. "Twelve knots, or I'm a mutton-eater," she said. More softly, "You trained me well, daughter of my father's sister." She turned to Shyll, clutching a ratline to keep erect on the canted deck. "Still doubt we'll catch her?" she said. "Go on, get your giant jackal ready, we'll be on them in half an hour."

He laughed, gave a whoop, made a flying leap with heels high over the quarterdeck railing to land on the main deck, rolled, sprang to Inu, grabbed the greathound's ruff and planted a smacking kiss on his nose.

"*Arooouff,*" the dog said, backing himself erect and jigging in place from foot to foot; his tail waved madly, beating out a steady *bong-bong-bong* on the iron neckguard of a crewman's helmet. The man lurched forward, turned, took the tail straight in the face and staggered back with a slightly stunned expression, shouldering a neighbor aside to make more room. Inu panted into Shyll's face and licked. The teRyadn pushed his muzzle aside, laughing.

"Got to feed you more grainmash, boy, your breath alone could stun a Ri. Come on, time for your collar and harness."

The dog dropped his ears slightly, but stood with strained tolerance as Shyll and the two Moryavska who had appointed themselves the greathound's servants equipped him for war. A leather coat sewn with bone plates covered his flanks and chest, ridged down the spine with orcas' teeth; a fitted helm strapped with steel protected head and eyes, and a spiked collar his throat. Shenka and Jakov knelt to bind on sharkskin leggings from paw to hock, boiled in vinegar for strength and rough enough to strip the flesh from a grabbing hand. A rumbling growl like rough stones grating in a mineshaft made his barrel-hoop ribs tremble beneath the fingers that buckled and strapped; half complaint at the constriction, half anticipation.

"Stand still and take it, you damn puppy!" Shyll said. "I'm not getting you killed because you're too hot in that! Sit!"

Inu sat and fluttered his lips. His pack was going to war, and he knew enough to obey the packleader's signals. The river might be too big to scent-mark, but it was *theirs.*

"What crew?" Rilla called to Boryis.

There was a pause; they had cut south of the *Kettle Belly* by half a *chiliois* and put about, ready to run north at her before the wind, safer than an attempt to board the high sterncastle. A merchantman had a higher freeboard all about, but it was lowest at the bows.

"Nobody I recognize," Boryis called down. Rilla's eyebrows rose in surprise; Habiku had dismissed and hired lavishly, but a good half of the crewfolk of the *Sleeping Dragon* were still those taken on in Megan's time. The *Kettle Belly* had a nearly intact crew, not worth the master's attention on a milk run schedule.

"There's . . . twenty of them at least, not counting any below," Boryis continued; dismay was plain in his voice. Half again the normal complement, and if they were new-hired, less likely to make a token resistance only. DragonLord's favor on Habiku or no, most of Megan's followers remained loyal to her and her blood-kin, Rilla. "More! They're standing to battle stations, all well-armed. Some of them are taking a cover off the sterncastle . . . Dark Lord swallow them, it's a steelspring!"

"*What?*" Rilla shouted, startled out of calm. That was a war engine, powered by steel skeins and throwing two-meter javelins; a monopoly of the F'talezonian river-fleet. "On the *Kettle Belly?* That's like putting a mailcoat on a milk cow!" A moment's thought.

"Out sheets; grapnelmen and archers to the bow! We'll lay alongside forequarter to forequarter, and board that way."

The *Kettle Belly's* length, crew, mast and rigging would be between her and those shipkiller missiles. The pulleys squealed again as the lines slacked, letting the booms swing out from the centerline.

"Captain!" Boryis called. *Marines! It's pig-sucking Marines! On the Kettle-Belly?* Rilla thought. *What in Halya have we stumbled on?* The wind was astern, now; the river straight north and south for twenty *chiliois,* and with near two *chiliois* of sailing room all that way. Feet thundered on the deck as those of the fighting-crew who favored the bow crowded forward, a deep throbbing sound as they plucked at their bowstrings in anticipation. The grapnelmen were roving the ends of their ropes to deck cleats; the three-pronged metal hooks they held ready for the circle-and-toss. The steel wire binding the ropes for a meter below the attachments glittered fierce and cold in the pale morning light. Boryis slid down a stay and handed her the spyglass by its strap.

The *Kettle Belly* was nearing the western shore, about to tack.

"Helm port three," Rilla said. *Zingas Vryka* had been nearly dead in the water with her sails luffed, bow rising and falling in short, choppy strokes as the wind put just enough way on her to balance the current. Now she slid forward, at first only a hint of movement, then gathering speed with a swift gliding rush like skis on powder snow. The hull spoke, not the complaining squeaks and rattles of holding station; this was an eager sound, the long flexing of the hull-strakes and the oak treenails that bound timber and plank, the drumming thutter of waves parting, slapping the hull like wet hands down half its length; the sails creaked and popped as they stretched, and wind hummed through the cordage.

Kettle Belly was turning, turning toward them; no choice, except to continue the tack to the western shore and ground her. The view of her changed, from three-quarters on to her port to the narrower head-on silhouette and the blunt rectangle of her sail, fluttering its baggy fabric and then steadying as it caught the wind. The merchantman was making three knots; *Zingas Vryka* thirteen, with a stiff wind coming in on her starboard quarter, even better than on directly following. The two ships closed with frightening speed; she could see the streaked planks of the old freighter's hull, a missing section of rail, tangled ratlines in her rigging.

Sloppy, sloppy, Rilla thought. Filthy *rokatzk* wouldn't spend on maintenance. A thread of smoke from her sterncastle; hadn't they doused the galley fire? Bad practice even safely at anchor, on a ship made of tinder-dry, tar-soaked wood and cloth. She opened her mouth to call for the sails to be taken in, this was far too fast for safe boarding, when the tubby shape began to shift again. Turning to port, away from her; trying to run before the wind, a square rig did better so, but the *Zingas Vryka* was still much faster . . .

Her eyes snapped wide. "Come about, *left* full helm. *Down, everybody down!*" she shouted. Even Inu dropped, hearing the urgency in her shout.

The ship staggered in the water, swiveling to port, heeled crazily onto her starboard side as she turned broadside on, her momentum and the wind pushing at her sails and thrusting her further down. Yells, clatter as bodies and weapons tumbled across the deck; the starboard rail went under, water fountained into the scuppers and the masts bent like bows. A line parted with a crack like thunder and whipped across the deck with a force that would have cut a human in half had any been in its path. For an instant forever long she was sure the *Zingas Vryka* was going to capsize, but the deep keel bit and the motionless moment passed as she began to slide toward the western bank on a shallow tack.

Too slow, too slow, ran through her mind. *Can't push, can't do anything.* They were pinned, ants scurrying beneath a descending boot; she could feel the jelly-like resistance of the water under the keel, the *Zingas Vryka* gathering way slowly, oh so slowly, under the steel gaze of the murder machine.

The *Kettle Belly* was broadside on to them, only a hundred meters away. Faces and weapons lined the rail, jeering; the squat shape of the springsteel hunched on the sterncastle, close enough to see the oily yellow flames and black smoke trickling from the bundle of pitch-soaked rags tied behind the barbs of the missile. So close she could see the crew making their last adjustments, the javelin point raising and swiveling as they turned the wheels. F'talezonian river marines in black-enameled leather armor trimmed in blue-green; one looked at her, and she could imagine the narrow dark eyes squinting under the bowl-helmet. The marine stepped back a pace, doll-figure beside model machine. A swift jerk at a lanyard.

Chinnnng. A sound like steel hammers on steel, deep in the forge caves. The javelin flew too fast to be more than a blur, but the smoke trailed it like a long black spearshaft. Rilla stayed motionless beside the wheel for the time it would have taken to blink and open her eyes again. The long shaft flickered by not two hands' width from her ear, and the wind of its passage whirled her about to see the black trail snick into the water a hundred meters south with a flash of white smoke.

The chaos on deck was sorting itself, Temuchin yelling, a pair of deckhands securing the broken stay and roving a new one through the blocks, and the gap between the ships opened, swelling as they ran their right-angled courses. Inu scrabbled into his place, splay-legged, still low, trying to obey the order to lie down.

On the *Kettle Belly* there was an orderly scurry about the springsteel; Rilla watched the marine who had pulled the lanyard turn and boot the buttocks of one of his squad, and they pumped at a pivot-mounted geared leaver. Swift hands lifted another huge finned dart into the trough, spun the aiming-wheels; Zaki work, nobody else could make gearing like that. She cursed her people's facility with metalwork as the enormous tuning-fork note of the springsteel sounded again.

"Keep down, everybody not on a line keep down," she called again, watching Deigjuburg the Moryavska rise and bend her bow; the woman ignored the foreign Zak words and loosed, a high arching shot. Deigjuburg's arrow winked as sunlight caught the head turning at the peak of its arc, high above. At a hundred and fifty meters the springsteel's bolt was barely even a blur; the Moryavska woman snapped back a meter and crumpled, a two-inch hole punched through her from chest to spine by the bolt. Deflected, it pinned a crewman crouched behind her to the deck, through shield and leg and half its length into the deck planking; he screamed and twitched. The mercenaries on the *Kettle Belly's* deck laughed and beat swords on their shields. The sound faded as the *Zingas Vryka* drew away; not out of range, that would take half a *chiliois*, but the springsteel crew were wasting no bolts on a dwindling target. The privateer would have to come close to do damage, and they'd be waiting.

"Annike!" Rilla called, her voice flat. "See to Yahn, get him below to Iczak. Get some people aloft, form a bucket chain and douse the sails." That would slow them, but speed was the least of their worries. "Wet sand to the deck." That was their ballast, there would be plenty. *Laugh at killing my crew, will they?*

Habiku. You are teaching me the color and taste of hate, the sticky feel of it on my soul, the thick sweet taste of it on my tongue. "Steady," she said to the helm and then, "Prepare to come about." Her voice was clear as the ringing of the steelspring.

Annike came up beside her. "Yahn doesn't look good," she said. "Iczak's trying to stop the bleeding . . . fever for sure, even if he does. How do we get past that thing?"

They looked north, across grey, choppy water to the merchantman ploughing straight upriver. Straight north at four knots, probably her best speed.

"With enormous difficulty," Rilla said sharply, then made a gesture of apology to the second mate; the question was an honest one. "All she has to do is keep twitching her ass end toward us like a horse that's about to kick; we can't close in, she's not very maneuverable but it'll be a job from Halya to get right in bows-on. Dark Lord kiss Ranion for giving Habiku that springsteel, what sort of a DragonLord . . ." She paused; futile, and besides, everyone *knew* what sort of a madman the current ruler of F'talezon was.

"Hmmmm," Annike said. "And whoever's commanding that tub is no fool."

Rilla nodded and turned to the helm. "Bring her about; three points to starboard." The wheel spun, and the privateer pointed her bows north and east, following the merchantman's wake but slanting to the right to increase the distance between them. "We're closing too fast," she said after a moment. "Reef, if you please."

Annike raised her megaphone. "Three loops in, main and fore's'l!" she called. The deck crew unstayed the lines that held the sails aloft, backed a practiced half-step. Others jumped to the booms, bunching the loose folds of canvas down on the wood and lashing them tight, making them fast with slipknots. The mass of cordage and canvas and wood flowed through their hands into new shapes as neat and functional as the first.

Rilla closed her eyes and saw the river in her mind; it tended northwest from here, F'trovanemi Isle was a long day's sail upcurrent. The F'talezonian river-base, a rocky islet armored with a castle like a dragon's scales; springsteels, rock throwers, a garrison of a thousand and half a dozen galleys with full crews, any one of them able to outrun or outfight her. It had been a calculated risk to lurk about Bayag Isle: the fleet had hung two shiploads of river pirates here only last year.

Worth it, because they were preying on the Sleeping Dragon alone . . . She opened her eyes again, looking north. The river swung about Bayag Isle, turned straight south and then southwest; the current slowed and dumped sand and silt, mostly in the shallows and marshes of the eastern shore. Not always. And it changed from day to day.

"Steady as she goes," she said. "Let's get ahead of her."

Annike frowned. "She'll just turn again and tack south," she objected. "We could keep that up all day, or until a patrol galley comes by. Or another merchantman; if they ran south together they'd be too much for us."

Rilla smiled, tapping fingers against her belt, shrugged her shoulders against the weight of the leather battlejacket. "Dark's no good, clear sky and full moon. But if they turn south, they'll have to tack. Port or starboard, and I'd say starboard, running south: notice now she's been hugging the western bank? Afraid of shoals."

Annike looked north, then over to the western bank. She grinned, hard and sore. "And if they tack to the east, we run 'em north and try again?"

The *Zingas Vryka* drove straight up the channel center, crowding her enemy toward the western bank. The *Kettle Belly* plodded north, the springsteel pivoting to cover the faster craft.

Rilla put the glass to her eye, legs flexing automatically against the steady rocking of the deck to keep the image clear in sights. The ships ran parallel for a moment at half a *chiliois* distance, and details sprang out at her. Twoscore and ten crew, at the least: Zaki, dark-clad and short; big, fair Aenir; a Rand warrior in fantastically-colored enameled armor leaning on a long-hilted curved sword. She could even see faces, scarred and hard; professionals, apart from the common river rats handling the sails.

And the marines, stolid professionals, each with another fire-bolt in the trough and a torch to hand. Five or six of those would fly into deck and sails if she tried to run in, the *Zingas Vryka* would be a singed bitch indeed. Many of the figures on deck were metal-armored fighters with no trade but war. *Not* an economical way to guard a cargo of blackrock and hides, obviously something special here.

Time enough to tally her cargo later, she thought. They were pulling ahead now, well below their best speed but still lunging past the *Kettle Belly* as if it were standing still. Cold spray wet her lips; the wind behind them blew strands of hair loose from her steel cap, long dark threads coiling forward about her face.

"Come about to port, helm," she said. "Annike, keep her so; sheet close, sails one point out as we make southing."

The ship slowed and rocked as they turned, keeping their left flank to the *Kettle Belly* a *chiliois* downstream.

"A point to port of south, helm," Rilla said. She heard the crewfolk grunt as they bent into the wheel, the jerk through the hull as the rudder bit and kept the *Zingas Vryka* pointing almost in to the wind.

" 'Ware boom!" Annike's voice as the poles snapped across the deck to take the wind blowing in from the starboard bow. The rear edges fluttered wildly, almost luffing; she was too close-hauled, pointing too near the wind to make speed. The banks slid by as they began to gather way, not more than six knots but almost directly south, tending only a little to the east.

"Captain, if the wind veers we'll take it bow-on," Annike called from the main deck. "I'll not answer for the tackle if we do, with all set!"

"Steady as she goes," Rilla replied, eye and spyglass trained on the *Kettle Belly*. The merchantman was six hundred meters from the western shore; would she . . . *ah*.

"She's turning to port!" Rilla called. "All steady!" She could feel the enemy captain's thinking: a short tack to the west bank, then another right out to midstream, right across the wind, easiest for his single-sail square rig. That would give him the most maneuvering room; he'd be trying to outguess her, imagining she intended to crowd him to the bank until he had no choice but to anchor his bow to the shore and wait.

"I might have tried that, too," she said happily. The *Vryka* continued her course, her motion a short plunging like a horse run on a tight rein. Details came blinding-sharp, the scudding mare's-tail clouds, a fish jumping off their bows, a loon's mournful call, the bat shapes of a pair of feral flittercats flapping around a treetop nest. *Come on. Come on.* The *Kettle Belly*, dangerously close to shore and still three-quarters of a *chiliois* ahead. The crew's tension, audible on some level far below ear-hearing, like the straining of a green stick bent almost double across the knee. *My crew are probably all wondering "What fish-stinking thing is she doing?"* Show them . . . come on . . . turn!

"He's coming about," she whispered. Quickly, too, for a ship in that condition. Sail canting, poled out from the deck. Turning, coasting, gathering way directly east, the bluff bows battering sunlit bursts of spray into the air, the round hull pitching as it cut across the direction of the waves. And—

A long yell from the *Zingas Vryka's* crew, long and gleeful. Another shout from *Kettle Belly*, of dismay; she *jerked*, like a man stumbling as he stubs his toe; her rear mainstay snapped with a deep, musical sound of pain that carried clearly through the shouting from near a hundred throats. The freighter's stubby mainmast leaned forward and hung with a crunch of parting wood, leaning drunkenly in a billowing tangle of heavy cloth. Another jerk, and she was dead in the water with that heavy finality that any sailor knows and dreads; the motion seemed slow, but the mast leaned further with popping sounds and she could see every figure on deck lurch, almost fall; a tiny stick-man screamed once and seemed to leap from the crows-nest in a curve ending in a foaming splash ahead of the *Kettle Belly's* bow. He bobbed up downstream and swam dazedly for shore.

"Didn't know that shoal was there, did you, Lady-forsaken bastard, did you?" Rilla shouted as she shook her fist in the other ship's direction. "Helm, come about, ten points to starboard, sheet sails out five." Another gesture toward the slayers of her crew. "Caught you fast and hurt you bad, mudfoot!"

The *Zingas Vryka* spun as agilely as her namesake, to starboard; there was the usual weightless pause as the bow came about, then an almost solid click as the wheel spun again and she settled into the groove her captain had chosen; straight west, across the river, toward the sandbank that held the *Kettle Belly* fast. Blocks squealed in protest and shed blue smoke as the deck crew paid out the sheets on the

Lady's sails to put full speed on her. Rilla swung the spyglass to her eye, squinted. There was blood on the other ship's deck, and figures that lay still or writhed; the dragging sail hid most of the deck, but she could see others staggering about, stunned. The mast was swinging, a band of splinters where it joined the deck and only the standing rigging keeping it half-upright.

A splash off the *Kettle Belly*'s stern: her captain was throwing an anchor, to try and warp her free and swing the undamaged war-engine on her sterncastle into use. Possible, with enough hands on the cable and enough time. Which Rilla did not plan to grant; the water was boiling beneath the *Zingas Vryka*'s bow, and the lupine figurehead would be dipping its fangs.

"How close can you take us?" Annike called, an anxious eye on the bellying curves of the sails. The *Zingas Vryka* carried far more canvas than the *Kettle Belly*, and had a deeper keel; a grounding at speed would be even more disastrous for her.

"Right up to her," Rilla called exultantly. "That bank shelves steep to the main channel, the current carved it out, it's only shallow on the landward side!" Her mouth was dry and she could feel the blood pounding in throat and ears, the ships closing with terrifying speed, feeling the sandbank curling up toward the vulnerable knife-keel of her ship. Temuchin was up in the bows, she could hear him:

"Everybody grab a line!" He took the hands of a Moryavska and placed them on the rigging. "Careful with those spears, everything's going to go flying, ready with the bows, get those grapnels up; two volleys then over the rail. *Back, you pi-dog.*" A hand slapping a nose, and a sound halfway between a snarl and a whine.

"Stand by to let go sails," Rilla said; Annike relayed it with her megaphone and the deck crew braced. This would not be a controlled lowering, and that much weight of canvas could be dangerous. The *Kettle Belly* was suddenly *there*, and she could see figures madly hacking at the rigging with axes, trying to drop the main yard, to give the sterncastle a clear view of the bows. A line parted, another, the sail dragged one side into the river—

"Now!" Rilla yelled, grabbed the sterncastle-rail with both hands—*I can see the damn spring but it's not cleared*—

The *Vryka's* sails boomed down in loose folds and Rilla could feel the loss of way, a silent coasting from the hull, like the top arch of a leap.

The archers in the bow loosed, once, twice, arrows a stinging hiss like vipers flung at the merchantman, and they stepped back, braking themselves; shafts snapped into wood, punched into sagging canvas and hung from the folds, sprouted from arms, bellies, thighs. There was a high, musical *tink* sound as some struck metal and punched through; at that range even the best armor was vulnerable. Not much fire came in return, too few of *Kettle Belly's* crew were on their feet and free to come forward. A few hand darts slanted over the narrowing meters between the ships, thrummed in the *Vryka's* rail, went *crack* into a shield, and then one into bone and lung with a crunching impact. A crewman looked down at the thick black shaft standing in his breastbone, touched it with a wondering finger, coughed blood, dropped.

The *Vryka* lost more way; grapnels flashed, swung out in looping casts. One snagged in the tangled rigging, another crunched into timber; there was a splintery groan as the cleats took up the strain and strong hands heaved at the ropes, the current pulling them around. The hull touched sand, a brief grating and Rilla felt a cold hand seize her heart; then the sharp reinforced prow was slicing into the steep outer face of the sandbank, a jarring thud and enormous hissing that ran through the hull and snapped her forward against her hands' grip on the rail. Above her, the mainstays hummed as the tons' weight of inertia flexed the masts forward, strong supple wood bending and the thigh-thick cables sounding a note that ran up the scale until her teeth ached with waiting for it to end in a disastrous snapping.

No break; instead a grinding crash as the two bows met, the smooth surface of the *Zingas Vryka* meeting the rough, lapstrake oak planks of the *Kettle Belly,* a sharp jolt throwing anyone standing forward and to port. The two ships pivoted, tied nose to nose, shifted on the sand and stopped as the greater weight and solid hull-grounding of the merchantman

held both against the river's thrusting. Current heaped the
water high against them, waves breaking over the starboard
rail of the *Vryka* as it dipped against the ropes that bound it
to its prey. The ruined mast and rigging of the *Kettle Belly*
leaned again, groaning, falling and tangling against the forward mainstay of the *Zingas Vryka*.

"*Grey Wolf! Grey Wolf!*" her followers shouted, pouring
forward. Rilla let go, snatched dartcaster and twofang, leaped
the quarterdeck railing and landed with a boom on the main
deck, started forward with the helmscrew behind her. The
mercenaries were already hacking at the grapnel lines, crowding to the rail of *Kettle Belly* and trading thrusts with spear
and twofang and boarding-pike with the *Zingas Vryka* crew
below; they were outnumbered now, but they had the advantage of height and better armor, and the springsteel could fire
over their heads to wreck the privateer if they held their line
for long enough.

Inu howled, a stunning sound, unbelievable even from an
animal as large as a saddle horse; the snarl that followed
ratcheted upward into an open-jawed bellow, and the hull of
the *Lady* rocked as he leaped. Even the grounded merchantman moved as he landed, soaring over the points that tentatively probed for him. A long boarding-pike thrust as he
landed, crouching as the momentum of nine hundred pounds
pushed him to the deck. He seized the ashwood shaft between his jaws, bit; it splintered, and he threw the piece that
held the spearhead over the side. An axe-wielder charged,
double-bitted weapon swinging; Inu's head darted out, snake-
swift, closed jaws on his waist. The dog braced his forefeet
and flipped his head, a rat-killing gesture, and the armored
man went over his back, struck a railing, and dropped into
the water.

Rilla could see the top of Inu's head behind the line of
points, heard his bellowing roar over the flat thuds and
unmusical, scrap-metal sounds of combat; then the enemy
line was breaking, as the *Kettle Belly's* fighters turned to
guard their backs. A man's voice on the other ship was calling
retreat, calling for archers to kill the monster, but another
shout of "*Grey Wolf*" echoed across river and marsh, and her

followers were over the bows and swarming up: Shyll's blond head was beside the dog, helmetless and laughing as he whirled and thrust with dagger and smallsword; Moshulu's great hammer boomed on a shield. It broke, and the arm beneath it; the Moryavska heaved the huge weapon aloft, swept it down on a helmet that crumpled with a clamor of yielding steel, stepped over a body leaking brains and brayed a warcry.

Above her head, sailors were fighting in the tangled rigging, knives and hatchets and bare feet cat-agile on the ropes. Rilla sprinted, vaulted from her ship's rail, touched the *Kettle Belly's* and came down with the dartcaster up. *Pick target— jolt of wood in my palm. Cast. Cast. Drop the caster—duck!* The foredeck of the *Kettle Belly* was jammed with naZak. *I can't even see my own crew—*

The Zak had the advantage in the tight space, the deck lurching randomly as Inu moved. Splashes marked people falling into the river. *Twofang block side, slash across helm, SWING!* The end of her twofang burred through the air with the sound of a banner cracking in the wind, slashing groin height. The Aenir leaped back, jolted into the fight behind him; knocked off balance, he almost fell onto her point.

Another *CHIINNNG* from the stern and a crescent-head javelin, points forward, tore through the *Kettle Belly's* sail and rigging, plunged into the tangled fight in the bow. The inner edge of the sickle-moon head was razor sharp and half a meter across; it cut one sailor in half. Blood splashed as if a bucket had been dumped and the decks were greasy with it. Someone had died, someone else was screaming in an impossibly high shriek that went on and on.

Damn you, damn whatever you're protecting. Rilla skidded on the oily, salt-and-iron stinking deck, caught herself from going over the rail into the river.

Inu was tossing whoever smelled wrong into the water, like a puppy throwing bones, but his growls were loud enough to resonate in the wood of the ship. The fighting was breaking up into knots where sailors and mercenaries tumbled and fought through the rope-littered deck, and the wounded lay and shrieked or crawled into the scuppers to tend their hurts,

or sat staring incredulously at the stump of a hand . . .
Halfway down the hull, the sail hung, folds tumbling to the
planking except where an intact line hung the right corner
man-height from the deck. Another javelin from the steelspring
through the sail; this one tumbled a *Kettle Belly* sailor in
pieces from the rigging and plunged through to slice a ratline
on the *Lady*. Faces turned as the merchantman's crew cried
protests at the blindsided firing that endangered them as
much as their foes. Splashes followed, as sailors threw aside
their weapons and went eel-swift over the side; Habiku did
not pay enough for them to stay and be shot in the back.

The mercenaries were truer to their salt, or perhaps simply
more heavily armed and less easy in the water. They broke,
but in order, retreating past the sail and setting their weapons to hacking it down from behind; a rearguard held the gap
between canvas and rail. The *Zingas Vryka*'s folk gathered,
made a rush, were cast back panting and holding their wounds;
except for one who crawled under the jabbing spearpoints,
sank down, lay still.

Her crew stood, growling, as Rilla came up. A brief silence
had fallen; she could hear the wind, the heavy breathing of
exhaustion, Inu's claws on the deck, a metallic chinking from
behind the curtain of sail that had to be some further devil-
ment with the steelspring. The mercenaries were shrinking
their rearguard, shuffling backward through the gap until
only the Rand stood holding it. He swung the long, curved
blade around his head, visibly relieved to have room to use it
properly. Not a tall man, though taller than any Zak, blocky-
shouldered, armored from head to toe in steel enameled with
violent patterns of yellow, green, blue, purple. The helm's
triangular visor covered most of his saffron-yellow face, concealed his slanted black eyes; the mouth below it was
expressionless.

A dart snapped forward, rang harmlessly against a curved
steel shoulder-guard. Another flicked toward his face: the
long sword whipped around fast enough to blur, and the
hardwood clanged off the metal of the blade. Two crew ran
in, four hands, four knives flickering; there was a series of
movements too fast to follow; a knife grated over the Rand's

thigh, his sword took both the wielder's arms off at the elbow, and in a turn-and-strike of the same movement he kicked the other Zak under the chin with an iron-toed boot. The woman flew backward and landed with her head at an impossible angle.

"Back!" Rilla shouted. "Shyll, Inu, Moshulu, you three. Quickly!" There were heavy ripping sounds, and blades appeared through the sail, ripping at the canvas. A steelspring bolt snapped through, aimed low this time, chopped through the deck; she heard it cut through the hull planking below.

Inu paced forward, doubly masked with steel and leather and blood, snarling endlessly; his head was held low, no more than waist-height, and he came at the Rand in a slinking, side-crabbing rush. Moshulu followed, at a trot that made the deck boom; Shyll ran at his greathound's hindquarters, long hair and headband bobbing, strands clinging to the sweat-dampness of his arms.

The Rand did not brace himself. Instead he waited, flat-footed but not heavy, knees bent and one toe behind the other, almost a standing version of a sprinter's crouch. The sword raised, point at Inu's throat-height, poised not in quivering tension but lightly, relaxed.

The greathound lunged, jaws darting down for a grip on the Rand's leg, jaws strong enough to crumple the thin metal of plate armor. The boot met his nose instead, with a thump that ran back through the dog's massive body to quiver his feathered tail; Inu hesitated an instant, then drove in again, snarling as the curved sword squealed off the metal spikes of his collar. It bit through: he yelped as it gashed the ruff above his spine and the heavy muscles of his neck.

Rilla heard Shyll yell, "Inu, DOWN!" The dog dropped flat, completely vulnerable; the Rand ignored the foreign shout, assuming the first hit had been enough to stun, lifted his sword for the killing blow. Light broke off the edge, still slicing-sharp after the battering it had taken; the Rand warrior stepped forward with easy confidence, ignoring the big Moryavska with his hammer. He was beyond the reach even of long arms and a long haft, and besides, so heavy a weapon would be slow.

Moshulu *threw*. The forging hammer flashed across the gap in an instant that stretched; even then the Rand was dodging. It took him in the upper chest with a *clang* that struck like a gong in the temples of his home city. He was flung back with a dent the depth of a fist in his armor. He stumbled back two, three steps, arms wide in spasm; not even a sword-pledged Rand could ignore the first pain of cracked ribs, and his gasp of pain levered them into metal bent too close to let him draw full breath.

The curved sword wavered, then froze as Inu sprang up and seized his right arm at the elbow; clung grimly with flattened ears as the armored fist of the left pounded on the whalebone-backed leather of the dog's helm. That stopped as Moshulu stepped near and caught the man in a bear-hug; Shyll was on Inu's other side, smallsword poised as he danced about for an opening.

Inu released the Rand's arm; the armor had not been pierced, but the limb hung limp and blood ran from the dangling fingers of the gauntlet as the sword clattered to the deck. Moshulu hoisted him up, grinning in the depths of his russet-brown beard; that turned to a roar of pain as the warrior snapped his helmetted head forward into the Moryavska's face, drove a steel-capped knee toward his groin. Moshulu took the knee on his thigh, spat blood and teeth, *squeezed* with a bull-bellow of effort. Metal squealed, bending, and at last the Rand was making a sound, desparate grunts to match his thrashing. The Moryavska roared again, raised the man over his head and slammed him down on the railing; it broke with a splintering crash and the body fell from his hands and into the shallow water of the sandbank to be slowly nudged away from the ships, barely submerged and face-down. One or two bubbles broke the surface, then nothing. Moshulu dropped to his knees, panting, dazed, watching thin runnels of blood drift downstream as the crew of the *Zingas Vryka* charged past him, cheering.

"Hold! HOLD! Lady take it! Stop right there!" Rilla shouted through her curled hands. "Truce!"

Silence fell as she stepped to the gap where the Rand had stood. She looked backward; barely half her crew were still on their feet, there must be ten dead at least, as many again too badly hurt to stand and fight. "Fight," she muttered softly to herself. "This is a massacre and it has to stop, right now." To her own:

"Annike—no, Piashk, light me a torch. Everyone else hold your places." There was quiet at last, quiet enough to hear the water gurgle and the snick and flare of a sulphur match. She took the torch and shouted around the gap. "Will you give truce?"

"Had enough?" a voice gibed.

Then another, the Captain's voice that had called for archers earlier: "Truce; oath by the Lady and the Lord's shadow." A Zaki accent, F'talezonian Middle Quarter; that oath would be kept, at least in public. She stepped through to the rear section of the deck. The mercenaries held their ground; about ten left, battered, bleeding, leaning on their weapons or making half-hearted efforts to cut away the tangle of rigging. The Captain and second mate standing among them, both Zak . . .

Zrinchka, she thought, recognizing him from one of Megan's gatherings in the old days; an up-and-coming captain of thirty or so, with a half-interest in his own vessel and the rest belonging to a consortium of small traders. The *Kettle Belly* was *not* his usual stamping ground at all. Behind him, the quarterdeck and the springsteel six marines and a HandLeader. He perched with a leg swinging on one of the leg-struts of his weapon, face calm in contrast to the tension of his troops. Thin, dark River-Quarter face, middle-aged, a professional who followed orders. *Probably disgusted to have his machine in civilian hands*, she thought. *Also thanking the Lady he's under a merchant skipper, not a naval noble who'd order a stand to the knife*.

Rilla sniffed, spat to clear her mouth, coughed to clear her throat. *I'm soaked to the waist in blood*. Bile rose thick at the back of her throat, and she choked down the overwhelming urge to vomit. *I don't have time to throw up*. She had seen death before . . . but so many, so many.

"Shyll, Temuchin, shields, please." Zrinchka's word she trusted, but one of the naZak mercenaries might risk a throw and his anger, for Habiku's reward. She called over the shield rims, her voice forced to lightness:

"Zrinchka, I didn't think you were this hard up. What are you doing aboard this tub?"

The man straightened and shaded his eyes with a hand, the twofang loose in his grip. "Dark Lord's dung, it *is* Megan Whitlock's *patrischana*, father's sister's child," he said, and then shrugged. "The *Wild Goose* was laid up with a cracked strake, and Smoothtongue offered me a one-time charter to run this bucket down to Rand; said he had an important cargo to transport quietly, and I needed to meet my payroll or put my crew on the beach . . ." Anger creased his face.

"I lost my bosun and four good hands to this." His eyes went to the torch. "And didn't Whitlock teach you better than to carry an unshielded flame on deck?" His face was pale too; a merchant skipper on the Brezhan could expect to see the odd skirmish, but river pirates were in the trade for profit, not blood—they rarely pushed home an attack against a well-defended vessel.

Rilla forced cheeks that felt stiff and numb to grin. "You pushed into a private quarrel, Zrinchka," she said. More formally: "Honorable Captain, we have the option of casting off. Unfortunately I don't believe that choice is open to you. Though I hesitate to burn one of my own ships, I will if I deem it necessary." She moved her hand toward the dangling, shredded canvas. "You can swim to shore before she goes up, of course. I wouldn't bet on being able to take much with you. Surrender and you can take your personal gear, and I'll leave you enough supplies to walk it upriver to the nearest settlement."

Zrinchka bit his lip, held up a hand for time, turned to speak to the marine NCO on the quarterdeck. Rilla could hear their voices murmuring; she could also see the mercenaries look at each other out of the corners of their eyes. The blood-rush of combat was fading, limbs and wounds stiffening; they fought for money and their reputations, coin was of little use to a corpse and nobody could fairly say they had not done an honorable day's work, with half their number dead.

"—not enough for my life!" Rilla heard the merchant captain say.

"All very well for you, Teik," the bandy-legged little marine was saying, crouched to bring his head within talking distance of Zrinchka. "I's the one what has to answer to the Teik Captain back at the fort for this buggering load of scrap." A thumb jerked over his shoulder toward the low-slung spider shape of the steelspring. "Much as my balls is—"

The ragged edges of sail flapped in a sudden gust of breeze. She could catch only a word or two: "orders," "papers." Behind her, she heard Shyll whisper to Inu, and a basso growl rumbled out; the mercenaries looked at each other again, openly, and one of the marines made an averting sign against evil. At last Zrinchka grabbed a folded document from the sergeant, scribbled angrily and turned.

"We accept your terms, pirate!" he snapped. "On one condition."

"Which is?" Weariness crashed down on Rilla like a blanket of resilient air, and she fought not to stagger.

Zrinchka's voice was grim. "That until we're gone, you keep that Dark Lord damned *dog* away from us!" Weapons clattered to the planks, and Zrinchka drove his twofang to stand, humming to match his frustration.

Rilla sat on the sterncastle of the *Kettle Belly* watching as they finished swabbing the deck. The marines and the mercenaries stood together on the starboard side, with the dejected look that prisoners always had; Iczak had attended to their hurts after seeing to the *Zingas Vryka's* folk, but the sheer physical misery of after-combat letdown was on them. Not to mention the pain of financial loss; hired fighters carried much of their profits on their back in equipment, and she was leaving them their clothes only, and one belt-knife each. It would mean long years of lower pay and greater risks, unless they could dun Habiku Smoothtongue for their losses. The marines were more philosophical, since the DragonLord would have to replace *their* gear.

Near them Shyll tended Inu's cuts. The dog whimpered, shivering as Shyll, frowning, carefully cleaned the wounds. His tail was tucked between his legs and he pressed his head flat to the planks in propitiation, flinching as the needle and catgut closed a long gash on his flank.

"Quiet, Inu. *Good* boy, *good* boy." A feeble wave of the tail, and the dog bent his barrel-sized head to lick at the wound. Shyll gently pushed the nose away. "*No*, Inu. Understand? *No*." The greathound looked at the teRyadn with melting amber eyes and laid his head down again with a gusty sound halfway between a whimper and a sigh. Shyll finished, straightened, glared at the prisoners with more anger than he had shown during the fight. Two of the marines were bouncing a pair of dice against the scuppers; they continued their game, but one of the mercenaries rolled his eyes at Inu and fingered his hair earring.

Rilla climbed stiffly to her feet and walked over to them, addressed the marine commander in high Zak.

"Teik." Her bow was exaggeratedly polite, and so was the form of address: the sergeant blinked in surprise and instinctively braced into the regulation rest position. "I'm so sorry to have deprived you of your transportation but I'm sure the short walk to F'trovanemi, no more than two or three days, won't harm you." A pause. "Do you know whose ship this is?"

"Ahhh, Teik Captain, some half-breed Upper Quarter ClawPrince with pull, is all *I* knows," he said.

Rilla shrugged. "Your officer will know who I mean. Tell him to tell Habiku Smoothtongue—" She paused. "Habiku Muttoneater that I'm still taking back the Sleeping Dragon. It was very kind of him to send me a steelspring for my *Zingas Vryka*."

The marine's face darkened, but the insult was not directed at him, and anyway, *he* was too unimportant for the Palace to notice. Word had it that the orders had come under Ranion's seal, but it was the Woyvodaana, the DragonLady, who had given the order. This Habiku might be a favorite of hers, word was also she had an eye for the men, though it was as much as the skin on your back was worth to say so in front of an officer. A sudden thought almost made him smile. Woyvodaana Avritha might still see that someone was punished if the half-Zak riverlord wanted it, but it would be his commander, high-born enough to notice, that would catch it. The siege engine was worth as much as the whole merchant ship, or more. He hesitated, twisted the knitted wool padding-cap between his hands, spoke.

"Teik Captain?" Rilla raised a brow. "Ahh, the old girl there," he jabbed a thumb at the springsteel. "You'll take good care of her? Don't leave her wound more'n a day or so, see the gears is kept proper and greased?"

Blinking, she nodded.

The Captain's cabin was the usual cubbyhole at the rear of the sterncastle, bearing evidence of a hasty cleaning that was probably Zrinchka's work, and under that a sour stink of old spilled wine. Rilla slumped into a cracked leather chair and looked dully up at Shyll, whose face was still speckled with dried red flakes.

"Shyll, how is everyone?" She made vague motions with her hands. "I thought I'd seen fights, but this . . . this . . ."

He limped over and laid a hand on her shoulder. "Inu's fine, if we can keep him from licking off the bandages; not very happy, though, he hurts and his lips are bruised. I left Shenka and Jakov with him."

Rilla felt a surge of anger at his speaking of the dog first, then pushed it down with an effort that left her more exhausted than before. Shyll was a teRyadn, one of the settled not-Ryadn who had failed to bond with a Ri. She put a hand to her forehead. He'd just never realized that he was too decent a person to bond with one of those things. He was a doglord, not a Ryadn. The bond to his greathounds was as close as kindred; Inu was all he had of his homeland. *And besides, I'm fond of the great lump myself.*

"Out of forty we lost ten—" She winced. "Boryis is bad," he continued softly. "Yahn's still alive but . . ."

"Is this worth it?" Rilla asked dully. "This was ten times worse than I thought it would be."

He grasped her shoulder. "We're here through our choice." His grin was tired but still brilliant. "Let's see what Habiku thought was so valuable. It couldn't have been this ship." Somehow she pulled a smile from inside somewhere.

The Captain's books were hung on the walls in the cabin, locked. It took them a while to find the keys. "Shit. Maybe we should just break open a few bales and so-forth . . . ah, Rilla. Here they are."

The supercargo's loadbook opened with a sticky crackle of bookbinder's glue, powdering. There were a number of loose pages in the back that Shyll took, as Rilla ran her finger down the column of goods, her lips pursed in a silent whistle. There was a thump and a creak as the jollyboat cast off to take the marines ashore and turn them loose.

"My. Sweet. Serene. Unruffled. Goddess," Rilla whispered. "Showtiger furs. Glass brick. Fine-steel. Ermine. Walrus ivory . . . What in Halya is going on—"

Shyll interrupted her with a whoop and a yell that had people running to see what was wrong. She looked up and he swept her and the book up and swung them around in a tight, limping circle, barely missing smacking his head on the ceiling. "*She's back! Fanged God, she's back. Rilla we were right! She's back—*"

Rilla managed to squirm one arm free and put her hand over his mouth. "What are you babbling about?" Inu was barking. Temuchin had wrenched the door open and half the crew was behind him. There were tears in the teRyadn's eyes. He set her down gently, put a crumpled dispatch in her hand. The smile on his face was like sunlight on water.

"The stuff on board," he said quietly, "is all, was all for bribes to the young prince's advisors in Rand to arrange an accident for Megan. An accident that won't ever be arranged!

"Megan. She's back. My—" He grinned again, sheepishly. "Our Megan's back."

Chapter 8

Megan handed Shkai'ra's binoculars back down to her. "They're telling us to stand off until they give clearance, the sheepfuckers. Piatr!"

He looked over the edge of the poop, "Yes, Captain?"

"What reasons do the Thanes have *now* for such high-handedness?"

"None, Captain, but Yannet says that the Aenir won the trading deal they were competing for from the Stroemfiar. All those who don't own their ships must rent passage from the barge-people and the Aenir had more of what they wanted."

"Fishguts." She swung down next to Shkai'ra. "Akribhan, you'd find this town easy to take, impossible to hold. They'd pick you to death with niggling complaints and finicky ways."

The Kommanza shrugged. "Hang them up, let them argue with the vultures."

"Wonderful, then you'd have to train collars of slaves to handle the river mine. Damn their arrogance. Hai, since this is only a layover, not a harbor stop, we don't have to conform to rules. Shkai'ra, would the brats be up to learning a new skill?"

"Hm. If it's blood you want, well enough, courtly grace and manners, no."

"Oh, nothing strenuous. Damn sheep-herders want us to lose *zight* waiting on them. Mateus! Oar count! Rough challenge, find out if anyone will match me."

He looked startled then grinned. "Aye! All hands! Any who will match in running the oars?" The crew's attention focused on the deck, and with a clatter the oars came out.

"Challenge? What is this?" Shkai'ra asked. Megan laughed and pulled off her boots. "Only a bit of fun, poking their rules in the eye. We close and maintain just outside the harbor, slow beat. Between strokes the oars are held out and you walk the rank, out over the water from one end to the other. It's a way of showing them that we can handle the ship well enough not to need their damn harbor. And rough challenge means that anyone on board who wants to, can try to match my number of runs. If you fall in the river you lose *zight* but not much. It's more of a laugh-with than a laugh-at because almost everyone who does it gets wet."

Shkai'ra looked out at the slow falling beat of the oars and smiled slowly. The ship slowed headway outside the harbor mouth and the oar-master signalled with a double *thump*. Then the slow-beat began; a crewman began a broken-cadenced song to the beat, keeping time. As Megan stepped to the gunnel the familiar lines brought an amused look to her eyes.

> Thy father was a Thanish goatherd;
> > THUMP, *Rang the beat.*
> And mother she did bleat.
> So if you drink with me my friend,
> Do so in another tavern.
> > THUMP.

She had the rhythm now and between beats stepped out onto the banks of outstretched oars that gave slightly under her weight. No one strove, this time, to throw her off balance by dipping their oar. She ran the rank once and rubbed the sole of one foot down her other leg to dislodge a splinter and looked back along the deck. "The next verse!" she called, beginning it herself.

"White wine only do I drink;
                THUMP;
Unless it be blood red."

Shkai'ra stepped to the rail and looked down. The arrow-stem of the *Zingas Vetri* was pointed upstream, just keeping way on her against the current. She was on the left side of the ship, the townward rail, and she could smell the silt in the banks of sediment traps that lined the banks; it mingled with the acrid smoke of the smelters and the sour scent of bad lowland drainage. The water pulled by along the tar-black lapstrake planks of the hull, cold and brown with sediment.

Frowning slightly, she glanced up to see Piatr leaning against a stay and cleaning his fingernails on a knife, whistling with elaborate casualness.

"If you've got something to say, say it," she said. "If you're a musician, I'm a sea captain."

She sprang sideways out onto the oar. It dipped under her weight and she crouched, toes clinging. Then she skipped to the next, and the next, remembering. *It had been the fall hunt, in her seventeenth summer; they'd cut out a small herd of buffalo from the river marshes and run them, riding close to strike with lance and arrow. She'd kicked her feet clear of the stirrups and jumped to a hairy, humped giant-back, on to the next before it could buck, tossing chaos and death a body-length away, from one to its neighbor to the other side of the herd and then vaulting to the ground, running and tumbling and shouting laughter to a sky bluer than bird's egg and sharp enough to cut with a knife.*

This would be easy.

She put her hands on her hips and skipped, doing a half turn in the air; almost missed the next oar; recovered with a cat-twist; ran the last three and swung inward to the deck. She tossed her head to feel the river wind through the thick, fine-textured mass of her hair, cool on her flushed cheeks, panting slightly. She nodded to Megan.

"It has its points. Who's next?"

"Piatr," she said. Shkai'ra turned in surprise. *The one-foot? Running oars?* He wasn't running. With the final line of the

verse, he leaped and began the next, hanging from under the
bank he moved the rank hand over hand. ". . . with three
Ieus camels," he sang off key as he tumbled over the rail next
to them. "Hello!" He said jauntily. "It's what I have to say, and
you're right, you are no sea captain." With a splash, Stanver
slipped and fell, spraying them with cold water. Amidst laughter they threw him a line off the stern of the ship. Shkai'ra
looked Piatr up and down, put one foot on the rail and looked
over into the water. "Wet damn river isn't it?" she said. He
chuckled. Megan cast a glance at the harbor. The row-tug
was on its way. Suddenly it was good to be home.

"Mateus! Race!" She whirled and jumped for the outriver
side of the ship, calling over her shoulder. "That song would
bring them quick, they can't hear the words but all anyone
has to hear is the tune!"

A sudden grin split her face and she leaped back and forth
between two oars, once, twice, then darted forward. She
caught a glimpse of Mateus's head opposite, racing the other
way and laughed, skipped an oar, and in trying again missed.
She came up spluttering and laughing, caught the rope with
one hand. The current swung her back, close to the other
head bobbing in the water. "I missed," Mateus said, then,
unsure of her laugh, smiled slowly.

On the deck Megan wrung out the edge of her tunic as
Piatr, Shkai'ra and now Sova went into the water with flailing
limbs trying to catch balance. The song was degenerating, the
oar-banks growing uneven as more of the crew succumbed to
laughter.

"Flap harder with the arms! You might fly!"

"Not so much noise, you'll scare the fish!"

"Fish, nothing! They'll scare the Thanes!"

"With bait that size who knows what we'd catch!"

Megan leaned over and looked at the cluster of heads
around the rope, strung out like beads on string. "Stop making so many waves!" she called down to them with mock
anger. "The ship is rocking!" Then she sobered. The tug was
there.

"All right! Well done! Oarmaster beat two-stroke. Let's
get my *Vetri* into anchor." She turned and offered the others

a hand over the stern. "Wet fun," she said. "*Zight* be damned, it was still fun."

STAADT RIVER MINE
SAME DAY

The throbbing whine of the water-driven turbine echoed and re-echoed in the narrow street. High walls to either side concealed smelters, brickworks, carpenters' shops, stables, the multifold outbuildings necessary to a large manufactury; ahead was the blank granite square of the river mine itself. Shkai'ra rubbed one hand across an ear, peering over the shingled roof to the maze of diversion channels and canal docks beyond; they would be lost to view as the road swooped down to river level. She could see young workers scampering monkey-agile, closing and opening water gates; a heavy silty smell filled the air, struggling with the sulphurous stink of the refineries, tang of fresh-sawn pine . . .

Must stink to Zoweitzum in the summer, she thought; it was cool even in late afternoon, now. To the man beside her:

"So what did the factor say?"

"What?" Piatr started out of some private thought, almost missing a hobbling stride. "The mine-kin would rather deal with the owner than an agent; Habiku pushed them, and they tore up his contract." He paused. "Habiku . . ." His voice filled with what a stranger might have heard as love.

The whine of the turbine died, and Piatr's tone became brisk. "The mine-kin are hard to deal with. Don't even *look* as if you're trying to steal their secret. Wringing copper and silver and gold out of riverwater is an art well worth killing for."

"Do I look like a miner?" she said, slapping her breast-plate. She was in the head-to-toe harness of a Kommanz lancer, and the fanged skull of Stonefort Keep grinned redly beneath the fingers of her gauntlet.

"Anyone," he snapped impatiently.

She shrugged. "We'll just talk at a distance, then. And

quickly; Megan will be feeding that Thanish harbormaster to the fish by now, and we'd best hurry if we want to help."

Piatr turned to her with a grin that froze at her expression as she looked over his shoulder. They had reached the end of the approach road; the door of the river mine was before them, a blank wall to their right; to the left was another laneway, making an L-shape.

"Piatr, I don't think those are miners either," Shkai'ra said softly. He turned his head. There were four, city bravos from their looks. All young, but with scars enough to show their trade; chunky, fair men in leather knee-breeches, bright shirts and three-cornered feather hats. They carried small round bucklers and sickle swords, blades that rose straight from the guards before belling out in a double-edged curve.

Shkai'ra's shield slid from her back; she thrust her arms through the grips and brought the rim up under her eyes; the long curve of her saber slid free of the sheath with a soft hiss, rising with delicate precision over her shoulder.

Possible, ran through her mind, a cool appraisal that filled her forebrain with calculation; she could taste the hot salty bubble of excitement that ran below it. *They've no harness and they're brawlers, not soldiers. Not used to fighting a different technique.* Her pupils widened.

Piatr limped to cover her shield side, drawing his belt knife.

"*Nia, bh'utut!*" she snarled in Kommanzanu. Then in Zak: "No! In there, into the building—I can hold them in the doorway."

He looked at her, surprise in every line. "What? They're Thanes." His voice roughened and he settled into the knifefighter's crouch. "I owe them," he said softly, then a grin flashed across his face. "And what would I tell the Captain if you get killed?" He moved back to the point where he was clear of her but could still cover her back. "She'd kill me!"

Shkai'ra giggled, the high-pitched, mocking titter that was her folk's reaction to the fact or threat of death. "I can't fight with a cripple to guard," she said, panting slightly, lips wet. "*Get in that door before I kick you in!*"

She elbowed him back and pushed; he rebounded from her backplate into the doors, and through them. The river mine had made examples enough not to need bars against uninvited guests. The Thanes jogged forward, spreading out, not wasting time with words. Shkai'ra settled into the portal, slightly back from the entrance; it was barely twice the width of her shoulders, narrow enough that they could come at her only one at a time.

She barely heard Piatr's squawk, "Cripple!", before the first Thane reached her. She could see the cracked front tooth of his grin as he slashed low. Her face was twisted in the semblance of a smile as she jumped, then stamped hard on the blade under her boots, pulling the Thane forward. His face just had time to register shock as the sabre carved through his neck. The second pulled back not to stumble over the body of the first, cast a glance at his comrades and they spread out to either side.

They're trying to force me back, Shkai'ra thought, waiting for them to come and die. There was an uproar rising behind her, shouts and cries of "Outkin!" "Take him!" "Stop . . . ouch!" "Hey!" "Grab him, you steerfucker!" "OOF!" that she paid no mind to. Then they were on her, working together to try and bring her down or force her back. *SSShrashh*, her sword screeched off the small buckler of the one to her left; she stepped in as he wobbled, off balance. He leaped back, not far enough and she opened him across the belly.

The others' blades jarred her shield as she stepped again and forced them back. "Damn, verdamnt Zak lover . . ." one panted.

"Shkai'ra!" Piatr's shout came from behind her. "Duck!" She bent her head, twisting to one side as the Thane hacked with the curved blade, hoping to get around her shield, slammed the edge into his face and flung up an arm to ward off stone chips that flew from the wall from where the thrown sledge hammer had hit, just above her head.

The Thanes were gone, overborne by the crowd of miners that ringed them, Piatr backed to the wall beside her. "No!"

he cried as her sword came up. "Don't kill anyone here! We have business!"

The saber made a ripping noise in the air as she whipped it back and forth to keep the mob at bay. "Tell *them!*" she snarled.

The thrown hammer wasn't the only one in the crowd. In hard, calloused hands were shovels, chains, rakes, lumps of rock and cargo hooks, hefted and ready to use. "I don't care about your *whulzaitz* river mine!" She could take many of them with her, but sheer weight of numbers would tell. It was no end for a warrior, beaten to death by workers with *tools*.

There was a heaving in the crowd; a spray of burly labourers staggered aside and the Minemaster stood before her, heavy, middle-aged face red between greying muttonchop whiskers.

"*Vat is der meaning of this?*" he shouted, the shiny skin of his scalp glistening through thinning hair.

Shkai'ra snapped her saber to one side, clearing it of blood and spattering the foremost of the miners with a spray of salty droplets. One of the bravos was still moaning at her feet. Irritated, she booted him in the back as she wiped her sword clean.

"It means," she said, "that two peaceful travellers coming to talk business were accosted by cutthroats on your doorstep, then set upon by your underlings when they sought refuge. *Die, damn you, and get it over with!*" she added in an aside to the Thane at her feet, following with another kick.

The Masterminer stared at her. "Peaceful? Und der is reason that such as dis should attack you?" He stepped forward, almost to within range of her sword tip. "Ve have no quarrel with you but with *him*." His hand snapped out to point at Piatr. "He vas inside and is not *montagee*. So why do you protect him, 'peaceful traveller?' "

"Thanks for pushing me there, Firehead," Piatr whispered and stepped forward as she spoke.

"Because we ship together. It's reason enough."

"Masterminer Verner," Piatr said quietly. "You know me. In the seconds I was inside I could not have seen anything that I understood. And I had no desire to be there, as your people can testify to." He nodded at one or two nursing bruises, just beginning to show.

"Iz no matter," the Masterminer said. "You are out-kin. Ve cannot allow out-kin to leave, having entered."

Shkai'ra rolled her eyes up. The Thane at her feet gurgled and was still. "I'll talk easier if you put down the shovels and rakes and tools of destruction," she said.

"I do have an idea that might solve our problem . . ." Piatr rubbed the side of his nose with a finger. Shkai'ra looked at him, then at the miners.

"Right," Shkai'ra said, looking down at the nick in her wrist. "You get to explain to Megan why we're late, *brother*. And why we're both very suddenly *montagee*." She fingered the small brown mark of a fish at her throat.

Megan was pacing the aft-deck when they got back. "Why—!" Her voice died as she took in the two mine-kin marks.

"I . . . ah . . . I have something to tell you, Captain . . ." Piatr began.

"No you *don't!*" Shkai'ra interrupted and stamped past them both to go below. "One-foot, don't say anything, I changed my mind. Nothing happened. Not one *zteafakaz* thing happened in this silt-stinking, louse-ridden huddle of flea's droppings you call a town. *Nothing!*" Francosz, in the rigging, snorted and Sova stifled a giggle. From below came the sound of a slamming door and a vengeful splash as another of Ten-Knife's offerings was pitched out of the sterncastle window. Piatr grinned sheepishly. "The Masterminer agreed," he said quickly as Megan opened her mouth. He stepped back. "I've got work to do, Captain."

As he swung down the ladder he heard a snort and Megan called after him, "I sent you to bargain with the miners, not get adopted by them!" He chuckled then.

The sun had set, and the night was very clear; the deck crew moved quickly about their tasks. The wind was only just enough to push the canvas taut, and even the nightbirds were silent; the only sounds were the low chuckle of water parting before the keel and a soft chorus of creaks and hums from hull and rigging. There was a smell of wet and chill, a vagrant hint of woodsmoke from some peasant's steading; the banks of the river were low here, and the light enough to see stands of sere, dead rushes. The river was broad and smooth, with an almost oiled sheen to it, like a rippled surface of black silk glowing slightly, the reflection of the stars deep within it.

The captain of the *Zingas Vetri* raised her face to the sky and her breath caught at the clarity of it, a road of shining silver dust across the sky from east to west, with the north star and the Gourd ahead. And another star, low on the northern horizon, very bright, bright enough to make a fairy light-path down the long reach of the northing Brezhan, as if she could leap from the bows and tread along a path of shining music to—

"Shamballah," she murmured. Megan lowered her spyglass and sighed, the stiff set of her shoulders relaxed somewhat. Then she called over her shoulder, "Shkai'ra, you might be interested in this."

". . . fifty. Up. Stay up on your knuckles. Don't move." Shkai'ra looked from the deck to the poop. "I'll be there, will it wait?"

"Yes."

The Kommanza turned to the two children. "Up! Sponge down. I'll be down to check on you in a moment." She swung up the ladder, landing soundlessly as Ten-Knife beside Megan, who handed her the spyglass.

"Have a look at the brightest star, there on the horizon." She smiled. "We call it Shamballah, it means *Paradise*," she said in Kommanzanu.

"*Ztrateke ahKomman*, that's a bright star," Shkai'ra said. "Noticed it since we made northing of Brahvniki." The Kommanza trained the glass. "Well, I'll be a sheepfucker! That thing has a disk." A soundless whistle. "And . . . tell me I'm imagining this, kh'eeredo. Are those panels—square?"

"You're not imagining it. One sect of priests in F'talezon says that that star was built; by their god, of course. It's always in the same spot, like the north star. We have lots of stories about it, no one knows for sure what it is. To me, it means I'm home."

Shkai'ra slung an arm around Megan's shoulders, feeling somehow set at arm's length. *Home. The only one I've had is more than a year's journey away.* She sighed. "Well, a whole town of witches ought to be interesting, at least." A glance at their wake: star-images tumbled in the broken water.

"I'm a very long way from home," she murmured. The constellations looked the same from the gaunt stone towers of her kindred's castle . . . How far away . . . oceans and mountains and rivers, cities and years? "It's cold," she said, pulling her arm away from Megan's shoulder, drawing her cloak about her.

The Zak looked up at her and her hand tightened on the spyglass. *In searching for my own way home, for my own revenge, I've forgotten to think of my steel-sister. I've been assuming she'll stay.* "If you want to, any home I have is yours, akribhan." She clamped the fear down under the locks and bars in her mind.

"Well, let's make your home city safe for you first, *nia?*" A sour chuckle. "Making Stonefort safe for me again would be more difficult; you'd have to kill all my relatives to do it." She pulled Megan closer, shivering slightly; went down on one knee to bring their faces on a level. Their eyes met for a long moment before they kissed; Megan's hands cupped the Kommanza's face, the razor nails resting with infinite delicacy in the angle of her jaw.

"Hmmp. Not so cold," Shkai'ra said, nuzzling into the thick black mass of her other's hair. "Home is where I choose, love: and I chose to be beside you. Haven't regretted it."

Megan closed her eyes and leaned on the other's shoulder, then shivered and pulled away as she hadn't done for months. *Habiku, I'm going to kill you.* She didn't see Shkai'ra's worried eyes.

Chapter 9

NYSNY TVER
FIVE DAYS NORTH OF BRAHVNIKI
TENTH IRON CYCLE FIFTEENTH DAY

"Captain! Mateus!" Yvar Monkeyfist called before he set foot on the wooden dock; there was someone slung over his shoulder, wrapped in a old red satin coverlet faded to a dirty salmon pink. The crowd along Nysny Tver's muddy main street ignored him. They were Aeniri, or mostly, managing to make even the straggling little trade town seem crowded; they did not make way for him either, and the Zak dodged between their stolid, baggy-pantalooned height like an eel among salmon.

The Zak ducked under a horse's belly and its rider shouted. The horse bucked, and she gathered the reins close as it squealed and half-reared, and Yvar was forgotten. His footsteps boomed on the oak planking of the dock.

The first mate had been speaking to the bosun, Agniya. Both turned to watch the sailor as he trotted toward them. They gave each other a single glance as they saw his face, strained and sweating and white under the rusty-black knitted sailor's cap, came to the gangway at a run. Yvar staggered up with one hand clutching the rope sideguard, the other looped about the body on his shoulder. It shifted bonelessly as they lifted it from him; Mateus wrinkled his nose at a heavy smell of mustiness, old sweat and a cheap herbal scent.

"Bosun, you don't know her." Yvar let Agniya take the

156

weight, fell to his knees on the deck and panted. "Mat—First Mate, you'll need your kit." He raised his voice again. "Captain!"

Megan came up the ladder from the *Zingas Vetri*'s narrow hold, with the supercargo's Arkan pen behind one ear and ink on her fingers. Her eyes narrowed at the sight of the shrouded body; her face didn't alter, but suddenly the blades at her belt were more noticeable than the clerk's tool. "Yes, Yvar, what is it?"

"Captain, it's Katrana. Healheart." He stopped and swallowed, setting his jaw. "She was in the brothel, I've asked Mateus to get his kit."

She looked at the vaguely stirring pink bundle and her eyes went blank as slate. "In my cabin," she said and led the way.

Sova started guiltily as Megan opened the door in front of Yvar. "Sova, out," she said. "I'll see you later." The girl backed up, her hands behind her, her eyes big. She sidled around the table, out into the corridor, as Yvar edged around to lay his burden in the bunk.

Mateus came in with his bag, closing the door. Yvar stood back, his hands clenching and unclenching. "Katrana doesn't recognize me, or anyone," he said, tightly. "The madam gave her to me because I was Zak and she didn't want any of the other girls or boys touched by one of the witch-folk."

Megan sat on the edge of the bunk as Mateus gently pulled back the coverlet. She made a sound, wordless, less of an exclamation than a belly-deep grunt.

Kat was naked, bruised around the shoulders, but the worst was that her head turned aimlessly, blank eyes staring past the ceiling, her fingers picking at the raw skin on her knuckles. When the coverlet pulled free she shifted to open her legs, raising her knees. A vague little smile appeared on her face and a trickle of saliva glistened at one corner of her mouth where red paint almost covered a lip sore. Her skin showed chalky pale against smeared face-paint and her hair had been cut and frizzled around her face, curls matted at the nape of her neck. She smelled of the herbal perfume and burned dreamdust. She hummed an aimless little tune that wandered up and down and around, again and again and again.

"Kat," Megan called. "Katrana?" There was no answer. "Katrana, you'll be all right."

Mateus tried to get her attention and when he failed, began examining her. Megan stood up abruptly and turned her back, facing Yvar. He unclenched his jaw when she faced him and said, "They drugged her with Thall and Gods'Tears, maybe dust, to keep her docile, stunt her witch powers. The madam was quite proud of her. I paid to get her here but I didn't have enough to buy her outright."

"I'll see to it, Yv. Off with you."

"Aye, Captain." Megan put her hands flat on the table and looked down at them. "Mateus, when you're done, tell me how bad she is. I'll try to reach her mind, if she's strong enough."

"Aye, Captain."

"Zemelya," Megan called to the supercargo as she came on deck.

"Captain?"

"Talk to Yvar; I'm authorizing the purchase of a bondservant from the . . ."

Yvar looked up from a coil of rope. "The *Bucking Mare*, Captain."

"That's it. Debt bond; see to the cancellation." Her voice was calm, a little abstracted; she squinted slightly at the birds wheeling over the choppy blue-brown of the river, folding her hands in the wide cuffs of her cloak. A spot appeared on the dark-grey wool of the sleeves, then another; blood, where the razor steel of her fingernails was slitting the desensitized skin over her shackle scars.

Zemelya, whose gift was to sense emotions, shivered and looked after the Captain as she turned away from him; like a breath across the shoulders and neck. Like something stirring under dark water, under the rotting pilings of an old wharf—he shook himself. *It's the cold*, he thought.

Megan turned away from him, wanting to get away from the pressure of crew around her. Pressing, like a city crowd that touched and brushed at back and elbows, or a soft net muffling— Nobody was touching her, but they were *there*.

There was no place to be private on an arrowboat, except the cabin and Katrana was there. Shkai'ra was ashore with the boy. *No place I can be alone to think.* Her skin felt tight enough to split, her head hurt as if there was some machine of steel and screws inside, driving bands out against the skull; the need to be alone was like the thirst she had felt in the slaver's hold in mid-Lannic, drifting in the doldrums with the water-butts dry. Ten-Knife looked up from the after rail and growled as she passed, but didn't move.

She paced the deck, and though her step seemed as light as always, it rapped on the pine boards; she scarcely stopped to vault the sterncastle railing: Ran along the deck, out along the bowsprit to stand face into the wind with her hands on the forestay. The breeze was like ice on burning cheeks. *Katrana was the first to treat me like something else than Captain's toy eleven years ago.* "—here now, lassie. He's bad." *She told me.* "But he'll hurt you less if you cry when he wants tears."

Megan looked up through the ragged ends of her dirty hair. He hadn't cut her hair again after he bought her and it was growing out again. She hadn't felt clean in days and had stopped caring. "I don't cry." Her tone was flat; no inflection at all. Her hands curled and uncurled, flexing and restless, never still and always empty. He was careful never to allow knives.

Katrana, ship's healer, pulled at one of her own long brown braids, making the Aeniri hairbells chime, sat down beside her and pulled out a knife and a chunk to whittle on. "Well, pretend," she said quietly. "You're still alive and have decided to stay that way." Silence for a time, then . . . "You'll have to learn how to use one of these," she gestured with her knife. "Once you get too old for him." The older girl smiled at Megan, bitterness in the expression. "We get some time, I'll show you." She'd shown Megan the way to really handle a knife. In her hands the blades were like water or sparks jumping from grip to grip.

Katrana had held her the first time she cried real tears after the Arkan had raped her. *She helped me stay sane.*

And later, much later when Megan was fourteen. "Kat . . . it hurts . . . Koruuuh! Hurts . . ."

"Shush, Megan hush. Here're my hands. Breathe . . . one and two . . . breathe deep and push."

"No . . . mine . . . hurts . . . Kat, it hurts. Ahhi, I can't . . ." Megan clenched her teeth on the scream tearing its way out of her, just as the baby was. ". . . has claws! Killing me . . . it's . . ."

"No, Megan, hush. It's only a baby . . . think of it as your baby. You're its mother. Here, lass, drink this." The world dissolved into a wavery blur where Kat argued with Sarngeld, stood up to him when he suggested that they let both girl and brat die. Wavery, hazy woman's hands that held her and blocked something gruesome happening somewhere below her waist that she couldn't feel.

Blood and swinging in and out of darkness and pain seeping back. *Katrana held me to life when I thought I'd die; held me when I knew that I'd never have another child. She held me when I cried, always swearing never to cry again.* Katrana had helped her when the Arkan had sold her son away. *I remember his crying as Sarngeld dragged him out of my chained hands, remember screaming his name as I tore at the links, trying to free myself. Kat came down with the keys, that night, and a set of knives. Kat.*

Megan backed down to the solid deck and paced, remembering, then went below to see if she could help Kat.

Sova dropped the dead rat over the side. *When Francosz gets back I'll just tell him that I couldn't hide it in their bed. Not this time.*

She saw the Captain come up and talk to Zemelya, then start walking the deck as if there were witches after her. *But that's silly, why would witches chase a witch? I wonder what's going on. Who was that?*

She washed her hands in a bucket dipped from the harbor; Piatr had told her that rats could make you sick if you weren't careful. Then she jumped, grabbed a ratline and climbed; not as quickly as Francosz, or the crew, but she could do it now. Right up into the rigging. Out of the way when the ship was at anchor, away from the crowding and jostling of deckhands and rowers. Down below, the hull was almost steady, with hawsers at bow and stern loop to timber balks on the dock. At the masthead, every quiver was amplified, a slight swaying roll and pitch, the surge and rebound of the northing wind catching masts and hull and rocking them against the cables.

I like it up here, she thought. *Mother never let me do anything like this.* The wind was blowing up the river; Nysny Tver lay south, sprawling over the hummock of rock that jutted out into the stream. The wind ruffled her hair and she squinted into it; Mateus had told her she'd get sailor's wrinkles from that. Sova climbed the final arm-up-and-scramble to the lookout's post, a simple crossbar three feet below the whale-bone cap of the mast, and wound her legs around the wood, locking her heels. The breeze was chilly enough to bring gooseflesh to her arms and legs inside the wool trousers and shirt. She pulled the knitted cap down over her ears and shaded her eyes with a self-consciously sailorly hand.

Maybe I can find out who that was, she thought. There were plenty of ships on the river, spread out below her like a map from the seventy foot height of the mast.

Sova rose to stand on the crossbar, looked down at the tiny narrow shape of the deck far below; the houses of the town beyond were scattered helter-skelter, new-built since the town was burned out in Enkar's War three years ago. There was a steep-roofed wooden temple with eaves carved with the head of Bogor the horse-god; a pair of flittercats dived and swooped around the yellow-painted spires, crowding a hapless pigeon.

The triatic stay stretched out before her, linking the mastheads. Sova looked down again and swallowed. It was a *long* way down . . . She bent, pulled off the rope sandals and stuck them into her belt, beside the sharp deckhand's knife with the saw-back for cutting heavy cordage. *Fear is useful as a warning*, Shkai'ra had said to her. *If you let it rule you, you're its slave*. The cable dipped slightly under her weight. She grabbed the stay and swung her feet up, breathed deeply, then spidered over with a whooping yell. The rough surface was a brushing reassurance; she ended the crawl with a swing, smack against the foremast and clutched it, laughing.

Yvar was beneath her; she cupped her hands to hail him, then swung into a shroud to slide to the deck. Suddenly she was hungry, pleasantly conscious of her own sweat. *Funny, I always hated sweating before,* she thought. *It doesn't really smell bad if you don't let it get stale.* Father's sweat had smelled of beer, sour somehow: she could not *imagine* her mother doing anything but . . . *glowing,* that was how she'd said it.

"Yvar!" she called again, dropping the last six feet and landing in a ball. Yvar was a friend, the best ropemaster and knotsmith on the *Zingas Vetri;* he'd promised to show her how to do the Monkey's Fist.

"Yvar, who *was* that you brought on board? Was it a robber? Did you have a fight?" The sailors would talk about dockside brawls and riots, sometimes; it sounded like fun.

Yvar looked up at her, and the brightness faded from the day. "No," he said slowly. "It wasn't a robber. Someone who'd been . . . robbed. Robbed of everything." His eyes focused, and he became conscious of the Thane girl's mouth making a shocked O of surprise. "It's all right, Sova-child. An old friend of mine and the Captain's; she's . . . sick, very sick, and we're worried about her. Don't talk about it to the Captain, she's upset. Look, don't you have anything to do?"

Sova swallowed; a vendor had come on board with hot honey-pancakes and set up near the gangplank, but she didn't feel hungry any more. *I wish Francosz was back,* she thought. "I'll find something, Yvar," she said.

Mateus closed his kit with a click. "She has lung-clot in one lung. A venereal disease. Someone broke a rib, but it's healed up well. She doesn't have anything that I can't treat. The problem . . ." He trailed off. Megan didn't react.

"Is she strong enough for a mind-healer to help her?" Her hands came out of her sleeves.

"I think so. I'll stay while you try." She shook her head, but he held up one hand. "It's safer for her."

Megan nodded and sat down next to Kat. Mateaus had washed the face-paint off, gotten her cleaned up; she looked almost like the old Katrana, except for the short hair. Megan brushed a curl off Kat's forehead, then took one hand in both of hers, took a deep breath and closed her eyes.

Center. Cool blue space behind my eyes . . . Megan reached for the place in her mind where all Zak alive were gathered. *I have just enough power to know that it exists.* An orange-red glow, like the sun seen through closed eyes . . . *That's me.* This place was like a sea, or ice crystals blowing on the steppe, a shifting curtain, or waves that surged and flowed around her. The dim spots near her were Mat and further away were the Zak crew. Far and yet not far was the whirlwind of fire that was F'talezon, weeks away up the river. Sparks drifting in and through the manrauq, the sea of power. Katrana was lost here somewhere, mind gone, driven out by the drugs.

Kat! Megan called and watched a mint-scented line of red coil out into the manrauq. *Kat, where are you? Katrana Healheart, Daughter of Wynn Nethand, Daughter of Binah Sailspinner. Kat. Koru, Lady Goddess, help me. Dark Lord turn your eyes away. Kat!*

There! No. The manrauq rang with Kat's presence, and her loss. *My edges are fading. I'm becoming one with the power, one with the cool . . . blue . . .* CRACK!

Megan shuddered, blinked and ducked under Mateus's hand. "You . . . you don't . . ." She couldn't stop the tears. "I'm all right. I'm back." Her headache was back, like a band of damp rawhide drying around it, her eyes hot as she tried to stop crying. "You don't have to slap me again, Mat. I'll have you up for striking the Captain . . ." She laughed like porcelain cracking, like a ship's timbers splintering on rocks, and put her forehead on Kat's hand. "I couldn't . . . I tried, Mat. I couldn't find her. I couldn't."

He put out a hand but didn't quite touch her back. She cried, and Kat stared at the ceiling humming her tune that went in and out and around and around.

Chapter 10

ON THE RIVER BETWEEN NYSNY TVER AND RAND
FALSE DAWN, TENTH IRON CYCLE, TWENTY-SECOND DAY

Sova snuggled deeper under the feather tick, pulling it higher up her cheek against the cold. Francosz sighed and rolled over. He pulled the covers half off and when she yanked them back only muttered and stuffed his head under the pillow. It was never completely dark here in the companionway; the Captain kept a *kraumak*, one of the eerie glowing stones that only the Zak could make, slung in a glass globe from the ceiling. That heatless glow was safest belowdecks on a ship. Sova had grown used to it, no longer waking up and imagining the baleful eye of witchcraft staring into her soul.

It's good and warm under the tick and we don't have to get out of bed yet, she thought, putting one hand under her cheek. She could hear the boards squeak and the pad of feet over their heads; watch was just changing; *It'll still be dark, except for the part of the sky that's sort of glowing silver, where the sun will come up*. The wind always dropped this early so the *Zingas Vetri* wasn't making much way against the current. The hull whispered to her through the floor and the pillow and the bones of her hand. *Like she's saying "Going, going, I'm going." Shift. Scrape. I like that. I feel funny. Full, kind of.*

She dozed, then snapped awake when she felt a trickle of

moisture on her leg. *I haven't wet the bed since I was a baby!* she thought indignantly. But it didn't feel like . . . She put a hand down to feel, then looked at her hand. Red. It was red. She reached down again, pressed herself, brought the hand out; this time the whole palm was covered.

"*Khyd-hird!*" She scrambled up and threw herself at the door of the cabin, crying with terror. The wood boomed under her fists and feet, and the feel of blood suddenly gushing down her legs lent the strength of panic. "*Khyd-hird!*" Francosz tumbled out of the featherbed behind her, asking what was wrong.

She burst through, staggering as the latch opened, to see Shkai'ra half out of bed with her sword already unsheathed, Megan up and reaching for her knives. "I'm bleeding!" she cried. "I'm bleeding! Am I going to die? I'm all bloody. I . . . I . . ."

Shkai'ra took her by the shoulders and shook her. "Hush. Where are you hurt? Tell me."

"I . . . between . . . between . . ." Sova sobbed and looked at her shift that had red patches on it. "Between my legs. I'm all bloody between my legs."

Shkai'ra stopped and looked at her. "Between your legs," she said. "Girl, you've just become a woman." She snorted. "Put a clout on, get washed up."

Sova looked at her, bewildered. "A, a woman? But I'm bleeding."

The Kommanza stopped in the act of sheathing her sword and turned up the light; lamplight rippled on the pale skin of her shoulders and arms. She turned, blinking in bewilderment.

"Look, *kyd*, I told you—" She stopped, turned to Megan. "You told me they had some strange customs, kh'eeredo, but—"

Megan put her knives down and padded over. "She's a Thane, Shkai'ra. They don't think women should know where babies come from until they have them. The Lady's truth, I'm not exaggerating. She doesn't know what's happening."

"Right. You mean I have to explain to the brat? Oh, sheepshit. Look," Shkai'ra said to the girl. "It'll happen every month. You'll bleed. Every woman does, until they're past their middle years. I do it, Megan does—did it, you're not sick. You're not wounded, you're not sick, you're not going to die. It means that you can bear, so you have to be careful when you fuck or you'll get pregnant."

Sova stood looking at her, her mouth open, her bloodied hand still held out. "But, but . . . This happens to *you*?" Behind her, Francosz snorted, "Girl's stuff." And went back to bed.

Shkai'ra settled back onto the bunk, glancing out the window. "Glitch take it, false dawn. Not much use going back to sleep."

Sova stood, with tears in her eyes. "Please," she whispered.

Megan sighed and flopped down on the bed behind Shkai'ra. "I don't think you've really grasped the extent of the ignorance you're dealing with, akribhan," she said. Her face remained calm, but a hint of malicious amusement flickered in the depths of her eyes. "You were the one who wanted to bring them along. They're your apprentices, so . . ."

The Kommanza groaned and reached out to guide Sova to the bunk. "Wait a minute, sit on this." She handed the girl a washcloth, rose and soaked another. "Right, pull up your shift and wipe yourself off with this one." Sova took the cloth, cringing. Megan studied the boards of the ceiling as if she'd never seen them before.

Cursing under her breath, Shkai'ra rummaged through a chest of gear set into the wall. "Sheepshit, where . . .bowstrings, wax, whetstone, armor-lacquer, birthherb, fuck it, *sponges*—" She looked over her shoulder; Sova blushed furiously and covered herself with the cloth. "No, get it all or you'll smell."

Shkai'ra picked up a sponge, drew her knife from the weapons belt and began to trim it, explaining the use of the sponge with a few blunt words. "You're smaller and you'll have a light flow for the first year or so, so we'll cut this down . . ." She paused to consider her handiwork. "Good. Now, do you do it or do you want me to?"

Wide-eyed, Sova snatched at the sponge and waited. "Aren't you . . . aren't you going to turn around?" she stammered. Shkai'ra threw up her hands in bafflement. Megan looked intently at her nails.

"You can make do with one. You take it out when it's soaked, every three hours or so at first; clean it in cold water—*every* time, hear me? Leave it and you get sick, it rots. Two is better. That way you'll be able to clean the one and wear the other. It shouldn't last more than six or seven days, if it does tell me. You may get pains in your belly; the best cure's hard exercise, or so they always told me. And—" She turned; Sova was standing with the stained and wadded shift clutched before her. "No problems?"

A shake of the head.

"You're sure? Good." She sighed again. "Here's a clean shift. Here's the other sponge." Shkai'ra paused, tossing a leather pouch up and down in one palm. "Look, you're a virgin, *nia?*"

"*Yes!*" Sova whispered, struggling gratefully into the shift; it was an old shirt of Shkai'ra's, and hung past her knees.

"Oh, well, then you won't need this." She tossed the bag one more time. "Even on your safe days, there's a risk, so you make a tea of this and drink it afterwards to make sure it doesn't catch . . ." She looked into blank bewilderment, and her confidence faltered. "You don't know about safe days?" A shake of the girl's head. "Baiwun hammer me flat, you know about *fucking*, don't you? I mean, you've seen grown-ups doing it?"

"It's . . . it's a bad word," Sova said, stress taking years off her voice. "One of the gardeners used it, but Mama slapped me when I asked her what it meant."

Shkai'ra slumped back to the bunk and gently hammered the heels of her hands on her temples. "Kh'eeredo!" she said. "*Help!*"

Megan took pity on her. "Sova, people say 'fucking' when they mean having sex with someone, making love." She narrowed her eyes at Shkai'ra. "Of course you only have to worry about getting pregnant if you have sex with a man. Thanes think that even pleasing yourself with your hand is wrong."

Sova gasped and covered her mouth with her hand. "Oh, I'd *never* do *that!*" Megan shook her head thoughtfully.

"Why not? Anyway, the bleeding is a sign that your body is ready to carry a child. Your eggs are ripening."

"Like a *chicken*?" Sova sat down with a thump. Francosz stuck his head in the door.

"What's like a chicken?" he asked. Megan started laughing and threw herself back on the pillows.

"Shkai'ra, I'll take turns with you, but what *he* knows he probably learned whispered behind the barn and it's likely wrong. You'll have to tell him too!"

"Tell me what?" Francosz said.

"Out!" Shkai'ra said, pushing him with the flat of a hand. Over one shoulder. "All right, I'll see to it." Megan climbed out of the bunk and knelt by Sova, putting a hand on her shoulder. The girl jumped and froze.

Megan sighed. *Is she never going to cease being afraid of me?* "Welcome to womanhood, little sister." The Zak hugged her formally, touched the top of her head and her chin. "This is the point where you really start growing up."

Sova looked at her wide-eyed. "Does . . . does this happen to *you*, too?" Then flinched as if expecting to get hit. Megan settled back on her heels.

"It used to. I had a baby too big for me and now I don't bleed anymore, and I can't have children." She looked away. "That won't happen to you, Sovee."

Sova stared at her, wide-eyed. "Why did you call me that? How did you know?" She edged backward an inch. Megan blinked, then got up and sat down at the table.

"It's Thanish, isn't it? Means little one? Nothing magical about it." Sova stared, then nodded. *I understand, I think. But why are you being nice to me?*

The murmuring outside the door stopped and Shkai'ra walked back through the door, shaking her head.

"Knows what goes where and nothing else," she said dazedly. "This is *strange*."

F'TALEZON, THE DRAGON'SNEST
WOYVODAANA AVRITHA'S CHAMBERS
LATE EVENING, TENTH IRON CYCLE, TWENTY-
SECOND DAY

"You are so beautiful, Avritha." Habiku murmured in her

ear afterward. He ran his hands down her smooth skin, felt his own drained satisfaction, watching the light from the fire flicker on her pale breasts. Her skin was slick with sweat and the long black hairs of the sable furs they lay in clung to them. Her head was flung back, her hair as glossy a black as the furs, flowing over his arm.

They were lying in the bedbox, an eight-foot circle of Ibresian mahogany, carved in the shape of a dragon biting its own tail, filled with brushed-cotton feather quilts, linen sheets and furs. For a moment he luxuriated in the sheer wastage of making love in sable, staining the priceless, lustrous mats sewn from hundreds of the six-inch furs. They came from the cold forests northeast of F'talezon, vast beyond imagining, that stretched north to the Dead Land and the ruined cities. He imagined trappers leaving their lonely shacks, dark little woods-Zak in ragged quilted parkas, skiing their traplines in hunger and fear of white tiger and Ri and the winter wolf packs. Then trudging through blizzards with mittened hands jammed into their armpits, pulling their sledges of sable and ermine to the trading posts, canoemen fighting the white water with the bales . . .

And all so I can ruin their work in a moment's passion, he thought, shivering, and said again, "So beautiful."

"Hmmm. And you are so warm." She turned into his shoulder, twined her fingers in the mat of brown curls on his chest, nuzzling close, her long nails scratching his skin. "You are so good to me," she whispered and licked the corner of his jaw under the ear. "I need you." The room seemed to press around her. Cover the floor with rugs and furs, hang satin tented from the ceiling, light candles to give a glow, put braziers behind the jadite fretwork screens until they shone comforting red . . . and it was still a stone box chiseled into the side of the riven mountain. Old, so old its markings bore traces of the tunneling-machines of the ancients, who had cut stone with rays of light. And cold, cold . . .

He gathered her into his arms and whispered, "I love you." *My dear*, he thought. *You are very good in bed, but you are too tiring to love. You ask far too much for the snippets of power you give out. But you'll never find out that I'm lying to you.*

She raised her head off his shoulder and looked into his face. "Habiku, there's something wrong that you're not telling me. I'm no shrinking violet to be protected. Tell me, love."

He rolled over and pulled her on top of him, touching and kissing until she writhed against him, then she stopped his hand as it slid up her thigh. "Don't distract me, dear. You haven't answered."

He kissed her, then put one hand behind his head. *Do this right*, he told himself. *Cuddling an angry Avritha is like cuddling her namesake, a viper.* "I didn't want to tell you," he confessed sheepishly. "Well . . . you know the favor you did for me, beautiful lady?"

She propped her chin in her hands, braced on his chest and tilted her head. "Which one, my darling?"

"The protection you gave me for one of my important cargoes . . ." He trailed off.

I received my own report on that fiasco, she thought. *But I was ignoring it. What will your excuse be, hmmm? I'll have to make you work very hard for my forgiveness.* She ran a finger down his face and squirmed against him. He wasn't ready yet.

"The marines and so forth," she said, narrowing her eyes at him. *That little favor cost me*, she thought. *The steelspring was worth as much as these furs but it would be ungenteel to mention it, especially to a ClawPrince.*

"It was lost to river pirates, Rilla Shadows'Shade, I'm afraid to say."

"Lost? And the marines?"

"Set free to walk home." He looked down and sighed. "I suggested to their commander that they be punished for giving it up so easily, but that's for you to say, dearling."

"I'll look into it." *If that was what you call giving up easily, love* . . . "As far as the law goes, it *is* her company, and the deceased owner was very careful to keep most of my influences out of it. I *could* mention it to Ranion, but he's been otherwise occupied and might get annoyed." She watched his eyes flicker as she said that. *Fear Ranion, my dear, and love me, that will do you most good.* "I've only been able to help you find the loopholes. Why was it so important that you protect *that* cargo?"

"Ah. Well." He smoothed her hair back away from her face, cupping her cheek. "The former owner, Whitlock, isn't deceased."

Her eyes narrowed almost to slits as he ran his fingers gently down her neck. *Your act is slipping, Smoothtongue*, she thought. *There's a note of sincerity there that wasn't before*. She held her silence, almost forcing him to go on. "That cargo . . . well, it was necessary to ensure that the former owner remained the *former* owner."

"Ah. Rand? The Jade Button of the Third Rank? Rather soon for a second accident; still, they know how to handle things, in Rand . . . . and she's not a Prince and Heir, after all. Nobody would notice. Poor love, it must have been a *large* cargo, to persuade a Third Rank to interest himself in a merchant's affairs." A frown. "The RiverBlade people are going to be *very* annoyed at losing the steelspring." F'talezon had a monopoly on those; only Zak mindsmiths could forge the sealed perfection of those coils.

Habiku nuzzled his head into the curve of her shoulder to hide the shock in his eyes. Her sweat smelled different from other women's, of the rare spices served at the DragonLord's table, and the Haian coconut oil she used to keep wrinkles out of her skin. *Bitch, bitch!* he thought. She was a Zak noble, not a sheltered Enchian raised in women's quarters. Uen's scheme had recreated itself in her mind on a casual suggestion. *Don't anger her*.

He turned his face back toward her. She smiled down at him, then her face went blank. With a tickle along his spine he recognized her gift. "Habiku Smoothtongue, become cage dweller. The door is sealed. The iron locked around your height." He shivered and swallowed, breaking out in new sweat but with fear rather than passion, wanting to look away from the eerie sight of her speaking without knowing what she said, hearing doom fall in that flat, even tone from her beautiful lips. Avritha's power was prophecy. More often then not she was right. She blinked and was back again. "Of course, the favors . . . Habiku, dear. You have that look on your face. Did I prophesy? What did I say?"

He pulled a smile out of somewhere and put it on. "Oh, something about me being iron." *Metaphorical, of course. She doesn't need to see much to tell me that I'm in a cage of sorts. Once she is dead, I'll be free of my troubles. It's all trickery anyway, witch tricks that a five-year-old could see through.* "Iron enough, my love."

She wiggled against him again and her smile grew. "Iron indeed." She stretched luxuriously, putting her hand on him. "Give me your warmth, dear."

"There is nothing I would enjoy more, my darling." He cradled her in one arm and began stroking her from neck to thighs, brushing careful fingertips over her nipples. *Purr, you bitch. Then I'll ask.*

"Mmm. That . . . that is so good." He blew a soft breath into the hollow of her neck and his tongue chased his fingertips down her body.

"Love?" His voice was muffled against her belly. "Could I ask you a favor?"

"Hmmm?" She grabbed him by the hair and pushed him lower.

"Could you use your influence with the Rand? You have power." He slid down and caught her wrists in his hands, kissing each palm, then licked along her sweetly curling pubic hair. *You please me well, so far, ClawPrince,* she thought. *Try harder.*

"Hmmm. Kiss me there, love. Hard. Mmm. I'm afraid I can't do that, dear. No, don't stop. My husband might notice if I deal with the Rand directly. Yes. That's right. Please me well, darling."

He ran his tongue along her folds, feeling the world drop away from him, fear clenching his stomach. *She's never said no, before. Dark Lord. Dark Lord. I have to convince her. She's never refused me before. Perhaps she's just teasing me. Bitch,* he thought as he kissed her lovingly. *Bitch.*

ON THE RIVER BETWEEN NYSNY TVER AND RAND
FALSE DAWN, TENTH IRON CYCLE, TWENTY-SECOND DAY

"This is *strange*," Shkai'ra said, letting herself fall back and rolling her head onto Megan's shoulder. "Kh'eeredo, you've got to help me with this impulsiveness of mine."

"Impulsiveness? What, you mean taking the two children away from their parents after we ruined them? Taking responsibility for two children for at least six or seven years? Impulsive?" She opened her mouth to continue and Shkai'ra sealed her mouth by kissing her. Megan smiled around the kiss. "Yes, I'll agree that it was dumb. But I love you anyway."

"I love you too. What little there is of you . . . Didn't anyone every tell you it's impolite to laugh while someone's kissing you? Just for that, I'm going to kiss your ear instead." She glanced out the window. "Hour and a half 'till we have to be up." A grin. "If I'm going to explain things to Sova, maybe we should practice."

"Don't forget Francosz. Prac-mmm—Practice sounds good to me." She pretended to scratch Shkai'ra with her claws. "You great lump, I'll have to cut you down to size. You've never asked me to help you with the children. Do you want me to?" She sighed and snuggled under Shkai'ra's arm. Then she reached up and dug her toes into one of the Kommanza's ticklish spots.

"Stop that!" Shkai'ra giggled hysterically and arched her back. "Oh, all right, you can help. *Please!*" Shkai'ra locked her legs around Megan's thighs and rolled on her back.

Chapter 11

ON THE RIVER BETWEEN NYSNY TVER AND RAND
EVENING, TENTH IRON CYCLE, TWENTY-SECOND DAY

"EEEEEEiiii—" Shkai'ra shrieked, the wooden practice blade scything around to impact on Sova's buckler with a gunshot *crack* of wood on wood. The Thane girl pitched backward, saving herself from a fall with a half-controlled dozen-step stagger that brought her back painfully against the rack of belaying pins about the *Zingas Vetri's* mainmast. She squatted, rolled, and dodged behind the mast in a defensive crouch as Shkai'ra followed up her charge.

"All the gods damn you, girl, stop *flinching*," Shkai'ra shouted.

Sova circled warily, keeping the thick pole between herself and her instructor, wooden blade held tight in her sweating grip. Sweat . . . she could feel it pouring down her flanks under the padded doublet, down her neck from the aching heavy helmet, stinging and blurring in her eyes despite the cork and sponge lining. She wobbled, mouth open, fighting air that was shocking-cold on her face but seemed to be warm, wet flannel in her lungs.

The long sword stretched toward her around the mast, seem-ing to blur toward her midriff; with an enormous effort she dragged the buckler around to meet it, and the oak tip punched the circlet of leatherbound wood back into her stomach, wrenching at her shoulder.

174

"I . . . am . . . not . . . *flinching*," she panted, as her stop thrust faded six inches short of Shkai'ra's knee; the Kommanza didn't bother to block. "I . . . feel so . . . bloated and—" she dragged the air in with the muscles of her stomach, relaxed one knee and let weight pull her out of the way of a backhand cut, as she had been taught "—*slow*."

"Are you going to tell a foeman you can't fight today, because it's your bleeding-time?" Shkai'ra said. "Force it, girl, force it, or you'll end up dead or chained to a millstone!" The Kommanza bounced forward suddenly, leaping away from the mast, and front-somersaulted in mid air; Sova found herself backpedaling again, using buckler and sword to block cuts and thrusts that swung in from every possible angle. Hard enough to jar her right back to the shoulder, fast enough that only an all-out effort with no reserve could stop each attack, and was humiliatingly conscious that Shkai'ra was moving at a fraction of her maximum. At last one thrust jabbed into her shoulder, with a force that spun her about and left her gasping with the pain of the bruise.

Astonishingly, Shkai'ra was grinning at her. "Not bad," she said, leaning on the wooden blade. Sova fell to her knees, wheezing; Shkai'ra moved to her side, unlatched the helmet and poured a dipper of riverwater over the girl's head, then another over her own. The Thane could feel heat radiating from her face and neck and arms; nothing in her life had felt better than the cool evening breeze sliding over the sweat, tasted better than the first mouthful from the dipper Shkai'ra offered.

"Not bad at all, considering how late you started." Hard callused hands felt at her shoulders and arms and back. "Tightening up nicely; now we need to get you stretched." Sova looked up and managed a smile around her gasps, distantly conscious that the woman was scarcely breathing hard at all.

"Mind you, any Kommanz ten-year-old could slice you into skunkbait, but it's a definite improvement." She turned her head; Sova looked over to see her brother still stretched out prone, recovering from *his* bout.

"Megan!" Shkai'ra called. "Hai, weren't you going to work

with Sova on the short blades?" She walked over to Francosz and nudged him in the ribs. "Enough rest, O Prince of Enchanted Sleep." He groaned theatrically, and received a harder nudge in reply. "Up! You should be able to run an elder like me into the deck. Up!"

Megan, also stripped down, looked up at Sova's startled face from the angle of her stretch, right leg stretched straight, left leg bent as if she were hurdling, right ear on her knee. "I told Shkai'ra I'd help out. She's the sort who likes going in at full screech, long sword spinning. Strip down to your shirt."

Silently Sova did, her fingers suddenly clumsy on the doublet. The wind was icy on her chest and back. She heard Shkai'ra yell "Fifty!" to Francosz, heard him start counting push-ups at the top of what breath he had left and wished she were with the teacher she knew. The Zak had never offered to help before.

"Don't get chilled, keep moving. You need to be limber for knife-work. Follow what stretches I do. Begin." The Zak seemed to flow from hurdle stretch to V stretch, and put her chin on the ground. Sova tried and stopped a foot high off the deck. "Don't overdo. Right. There's a difference between stretch and tear. Shift. The first rule of knife-fighting," Megan said. "The winner goes to the healer, the loser's dead." Sova found herself sweating all over again. Her *Khyd-hird* had shown her these stretches, but the Zak could do them unbelievably well.

"Ky—" she stopped. *What do I call her?* "Captain? I can't do this, my muscles won't stretch that far."

"Never say *I can't*. I started worse than you. Up! Follow me." Megan led her at a run around the deck, dodge coils of rope, leaping over barrels. Then she headed into the rigging. Sova groaned, set her teeth and followed. Up the lines then down, hand over hand, upside down, sideways. She was panting again, mouth open and dry, her arms and legs ready to fall off. Then down to the deck.

"Kneel. Catch your breath by the tail. Don't grimace at me, that lets everyone, including you, know that it hurts. Pretend it doesn't; after a while, it won't. You know that much."

The railing in front of Sova was greying, swaying as she wavered. She heard Shkai'ra's voice, the crack of wood on Francosz's buckler, smelled roast beef that Piatr was cooking. Her stomach grumbled but she felt so full. Then things settled again.

"So. Here we have practice knives, three or four weights and balances. Try them." The knives that Megan laid out on the deck were different shapes, made of dark polished wood like the sword Shkai'ra had made for her. They felt like satin.

"These are yours until you can make your own. I want you to try this every day, whenever you have a minute." Megan picked up a wooden blade, seemed to drop it. It spun round and the hilt smacked into her hand. "It's the first recovery. I'll show you slowly." Her hand flicked, the knife hilt rolled over her knuckles and continued the circle to smack into her palm again. Sova tried it; the knife clattered on the deck. "Just keep trying until you won't cut your fingers off with true steel.

"If you're interested, I have a book describing the way knife-fighting developed."

"Ca . . . Captain." Sova felt the blush rising up her neck and clutched the hilt of the wooden dagger hard enough to bring the knuckles white. "I—can't read. I'm just a girl."

Megan snorted. "Fine fix I'd be in if I couldn't read. That's another lesson I'll be teaching, I guess. Your brother, does he?"

"Yes."

"We'll worry about that tomorrow. Too much talking. Knives away. This is the basic stance. Feet shoulder-width apart, weight on the balls of the feet. Knees bent. One hand for blocking. If you're lucky you'll have a cloak or a gauntlet."

They circled. "No, no, we're moving to keep our knife-hands forward. Stop." Sova froze in place and Megan continued the motion. "See how I can come around you and cut your arm? Now—"

The supercargo cleared her throat. "Captain." Megan blinked out of her concentration, backed three steps and crouched to lay the imaginary knife on the deck.

"Yes, Zemelya?"

"Captain, we *have* to go over those books from the Brahvniki office if we're going to find out where the cash was coming from. Lady knows, it wasn't legitimate operations and I don't think the slaving or dreamdust would bring in that much either . . . and it's too irregular . . . I can trace the numbers, but . . ."

Megan sighed and turned to Sova. "Looking at figures in ledgers is a *big* part of being a captain. Here." She tossed one of the wooden knives, picked a stick of charcoal from a sack by the water-butt and walked to the rise of the poopdeck. There she sketched the outline of a human figure, reaching up to draw the head at arm's length above her own; the burnt wood went *skrit* on the smooth oak planks.

"Throat, stomach, groin, inner thigh, hamstrings. Get into stance, *so*. Lunge, *so*. No, don't hop: *skim* your foot forward and keep the back foot with toes angled out and weight a little to the front. Switch your center of gravity, but not so far forward you're pinned; move back with your knee . . . good. Ten times each target, then switch. Don't fall into a pattern, and just *touch* the point to the mark."

Sova weighed the smooth curve of dark wood in her hand, scowling fiercely at the black outline and trying to put a human likeness on it; the only one that came to mind was the chimneysweep who had come last year. Legend said sweeps would steal bad children away; he had frightened her into crying when he mock-threatened it, she had known she deserved it and her parents would not care . . . She lunged, and the point went *tock* against the stomach-cross.

"No, too hard for a beginning. Control it."

"Why no mark for the heart, Captain?" she asked, without looking aside, as she had been taught. *Treat a target as real and a practice weapon as steel*, that was what the *Khyd-hird* had said.

"Too many ribs in the way. Practice on that until I come back."

Sova lay and stared up at the *kraumak* in its globe, the bubble of Francosz's almost snoring next to her ear, and couldn't sleep. Every knot in the planks under her pallet seemed to be bigger than her fist. She blinked and swallowed against the big lump in her throat, her chest felt tight and thick and the air all around seemed to press on her. *I want to cry.* She could feel the tears aching to be shed, and sniffed. The feather tick was too warm and heavy. Her stomach cramped, then eased again.

She sniffed but the tears wouldn't stop. She shifted out from under the blankets not to let in a blast of cold air to wake Franc. *I don't want to cry in front of him.* She padded up to the deck, nodded at Stanver who was on watch.

The moon was down, but the bright spot of Shamballah was up over the port bow, shining in the ripples of the ship's passage. She leaned over the stern rail, looked down at the velvet black and flickers of the water coiling out from under the ship. Behind her at the wheel, Stanver called, "Sounding?" Another soft voice from the bow answered, "Three fathoms, showing brown!"

The steady wind blew Sova's hair off her forehead in spidery wisps and the reflection of stars seemed to blur and shiver as her eyes filled with tears. *I want to go home.* She put her head down on her crossed forearms. *I want to go home.* Then she pulled her head up and wiped at her face. *There isn't a home to go to, anymore,* she thought. That brought a sob up from her chest to clog on the tightness in her throat.

She slipped over to the port ropewell, slid down to sit on the coil of the anchor rope, buried her face in her hands and sobbed until her eyes felt burned and ashy and her chest was empty and hollow.

"Do you want some company?" The Captain's voice over her head made her jump as if speared. Megan slid down to sit next to her, a shadow in the dark, wrapped in her dark cloak.

Go away, Sova thought. *You're a Zak. A witch. What do you care?* She put her head down on her knees and closed her eyes, trying to stop the last tears squeezing out of the corners.

"I used to sit in the ropewells and cry," Megan said quietly. "It used to be the only place I could hide on board a crowded ship."

Sova looked up, surprised. "You cried?" *The Captain?
Crying?* Nobody could ever make the Captain cry. That was
impossible. Like the *Khyd-hird* being a baby or the sky falling.

"Oh, a few times. I had someone who cared enough to
listen to me to cry on, and she didn't mind getting her
shoulder wet. When I was your age, the whole world fell
apart and it was like your Thanish Halya." She held open one
fold of her cloak. "Are you cold? You're only wearing shirt
and trous. It's clear enough to be going on for a real cold."

Sova hesitated, looked down at her fingers twisted together
in her lap. *She's not so bad, even if she is a witch.* She edged
over the coil of rope and squeezed in beside Megan, who
wrapped the cormorenc feather cloak around her. "It's a good
thing you're no bigger than I am," the Zak said. "We'd never
fit."

They sat in silence for long enough for Yannet to make a
full round of the deck above them. "Sounding!" "Four fathoms, rocky!"

"Anything wrong that I can help?" Megan asked. "If I
know Thanes, your brother isn't listening to you much."

Sova blew on her cold fingers and shivered. "N—o," she
stammered. Then the tears came back. "I want to go home!"
she wailed softly. "I just want to go back to being *me!*" She
gulped, sobbed tearlessly and suddenly realized that she was
controlling herself the way the *Khyd-hird* had taught her:
with breathing. But that was almost worse. "I don't know
what I am anymore. I'm tired and my bruises hurt and . . .
and I can't do it well enough. I never will!"

She choked off, stuffing a fist in her mouth. Megan brushed
the hair off her forehead. "Home. Well. We can't do much
about that. Sova, I realize that apologies don't really help,
but for my part in your father's trouble—" She caught herself, took a deep breath "—your father's ruin, I'm sorry. And
you are yourself. Sova Schotter's Daughter. Someone . . ."
The Zak put a knuckle under Sova's chin and gently pushed it
up so that they were looking at each other. "Someone who I
heard Shkai'ra say 'good' to, not a few hours ago? A 'not bad'
and a smile from her is an equivalent to a triumph in
Brahvniki." They looked at each other, Sova seeing the spar-

kle of reflected starlight in the Zak's eyes. "Hmmm, little sister?"

Sova nodded and buried her head in Megan's shoulder. "So," the Zak woman said quietly. "If you really need a shoulder and we're both up at an unGoddess-blest hour, ask me." She smiled. "If you don't mind being friendly with a Zak."

Under cover of the cloak, Sova sniffled and wiped her nose on the back of her hand. "Doh, um, no," she said as her nose cleared. "I, um, I don't mind."

They sat together a while longer, the wind blowing steadily over Megan's shoulder, coiling around the ropewell, tugging at them. "Here," Megan said. A coin appeared between her first two fingers. It was a Thanish silver. It disappeared and reappeared. "My father showed me how to do this." One hand passed over the other and the coin vanished again. "Anyone can do *this*. Why don't you try it?"

For me? Sova thought. *She just wants me to try it. Don't drop it in the river.* She took the coin and slowly, fumbling a little, she made the coin "disappear." "I did it!"

"You certainly did." Megan watched as Sova tried the trick five or six times, getting smoother every time. "You might as well keep the coin to practice with. It's yours."

Sova hugged her and turned the coin over and over again, made it disappear again. "Really? Truly?"

"Really, truly."

"Sounding!" "Three fathoms, showing mud and sand!"

The sounding cry happened three more times as they sat there and Sova's head gradually became heavier and heavier on Megan's shoulder. Finally the Zak stirred and said, "Bedtime, Sovee, come on."

Shivering, sleepy-eyed, Sova stumbled after her, up out of the ropewell, down the poop ladder and belowdecks, shuffled over and crawled onto her pallet, pulling the feather tick over herself. Megan tucked the edges in around her, noticing that the closed fist she stuck under her cheek was tight around the old coin. As she straightened, she looked over into Francosz's gaze.

He looked at her over his sister, expressionless. Megan

raised an eyebrow and stepped away. Back up on deck she retreated to the rail above the ropewell once more, her claws digging into the wood. Once, she looked down at the name "Habiku" graven in the oak and scratched it out viciously.

The sterncabin was as bright as the corridor, with starlight reflected off the wake and through the windows; they were closed all but a crack, and the little room smelled companionably of wool blanket, lamp wick, oiled leather and Shkai'ra. The Kommanza lay on her back, as usual; taking up most of the bed, also as usual. One arm was curled up behind her head and her cheek lay on her bicep; Megan looked at the sleeping face, relaxed and washed young by the pale light, the smooth, heavy arm and crinkled hair bright against the pillow. Shkai'ra rarely had trouble sleeping. She could brood, none better, day after day of black silence and slitted expressionless eyes; the Zak remembered her saying once that her people's neighbors sometime called them the "ice-lookers."

But she rarely lay awake with it. Come full dark, when the work of the day was over, for her it was time to eat, make love and roll into the blankets and unconsciousness. *I envy her that*, Megan thought as she undressed silently. *I wish I could banish my ghosts so. If only for the hours of the night. She leaves me behind in my darkness, uncaring.*

Perhaps it was her childhood; down in the River Quarter, there was always darkness amid the narrow rubbled streets under the cliffs, but never really night, never a time when everybody slept. Never a time when you could completely *rest*, either. She remembered lying awake listening to Mother and Father talking. It had been a warm sound, usually. Most so when she was very small, in the old family house in the Middle Quarter, where their voices came from the wallbed. Later, when they had to move downcity, there was strain in it as well as love; once she had heard her father crying, because they had to chose between having her boots patched and meat for the soup.

Megan shook herself back to the present with an unvoiced sigh, stretched. *You'd be awake enough if I tickled you there*, she thought, looking at the tuft of armpit hair that Shkai'ra's position exposed, an absurd little vulnerability.

"Doan' even think about it," the other woman mumbled, opening one eye a crack and holding up the blankets. Then, "*T'Zoweitzum*, you're cold."

They curled together. Megan laid her head on Shkai'ra's arm, her cheek against the other's throat; pulled her close with an arm and a leg looped over her waist. The Kommanza mumbled again and shrimp-curled, tucking her chin over Megan's head and bringing one long thigh up behind her.

"I only ever tickled you like that once," Megan whispered. Shkai'ra used her free arm to rearrange the blankets; through closed eyes the Zak could feel the greater darkness as they shadowed her face. *This feels good*, she thought; let the sigh be audible, this time, and relaxed, listening to the strong slow pulse under her ear. Strange to be so comfortable so close to a naZak, but the years had made it so; you learned each other's bends and crannies, until somehow you *fit* with a person.

"And I like to brained myself on the beam over the shutbed when you did," Shkai'ra replied. "Ah, well, you were drunk," she continued charitably. Megan lay against Shkai'ra's warmth and felt colder than the steppe.

An anxious *chruuut?* came from under the bed; Ten-Knife scrambled up to the covers, walked over their hips and ribs and thumped down to the pillow, curling up behind the Zak's neck and butting a cold, wet nose against her shoulder.

Shkai'ra sighed and gathered her close, drowsily, sliding down back into sleep. Ten-Knife purred at Megan's shoulder but it didn't help as the Zak lay in the dark, listening to her lover's distant breathing. *Even in your arms I'm alone, Shkai'ra. Why can't I make you see?*

Exhaustion dragged her into sleep as false dawn tinged the sky.

Chapter 12

The *Zingas Vetri* oar-walked into Rand on a bright cold morning that crackled with hoarfrost. The bare feet of the deck crew left prints dark and wet on the frosted planks; rigging chimed with blue ice shards, as delicate as the fragments left by hatchling hummingbirds. Chips spun free and ran downwind, sparkling. Breath smoked; Shkai'ra felt the chill wind pouring over the high rim tighten the skin of her cheekbones with a kiss that tasted of home.

Steppe country to the east, she thought. Megan stood by the wheel, wrapped in the cloak of dark feathers and silence. *She won't tell me what's wrong anymore*, Shkai'ra thought. *I don't understand you any more, kh'eeredo-mi. Revenge isn't that important.*

The river narrowed, swinging east of north. The *Zingas Vetri* dipped her sharp prow; the mallet-beat quickened as the long, narrow hull rolled, shipping water the color of jade across the foc'sle deck, to fall back in white froth through the scuppers. It smelled of cold purity, rock and distant glaciers.

"Quarter-point to port," Megan said quietly. "You know the drag under the Watchers." Then: "Mateus, peace pennant to the peak, we're coming up in the Shadows."

The first mate's whistle fluted, and a narrow green banner ran up and snapped free in the east wind. Ahead, the Brezhan surged between cliffs that rose sheer barely a *chiliois* apart; the current ran deep but very swift, rising in long, smooth wells like the muscles in an athlete's legs. The steersman grunted, leaning into the spokes as eddies jerked at the rudder, and the rowers braced their feet and shortened their stroke, chopping the slender ash blades into the water as the river gripped keel and planks like a hand.

Megan ignored the Watchers; four black pillars, two hundred meters high and thirty through, smoothed by water and patient labor. Her eyes narrowed on the face of the river where it rushed past their feet. The Watchers stood where the river had crashed through the crater's lip; folded against their sides like wings were the cranes that could swing thick chains across the current.

For a long moment the *Zingas Vetri* hung between two of the monoliths, shuddering as the rhythmic thrust of the oars hung in balance with the power of the water. Then the motion smoothed, and the galley surged into the calmer waters beyond as if slipping downslope on a gentle hill.

The basin was an oval ten kilometers across, as if the earth had opened an eye to gaze at heaven. The walls stood sheer, rippled in a regular pattern of grooves and swellings. Volcanic rock, pearl-grey granite, green marble and onyx-colored basalt. Nearby, where the wall fanned out on either hand, the colors glowed softly in light reflected from the water and beneath it as the long rays of the morning sun glanced back from the surface. Westward they blazed, as bright as the disk of sun rising over the cliffs.

Ahead stood the islands of the same stone, in a cluster from the center of the caldera. Rand, they were named in the old tongue: the steepness where the world ends. Some were tiny, thread-thin at a distance that made children's toys of ships; others bulked almost squat, their sloping surfaces larger than farmers' fields. From this distance the eye could link them into the shape of a great flat-topped cone.

The bridges heightened the likeness, slender arches soaring from shaft to shaft; on the upper slopes were gardens, terraces and mansions carved from the rock. Below, the vertical stone was worked in balconies and doors, where sleepers could wake to see mast tips swaying by; spouts channeled off springs to fall for long seconds in silver threads before they misted into clouds and merged with the canals below.

Shkai'ra glanced over the rail. The water was very clear; she could see long slopes of smooth rock below, a bowl of muted color sloping down into darkness. The shadow of the *Zingas Vetri* sculled across those curtains of stone, tiny, as if they floated in unclouded air ten times mast height above the ground. For a moment she felt giddy, feeling the ship about to fall. A school of Brezhan gar slid beneath the keel, seven-meter river wolves as narrow as eels, with the undershot, toothy jaws of pike. She blinked, looked up again at the city of islands.

"Looks like a firemountain, what's the Zakos word?"

Megan started. "It is," she said. "A *flahmbrug*, a volcano."

She looked at the group of islands as if they were new-sprung from the river.

"When the Phoenix rose to burn the world, the land blew up in the river's path. That made the cup." She waved a hand at the walls of cliff around them. "Then from the bottom a new *flahmbrug* broke through. Since the river had a hold on the stone when it formed, it wore through when the Worldfire died." She was silent a long moment, and the only sound was the oarmaster's beat. "The Rand have been here, they swear, ever since. Even before Iyesi fell. I don't know if I believe them, but they treat all foreigners the same; like dirt."

RAND, BOTTOM LEVEL, HSIANG ISLE
LATE AFTERNOON
TWENTY-FOURTH DAY

pain. pain in my chest, lungs are like stone. stone all around, always stone.

He crouched below the lip of the tunnel, in darkness. It was always dark here, air was too precious to waste on flame. The child cutters who followed the twisting vein of *cardamorine* could read the rock with their fingertips.

better no light, need no light, feet know the stairs like hands knew my wife's face—

A grunt, loud in the small space, echoing over the *drip-drip-drip* of water. It had softened the scabs on his back; the rag pad on his shoulders was moving, and he reached a hand up to adjust it. A whistle, and a slab pushed out.

bend shoulders. pain! rough hard on shoulders flesh too thin, ulcers weep . . . turn, not to see, not to feel. one step up, brace, push. seven thousand steps to the light. second step. breathe: lungs thick with rockdust. push. better to hurt than to think. push!

A thick, gobbling noise filled the tunnel, and the tongueless man climbed the stairway without end.

RAND, TOP LEVEL, HSIANG ISLE
LATE AFTERNOON
TWENTY-FOURTH DAY

Piatr looked around the crowd at the entrance to the lower levels. Nobody touched them; Rand courtesy, perhaps, or the fighting-knife Shkai'ra was stropping on a leather strap wound about the knuckles of her left hand. But the bubble of space about them was uncomfortably small. This folk lived with crowding even more than most city dwellers, and the distance-of-courtesy was less than among his people, much less; something at the bottom of his mind was perpetually uneasy.

The crowds were worse here, of course. Height and class were one in Rand; the city was one huge, multilayered structure, tunneled down into rock, carved and sculpted and vaulted above. On the surface the buildings rose in tiers with graceful sweeping roofs and gables wrought in scarlet dragon shapes, inlay and carving that cunningly followed the patterns of the rock lent color; so did rooftop gardens, potted waterfalls of flowers, hangings. The nobles and court and merchant princes of Rand lived there, in the sunlight, while the mass of the city dwelt below, honeycombed into the rock. Here it teemed with them: his memory prompted with remembrances of anthills he had broken open as a boy.

The Zak leaned back against the wall, hooking his thumbs in his belt and leaning on his stump for the pleasure of feeling healed flesh and smooth-fitting socket.

They make my skin crawl, he thought, scowling at the throng. Dark eyes that stared at you and through you, from under the heavy straight-cut black hair. Saffron skin and slanted eyes like cats. Hostility from those in the plain blue of the commons, laborers, dock-wallopers, porters. A thin disguise drawn by greed on the shopkeepers and craftsfolk; overwhelming haughtiness that ignored their existence from magistrates in brilliant silk and scholars in their robes. Pedigreed flittercats blinked, as disdainfully as their owners, from the sweeps of roof. Impassive appraisal behind the faceless beast-masked helms of warriors in leather and enameled steel, plumes nodding as their heads turned. Gloved hands tightening on the hilts of curved swords, grips of long bows of bone and bamboo, spears whose heads were fantasies of hooks and spikes. Lord and worker, student and merchant, thief and warrior, all were Rand. You were not.

A street festival passed, clashing drums and leaping, many-legged dragons of paper and gilt; meter-long streamers of colored silk on the ends of poles wove and spun in intricate patterns; gongs blared . . . Children followed, running and shouting; vendors with carts that were piles of wicker baskets over vats of bubbling water, each tray holding a different delicacy in buns of steamed dough, or deft hands rolled lumps of rice between palms with green paste and raw fish.

Shkai'ra grunted beside him. "I want to find that jeweller, and the girl-brat needs a blade. Damned if I'm going to stand around like a yokel seeing my first city, jaw drooping and grass seeds in my hair."

"Perhaps we should wait for the crowd to clear?" Piatr shouted to be heard.

"Plague or sack 're the only things that would work, and I'm not waiting for either," she said, snapping the knife back into her boot and tucking the hone into her belt.

The entry ramp was even more crowded that the street outside, if possible; the ceiling was arched, and the peak cleared Shkai'ra's head by a bare handspan. She kept to the center of the street, left hand holding the scabbard of her saber just below the chape that hung it from her belt. That left it horizontal, in perfect position to jab with the brass pommel or the ivory-shod wood of the sheath's tip; the Kommanza walked with an arrogant swaying stride that sent hints of trampled heels and jarred elbows ahead and to the sides, winning them added inches.

"Like a black fur rug with occasional hats," she called back over her shoulder to Piatr.

He caught himself grinning. In this city he'd kept mostly to the Zak enclave; it was more comfortable. He was only a bit taller than most Rand and had never thought what it would be like to look down on the crowd. Their eyes slid off his, worse than most naZak. He felt as if they barely realized he existed. He smothered the grin and the wish that he had enough power to make them notice him. The Captain had enough but it was never smart to show off to naZak. They tended to notice you by seeing how long you took to burn.

The tunnelled roadway curled downward, broad enough for two; the air was damp but fresh, smelling of fried fish and vegetables and spice. The light was diffuse, a soft glow with no obvious source, unless it were the occasional square well in the ceiling overhead. "Have any idea why it's not smoky with torches?" Shkai'ra asked over her shoulder.

" 'Course, little sister," he said, looking up at her. She grunted. "They do it with mirrors. Arkan-glass mirrors."

She raised a skeptical eyebrow at him, and slowed so he could keep up. "Truthfully, yes," he continued. "They sink light shafts from the surface and use Beornholm or Arkan glass for reflecting. See?" They were under one of the square openings in the ceiling. He gestured with his thumb. She looked up and away, squinting from the point of brightness.

"Smart enough," she said and continued down, hand resting on her saber. "Hate to have to fight my way into this place: not a good town to besiege, either." The moisture in the air was thicker as they got closer to the river surface tunnels. "Wouldn't mind looting the place, though."

"Loot and kill," he grunted. "Is that all you ever think

about?" For an instant there was a memory of fighting underground in her eyes; packed dark with dying, bleeding bodies.
Then it was gone and she grinned at him amiably.

"No. I think of sex, too." She paused at a cross-tunnel and
as she turned, her eye was caught by a carving in marble in
one of the booths opening on the tunnel. She paused to pick
it up and examine it.

"I thought you were in a hurry."

"But not that much. Megan knows how to deal with customs clerks and officials better than I do. I'd want to carve
the sheep-faced little bastards into fish chowder."

"*Dah*, so would she if she could."

Shkai'ra nodded and turned to the sculptor.

*step. straighten the leg. its not so hard. only four thousand
more. harsh-grinding on my back—don't stop if i stop i wont
start again. yes i will.* The stone carrier staggered sideways a
step, head down, panting. *no extra steps. waste of steps.
hoard strength like sand in two cupped hands. knees hurt.
the block—dont drop it, crack it—flogging.* He vaguely tried
to think of something else, a child's face; couldn't remember
it. A child's laugh. *no laughter from the cutters only lonely
tears. turn ahead. space to rest.* He could feel the warm sting
as the corner of the block wore through his skin where the
pad did not reach, and wondered if he was bleeding again, or
just sweating.

Shkai'ra watched the sculptor work a moment then asked,
"This local stone?"

The man looked up and clasped his hands, bowing, his
accent sing-song. "Ah yes. Very deep. Down . . ." He pointed.
"They dig, yes. More come now."

He had pointed to the approaching figure. The porter was
not a Rand; as tall as Shkai'ra and big-boned, light-skinned
with the pallor of someone long underground. He had been a
strong man once; now he staggered under the block of stone
and the thin rag pad that covered his shoulders was sodden
with red where the block had chaffed.

Another porter, Piatr thought. *Poor bastard. Wonder how*

he had the shitty luck to be sold here. He turned back to the stall, nagged by another feeling that made him itchy, but he couldn't quite get at what was making him nervous. "Are you going to buy . . ." His voice choked off and he wheeled back to the slave. He found himself looking into the ruins of someone he knew. The porter's brown hair, locks pulled loose of the sweaty headband, fell over his face as he looked down, away from Piatr.

"*Tze?*" Piatr took one limping step to where the other man had lowered the stone and knelt beside it, chest heaving. The man did not look up. "Tze? I know you. Tze?"

The porter made a thick, garbled sound and shook his head, looking away. "Tze Riverson!" The slave reached over his shoulder, fingers dabbing in the blood on his back and faltering, as if remembering something from a dream, scrawled, "was tze" on the stone. He staggered to his feet and, groaning, lifted the block again.

"No! Put that down, Farshot, help me, the Captain would want him. Carver, who owns this man? Tze, stop." Piatr held the porter there by one strap on the stone. The crowd around them was edging past the scene, or pausing to watch covertly. "Put it *down*," he said again.

"Megan knows this man?" Shkai'ra said, blinking in puzzlement.

"Of course, the *Captain* knows him—he was her first mate on the *River Lady*, the dog-sucking DragonLord's people took him, we thought, just before Habiku—" he stopped. "Habiku came on board," Piatr said wonderingly.

There was a splintering sound as the block of stone hit the pavement. Tze braced one hand against a larger fragment of stone; fresh sweat cut runnels through the caked stonedust on his face as he strove to speak, coughed pink froth, seized Piatr by the arms and tried to shake him. The tall man quivered with frustration and an anger that Shkai'ra could feel even from behind him.

Piatr seized the hands on his shoulders and gripped them between his. "Easy, Tze, easy. The Captain's going for Habiku. Easy."

Shkai'ra watched with narrowed, considering eyes and a

corner of her mouth twisted with an increasing disgust. *Habiku*, she thought. *The man is a jackal*. No, a hyena. He tried to kill Megan. *Everyone has enemies, I'd kill him for that*. But this. What did this man Tze ever do to him? *Habiku, I'm beginning to . . . dislike you*. Silently, she watched the two men.

Piatr was lowering Tze to the floor, an arm under the bigger man's to avoid touching the raw sores of his back. The slave's face had the lifeless stillness of dough left too long, that collapses after rising. A flicker of life ran over it at Habiku's name, even as the hands made faint grasping motions at a block of stone no longer there.

She turned to the sculptor. "What," she said quietly, "is the price of a stonechopper in this warren?" Her voice was calm, a husky alto burr under the liquid sibilants of the Zak tongue. He looked away, thinking. The outland porter was worn out, it would not be worth haggling overmuch.

Megan controlled her temper with an effort, clasping her hands and bowing to the official. *Bow and bend your neck*, she thought.

Always smiling that poisonous, superior smile as you regrettably inform the stupid foreigner that of course the fees and bribes are high, but unfortunately the High Lord . . . Sorry, so sorry, not possible, perhaps tomorrow . . . Her own smile grew tight and sore; her fingernails gouged splinters from the table, unnoticed.

"By courtesy, a cup of tea, Honorable?" He would refuse, they always did, but you had to offer it or lose *zight*, since it was a notion they claimed to have invented. *Would you'd take it, would Marta had brewed it, then I could get some use out of having a poisoner for a father's sister*.

The thought was a cold shock, not removing anger but focusing it. This scroll-shoveller was no worse than any other jack-in-office, no worse than a thousand she'd dealt with in half a thousand ports. Fat faces and thin, blond or black or saffron-skinned. Petty cunning and stupidity, and always the outstretched palm; it was like rats in the bilge, you cleaned them out when you could, endured them when you must.

But I want him off my ship, she thought, with a venom that was no less real for her knowledge that it was born of frustration.

After all the bowing and smiling and smiling and bowing required to get the official down the rope ladder and into his gondola-palanquin, she allowed her face to relax in a scowl, and went down to the cabin to write the letter to the Shrine of Joy, the healer shrine of the Grey Brothers, a sect answering to Saekrberk, where they'd have to leave Katrana.

She sits and smiles all the time. She can do simple things, if you speak slowly. Megan dropped her face in her hands. *I've cried again*, she thought, *just as Katrana said. My tears won't do anything for Kat.* She pressed her hands to her face and sobbed dryly. *She was my friend. He hurts my friends. Anyone who had more of me than he did. He wanted me, and all he ever got was the Captain, untouchable, in control. It festered in him, respecting me. Kat.* Her shoulders shook, then with a crack she slammed her fists on the table, sending the inkpot bouncing onto the floor. *No, I can't cry, even for a friend. It won't serve.*

She unclenched her fists and forced evenness on her breathing, at last opening eyes squeezed shut against tears. She looked at the spatters of ink on her boot and puddled on the floor. *Sorrow won't serve; but hate will. This hate growing in me, ready to burst forth and poison like the amanita slipped into a dish of innocent mushrooms, lying like acid in my guts, it's the only thing that will serve me now. Nurse it, culture it, that it grows strong*, she told herself.

There was another bustle on the deck that she ignored. *Perhaps if I think of what to do to Habiku when I have him in my hands, perhaps that will make me feel better.*

"Captain." Outside the door, Piatr's voice was hesitant; that was unlike him. She'd heard his step, the soft scuff of his boot and the harder thump of the wooden foot. Slower than usual.

"What is it?" she snapped, flinging the door open. His face stopped her.

"Tze," he said. "We . . . found Tze. He's here, on deck."

For a moment, relief washed up from gut to neck, relaxing

muscles that had corded like iron down the sides of her spine. *Not everything is lost*, went through her. Then, *That isn't the face of a good-tidings bringer*.

"What is it?" she asked quietly. "Tell me." Her hand closed on his shoulder. "Tell me!" she shrieked.

Piatr's face twisted. He wrenched himself aside, heedless of the razor edges tearing through his blouse, tearing tracks through his skin, sank to the floor and cradled his head in his arms. *Please, don't let her speak please, I can't tell her I can't hurt her any more . . .*

Feet walked past him, slowly, with a heavy tread utterly unlike Megan's usual cat-light step. They passed him, down the corridor, up the companionway stair-ladder, to the deck, paused. Piatr waited; waited for the sound, biting his lip until the blood came, tasting grief thicker than pain. There was no cry; only the heavy steps, returning. They paused by him.

"No one," a voice said, in syllables of cold ash, "for any reason, is to pass this door." The door shut with infinite care.

Piatr sat on the sanded oak of the cabinway. There was not enough energy in him for movement, only enough to flinch, as objects broke against the door and wall; something heavy went through the sterncastle windows and splashed into the river. The sounds of breaking settled to a steady chorus of splintering and crunching. Behind it was the sound; it had started as a scream that broke and settled into a keening wail. It was sorrow, cold and grey as city slush in the last tired month before spring; it was loss like a child's too young for acceptance; it was a ship's hull moaning and tearing as the bow slipped below surface and the deeps had their way with the timbers. It was fury, and madness. The one-legged man felt the bile of fear mingle with the salt of tears on his tongue.

Sova lay on the poop, enjoying the mild warmth; the *Vetri* was berthed in a narrow slot cut into the black basalt of the island, and a day's sunlight was radiating back into the timbers of the ship. Behind her a carven dragon's head curved from the cliff, thirty meters up; its mouth was a spout that channeled a spring's runoff, and occasional droplets blew to her, a pleasant shock on warm skin. Her chin was through the railing, watching crewfolk about their work along the narrow deck; her hands were behind her, pulling one foot down towards her shoulder in a stretching exercise.

The official had been interesting, in the pretty silk robe and the funny little black hat with the wings. Sova would have liked to have a robe like that, pale blue with lilies woven in; he had smelled like lilies, too. The Captain didn't like him, even if she smiled and was polite. Sova's mouth turned down slightly; it had been a good joke, to walk after the Rand holding the hem of her tunic up the way he did his skirt. The impassive, slant-eyed face hadn't moved when he turned, but his pupils had widened, then gone pinhead sized. *Shkai'ra says you can always tell by the pupils*, she thought, and it was true. She giggled again, remembering; she had giggled then, too, and run up the ratlines to the main spar. Mateus had turned his head to hide a smile, but the Captain had been too angry to notice.

She's angry an awful lot, Sova thought. *I wish I knew why, it's scary even if she isn't mad at me.*

There was a stir on the dock; she turned to see, sitting up with legs straddled and bending her chin toward the deck. Can't get up speed on a footblow without stretching the hamstrings, Shkai'ra said. It made everything easier, too. Tall, redheaded . . . Yes, Shkai'ra; she was carrying a man in a fireman's sling around her neck. A big man, he must be heavy to make her step carefully like that. The gangplank boomed under her boots; Piatr limped by her side, one hand on the man's arm.

The Thane girl controlled a pout. Her *Khyd-hird* and Piatr had left earlier, and given her a curt, "No," when she asked to come along. It wasn't fair; Francosz was in the city somewhere, looking around, with Yvar. She wouldn't get to go ashore until tomorrow.

She slid down behind the rail separating lower and upper decks, hands gripping the wooden uprights that she peered between, curiosity overcoming the resentment. Then her breath went out in an O of shock. The man's back was a mass of weals, new ones scabbed and red, some half-healed, others twisted masses of keloid scarring white even against the corpse-paleness of a fair man long away from the sun. She had seen slaves her father had beaten, but nothing like this. A whiff of something reached her and she gagged; it was worse than the leper beggar that had waited outside the gate, filth and flesh rotting alive. She stood staring, hand pressed to her mouth. It scarcely even touched her when Shkai'ra's gaze flicked across her with an impersonal scorn at the squeamishness.

"Mateus, get your kit. We need you." There was movement past her, figures kneeling beside the man. His face was turned toward her; she could see the flat emptiness of the eyes, the thick ribs like hoops stretching the skin tight, falling in valleys between them. Yellow fluid ran from the deep ulcers on his shoulders; his skin twitched at the touch of water and cloth on the sores.

Mateus was there now. He had stood for a moment with his hand on his knife, the other raising the chest of medicines with a gesture of furious helplessness. He had ignored Shkai'ra's snarl of impatience, and he spoke to himself as he knelt beside the big man. Spoke Zak words she had never heard, softly, venomously; she could tell it was cursing from the tone, and the way Zemelya glanced sidelong at him from the corners of his eyes.

Sova blinked and listened. Shkai'ra was talking to Piatr: "Perhaps I'd better tell her . . ." She looked steadily at him for a moment. "No, you both knew him, it's your right."

Piatr had nodded, his skin grey, and turned to go. The Captain came up.

The Thane girl had been staring; she was shocked, but as a child is at a wonder, half excitement and half not understanding, fear that is a fear of an adult's incomprehensible distress, as a dog scents its master's, and howls without knowing the reason why.

This was different; she felt it come in the slow, heavy steps below her in the companionway that lead to the sterncabin. The Captain's face was a different thing, ice, a weakness in the heart of bones. Yet Megan simply stood, staring downward at the man on the deck. Shkai'ra began reaching out, began to speak, let her hand fall in silence. There was a great stillness, broken when Mateus let drops of a clear fluid fall on the man's back. An animal grunt, then a liquid sigh, unconsciousness.

Megan made a sound, faint, a beginning uncompleted. Her face rose; the eyes met Sova's without seeing. The Captain turned; she walked away, back to the ladder and the cabin. The girl felt a tense hush: awe, and a stillness like seeing an avalanche begin, before the sound can reach you. She felt a whimper beginning, suppressed it, felt a loss, a clearing, as if the sight had pushed her over a threshold in her soul, to a place where such things could be. Where there was no safety, and even the Captain, her friend, could be lost.

Then the sound began from below. Sova cried out and pressed her hands to her ears, bent her head to the deck and wept, wept for the broken man, for Megan, for her own childhood. Wept without hope of comfort, even when Shkai'ra's arm encircled her shoulder and held her, for where was refuge?

Stillness lay over the ship like a cloth on a wound. In the dark people sat, looking everywhere but at each other in the pale glow of the lamps on the dock. The rattle of dice on the deck, as sailors tried to bring normalcy back, was empty and faint, like the rattle one fears at a bedside watch, and those that made frantic love did so to comfort themselves.

There had been no sound from the cabin for most of the evening watch. They'd all heard the wail grow hoarser, collapsing into discreet words occasionally, damning *his* soul to every Halya. Curses filled with tears as something else smashed. Then silence.

Shkai'ra came down the companionway and found Piatr still sitting by the door, his head leaning back against the wall as he listened. Next to him a shadow uncurled itself and blinked solemn green eyes at her. Ten-Knife stretched and curled around her boots, but did not purr. She stood a moment looking down at the two of them, then nudged the dead rat away from its place by the door, putting out a hand to open it.

"Wouldn't," Piatr said, voice final, just above a whisper. "She said no."

Shkai'ra sighed. "Someone has to. She keeps this up, she'll get crazy enough to be left with her friend at Joy Shrine."

"She said no," he repeated but his voice was less certain.

"Then she'll have to tell me herself," Shkai'ra snapped and opened the door.

The only light was from the *kraumak* behind her and when she closed the door, from the outline of the window, broken bits of wood swaying slightly in the rocking motion of the ship. As she stepped in, something crunched under her boot and there was a movement from the darkest part of the room. "Leave me alone." Megan's voice was ragged and torn like the room. Not a whisper but a sound that has been used too hard.

"Megan."

"I like it like this."

"Megan." Shkai'ra's voice was soft as she stepped forward. "Let me put on the light—"

"NO!"

The Kommanza put out a hand toward the dim figure in the dark and only her flickerswift reflexes saved her from being clawed. The Zak was still again after that one strike as if she had never moved.

It felt right, in the dark, Megan thought. It had surged up and over what defenses she had, flowed through her like oil-sludge. Hate and fear were nothing compared to this monster that sat in her limbs and mind while she watched from somewhere a great distance away. The dark was as cold as the slushy river outside, and since the rage had died to ashes she had been that cold.

Shkai'ra paused. Perhaps Megan had gone truly crazy. There had to be some way to reach her.

"Megan," she paused, floundering, almost angry. She was no damn nursemaid, but . . . Megan needed her. "When we met . . . when we loved . . . Together, you said. Together we defy the storm." She paused. There was no sign from the Zak. "Kh'eeredo, you're alone in it, while I'm here."

One heartbeat. Two. Three . . . With a solid impact Megan

threw her arms around Shkai'ra, ignoring the Kommanza's instinctive defensive move.

"I'm going mad, Shkai'ra." Megan's voice, ragged as torn paper. "This is killing me. I'm going mad. I hate him. I want to tear him into bloody shreds. He hurts me by hurting my friends. I won't be able to have friends. They'll be hurt—"

"Kh'eeredo, I'm here. I'll help you kill him if you need it. You're not crazy. I know. You're strong enough that he'll never touch you again." Megan held to her lover as if she were falling, and shivered.

Chapter 13

SLAF HIKARME, F'TALEZON
TENTH IRON CYCLE, TWENTY-THIRD DAY

The Slaf Hikarme was silent under the snow. Silent except for the hoarse, inarticulate shout of rage from the private chambers of the master of the house. The servants and slaves in earshot tried to keep on with their tasks, flinching when something heavy broke, trying to pretend everything was as usual.

It had started when the master came home from Dragon's-Nest the night before. He had slammed in the front doors, shouting for his slave Lixa. When the butler had informed him that she was not yet back from Zingas Uen's, Habiku had gone silent, turned on his heel and stalked into his chambers.

"That BITCH! Avritha, the Viper as a name *suits* you! She refused me! Bitch! Viper in heat! Whitlock, I'll have you still!" The shouts from the inner chambers had been accompanied by smashing of priceless furnishings, the lapdesk flung straight through the west window. Now everything was silent.

The butler, hovering nervously in the corridor, glanced at the valet who shrugged and looked away. The door opened and Habiku, disheveled, clothing torn and disarrayed, one of his hands cut and bleeding, looked out into the light. "Get in here," he said hoarsely. "Get things straightened up."

"Of course, Teik, at once—" Habiku cut the butler off

mid-word, brushing past him, leaving the door swinging open behind him.

"Enough of that." He looked down at the cuts in his palm thoughtfully. "Have a bath poured," he said absently. "I'll just have to think of another way."

"Teik?" The valet stopped as he signalled one of the slaves, looked back at his master.

"Oh, nothing. I'll be in the Library." Habiku tried to straighten his clothing, folded his hands behind his back and paced down the hall, head down, thinking. He missed the look his servants exchanged over the devastated rooms he left behind.

"Yes, Teik."

RAND, HSIANG ISLE
TENTH IRON CYCLE, TWENTY-FIFTH DAY

Megan had gone to the metalworkers' street with Piatr, wrapped in a mood darker than her cloak; Piatr, and a banker's draft large enough to make the supercargo wince. Shkai'ra was alone on the quarterdeck, washing down after sword-dancing, when they returned. She paused with the bucket over her head, poured, then vaulted the railing. Francosz looked up from book and slate as she did. Sova was concentrating on copying the outline of a letter in the waxboard. She paused and nibbled on the end of the stylus but didn't look up.

Megan was directing as a dozen porters wheeled the cloth-covered dolly down the dock, its wooden wheels clattering on the worn stone.

Whatever it is, it's small, Shkai'ra thought, scuffing at her hair with a rough length of toweling. About five by three, but heavy, from the way they were handling it.

Megan stood by with a tension more evident than pacing, and her eyes flicked up to the rigging.

"Mateus!" she called. The first mate yawned up from below, from his bunk. "Turn out the crew. Rig the forward boom for cargo hoist; it's a—" she paused to estimate "—ten times manweight load."

He blinked, shrugged and began to bellow. Most of the deck crew were on board; they had duties of a sort during daytime, repairs with the rigging and gear, and stayed aboard while the rowing crew took liberty. Shkai'ra moved to the gangway railing to be out of the way, propping a leg on the rope to towel it and puzzling at the shrouded bulk. Francosz put the book down, said, "Keep on copying, Sovee," and came over next to Shkai'ra. The crew had readied the main-sail yard to use as a crane.

The parcel had a four corner tie already looped over the canvas; Piatr stumped to grab the hook as it jerked down-ward, leaned to fix it expertly in the center knot of the rig.

"Ease away!" he shouted. A half-dozen crew had the other end of the lift rope; it slid through their hands, coiling neatly at the feet of the last. Shkai'ra leaned her buttocks against one of the poles of the gangway railing, drying her feet and watching the way the outboard slack of the rope tightened. Another sailor had dashed past her with a coil of line and run a loop through the slack of the rig beneath the hook; she would control the movement from the dock. Two more had a holding line about the head of the boom, below the block.

I've commanded soldiers less disciplined, Shkai'ra thought. Mateus raised his speaking-trumpet.

"Haul her free . . ."

The weight on the dock lifted, swayed, steadied.

"Haul away!"

The rope-gang bent to their work, quick regular underarm snatches at the rod-straight sisal cord; Shkai'ra could hear the rasp of their work-roughened palms on the scratchy surface. The load swung up to twice manheight over the railing and hung with its cover dangling.

"Warp her home!"

"Easy, easy!" shouted the sailor on the dock, as the boom moved slowly to come in line with the keel.

"Make fast on the stayline," Mateus called. The rope con-trolling the boom was stubbed to a bollard. "Slowly—ease her down!" Another squeal from the block, and the rope-gang's hands moved in unison to pay out the rope, like the many legs of a centipede moving in unison. The boards creaked as the load came to rest on the deck, still covered.

Megan came up the gangway with a quick, nervous rush. Francosz edged away. He tapped Sova on the shoulder.

"All right, kh'eeredo, I give up: what is it?" Shkai'ra said.

The Zak halted, close enough to Shkai'ra that she had to lean back to clear the Kommanza's breasts and see her face.

"It's revenge," she said with a tight, glittering smile that left Shkai'ra feeling slightly alarmed; it was unlike the Megan she knew.

"Perfect revenge—it's an inspiration from the Dark Lord, Shkai'ra. You'll love it, even better than feeding him to dogs or hanging him under the waterfall by his armpits."

She whirled as the ropes came off. "Mateus, announcement. Get everyone here. I'll need someone to translate into Rand. Jump!" He didn't stop to ask any questions. Megan seized the ties to the covering over the mysterious package and snicked through them with her claws. The burlap fell away, exposing the gleaming steel bars of a cage.

There was no welding seam visible on it at all, as if it had grown into its shape, solid bottom, five feet tall, three feet wide, three feet long. The door was one side, tied shut because the brass pin wasn't in the lock. It was made to be hammered shut and never opened again.

"Habiku's six feet tall," Megan said. "Koru grant him many, many years of life." She pointed to the top of the cage, where a steel ring was welded to the bars. "It'll hang in the covered court of the House of the Sleeping Dragon. For years! *And he'll still be alive!*" Piatr grinned, and Tze, who had been carried up from belowdecks, made a thick, gobbling sound that Shkai'ra took a moment to identify as laughter.

Francosz froze at her shout, and Sova grabbed him around the shoulders. *Great Gothumml*, he thought, putting a protective arm around her shoulders and doing his best to ignore the unfamiliar sensation of his testicles trying to draw themselves back up inside.

"He . . . he must be a *very* bad man," Sova whispered.

"*Nobody's* bad enough to deserve *that* witch after him," Francosz said with conviction. He felt his sister stiffen and pull away slightly. "Hey," he whispered. "Don't let her fool you."

"You didn't see the lady Yvar brought in," Sova snapped.

Megan wheeled to the northeast, toward her home city; her hands were over her head, clawed, and a red-orange nimbus played about them. "I call ye forth, I call ye forth, I call ye forth." She paused after the ritual summoning and the crew quieted; she closed her eyes.

"Habiku Smoothtongue!" she called, as if he could hear her. "By *Koru Vetri*, I swear! You bring my revenge on you like Her winter! What have you done! I'm coming, Habiku Treacher. I know, I know each of your deeds; every one is recorded, every one will be held against you. *Justice is coming, Habiku!* If the Great Phoenix came again it would be better if you burned in Its fires than face me! Better for you if the sky fell on you, better for you if the earth swallowed you, better for you if you had never been born than to be alive in F'talezon when my foot touches that rock. I'm coming to you as one of the Dark Lord's Eagles! Lie awake in your stolen bed, you filth, and *wait!*" She opened her eyes and gazed north.

Sova looked at the orangey light reflecting in Megan's eyes and steel claws. *Maybe Franc's right*, she thought, standing and twisting one foot over the other in discomfort. *But she was so nice to me*.

Megan's hands snapped down, the light going out. She looked down at the assembled crew. "You've heard," she said in a hoarse voice. "Hear me again. You all know. Hear my words. *Habiku Smoothtongue. I curse you living. I curse you dying. I curse you in sitting, in standing, in lying. I curse your footfall and the food that you eat. I curse you at home and in the street. I curse your seed, and your source, your flesh. I and my kin-blood curse you till death.*" Her crew were mostly grinning.

Shkai'ra could hear the murmur of the Rand translation just finishing. *Baiwun*, she thought. *A show like that will be all up and down the river faster than a horse can kick.*

Megan said, "I call you to witness. Dismiss."

*   *   *

"Sure you don't want to want to come along?" Shkai'ra said. She was dressing carefully, slipping a double-layered leather vest over her undershirt. The leather was thin and supple, but there were perforated bone buttons between the layers, enough to turn a knifeblade in a pinch but less cumbersome than real armor. Chamois pants, long linen blouse dyed green, tooled boots and belt, saber, dagger, a well-filled pouch.

"No," Megan said shortly, sitting on the bed and staring moodily out the sterncastle windows. It was dusk, and the harbor was doubly dark as the sun vanished behind the rim of the crater and the huge bulk of the rock above them. The riding lights of the ships were coming on, yellow eyes winking against dark wood and stone and water; brighter lights showed where fishing boats were putting out, the lure-lamps at their bows. In those lights the first swirls of feathery snow spun.

Am I truly going mad? Megan lowered her head. *No. I feel as though I'm made of cracked rock but I know* exactly *what I'm doing. He's going to pay. For my company, the loss of the time I could have taken to search for my son, for Mat, for Piatr, for Kat, for Tze and his wife and two sons, for all the lives he's maimed. He'll pay. For me.* She leaned her head back against the wall, the odor of teak oil and glue strong where the wood had been repaired. *I've got to hold myself together. With hate if nothing else.* Her stomach twinged and she pressed a palm flat against it, breathing deep to try and force calm on herself. Shkai'ra said something. "Have a good time," the Zak replied and kept looking out the window.

"Don't worry, kh'eeredo," Shkai'ra said. No response. "We'll just be out for a while." No response. "There are six river gar on the mast," she tried.

"Have a good time," was all Megan replied to that.

"Well, I did promise the little bastard I'd take him out," Shkai'ra sighed. "Look, we'll be back by one . . . It would really do you good to come in and get drunk, throw some dice, maybe break a few bones . . ." She stamped her feet into the boots to settle them; they were broken in, but only just. She braided her hair with angry jerks. "All right, *be* that

way." She swirled the cloak around her shoulders, fastened
the broach and cast it back from the right to free her sword-arm.

Francosz was waiting outside, in the new-bought best tunic
and breeches; his equally new shortsword was at his belt, the
pommel glittering with polishing. Shkai'ra sighed and hooked
it loose, dropping weapon and scabbard on her bedroll beside
Sova, who was hugging her knees, sulking.

"Why—oww!" Francosz rubbed the ear she had tweaked.

"Because, boy, some of the places I plan on going, wearing
a sword is considered the same as saying you can use it." She
nodded at his knife. "You remember what Megan said; as
long as that stays in the sheath, it's for roast meat. Draw it on
a living human, and you'd better be prepared to use it."

Sova mumbled something inaudible. Shkai'ra squatted and
put a hand under her chin. "Sova," she said softly. Then
more harshly: "*Sova!*"

The girl looked up sulkily. "Yes, *khyd-hird*?" she said, her
lower lip protruding.

"Sova, Megan is not . . . she's not feeling well," Shkai'ra
continued in the same almost-whisper. "You understand?" A
reluctant nod, and a nervous glance toward the cabin door.
"Now, she's very angry, because Habiku hurt her friends to
hurt her. She doesn't want to be with me or anyone she's
grown-up friends with, because we might quarrel. You understand that?"

Sova knitted her brow, considered, nodded. "It, well, it
doesn't seem very, well, grown up," she said. "She was so
mad, I mean, *I've* been that mad but she's . . . Well, it was
scary."

"You're growing up fast, little one: adults can't afford to get
as angry as children, because they can really hurt people
instead of just wanting too. Now, I need you to help me."

"Help you?" she said, the pout fading a bit.

"That's right; I'm not just leaving you behind—" *although
all the gods know you're a few years too young and a mite too
tender for the sort of dive I feel in the mood for* "—I need
you to help with the Captain. She won't get angry with you,
because she knows you're an apprentice and too young to
quarrel with." *I hope.* "So I want you to take her her dinner

when Piatr has it ready, and ask her to give you your next reading lesson." *Give Megan words and she can forget what hurts her*. "Don't be upset if she says no, just say you'll sit outside the door and practice, and she can call you if she needs anything. That way she won't get so wrapped up in things. Understand?"

Sova took a deep breath and firmed her jaw. "I understand, *khyd-hird*," she said resolutely. "You can count on me."

"Good," Shkai'ra replied, giving her a slap on the shoulder. "Don't wait up."

The lower bulk of the mountain city was hidden in darkness when they went down the gangplank. Francosz strode out jauntily, resting his thumbs in his belt. *All the girl's stuff and hard work and worrying about boring businesses is dumb. I'm learning. She said so. I wish she hadn't made me take off my sword. I'm a man now and should carry one*. "Why do you put up with all that fussing of Sova's?" he asked. "She's just a girl."

Shkai'ra reached back without looking and cuffed him behind the head. "Ow!" he said. "What was that for?"

"Boy, there was a time when *I* was just a girl, and don't forget it. Now, shut up and listen. When we go in, you sit behind me to the left. *Left*, understand? Don't get too caught up in what's ahead of us, and keep an eye out behind if we're not back to a wall. Don't drink anything unless I say you can and it's paid for. Incidentally, always pay for your drinks when you get 'em; oldest trick in the book is to wait until you're fuddled and add a round to the score."

He caught sight of a Rand fire-eater, standing in an overhang and twirling his flaming rods, running them up and down his bare arms and into his mouth, then juggling them in arcs and streamers of fire. The thickening snow hissed around him in the halo of lamplight that came through the peacock's fan of colored glass above the tavern's door. Shkai'ra reached back and snagged him by the ear. "Not that one."

"Why?" He rubbed the side of his head. *That hurt*. "It

looked like a good place. Why are you always grabbing and
hitting me? *Khyd-hird*," he added hastily.

Shkai'ra looked sideways at him and laughed. "Habit. Remember my back? That's the way my people handle young-
sters." She grinned at his worry. "But I've gotten soft among
outlanders. As for that place, remember what I told you
about women?"

He tried to swagger, slipped in the slush and looked back
at the man who was spitting a tongue of flame out into the
air. "Certainly."

"Well, maybe I ought to send you in there. It's got a
peacock's fan over the door." He looked puzzled. "It's a
high-class whorehouse. Overpriced drinks, and the games
might not be honest."

"Oh." He blushed, the feeling hot against the cold air, and
pulled up the hood of his cloak. They plunged into a section
of tunnel, a staircase-road with gutters at either side running
with snowmelt, black with only a glimmer from around the
curve of the road. Shkai'ra began to whistle, loudly and only
near the tune.

"Never sound furtive in a dark place in a strange city," she
said as they rounded the curve. "Alley-leapers can sense
weakness the way wolves do in herd-stragglers . . . Ah, now
that's worth seeing."

They stopped, looking up the terraced mountainside. The
temples and villas of the rich were like rubies and sapphires
scattered up the steep slope; great glass lanterns cast shadows
from dragon-carved eaves and gilded, sweep-sided roofs,
blurred through the gathering snow. Moving lights marked
palanquins and carriages on the spiderweb of bridges that
connected the peaks. A gong rang steadily, faint and mellow
and golden. Francosz felt excitement humming like jittery
sunlight in his blood at the sight; vague tumbled stories of
heros and princesses and treasures in ruined castles fell through
his head, and he came to himself with a jump when Shkai'ra
nudged him.

"Here's the place," she said. He looked around, bewildered, then saw the small door set into the cliff-face to their
right.

"Don't be so disappointed; it's bigger inside. More to the point—" she pounded on the black stone portal, a faint dull thudding. A trap opened at eye-height for a Rand, level with his brow and her throat. "—Mateus said they don't mind non-Rand here."

The door swung open, letting out a blast of noise and heat and smoke, smells of food and sweat and beer and wine and acrid dreamsmoke. The keeper was naked to the waist, a Rand squat enough to look almost square, blubber-smooth but with a dimpling ripple that spoke of muscle under the fat; shaven-skulled save for a topknot and sporting a thin drooping mustache. He looked at them suspiciously, fingering the meter-length, steel-tipped hardwood rods in his hands, then grunted in satisfaction as Shkai'ra showed a single silver coin. They ducked through, onto a dais that overlooked the long room.

"Don't look hungry, and don't show too much," Shkai'ra shouted over the uproar. "And stop goggling, boy: never been in a port city tavern before?"

Francosz shook his head wordlessly, forcing his mouth closed. There was a bar all along one side of the room, fifteen meters back into the rock, with red-lacquered mirrors and round spigotted ceramic tuns labeled in the spiky Rand script. Bowls and plates were displayed, warmed over spirit-lanterns and giving off spicy alien smells and smokes. Pasted-on strips of calligraphy covered the other walls, where they were not hidden under slateboards chalked with much-corrected messages. The rest of the ten-meter width of the room was crowded with low tables; men and women sat about them, drinking and eating and playing incomprehensible games with dice, cards, ivory plaques, board games with colored stones, chess . . . and money was changing hands on each and every one, onlookers hanging over the players' shoulders and shouting their odds.

"Ahh," Shkai'ra sighed. The far end was curtained off with a thick, hanging fringe of strung wooden beads; it was warm enough to bring a sweat to her forehead, dim enough to let the flames and mirror-reflected light cast a smoky red glow over furniture, faces, eyes. She swaggered down the stairway and slipped into the crowd, shouldering her way toward the bar with a decent minimum of elbow-work.

"Now's the time to keep your hand on your pouch," she shouted back over her shoulder to the Thane boy. "Better still, put it under your shirt." She unhooked her own, opened the neck of her blouse and hung the soft leather bag between her breasts. He followed suit, fumbling and scowling about.

"Are there thieves?" he shouted back. In the crowd the noise was worse, and he was uneasily conscious that most were two inches taller than he at least. Only about half the crowd were Rand, the rest a mixture of all the folk who lived along the Brezhan and some from the shores of the Mitvald; none looked too ragged, but there was a disconcerting number of scars, broken noses, enlarged knuckles and worn-looking swordhilts pressing in on him from all sides. He stumbled slightly, caromed off a hard-muscled shoulder that threw him back like a wall. The owner whirled and cursed, a black, one-eyed Ibresi woman with a gold hoop through her nose, wearing Yeoli steel bracelets that had to have been plundered and a broad machete-like chopping blade across her back.

She snarled and reached for his throat with a gloved hand whose fingertips glinted sharp. Shkai'ra looked back and rapped a polite knuckle into the Ibresian's shoulder, just where the nerve bundle surfaced.

"Sorry," she said. To Francosz: "Thieves? Oh, no more than usual. Mateus said nobody much under quarterdeck rank gets in here. And professional gamblers, of course; dreamsmoke merchants, whores, mercenaries . . . cutpurses everywhere. Ahi-a, here we are."

They reached the bar, a solid plank structure fitted like a ship's bulwark, the outer rail scarred and pitted and worn greasy-smooth by hands and bellies. Shkai'ra whistled piercingly between thumb and forefinger, pointed, waved a coin, a F'talezonian halfClaw. The expressionless Rand woman behind the counter turned and shouted orders in sing-song, reached and poured. A tall wooden stein of beer appeared for him, the same for Shkai'ra with a small tumbler of clear yellowish liquid. Then a tray: two cheap ceramic bowls, full of steamed wheat grains and grilled lamb and fish with a brown sauce full of chilies; two pipes also, with an ember in a clay stand and a container of shredded leaves and stems.

"*To Death*," Shkai'ra said, raising the tumbler to her lips. She took a slow mouthful, then swallowed suddenly. Her eyes closed, and she blew out with satisfaction, following it with a draught of the beer.

Sova tapped on the door, balancing the wooden tray with one hand. "Enter!" Megan snapped. Sova started, the tray tipped and she grabbed for the saltcellar just before it slid off. She steadied everything, tip of her tongue between her teeth, hoped the lid on the borscht hadn't slipped, opened the door and Ten-Knife strolled imperiously in with her, right between her feet.

It had been cleaned up since yesterday, the floorboards scrubbed, the scars in the wood filled and sanded and oiled. The window had been replaced with rose-colored glass, the hand-sized, diamond-shaped panes set in strips of brass. The oil lamp was lit, but turned low and Sova couldn't see into the shadowy corner of the bed.

Ten-Knife batted at a missed feather, sauntered toward the bed then changed direction, folding his greying paws under his chest beneath the dry-sink. Sova stood for a moment, then put the tray on the table, clearing her throat. "Umm. Piatr made your favorite."

"Thank him for me." Megan's voice was calm, flat, dull. The Thane girl shifted from foot to foot, looked at the floor, at the ceiling, at the cupboards, at the tray. *What do I say? She said . . . when she was nice to me, what did she say that made me feel better?*

"Umm. Care for some company?" She almost felt the second look Megan must have given her. There was a brittle sort of laugh, a rustle and the Captain slid out of the dark, blinking. Her hair was loose, the first time Sova had seen all of it. It hung to below her knees. She looked Sova up and down and her eyes glittered as if there were tears there, but none showed on her cheeks. *Maybe she'd feel better if she cried, like me*, Sova thought.

"I'll eat. You don't have to baby-sit me."

"Oh, I wouldn't do *that*! You're no baby." Sova settled down on her *khyd-hird*'s chest as Megan pulled the chair out and uncovered the tray. "Umm. Francosz isn't here tonight and I sort of need to do my next reading lesson, could you show me?" Megan looked up from where she was shredding a slice of bread into a pile of crumbs. Sova squirmed a little. *It sounds so . . . fake. Maybe she's seeing that Shkai'ra told me to ask her. She looks . . . I don't know how she looks. I've never seen anybody look like that, except when Mama sold Malae.*

"Right." Megan pushed the tray away. "Get your waxboard." She unslung an ornamental blue-green ceramic bottle from its niche in the wall and poured a thimble-glass full of green liquid. *Saekrberk*, Sova thought, leaving the door swinging behind her. *I know what that looks like.* "Korukai." Megan toasted the air and drank it in a gulp, then poured herself another, left it standing on the table. It was still there when Sova scampered back into the cabin.

Francosz finished the last of his beer as they sat by the dice table and fanned his tongue. That sauce had been good, but it was *hot*. He positioned himself to Shkai'ra's left and sank down on the low padded bench, with the extra softness of his folded cloak beneath, looking around the circle of gamesters. Sweat glistened on their foreheads, but their features and hands were steady; piles of coin, rings, chains, jewelry sat before their places. What had Shkai'ra said? Ah: *Look where they wear their knives. If they're sitting on the sheaths with the hilts next their right hands, walk out. If the blades are standing point-up in the table, run.* Here the blades stayed on the belts; it was the eyes that stabbed.

"More?" The voice spoke in his ear. He jumped, turned his head and found himself staring down the serving girl's tunic as she bent to speak to him. It was half-unlaced, and the breasts within were unbound; full, pear-shaped, dark-nippled. His tongue locked, and he gasped after breath. She leaned forward, and the rounded softness pressed into his shoulder, he could *feel* the nipples through the thin fabric of their shirts. Lines of heat and sweet, thrilling chill stabbed down from the spot to his groin, and the passage of his throat closed completely.

"Ngggghhh," he choked, and forced his eyes up to her face. She was young, only a few years older than he; half-Rand, moon-faced and plumply pretty. Her eyelids drooped, and she moistened her lower lip.

"More beer, young sir?" she said again. He could feel her breath on his cheek, warm and smelling of the mint leaves she had chewed; her body gave off warm scents of sweat and floral scent.

"Aggghk," he grunted, and nodded frantically at his stein. She raised the pitcher and leaned forward further, pressing herself harder against him as she poured. He raised the wooden mug without moving his eyes, hand wobbling and cool tingling wet sopping down his wrist. Took a mouthful and tried to swallow, coughed and blew foam out his nose.

Shkai'ra glanced back and gave a shout of laughter, nudging her mug close. "Me too: just the beer." The barmaid complied, pouring for the Kommanza and then helpfully offering her apron for Francosz to wipe his face.

"Here," Shkai'ra said, tossing a coin that flashed unnoticed silver past the boy's head. The maid's free hand plucked it out of the air with the quick motion of a trout rising to a fly and slipped it into her pants pocket.

"More later, come back for our refills," the Kommanza shouted, her clear husky voice cutting through the crowd's roar. Over Francosz's head she winked broadly at the girl and jerked her head downward at the boy. The girl fluttered lashes, rising and turning in a way that accidentally brushed the surface of her bodice across his lips. Francosz twisted his head to follow her swaying retreat, the full buttocks twisting against each other in the tight cotton knee-breeches.

Shkai'ra thumped him on the back to help the last cough. "Breathe, boy, breathe, you're turning purple and the night is young!" She cut a nick of resin from the small cube, warmed it and put it in the pipe, handed it to him with a match. "Here, calm down. Breathe, I said. Light this and draw on it, then a swig of beer; hold the smoke in your lungs."

Franc fumbled with the clay pipe, struck the match and puffed as he'd seen her do, trying to look as if he'd done it thousands of times before. The smoke coiled at the back of his throat and burned. He gulped, coughed, choked, and Shkai'ra pounded on his back again, absently, her mind on the dice. "Are you trying to kill yourself? Inhale it, don't swallow it!"

He tried again and this time managed to inhale the pipeful of sweet herb smoke. His head was floating a little and it was as if the smoke detached his mind from his head completely. He exhaled like a dragon blowing a small cloud out of his mouth and soothed his throat with more ale. "Here." Shkai'ra handed him the brown cube. "Enjoy yourself, don't stray too far. The barmaid'll find you to refill you."

Francosz looked down at the pipe in his hand. *Why am I moving so slowly? Who cares? I don't. Look at the blue haze twist as people move through it. That's funny.* He saw the barmaid passing behind another table; she turned and waved with the tips of her fingers. Francosz slid lower on the bench and took another puff; puff and sip, that was it. *The lights . . . the lights are so* interesting, he thought.

". . . and the Great . . ." Sova stumbled over the word and stared at it for a bit. "Puh . . . Poh . . ."

"Ph is pronounced 'f'," Megan said patiently. "F-ee-nix. Phoenix." She ruffled Sova's hair. "Enough of that. Why don't you go see if Piatr has something for you to do?"

"He'll just have roots for me to peel, or something." *The Captain doesn't look as bad. I can help.* "Can I stay with you a little longer?" Megan was locking the book and hanging it on its peg. She looked over her shoulder, surprised.

"All right." She came back to the table, looked at the cold remains of her untouched dinner and the glass of Saekrberk.

"Well. We've been left while everyone else goes to town. It doesn't mean we have to be dull here. You may have *one* glass of Saekrberk with me. We never celebrated your becoming a woman, why don't we do that?"

"Oh!" Sova blushed, then looked up with a shyly radiant smile. "You don't think it's, you know, dirty?"

Megan snorted and drained the last of her glass. "If it were dirty, half of all humans would be dirty." She refilled her own and one for Sova. "Like Arkans." She poured another and stared down into it.

Sova sniffed the glass and blinked. *The smell goes right up inside your head.* "Do I . . . do I say anything?"

"Oh, a toast. You can if you like." Megan refilled her own glass again, set the bottle down with a thump. "I toast the Goddess. Or you can toast . . . Well, it's your womaning celebration. Here's to being a woman with all the pain and joy of bearing children." They drank.

Gothumml, I'm dying. My throat's on fire, I can't breathe. I . . . I . . . Her breath came back with a wheeze and she tried to see through watering eyes.

"And here's to the goddess-damned bastards who hurt women, or try. May they . . . rot . . . in . . . Hal . . .ya." The sob came hard as if every tear were made of ice. Megan set the glass down with a chime as the stem broke and put her face in her hands. She clenched her teeth and dried her face. "Tears are no good to anyone else. I'm going to get good and drunker than I am. Sova, off to bed with you. It's late."

"Six," Shkai'ra shouted happily. The others around the table had dropped out, sitting silent. That was the only silence in the tavern; the noise had peaked, a continuous thudding roar that echoed back from the solid stone of the walls.

The Kommanza reached out to rake in the final pile, chortling happily. There was a buzzing in her ears and the room was hazed; not enough to spoil the twist-the-gut tension of the dice, just enough to enhance it. She swallowed to break the smoke-dryness in her mouth and looked up to see the dark half-Lakan face of her last adversary taut with anger.

"I think," she said, nodding at the meager stack of coins and single necklace left before him, "that you're sacked and pillaged, my man. Empty, drained, out of a stake and out of the game." She giggled, an odd sound from a woman her size.

"I think," the man grated in heavily accented trade-Zakos, "that you should stake me to another game. With fresh dice."

His sword hand clamped down on hers, quick and very strong.

"Oh, friend," she sighed, with a genuine smile. "This is perfect. So perfect." Shkai'ra blinked back moisture. It *was* perfect, after a day when every god with an orifice had shat on her head. Her left hand shot across, under the table, between the man's thighs.

And he's not even wearing a cup, she mused happily, clenching and twisting with all the strength of thick wrist and corded forearm. The slitted dark eyes flew open wide, bulging; the man's mouth opened, but no sound came out, only his tongue, waving like the feeding-frond of a deepsea fish. Shkai'ra rose and the man came with her, shuddering; the table tipped and spilled.

His grip on her wrist lost strength, turned to a feeble pawing. She flicked the hand free, cocked a fist behind her right ear. "Juuust hold still, friend . . . yes . . ."

The blow landed with a snapping twist, just as she released his testicles; the aquiline nose squashed flat with a satisfying crunch of cartilage and the man went over on his back, glazed eyes staring at the ceiling as slow red bubbles formed and popped around his nostrils.

Shkai'ra licked her knuckles. "Zaik smite me, not too drunk 'r smoked to judge it," she muttered soundlessly under the sudden increase of the tumult. Half a dozen were glaring at her, and others were turning; she could feel the focusing of their attention. She was not a regular here, and the crowd just might be chancy enough to mob a stranger . . .

She came to her feet with a handful of the scattered winnings, and shouted in a voice trained to carry over a battlefield, *"Drinks on me! Drinks on me all around!"*

The middle-aged Rand woman behind the bar swiveled her head like a catapult on a turntable, arrowing in on the sheen of precious metal. A hush had fallen, or enough of one that the clanging strike of a gong from behind the bar could be heard above the buzz of customers asking their seatmates what had been said. At the second clang, true quiet fell, enough for the proprietor's voice to be heard:

"One beer ever'body, all same red-hair lady pays! No come

bar! We bring!" The half-Lakan's friends looked about themselves, at each other, shrugged, and bent to carry the bleeding gambler out.

A great cheer lifted from the tables, hoots of laughter, beating of fists and cups and boots on wood and stone and sometimes unconscious neighbours. Shkai'ra dumped a double handful of the winnings on a waiter's tray, accepted salutes and backslaps with a grin, dislocated the thumb of a hand that groped up her thigh and flick-kicked the wrist of another that was edging toward the scattering of wealth where the table had stood.

"Francosz!" she called. "Get that cloak out from under your ass and get to work."

The boy started out from a dream of soft breasts under his hands and rose. *Floating*, he thought, as he spread the wool of his cloak. *I'm so light I could just float away. Wouldn't that be* funny. Shkai'ra knelt beside him and helped scoop stray coins and bits of silver wire onto the cloth. Their eyes met, and they laughed, laughed until the wet was streaming down their cheeks.

"Ahi-a, Francosz-boy, you bring me Glitch's own luck; plenty of it, good and bad," she wheezed, wiping at her cheeks with the backs of her hands. "Tell you what, boy. Wha'd you say to getting laid, hmmmm?"

He blinked at her, then suddenly recoiled. She laughed afresh, howling and hammering the flat of one hand on the floor. "No, no, Jaiwun *bless*, boy, not *me*. Wouldn' be proper. Your little charmer with the stein. I'll fix it up. Wha' say?" Her finger poked him in the ribs. "Get's moldy if y'don't use it, saa?"

The Thane boy could feel the smoke-calm leave him; his throat throbbed, then his temples. "You—" His voice broke in a squeak; some distant portion of his mind was surprised that that did not bother him. "You *will*?" He was nodding, frantically, before the words could force themselves out. "Ah, yes, *khyd-hird*, yes, *ja*, *deedly*, thank you, *yes*."

"Right." She folded the cloak, drew herself up and helped him to his feet before handing it to him. The bulge of the winnings was small, but surprisingly heavy. "You hold on t'this. Look fierce, now, apprentice. Back soon."

Shkai'ra shook back her shoulders and walked out into the crowd in a careful straight line; it parted for her with friendly hails. *Oh, Gothumml,* Francosz thought, amid rising glory. *It's happening, it's really happening.*

Minutes passed, like hours, like seconds. The tall, red-blonde figure returned with the barmaid and a young man similar enough to be her close kin. A wide grin split Shkai'ra's face; Francosz suspected his was silly-looking, but it mattered very little. The girl slid close to him, warm and soft; he swayed, and her arm went around him.

"Francosz," Shkai'ra said, "this is Tsu-Choi an' her brother Tsu-Li. Tsu-Choi would like to . . . what was it you said?"

"Open the Gates of Paradise for you, young sir," Tsu-Choi said, but the words were spoken to Francosz. Their stomachs touched, and her pelvis brushed his with a slow, light side-to-side that brought an involuntary jerk and a moan that was half pain from the boy. "My brother and I have a room, this way, young sir. You and your patron are *most* welcome."

"Hmmm?" Francosz forced himself back from a gathering focus that demanded he exclude all things but one. Shkai'ra was standing with her arm around the young man's waist, smiling with a warmth he had seldom seen on that cruel eagle face. "One room?" he said, embarrassment fighting a losing battle with sensation. His arm was around Tsu-Choi; she took his hand and moved it up to cup her breast, leaning her head on his shoulder.

"Certainly, apprentice." She nodded judiciously. "These seem like ver' nice peoples . . . people? All the' same, I'm *not* having you rolled; another rule, never drop your pants alone an' drunk in a place you're jus' passing through. Bad habit an' gets you deaded. I mean morted. I mean killed. Not here, sometime. Gotta teach you."

Tsu-Choi swayed against him. "But, uh, *khyd-hird,* I thought you and the Captain—"

Shkai'ra nodded again, sidestepped and caught herself with a graceful sway and dip. "So we are, boy, but I gotta remind myself what it looks like in action sometimes . . . Anyways, you wan' stand here and talk all night or fuck that nice girl, or what?"

The barmaid stopped his lips with a kiss and began to walk backward. He followed, stumbling, utterly unwilling to break the soft contact. Her tongue probed between his teeth; he started, caught at her. *Gothumml*, now *what am I supposed to do*, he thought. *Nobody told me she'd put her* tongue *in my* mouth, *oh, Gothumml* . . .

She broke the contact, laughing, seized him by the hand and led him through the room to the screen of beads amid ironic cheers from those at the tables; he could taste her on his lips, mint and garlic and wine. Up a winding staircase through the coarse pumice rock. Into a cubicle, narrow, utter darkness, stuffy—a collision behind him in the doorway, giggles. The scritch of a sulfur match, and a smoking taper flared redly. He looked about: two low narrow bedsteads, with cotton ticks and thin pillows, a stand with jug and basin and a few changes of clothing folded underneath it.

Tsu-Choi turned from lighting the candle and smiled at him, slowly undoing the lacings of her tunic and drawing it over her head. His hands seemed to reach out of their own wishing, trembling, closed on the soft roundedness of her breasts and kneaded. The Rand girl hissed and closed her eyes, back arching, hands urging his head down to her; he took the hard smoothness of a nipple between his lips, oblivious to her fingers releasing the fastenings of his clothes. Oblivious until suddenly he was naked and the small work-hardened hand closed around the shaft of his penis. He cried out again, and tears flowed from under his closed lids.

"Oh, young sir, you're in pain," she whispered. He blinked through lashes starred with tears to see her dropping breeches and loincloth to the floor, lying back on the pallet, opening arms and knees. "Here," she said.

"Come *on*, boy," Shkai'ra was saying, with a grunt as she pulled on her boot. "It must be thirdwatch at least."

Francosz stayed kneeling beside the pallet for a moment longer; he was fully dressed, except for the undone lacings of his shirt. The second candle had guttered down to a stub, and

the tiny room smelled of tallow and late night and musky sex.
He could see the Rand girl smiling at him through a tangled
mist of black hair; he felt . . . *empty*, he decided. *A little
sore. Sad. Happy. As though the whole world is different.*

Francosz picked up her hand and patted it awkwardly.
"Thank you, Tsu-Choi," he said. "That was . . . thank you
very much."

Tsu-Choi stretched and raised herself up on one elbow to
kiss him a final lingering time, without heat. "Your very first;
you remember Tsu-Choi always, eh, young gentleman?" He
nodded. "So. You remember Tsu-Choi, be nice to all your
girls like tonight." She lay back and sighed, stretched again.

Shkai'ra's arm was around his shoulders as they ducked out
of the tavern door; the snow had stopped, fallen a handspan
deep, but the cold struck through his clothes to dry the sweat
on his skin with shivering. The Kommanza drew her cloak
about them both; his was still bundled about her winnings;
looked up at a night dense with stars.

"Life's full of good things, *nia*, youngling?"

He nodded wordlessly, too full of the evening to speak.

She yawned hugely. "Like hangovers . . . Pint of water and
then to bed."

Shkai'ra closed the door of the cabin behind her after
Francosz settled in next to Sova; the look of stunned revela-
tion was still on his face as he pulled the tick over his
shoulder and dropped instantly unconscious. She stood a
moment looking down on them, shook her head and bent to
tuck a corner of the quilt about Sova's hand. The girl had
been already fast asleep, huddled under the feathers, her
hand clutched around the coin she'd bored a hole through
and strung on a thong.

The Kommanza heard a raspy snore in the dark as she
entered the cabin and swung the door quietly to, struck a
match. The lamp had burned out, empty, and the glass
chimney was thick black with soot. She sighed, wobbled out
to grab a candle from the cupboard.

In the wispy yellow light she saw Megan sitting on the
floor, head tilted back on the bed, mouth open, snoring.

The tray stood on the table, all the food congealed, cold. The Saekrberk bottle stood next to her and two glasses, one broken off its base. Ten-Knife lay on the bed, curled up on the long black fan of Megan's hair.

She sighed, dumped the contents of the plates out the sterncastle windows and stacked them on the tray, undressed and lifted Megan to the bed. The Zak stirred and muttered as her lover pulled off her clothes and tucked her under the covers, arranged the pot and the pitcher of water within easy reach, blew out the candle and climbed over her by starlight to slide beneath the blankets on the outboard side.

Ah, Megan, my heart's delight, she thought drowsily, as the Captain of the *Zingas Vetri* nuzzled closer in her sleep, her breath carrying the strong green smell of Saekrberk. Her hand stroked the other's cheek; she smiled in the darkness, ready for sleep but not quite to relinquish the contentment of the moment. *How I wish to make all things well for you.* She closed her eyes, listening to the soft breathing beside her cheek and the lapping of the harbor beneath.

"It's a cage," Uen said.

Habiku's expression stayed one of polite interest, but the Arkan pen bore down on the linen paper of the ledger on a growing blot. He looked down at it with a brow-arch of polite interest and turned to Lixa.

"Blot this," he said. "Then finish the totals. Not here, you brainless cunt, take it out." To himself, wonderingly, "It was a coincidence. Those prophecies, they're mind-sickness and hysterics. Nothing!"

"Prophecy?" the Zak noble said, reaching for a candied fig. He bit into it, worked sugared syrup off his teeth with his tongue. "I wonder what these are like fresh?" he said idly.

Habiku cleared his throat and looked up, up the three stories to the alabaster roof and the stars beyond. "I hope Lixa was satisfactory?" he asked.

"Oh, most," Uen said. "Thank you again. A little too passive and docile at first, but with the right stimulus . . ." He watched the red flush creep up the naZak's neck with satisfaction; a humiliation to him, and the punishments would be just recompense to the cold-loined bitch of a bondservant as well.

"And this cage?"

"Oh, a conceit of Megan Whitlock's; very . . . very Zak, if I may say so. Perhaps a little old-fashioned, rather Middle Quarter. The homing bird report waxed quite detailed, considering the cost—it must have impressed the audience no end. The cage is of steel bars, set in a mesh; just the size to confine a man . . ." He looked at the tall form of the naZak in the lounger. ". . . a tall man, so that he could neither sit nor stand. A lock that can only be fastened once."

He lifted a finger to the arch above them. "And a steel ring to hang it by: the report says she stood on the deck of her ship, *Zingas Vetri*, and called the Cold Curse on you, sir ClawPrince: and that you would dwell in the cage, hung from this very roof, until you died." He laughed. "A pleasant conceit, is it not?"

Habiku looked up; his eyes narrowed.

Uen was standing, and Habiku was suddenly conscious of having no recollection of how he had come to be so, or of the passing time.

"Well, the DragonLord awaits." The usual formalities passed more emptily than usual.

Chapter 14

**THREE DAYS NORTH OF RAND
FOUR DAYS SOUTH OF AENIR'SFORD
ELEVENTH IRON CYCLE, SECOND DAY**

Megan rested a hand on the wheel to judge the current's pull on the hull, and called forward, "Ilge, Mateus, stand by!" The sail came down with a rattle and she called again, "Pull! Rudder full starboard."

The helm crew spun the wheel, while the *hortator* relayed commands to the rowing deck.

"Hard starboard pull!" The oarsmen on the right leaned into the stroke, the port chopped their oars down into the current and braced, and the *Zingas Vetri* swung smoothly into the shelter of the bluff, the last sun of the day reddening the black-flecked, grey rock outcropping.

Megan nodded. "Away anchor!" The two deckhands in the bow swung their mallets against the wedges holding the anchor. The spokeless capstan whirled, blurring, with a hint of frying oil, as the greased wooden bearings squealed. A splash, and the hum of cable paying out of the ropewell; the eddy in the still pool turned the ship's stern downstream.

"Well done," Megan said. "Francosz, you can take the first watch with Stanver and Alexa and the others."

The boy looked about, shivering, then saw his sister watching.

He drew himself up with a casual air. "Aye, Captain," he

called. Sova stuck out her tongue at him and fled giggling up the ratlines to the crows-nest as he jumped down from the foc'sle and pursued, whirling a rope's end in mock ferocity. Shkai'ra looked after them, then up at Megan; she raised an eyebrow as she strolled nearer.

"Aye, Captain," she murmured. "Splice the mizzenmast; look hearty now . . . I can see why I've never been enthusiastic about being a parent before: their energy ages you."

"Of course, as teacher," Megan replied *sotto voice* as the chase came around to them again, "you have to stay ahead of them, old *baba*." Francosz lunged after Sova; his sister retreated squealing, then dashed around Megan and Shkai'ra to kick his backside before he could catch up or turn around.

"Right. Look here." Megan's voice rose as the two children spun around them, almost grabbing, dodging back and forth. "Since you have so much energy, Sova, you can take the second watch." The girl slowed. Francosz ran into her, and both of them piled into Shkai'ra, who stood with arms crossed, looking severe. They stopped, aghast.

"You're not ready to braid warrior's locks yet," she growled. "Go bother Piatr, he said something about needing help with that sweet-biscuit batter. Fast, or you'll do it standing!" The Kommanza watched them dash forward, one corner of her mouth quirking upward. Sighing, she pivoted on one heel and examined their surroundings.

"You know," she said, "once we settle things in F'talezon, I might adopt them. Of course, I'd have to be married, you need a couple of parents at least. Like to have a couple more of my own, too."

Megan turned toward her, eyes lighting with the almost-smile that rarely touched her lips. "Why, *akribhan*," she said gently, reaching out to touch her on the arm. "Is that a proposal? Shall we consult a *bayishka* to settle the portions?"

"Something to think about, at least," Shkai'ra said, returning the touch and glancing up at the overhang.

"Indeed it is," Megan said. Her tone grew somber. "My son . . . Sarngeld sold him away, before I killed the Arkan filth. That remains to be done, once the House of the Sleeping Dragon is cleansed."

"Right," Shkai'ra said. "We'll find a way . . . Gloomy damn place to stop, *nia*?"

Astern, upstream, the Hanged Man's Rock was darkening. The west bank of the river downstream was bluffs, fifty meters high and jagged, scrub oak shaggy with mistletoe, thickets of holly drooping branches into the still water. Beyond, the bank curved still more sharply; she could hear the racing current upstream, where the river narrowed. Eastward were marshes, rank odors drifting from a maze of channels and islands and mudflats; abruptly a heavy, coughing grunt came over the air, deepening into a roar.

"I can see why you'd stop here before making the run up the narrows, though. Good spot to rest the rowers; I'd have expected a settlement."

Megan lashed the wheel back to its chocks, cocking a critical eye at the deck below, where tarpaulins were being lashed down and night-lanterns set.

"There was. A settlement here, I mean: over there, where the swamp is now, eight–nine hundred years or so ago. Ilge," she called, interrupting herself. "Second anchor tonight."

"Aye!"

"Anticipating the foul weather, then," Shkai'ra said, looking up at the feathery clouds called mare's-tails.

"Yes." Megan closed the lid of the navigation box set just before the wheel, and sealed it, continuing, "It was called Ore-Yinsk, but nobody remembers who the people were; the Thanes burned it, when they first came to the Brezhan."

Task finished, she moved closer to Shkai'ra and leaned against her, pointing up to the pinnacle on the left bank. "Then they took their captives up there—the opposite slope's more walkable—and forced them to jump. The legend goes that the last one turned and cursed the Thane leader, him and his descendants."

Megan turned, gestured, right hand then left. The familiar shiver/tingle of the ship-wards sprang up, the orangey-red flicker that faded to a dusty feeling on the back of the teeth; she turned back to the Kommanza.

Shkai'ra shivered and made the sign against ill luck with her sword hand. "Did it stick?"

"For him, at least. There weren't many of the Thanes then, those were the first, a trickle before the torrent. The other towns upstream and down made an end of them; attacked their new settlement in the night. The Thanes made their last stand on Hanged Man's Rock.

"The Zaki took the leader and hung him there at dawn, along with the others who surrendered, though his son and daughter weren't found. Their bodies were thought to have been lost in the river. Since then, this spot's been considered unlucky: people have tried to found a town now and then, but something always happens: nosferatu, or werewolves; monsters, if you believe the stories. There are even tales that sailors jump ship here, although a more unlikely spot to desert couldn't be found."

Shkai'ra looked up; the moon was nearer full now, bright, but occasionally veiled by ragged ends of hard-driven cloud. The wind was rising.

"You know how to make a person comfortable, don't you, kh'eeredo?"

"You asked," Megan said. "By now you should know better than to ask a storyteller's daughter. That one's usually kept for scaring children." There was a quiet smile hidden in the words. "Children, hunh." The tall woman shook her shoulders, looking down at the top of Megan's head. "Let's go eat. If we don't hurry, I suspect Piatr's sweet biscuits will all be roped and branded."

Francosz had spent most of his watch pacing about the deck, fighting the effects of fresh air, hard exercise, two bowls of fish stew, barley bread, ale and a biscuit-eating competition with his sister. *Hand of the Hunter*, he thought, rubbing his stomach with a belch, *the little wench has hollow legs!* She was good company lately, better than she had ever been before. He pulled the collar of his sheepskin jacket up and sank down against the mainmast, hugging his knees, yawning and watching his breath puff before the chill breeze swept it away. The stars that you could still see between clouds were very bright in a night that crackled crisp with frost; it would be good to squirm into his pallet, pulling the feather tick up to his chin, its warm weight comforting. Tomorrow, Shkai'ra would start him on the bow; she'd said he was late for it anyway, but he might show well enough to use a wheelbow of his own. *Barbarian*, he thought from habit, and yawned again. *But she knows some good tricks.* The five sailors were all at their posts; he wouldn't sleep, just lay his head on his knees for a moment . . .

Alexa leaned over the rear rail. There was little reason for so many on the watch. What could happen, here? Still, you never knew. This place was cursed, you could almost smell it—then she checked herself. A sound—like oars, but there was enough light from the moon to see that no hull disturbed the waters. When the three-meter turtleback shape broached beneath the stern she paused for a moment, eyes giving information that mind could not understand. *A beast?* she thought. The top of the shape folded back, moonlight glinting off the oiled leather of the covering. It was the smell that snapped her attention back; old corruption, excrement and rotting flesh and bodies that had never washed; the smell of a prison, a slaughterhouse, a slave barracks. She opened her mouth to shout; there was a moment's pain, the sensation of falling, then nothing.

The Karibal caught the unconscious body, a dozen hands reaching up from the pikeboat to help him. Quickly he unwrapped the leather cord of his bola from the Prettie's neck, slapping away the taloned fingers of his sibs. "For the cave, for the cave!" he hissed, despite the grumbling protest of his stomach. "More, fresh, Now-Meat—go up."

Vilelem was one of the Wise Ones; he knew what must be done, and remembered words. "Quiet. Quick," then the series of tongue clicks for emphasis that they understood better. With a whining slobber, they followed him over the rail.

Ilge had been facing forward. There had been no sound behind her, rather a movement of the air. She wheeled, saw only shadows as a cloud covered the moon, then the light shining from corpse-colored eyes, spidery arms and legs swarming over the rail and the bola trapped the lungful of air she drew to scream. Her hand was caught to her neck by the weapon; the night-lantern fell to the deck and broke, splashing oil that burst into flames.

They swarmed over her in silence. The other boat had taken two more of the deck crew, but there was still the last to be taken. And it must be done without sound, or they would have to take the ship; very bad, to sink too many. Too many, and the Enemies might guess. They rushed forward, flanking where he was just turning. One of the Karibal, intent on prey, fell over Francosz who woke in tumbled confusion, sprawling on the planking. All he saw was the flicker, yelled, "Fire!", was clubbed into silence. Mikail shouted and went down. On the afterdeck, oil-flame sank into dry timber. The creatures dragged the two crew members with them as they fled.

"FIRE!" Below, the cry had been taken up. The boy felt unseen hands gripping him, thin but wire-strong; the world twisted by in bewilderment; he saw the Captain and Shkai'ra burst onto the deck just as he was pushed overboard.

His head cleared as he hit the water. Naked stick-men held him and dragged him into a boat.

"What . . ." and the smell hit him, thick and clutching. He gagged then, retched, vomiting helplessly as his hands were lashed together by the one that looked most human.

"Quick!" it snapped. "Row fast!" Behind the four rowers, another was clutching Ilge close to it. "Prettteeee . . . softpretteee. Nice-nice," it crooned and stroked her. She was still unconscious.

He opened his mouth to scream in the hooded darkness of the boat. The human-like one hissed, and a fist clubbed him over the ear. "Quiet, Fresh-Meat."

The wards broke. Once set, they needed little attention; it was like walking while you sang, like breathing. The rupture was missing the last step and smashing a bare foot into a pit of broken glass; it was inhaling hot oil; it was a steel cord stretched between the ears snapping and rebounding off the inside of the skull. Megan's cry of pain was wordless as she convulsed in her sleep, clutching. The cry of "fire!" and Shkai'ra's shriek followed, as ten sharp steel nails closed on the Kommanza's back. Shkai'ra spun into the center of the cabin, the long dagger from under the pillow in her hand.

"—like sleeping with a rabid wolverine—" she half-snarled. Then the narrow blonde head snapped up.

"Fire!" They plunged into the corridor. The crew were up and moving. A tar-soaked wooden ship, old and sun-dried, piled with bleached canvas, hempen rope like a slow-match; fire was the monster that would eat them. Shkai'ra hurdled Sova with a raking stride, bending her head to avoid the beam.

"UP, this is no *zteafakaz* drill, *move*, girl."

Megan clawed her way up the ladder, heedless of the solid smack of rungs under feet, hands that struck rather than gripped, throwing her body upward to burst through the open hatch. *Mine!* went through her as she landed crouching, the unnoticed chill roughening her bare skin. "My ship, my people—"

The last of the Karibal was disappearing over the rail as the Captain of the *Zingas Vetri* gained the quarterdeck. Two of her knives had come with her, the tips of the slim hilts gripped between knuckles to leave her free to grip; her right wrist twitched and the point was between thumb and fingers, hand cocked back over her shoulder, the motion oil-smooth and accurate. The creature was man-shaped; poised on the rail, she saw it jerk, spasm, arch backward to fall and drum its heels. As it fell, the second throw faded to a flip that put the hilt in her hand. She wheeled. The fire was a pool, spreading, licking at the base of the rear mast.

"Mateus!"

"Aye! Bucket chain read—"

"Not water, sand! That fire's oil, water will spread it. Sand first. Crew count—" The orders flowed, as smooth and hard-driven as the knife casts, the crew acting as the fingers of a hand. "—and I'll light the storm lamps."

"Teik Captain, do you think that's necessary?" Megan turned to her first mate, a blackness against the deeper black of the bank, darkness laced with the grey of rigging.

"It's tiring, but I want light to see what's out there. Finish that crew count!"

The slight Zak put both hands before her and began to hum, a sound that began deep in bone and spiralled up past hearing. Her mind sank into the sound, expanded, grew conscious of the mast and stays as a pattern of contained, whirling energies. Energies that could be tapped, pushed, manipulated. There were two spots on the cross-spar that were presensitized to her thought; costly, valuable in saved energy. Her hands snapped apart, stabbing to point at them. In answer, orange-red light glowed on the wood, witch-fire spreading to outline the furled sail and the heavy lines that anchored mast to fore and backstay. Witch-fire that gave light but did not burn.

Her face set, she turned to Shkai'ra, holding the backlash of power at bay by the force of her will. Air and river and night supplied the power for the light, but her own body's energy must guide and control it. The moon was a dull-pearl glow behind low cloud, and she was suddenly conscious of the cold, a wind that bit on her bare skin and smelled of the iron damp that ran before an early winter storm. She shook her head. Behind her, the crew was killing the last of the oil-fire and there were more things to think about. The thing. The Kommanza had kept sensibly aside while the trained teamwork of the crew dealt with the fire. She had focused on a human enemy, or at least an enemy of flesh; she knelt by the form of the one Megan had killed, her round shield leaning against her shoulder. Cold iron dimpled her skin slightly, gathered hoarfrost that sparkled in the ruddy glow of the light.

"Ahi-a," the Kommanz said, examining the body. It was small, no more than 130 centimeters; male, and thin almost to emaciation. Shkai'ra wasn't fastidious, even now that she had left the ways of her homeland and taken to bathing more than once a month, but the curdled stink of it was enough to make her gag; worse than a battlefield three days old under hot sun. The creature's face was covered in matted hair that might have been dirty blond under its coating oil, all except for the enormous eyes, now glazed, eyes of a night creature. Thin black lips were drawn back from sharp yellow teeth; bits of rotting meat were caught in the beard, lumps of filth and excrement in the almost-pelt that covered its body. That was mold-white and naked, except for a leather belt and necklace of bones. Megan pulled her knife free, careful to touch only her dagger, clotting blood dribbling on the deck as it rolled to its back. "What . . . what is it?" one of the crew asked.

"A man," the Kommanz replied.

"Captain—" Piatr began. Sova interrupted; she'd been carefully not looking at the body, and had had time to look around.

"Francosz!" She called, then turned to Shkai'ra. "*Khydhird*," she whispered. "Teacher, where's my brother?"

"—the night watch are missing: all five, and the Thane brat."

"I know why," Shkai'ra said, lifting the corpse's necklace with a belaying pin. "These are human fingerbones, they've been charred and split—this leather, in the belt . . ." She looked up at Sova and didn't finish what she was going to say. *Human leather*. The Thane girl swallowed, choked, swallowed again. Shkai'ra continued, "So we know why they took the bodies . . ." She scanned the deck, her eyes narrowed; the witchlight was nearly as good as daylight.

"Not enough blood for them all to have been killed." The Thane girl felt the edges of her vision blacken and saliva run into her mouth; the world spun. The strength that stiffened her spine came from within: fainting won't help.

"We've got to . . . to find him!" she half shrieked. Megan looked up to where Danyai stood at the junction of mast and yard.

"Nothing, Captain! Water's bare as a baby's backside!" The crew shifted, their eyes pale in the glow of moon and storm light. Her skull felt empty, like the water around them. Where had they gone? It was impossible.

"Where are they?" Clouds were thick across the moon's face, the sharp knife-edge of the frost riding the wind, rattling the sails. Her eyes swivelled from Sova's frightened face to the body, her arms hugging her bare torso against the wind. She tested her tiredness like the cautious probing of a tongue against a loose tooth.

Megan eased on her control of the light and it dimmed to a

flicker, put out her hand to Sova's forehead. *Storm light control easing. Thought-kin. Energy puddled in the living. From her hand, warmth. Color. Lifebeat speeded—close, closer—and matched. Blood knew blood.* The girl's hands fell limp and she swayed slightly; Shkai'ra steadied her before she could fall.

Megan went rigid, her voice a harsh mutter. "Blood to blood, kin and kin. Find him, child. Feel with yourself. Find him. As if your hands could reach and touch his shoulder. Your brother. He teases you, makes fun of you, loves you as his little sister. See him—" her voice was speeding, "—lock of hair falling in his face when he laughs . . ." and had eerily taken on the rhythms of Sova's speech. Both their heads turned to Hanged Man's Rock.

"Down?" The Zak muttered. The strain was mounting, and the direction made no sense. Down? There was nothing there but the Rock, a solid kilometer of it. "Darkness," she murmured. "Stink and moving . . ." The sensation came through. That was a boat, unmistakable, the fluid rocking surge; the panting rhythmic grunt of rowers . . . A hide boat, but why the . . . dimpled feeling of pressure where the boy's hand rested on hull-frame and covering? And the darkness was absolute, not night-dark but cave-black, absolute.

"It makes no sense!" she spat, coming to herself a little.

Shkai'ra watched the pointing hand. Her face was tight, immobile but somehow ugly with controlled passion, a winter rage that left her mind as clear as glass. "Try harder!" It was impossible for the attackers to have gotten out of sight anyway . . . But a precise fix was their single hope. Her head turned to Megan. The Zak hadn't often heard Shkai'ra use the snarling rasp that was the command voice of a Kommanz aristocrat, but there was no mistaking it.

"Try harder, woman! That kinless little bastard is khyd of my herd, no maneater's going to split his bones for the marrow! We're finding them and going a-rescue." Shkai'ra clamped control, and thought: *or to avenge.*

For a moment sheer fury almost snapped Megan from her concentration. *She's got no right to command me, not on my own deck.* The anger was unlike her companion; it was rooted in concern for the boy; the two of them had been together three years now, and still surprised one another. She breathed deep, caught hold of the manrauq and steadied it in her mind. Steel-Sister, or no . . . Akribhan—Her lips tightened.

"Your suggestion has merit. Mateus, see that carrion pitched overboard." She firmed her link to Sova.

The girl's thought tightened, clamping the line to her brother. *Francosz, brother. Dislike, love worry, Francosz, Francosz, Francosz*—Megan was stretched to the limits of her strength, her mind pulling like a piece of heated caramel candy from a street vendor on Jahrand-day stretching thinner and thinner . . . She threw her head back, teeth showing, eyes blind and, unnoticed, the witchlight flared from red-orange to brilliant orange, lighting the water and swelling against the dark, stark shadow and bleaching light on the faces of the crew. Then yellow, a flicker of green-blue, violet and the color beyond that the eye cannot see. Her hand rose further, then dropped.

"Down," she gasped, throat straining to reach a strange voice, then dropping to Francosz's baritone. "Down, underwet notnice, they say. There, there, rockthroatswallows—where are they taking me? Help me *khyd-hird*, it stinks, Sova, Captain, Father, cave under stone. Cave. Cave in the rock. NNNOOOOOO!"

The Zak's eyes rolled back into her head, leaving only the white; shaking tension turned to bonelessness. Shkai'ra and Piatr were there as she struck the wood, easing the fall, while Norvanak steadied Sova.

"You did it," Shkai'ra said with quiet exultation. Then with quick concern, "She's going into shock—quick, blankets, gather below."

"No . . . not yet. Down—in a cave. Entrance . . . there. Go, quickly, damn weakness . . ."

Shkai'ra eased the tiny form of her lover to the deck, feeling the shaking of the small, compact body. The witchlight faded; there was a hissing from the north, and the moon dimmed as denser cloud swept in. Stinging, the hard-driven sleet struck her back. For the briefest of moments she stroked Megan's hair. "Well done, kh'eeredo-mi," she murmured, then straightened. "Get her below," she repeated. "Warmth, something hot and sweet to drink when she can take it."

"I know how to treat overstrain!" Piatr snapped. Sova came up from below where she had disappeared when Megan's collapse had released her. She was trembling, stripped to her clout and shirt. Belted about that was the daggerbelt Shkai'ra had had made for her; she bore the Kommanza's weapon-harness and saber. Shkai'ra hesitated, then did not forbid. *Kin-tie*, she thought. The crew hesitated. "We're going after them, Mateus, aren't we?" a voice called.

"I'll go." Jimha stepped forward, then Yuri and Vodolac and Osman, who Habiku had cast off with no recourse in Volhinios.

Mateus inclined his head but said, "My duty. I must stay. She'd kill me if I left the ship with her unable to command." Shkai'ra nodded.

"Objections to who leads?" she snapped. "Good." Piatr began to speak, but she cut him off. "Your courage isn't in doubt. If you volunteer, your sanity is. The rest of you, get a weapon you can use in a confined space." She strapped the crossed belts over her chest and secured the saber to her back, stepping to the rail. Water was black below. "Piatr . . ." She paused. The cabin-kid, Bocina, was just coming up with a wooden crock that she placed on the deck.

"It's butter," Piatr said. "Grease to protect you from the water." She hawked and spat.

"Good. Five minutes is all I'd have given us, in that." The volunteers were coating themselves from the crock while she spoke. "Breathe deep while you wait! Who's the best swimmer? We'll need a scout."

They looked at each other. Vodolac stepped forward with a forced grin.

"I swim best; swim like a river otter, I used to dive-fish for lobster on coast when I was a lad."

Piatr greased Vodolac's back, then Shkai'ra's. His face was drawn and set. *Shouldn't squeeze through my fingers like that. Get it on her, not the crock or the deck.*

"Don't forget the neck . . . All right, Vodolac: no heroics, just find out what's down there and back." He nodded, staring over the side as Osman slapped him encouragingly on the shoulder. Then he hopped to the rail and dived, scarcely even a splash in the sleet-dimpled water. Shkai'ra grunted: he did look to be the best. Her own water skills were good but no more, natural strength and wind compensating for a late start. No knowing if there was air within swimming reach of the cave entrance. No knowing at all, and drowning in the dark if they guessed wrong.

She felt Sova shivering beside her. "*Hoi, wadiki,*" she said. The flask came; she took one long swallow and passed it around. "Just a little; a little makes you feel warmer, even if you aren't." Water might not be her element, but she understood cold well enough. Stooping, she spoke quietly to Sova, holding the girl's eyes with hers. "Just remember what I showed you. That knife's long, and sharp. Remember Megan's lessons. To kill quickly with a knife you have to slash, less chance of losing it on a bone or a muscle-clamp, too." She felt the sleet sting even through the grease, soaking to the scalp, beating on her shoulders. "Keep your thumb on the guard, point down and cut backhand and up; across the belly if you can, or along an arm that's reaching for you. And don't think, just do, understand?"

Sova's face was still, but there was less wildness in her eyes. And Vodolac broke surface, gasping.

"Just where the Captain said," he said. "Never would've got it without, there's an overhang—goes up once you're inside. No sign of light."

Shkai'ra jerked a hand at Mateus. "A closed firepot," she said, hoping it would last the journey. "Torches." The things' eyes were huge, night-eyes; they would need a flame. It came, and one of the crewfolk hitched it to his knifebelt.

The Kommanza stepped to the rail. "Let's go," she said, and leapt.

Megan opened her eyes in time to see them go over the side, trying to rise on one elbow, shaking muscles too weak to hold her. She gritted her teeth and locked her elbows.

"I'm . . . I'm all right!"

"Aye, Captain," Piatr said but didn't move from his place, and caught her when she fell back, her mind flickering in and

out of the minds of those she had just touched, with no
control; contact raw, like a harsh brush on sensitive skin. Any
touch was painful and clear as the Lady's Fountain.

*I'm wet. It's dark and stinks. No Khyd-hird! Who's scream-
ing? Alexa? No, get away! It bit me. There are more,
get away . . . Child? Eyes in the dark. No don't touch
me. He's still alive. No legs, one arm—he's staring at me.
Don't touch me . . . Sova! Captain! Khyd-hird! Aaah, no
you little vermin get away from my ankles. I'm bleeding,
getawaygetawaygetaway . . .*

Uncontrolled, she slid away from Francosz's panic, spiral-
ling into Sova.

I can't see in this. My skin hurts. My lungs hurt. With a
snap and a jolt Megan tried to find her own body, looked out
of eyes, felt her hands and legs and lungs dragging in foul air.
Still in Sova. They looked around from the crouch they were
in. A small cavern from the echoes. Dirt and crusted feces
crumbled till her groping hands broke through to slime and
then stone. They were in the shadow of one of the leather
boats. She swallowed hard when she thought of what leather.
Francosz. I'm afraid.

Then disgust caught at her throat, and the beginnings of
hysterical anger. The others were around her. She could see
dimly now in the faint yellow glow of the creeping patches on
the walls. With a sucking noise one near them dropped loose
and blindly started creeping toward their warmth. She shoved
a knuckle in her mouth and bit down on it, not noticing tears,
and kept still. There was someone, somewhere, screaming. It
echoed, and she didn't want to know where it came from.

Another wrench and Megan touched Shkai'ra, the rage
almost comfortingly warm. *Naik Zhaiz,* she thought and gasped
strength into her with every breath. *Much longer tunnel . . .
at least no damn alligators on my heels. Guard? Only one.
Interested in picking nits off his skin and watching . . . what?
Ah, tunnel to a deeper hole. Zteafakaz echoes. Might be
where he's looking . . . the leather . . . oily enough to burn?
Light.*

Then Megan was swinging in dizzying, nauseating circles
around a darkness. "No, I have to SEE!" She said and struck

out at it, at the smothering dark. "I can't, have to stay
awake . . ."

"No you don't, here," a voice she should know said. "Don't
throw off the blankets. Lie still."

The Karibal leader had thrown back the upper cover of the
turtleboat with relief. The leather was very old; one day they
would have to replace it. They would have to give shinies to
the Enemy who came to the upper cave. He frowned. Why
did the Enemy want shinies? He frowned again: hadn't the
Enemies-who-give-good-things stopped coming, when one of
the non-speakers was at the entrance and ate . . . His brow
cleared. No, that had been long ago; the new Enemies-who-
give-good-things were still coming.

They had said to take the next ship to come alone and they
would, once they had eaten. It was good to have more who
remembered words. Old Father remembered words. He noticed one of the rowers whining and pulling at the coverings
of one of the captured Pretties, making rocking motions as he
fumbled and ripped. Another had a mouthful of a dead man's
arm and was sawing clumsily beneath it with a rusted knife.

"No!" He said. "Take to the Pretty cave, for all Men. We
share; Old Father said to share all thing. For we are Men!"
He kicked the overeager eater. "Put on cloth! Old Father
said to wear cloth. Take Fresh-Meat to Meat Cave. Not start to
eat! Fresh-Meat go bad!"

Proudly, he straightened. The low ceiling of the Boat Cave
was comfort, home. From the low entrance came the excited
cries of the little ones, and the makers. The huge pupils of his
eyes expanded, away from the hurting brightness of the outside, with its bad-lights in the Up. Here the Up was dark,
only the faint yellow gleam of the movegrows. Strutting, he
walked into the Home Cave, followed by the others. It was
long and twisting, always as wide as many Men, sometimes
more. Vilelem halted before a niche, squatting; behind him
gathered the boat-men, carrying the Fresh-Meat, the Now-
Meats, the Pretties. He could smell the blood of the Now-
Meats, rich and salty, smell the Pretties. In the niche was a
skull, larger than the Men he knew, straighter. It had puzzled

him, why Old Father's skull looked like an Enemy's . . . Below it was a sickle-sword, deep-eaten with rust; the pattern was years before.

"Old Father," he said.

Some of those behind him muttered the words; others grunted. There was a moan as one of the Pretties stirred. "Old Father, we be good," he recited in sing-song. "We quiet, no enemies find us. We remember we are Men."

There had been more words once, he thought. But that was all he needed to say. "Go! Go!" he muttered, rising and kicking. "That one, that one—" He pointed to two bodies. "Eat. Others, Meat Cave. Pretties, Pretty Cave." He stopped to wrench loose a thumb, hacking at the joint with a rock; jamming it in his mouth, he led the way. There was no need for Words, this was old custom. The men followed, those who were not too hungry; they settled by the bodies, cuffing the little ones and makers aside to wait their turn. There was only one Pretty in the Pretty cave; many became Meat before long. She cowered aside as they entered, giggling as strings of drool fell on her swollen belly. That was good. The little ones the Pretties made often learned Words; even though the Wise Ones must watch, that nothing ate them. The others were busy, ripping off the clothes and weighing the new Pretties down, many to a limb. One was stirring, mumbling; he knelt between her legs, gripped her, entered, began to pump. The other Men grunted and rocked in chorus. Her eyes opened.

Megan wrenched out of Piatr's grasp with a shriek—"NO, NEVER AGAIN!"—eyes blind; seeing through Alexa's eyes, not her own, clawed and screamed as Alexa could not—mouth blocked by eager, pawing hands, and mouths, weighed down by bodies that rubbed themselves against her, waiting their turn. Alexa got a garbled scream free—anger, horror, rage, fear—and fought with the strength of utter despairing. Alexa, though a Zak, had no power; but Megan did. And for seconds she could "touch" her crewwoman with it, at cost; a killing drain of her power. Piatr slapped her once, twice, trying to break her out of the deadly cycle. He could almost see her

failing, cheeks hollowing, falling in, not even strength to keep
her heartbeat regular. He cut off the arteries in her neck,
barely enough to knock her unconscious, cutting off whatever
she was feeding.

Alexa's body grew hot under their hands and suddenly they
weren't holding a Pretty but a snake that writhed in their
hands and Vilelem tried to push away from what wrapped
around him.

Snake! It had been a snake that killed Old Father's Father!
Wrapped around his neck by the Enemies! Snakes came in
and ate little ones, squeezing, squeezing! Screaming, he voided
bowels and bladder, rearing backward, flailing. The others
exploded outward from the writhing shape, not caring that
their eyes and hands told different tales. Even the group
moaning and rocking by the other Pretty started up, although
not the one mounting; his eyes were squeezed shut. Blindly,
Vilelem struck out. And suddenly was fighting the Pretty
again; an elbow crashed into his throat, and he dropped. The
Pretty was screaming too, tiny Enemy eyes stretched wide
into the dimness. She turned, ran. Her skull met rock with a
dull chunk, and she fell to the rustling dung-matted grass of
the cave's floor. Vilelem moaned, waiting as his breathing
slowed. The Pretty stayed a Pretty. Faces crowded back to
the entrance of the Pretty Cave, those who had fled: the
others had not had time to notice anything unusual, there
was often commotion when a new Pretty was brought in.

"Quick, quick," he gasped hoarsely. "Bring wrapwrap,
wraptight, take to Meat Cave!" But for all his cuffing, none
would approach her. Shrinking, he forced his way back to her
and laid the first loop of leather rope around her. That made
the others bold: they crowded near to finish the binding, and
carry her out. The group about the other Pretty unfroze.
Vilelem clutched his genitals in shock; they were comfortingly present, but he wanted to be sure. Bent over, he ran to
the niche of the skull and crouched beneath it.

"Old Father, make strong," he crooned. "We be good. Old
Father, Old Father! Are we not Men!" There was fresh

screaming from the cave of the Pretties, but it did not reassure him as it should. He would stay with Old Father.

Shkai'ra's head broke surface, and she forced herself to breathe in slowly through her mouth, reaching down to pull Sova up beside her. The others broke surface quickly, moving up the slippery rock slope. The stink was like a blow, numbing the nose and taste buds; the darkness lay on their eyes like spoiled liver, and a confusion of screams, shouts, wails echoed directionless from rock all about them.

"Fire!" she whispered harshly. Jimha fumbled the lid of the firepot open, and they stripped the torches from their fishbladder covers and thrust them into the pot. "Careful, careful, don't put it out for the love of each and every god." She was afraid, she realized with a start. It was a very long time since she had been afraid of danger; the darkness weighed down on her with a physical presence. This was not war, it was like being shrunk tiny and hunted by maggots through their tunnels in a corpse . . .

The light flared. Her sigh of relief turned to a snarl as she saw the sentinel waiting by the narrow exit, starting up and throwing a spindly forearm before its eyes. This cave was small, there must be . . . That was a human voice screaming. She started forward; the shore was slime, then dry, crusted filth on a base of leaves and straw. Her hand went over her shoulder; enough room to draw and strike . . .

A small form darted past her; the torchlight glinted red on the knife in its hand. The Karibal was just straightening up when Sova struck him. Her knife was nine inches, battle-poinard; only the breastbone stopped her hysterical, ripping stroke.

Shkai'ra lunged and dragged Sova back, free of the gutted body. The Thane girl rose; her face was clenched in the torchlight, wet, still sobbing, white about mouth and nose, but the knife in her hand trembled only slightly.

"No time for plans; they'll have seen the light, even with all that noise. Follow me!" Shkai'ra plunged through the slit into the cave beyond. The crewfolk followed, with torch and bared steel.

*   *   *

Francosz was staring fixedly at the man on the floor next to him. The one who was still alive. With no legs and one arm. The screaming and shouts changed pitch once, but he almost didn't notice. Even in the dark, there was enough light from the patches of yellow that were crawling on the man to see that his nose was gone, raggedly, as if worried free of his face. He rubbed leather-bound wrists slowly over the ragged edge of something that he lay on, a bone perhaps.

Mucus was running down his face, tears as well, but if he could wear through the binding . . . "Maaah . . . ahma," he whimpered. "Sssovaah, Shkk'aiii . . . ahhhn . . . nybody." It was a low, dull monotone. The little ones would be back soon. Very far away he saw flicker of fire, shut his eyes, looked again. It was stronger. The screams were changing to panicked squeals as the creatures tried to hide from the light. He heard his name, others, blinked and began to shout, trying to get up on his knees, kicking out against old bones that crumbled.

Megan opened bleary eyes to lie for a minute staring at Piatr's worried face, too weary to do more than lie there and breathe. His face was bloody.

"Did I do that?" she whispered. "Sorry—"

"It's all right, Captain, no worse than a cat." He held a cup to her lips but she turned away.

"What's happened? Are they back?" She turned her head from one side to the other, slowly, every muscle in her neck aching. "I can't even feel your presence, Piatr. I can't—"

"Hush. Overstrain like that could kill you. I don't know what's happening. They'll be back, drink this." Her eyes were already closing and she tried to avoid the cup again, then took it and lay still. She didn't see the worried look Piatr threw out in the direction of the cliff. *Of course they'll be back. Koru, I wish I knew what was happening.*

The things ran before the fire, squealing, blinded, almost spitting themselves on the crew's swords. Shkai'ra hacked through them, shouting for Francosz and the others. With a slow crackle the leather boats caught fire, and the grass on parts of the floor. She felt a strong draught start at her back, heat striking from behind. *Like in a chimney*, she thought, then, "Osman! There might be another way out! Cut them off if you can."

He was to her left and disappeared into the smoky dimness, following the breeze to its way out, to kill these things before they escaped if they could flee through the holes the air used.

Shkai'ra raised her torch and stepped into an annex cave. A movement from the corner of her eye and she wheeled, lashing out with her foot. Her heel punched into the pigeon chest of a Karibal, sending it back against the rock with a crackle of ribs, a rock dropping from its dying hand. A woman was huddled in one corner of the triangular opening, a human woman, hugely pregnant; she blinked and squinted against the light, running her hands over the curve of her stomach.

"Ba-be," she said, and giggled. Shkai'ra looked into her eyes for a moment; the Kommanza's mouth twitched, and she placed the point of her saber against the woman's neck and pushed. There was another figure lying more to the center, spread-eagled; Ilge.

Shkai'ra thought she was dead, then caught a slow rise of her chest. Her body glistened, wet with blood and mucus and semen; there were no serious wounds. "On the body," Shkai'ra said hoarsely. "On the body." Carefully she reached down and stooped to throw the limp form over one shoulder. The main cave was brighter now; the ground cover had caught, and the layer of rancid smoke was falling quickly from the high ceiling, building faster than the draught could carry it away.

Misshapen forms scuttled, most of them very small; the crewfolk stamped and struck with glazed, hysterical passion. She heard Sova call out from another narrow slit, "Francosz! Francosz!"

The Kommanza started forward, coughing with the thickening smoke. She wasn't conscious of that, or the weight on her shoulder, nor of eyes glaring too hard and sore for complete sanity. But when a Karibal darted at her as she strode over smouldering punk she turned, driven by reflex deeper than mind. Alone of the ones she had seen, this one wielded a sword, one-handed, and even in the dim light she could see how time had eaten it. His other paw clutched a skull to his breast. Her automatic parry met it in mid-air, and it snapped. The Karibal froze, unbelieving. Her return snap-thrust speared through his chest, and the skull dropped to the floor where wisps of smoke were rising. The almost-human mouth leaked blood as it fell to its knees, scrabbling for the ancient bone.

"Vadda," it mumbled. "Vilelem isch . . . gud yhunga . . ." and collapsed, great eyes staring.

Shkai'ra halted for a moment, kicked it out of her path; an impulse made her stoop to pick up the broken hilt. "What—" she began as she sidled into the smaller cave, stopped, turned her head aside, forced it back. Sova was withdrawing her knife from the mutilated figure lying beside her brother and Mikail, the two still alive. Wordless, Shkai'ra cut Francosz's bonds, slapped him sharply when he swayed.

"No time for that! Get Mikail, this place is going to burn!" They retreated, coughing, crouched to avoid the worst of the thick smoke. Francosz kicked one of the little ones loose from Mikail's leg where it clung, gnawing. The others joined them at the pool. Furnace heat was on their skins; the air seemed thin to straining lungs, eyes dried; Shkai'ra could feel the draught of the fire increasing, beginning to pulse.

Vodolac was the last out of the main cave. "Other way out . . . I blocked it, Red-hair. Don't think any are left," he coughed. The one boat was a roaring mass of flames, the other was smoking. Shkai'ra could feel the hairs on her arms crisp and curl, smelled scorching hair. Beneath her feet, the smouldering punk was becoming painful.

"Out! Yuri, take Alexa, Vodolac—Mikail, Sova—help your brother. Out!" she slapped Ilge's face lightly. "Ilge! Wake up, hold your breath, hear me? Hold your breath." She hoped that there was a spark of understanding in the woman's eyes, thrust Ilge's hands under the weapons belt to free her own arms for swimming; the woman a dead weight on her back. *Don't drown now*, she thought, and plunged into the wel-come relief of the cold river.

*   *   *

The sleet was still hissing against the sterncastle windows when Megan awoke; grey afternoon light lay on the wool, a sad undertone to the warmer flicker of the lamp. Shkai'ra rose as she saw the Zak's eyes open, knelt to put a supporting arm under her shoulders and hold a cup to her lips.

"Beef tea," she said with a smile. "You look like a reject quarry slave; whatever that spook-pushing does, it takes energy." Megan drank, then hugged Shkai'ra closer. "I saw . . . bits," she said. "Did you get everyone out? My crew? And what was it . . . like in there?" Shkai'ra looked out over her shoulder, at a rock where smoke still whisped from crevices.

"Ilge, Alexa, Mikhail, Francosz . . . Safe. The others are dead; dead and cremated, with everything else in there. As to what it was like . . ." She paused. "You don't want to know," she said. Megan nodded, then a faint, puzzled frown crossed her face. "I . . . was angry with you. Did I dream that?" The Kommanza laid her back on the pillows.

"I don't remember it," she said and nodded to an ancient, broken sword in the corner.

"They had that," she said. "Seemed to think highly of it. What the hell is it?"

Megan blinked, focusing. "Sickle-sword," she said. "Thane, no doubt of it. Old, old, though. I've seen drawings of swords like that in records of the Thane migrations, from when they first came to the riv—" She halted, stiffening, turning to glance at the rock and back to Shkai'ra. "Hanged Man's Rock," she whispered. "The Thane leader's son and daughter—*nine hundred*! Koru, nine hundred years in there!"

She blanched and fell back onto the pillows. Shkai'ra hastily picked up a slat of board wrenched from the type of box used to ship Zak dried beef. There was a symbol branded into the thin wood. "Osman picked this up," she said. "In the outer cave, while he was blocking the main land exit. They had some gauds piled up there, bolts of cloth, that sort of thing: I'd say they'd been taking ships as well—at a guess, boring holes in the bottom. And fencing the loot to somebody."

Megan stared wide-eyed at the board. Her hands clenched on the bedframe. "That's the trade-seal of my House. Habiku!

Habiku was dealing with those things, he probably set them on us . . ."

"Hush, think about it later, sleep," Shkai'ra said.

"Sleep! I . . ." Megan stopped, blinked and yawned. "More exhausted than I thought," she mumbled in a small voice.

Should be sleepy, with the draught in that broth, Shkai'ra thought, stroking her hair and humming until Megan drifted into troubled sleep, lines still creasing her forehead. *Habiku*, the Kommanza thought, looking at the board. *Habiku, I would have killed you for my kh'eeredo's sake. Now you're piling up a debt to me personally.*

Chapter 15

AENIR'SFORD
ELEVENTH IRON CYCLE, SEVENTH DAY

"Get—back—into—bed!" Shkai'ra said, as the tunic settled over her head. Megan pulled her foot back from the rug and sat cross-legged on the rumpled bunk, her back to the ledge and sterncastle windows. Outside, the last of the night's snow was flicking past, big soft flakes turning dawnlight to a pearly grey.

From somewhere came a faint rhythmic chanting and creaking, as a ship was warped out of the water into a winterquarters slip.

The cabin was dark, and chill enough to raise ridges on Megan's skin. Both women ignored it, being used to worse.

"Why?" Megan asked. "You going to stop dressing and come back to hand-feed me something hideously expensive like peeled grapes?" She felt around on the floor for her boots with her feet, not wanting to tilt her head around far enough to look; it might make her head hurt worse. "When we're married, will you nag me like this whenever I'm sick?"

"Incessantly," Shkai'ra said. "And if getting back in is the only thing that will keep you flat . . . all right." She began pulling the tunic back over her head. "If you really *want* me to come back to bed, it's a better way to spend the morning than arguing with chandlers, but you're not getting up or doing anything strenuous until you've recovered."

AENIR'SFORD
TWELFTH IRON CYCLE, SIXTH DAY

hose-stream from a second pump-barge struck the burning mast. A huge soft *thump* of steam, and then a cannon-crack as the tough white pine pole split, crashing, hissing as it fell, and the upper half plunged into the harbor. Some distant part of her cursed the bargecrew for idiots; that could have fallen on them, or back along to the stern and guaranteed the loss of the ship.

The prybar-wielder spoke again: "Teik Captain, the sterncastle windows're open, if we bring the door down the flames—look, you can see light from under the sill, there must be fire at the base of the stairs."

"I have people in there. *Open the door!*" The two harbor workers looked at each other, shrugged, pulled the water-soaked clothes back up over their faces and attacked the wood. The door had jammed into the frame as the ship twisted in the water, groaning. It opened in a shower of white oak splinters, and there was a belch of smoke and hot, dead air as the door opened. The fire at the base of the stair-ladder had been small, for lack of draft; now it sent a tongue licking up at them, and the axeman stumbled back with a yell.

A hand thrust a wetted cloth at her. She snatched it, held it over her face and crowded recklessly close.

"It's small," she said, retreating and snatching at a fresh cloth; the first was dry. "Quick, sand—*there, that barrel there, fishgutted fools*—"

Shyll and Shkai'ra came up at a stumbling run with the hundredweight burden of the chest-high cask between them; sand was always kept under the quarterdeck railing, but the Aenir had not known it was there to use. The two ran the open end of the barrel into the deck-lip at the head of the stairs and stood to it as the damp sand cascaded down, heads craned back from the heat, gasping breaths sucking the wet clothes across the shape of their lips. Megan and Rilla and Sova gathered swift armfuls from a pile of soaked burlap sacks and pitched them through as Kommanza and teRyadn shook out the barrel and threw it bouncing and rattling down the deck toward the seven-foot stump of the mast.

Megan tucked one of the sacks about her head like a shawl,

tied the ends into her belt and dove through head-first,
landing crouched and scuttling forward along the companionway. The smoke was thinning in the upper section, and cold
air was coming in in pulsing blasts from the sterncastle windows, but she could feel a glow like a smith's forge from
overhead. The stubborn oak planks were not burning, not
yet, but the heat from the sail locker overhead was enough
to warp and buckle, the mahogany treenails screaming in
protest as they were ripped from the framing. Embers fell
through, and shreds of burning canvas.

Thumps behind her as the others, Rilla, Shkai'ra, landed.
And another groan hit their ears; a human one. Yvar Monkeyfist
lay where he had crawled, halfway down the corridor from
the ladder.

Sova swarmed down the way, knee-and-handing through
the coals and glass shards to kneel beside the man; his face
was distorted, as if something heavy had struck it on the side
and the bones had flowed away. Blood glistened black in the
fire and *kraumak* light, rough-surfaced with clotting. On his
face, and from the hip joint where the broken stub of a dart
jutted, quivering as he arched to keep it from grating on the
deck, braced on knee and cheek. More blood from the cracks
on his feet where they had lain in the fire before he came
conscious enough to crawl. One eye swollen closed; the other
swivelled to see her, but she couldn't tell if there was anything in it, anything but pain.

"Yvar, lie still." Megan beside the wounded man, sliding a
balk of rope beneath him as Shkai'ra and a dripping Shyll
helped; the heavy wool of the doglord's clothing was already
drying and shrinking. Yvar's mouth moved, but only bubbles
came out of it, and strings of red and gluey white.

"Lie still. We have a litter coming, and a Haian," Megan
said, her voice trembling as much as his bloodsmeared hand,
already hoarse with the need to shout over the noise and the
rawness of smoke. A glance back; the Aenir had turned the
hose on the base of the ladder long enough to quench it. She
braced herself on the wall and put her hand on the wound in
his side that was seeping his shirt red.

"I've got him," someone said. Megan didn't notice who it

was. Crouching, she scuttled down the remainder of the companionway, the light of the *kraumak* shining from the floor in the midst of shards of broken glass.

The cabin door was open, swinging back and forth on its hinges, banging against the warped frame in the fierce draught from the windows; the glass was broken out of them, and the wind howled through the hanging brass, blowing snow into her face, even as the blackened patch above grew and turned coal-red in the center. It was cooler in here, a little, but the heat grew from second to second. There was a body by the door, face clawed, Francosz's shortsword in it, jammed up between the ribs and stuck fast; it still grasped a short, forged-steel mace in one hand. Shkai'ra touched the hilt of the boy's sword; the body rocked, but the blade stayed rigid.

"I told him not to aim for the heart," she whispered.

The snow cleared for an instant, and in the watery daylight Megan could see Francosz sitting braced against the bed, Ten-Knife on his lap. She thought *he's all right*, then took in the dark red splattered around the both of them, the drag-marks where Franc had pulled himself up.

The boy was still alive. He raised his head as they came in, tear-trails on his bloody cheeks. One hand cuddled the cat, the other pressed to his side, his fist clenched. "*Khyd- . . . hird*, Cap—t—ain. I—tried. Ten—" He gulped and whimpered. "—Knife tried. They—cut . . . him in . . . h-h-al—f—I— hurt." The cat was already rigid, bloody fur standing in spikes around his claws and over his face, eyes open, staring.

Shkai'ra moved past her to kneel beside Francosz. The fist was clenched over a deep cut in his right side, toward the back, just below the short ribs. Blood all down the side, clotted in sheets on his tunic, but the flaps of the wound were still gaping, and more dribbled. She bent to look. There were bubbles along the edges. She glanced up again, and his eyes were half-closed; there were snowflakes on his lashes and in the tousled brown hair. The room shook again, a vibration like a wagon at speed over rough road, as the hose washed across the deck above. Wood splintered, and water dripped through onto her back, hot enough to scald. Shkai'ra leaned over the boy, shielding him.

She touched him on the cheek, with infinite gentleness. The eyes flickered wide open, awareness upwelling slowly, like a muddied current near shore. Shkai'ra waited until she saw he knew her.

"You did well, Francosz," she said, slowly and distinctly. "I am proud." His mouth worked, in an attempt at a smile. She continued, "Your blood is mine." Turning to Sova, "Quickly. But don't try to touch him!"

Only the boy's eyes moved as his sister knelt and reached out a hand black with soot, blistered; a hand that halted, hesitated. He sighed, or it might have been, "Sovee." She shuffled closer, and her knee brushed unnoticed against his leg; Francosz went rigid, mewled, slumped. Shkai'ra's hands blurred to catch him, lay him down on the uninjured side and pack the wound with sheeting.

"He's going to be all right, isn't he?" Sova clutched at Shkai'ra; the Kommanza lifted a blank face and shook her head, a single slow motion, completed the bandaging and stood.

"Tell me he's going to be all right, *khyd-hird*. Please."

"No. Sova, your brother is going to die; only a god could save him. If he is lucky, he will die asleep." The Thane girl sagged against the wall with a small sound, cramming one fist into her mouth. Shkai'ra bent, still expressionless, and picked up the cat to lay it on the bed.

"Goodbye, *Zn'Aiki*," she said. "Warrior rebirth for you." Reaching down, she smeared some of Francosz's blood onto her palm, mixed it with a little of the cat's, then drew a line with it down from brow to nose, repeated the process with Sova. The girl threw herself at the tall woman, who hugged her with brief ferocity. The heat from above grew.

"You must be strong for his spirit," she said. "Do you understand, girl?" A long second, and Sova nodded.

The Kommanza knelt again, sat back on her heels, closed her eyes and brought her hands up above her head, palms up, took a deep breath. Then she opened her mouth and *keened*, a long, wailing cry of naked grief and anger; Megan stood immobile, then threw back her head, joined her grief to Shkai'ra's, the double note of anguish rasping cold teeth down the others' spines. The Aenir outside started and shivered at the chilling ring of it. It lasted a full breath, and then Shkai'ra rose.

"Ten lives to make hellwind for you, Francosz," she said. "Five for the cat, who was a better warrior than many with hands. It will not be enough."

Dead. Francosz is going to die. My crew, dead. Yvar might die. Megan looked at the washbasin lying overturned on the floor, thinking, *someone should right that. And we should get out. I've obviously seen enough death that it isn't affecting me much or I'd be going crazy right now.*

"Rilla," she said. "Get the litter here. Get the Haian here." Her cousin went out into the corridor in a crouching run. *My voice is shaking like my brain.* She reached out and petted Ten-Knife's head, scratching where he liked it, along his jaw, along his fixed snarl, pulled her hand away as if it were on fire rather than cold when she realized what she was doing. She backed up a step or two, put an arm around Sova. "Get on deck. They might not be able to stop the fire."

AENIR'SFORD
EVENING, ELEVENTH IRON CYCLE, SEVENTH DAY

"Well, that's the lot of them," the Aenir magistrate said.

Megan stared dully at the row of prisoners standing on the deck of the watch-barge. Five of them, none unwounded. Zak faces, triangular and dark. River Quarter faces, thin and prematurely aged by hunger and overwork, bitter, feral eyes that trusted nothing and hoped for nothing. As she might have been, if the fates were otherwise.

The barge rocked beneath her feet, and the short, early winter day was dying, leeching the sky to the grey of charcoal. Behind her the wounded *Zingas Vetri* was being towed toward the pulling-up slip, her bows almost out of the water, the melted tar leaving bluish oil in her wake. The Aenir made a sound in his throat; he was a big man, in a leather breastplate strapped with brass, leaning gauntleted hands on the haft of a long axe. There were scars on the armor, and nicks and blood on the edge of the weapon; his second stood behind him, with a headsman's sword over her shoulder.

"The others were just sailors, acting under orders. They'll get fifteen years in the quarries for breaking the city's peace. These are the ones that attacked your ship; there are a dozen witnesses, no need for formalities. We'll have their heads off right here, or whatever you want, as the injured party."

Megan stood without moving or speaking for a time that made him frown and shift the grip on his axe.

One of the prisoners spoke first. "Give us to the birds then, waterrat." He spat, lifting the glob of phlegm toward her. "Dark Lord's luck, that you weren't sick in your bunk like we were told; I'd have cut you then, bitch, worse'n I cut your little Thanish whoreboy."

There was a low *chinnng*, the sound of a blade leaving the bone-rimmed mouth of a scabbard. Sova stepped out, face to face with the Zak. He was a young man, with pockmarks and the wispy beginnings of a beard and one eye purpling from a blow. He had time enough to open his mouth; it might have been for a plea, or defiance, or a question. Sova moved, without taking her eyes from his; her mouth quivered, but the hand moved as it had been taught, a straight upward thrust under the breastbone, angling to the left. The knife was double-edged, nine inches of F'talezonian water-steel with a rondel guard. The jarring impact of the guard on his breastbone hurt her wrist.

The black eyes were only inches from hers; close enough to see the pupils flare open. Disbelief, for an instant. Knowledge of death. His mouth made no sound, only an exhalation of breath that sprayed droplets into hers, saliva and blood. He slumped against her, pushing the knifehilt back painfully against her ribs. Mouth moving again, but again he made no sound; it was the Thane girl who screamed as his head lolled forward on her shoulder and the whole bony length of his body rested against her. She pushed, pushed again, and the dead man's head rolled toward her, the surprise still in his eyes, and the snowflakes landing on the unblinking whites of them, half-melting.

"*You killed my brother!*" she wailed, as the corpse dropped away from her, drawing her forward one step, two, as muscle-tension locked on the blade. It pulled free with a sucking sound, and the pit of her stomach heaved uncontrolled, shooting yellow-green bile and pieces of mangled roast beef onto the dark-clad form at her feet. Sova dropped forward, body arching with the spasms, coughing and retching thin acid between clenched teeth and through her nose, the screaming climbing to an intolerable shrillness as she stabbed, and stabbed and stabbed.

"*You killed Franc! Francosz, Francoszzzzzz*"— Then she was sobbing, not child's tears but the deep sobs of a human old enough to know loss is absolute. "*Give me back my brother. I didn't have enough of him,* give him *back!*"

Shkai'ra stepped to her side, lifting her up as she dropped the knife, lifting her and wrapping her in a cloak, holding her as she wept.

Megan spoke at last, soft, a whisper. "You don't even deserve the Goddess's mercy and you'll never get it." She raised her eyes to the Aenir. "Burn them," she said. "I don't care if they're alive or dead when they burn. Bury the ashes in stone."

Chapter 17

The wind howled outside, shaking the windows with its fist of snow, the first blizzard of the winter pounding on the closed shutters of the city. They would have piled rocks on their roofs down in the River Quarter; in the morning the children would slide down steep cobbled streets on cloaks and bits of board. Silence, shadows, creaking as the huge, soft pressure of the air leaned against the House, probing, seeking, looking for weakness . . .

Habiku set down his cup and excused himself from his mother's table. In the office he looked out at the wall the storm had thrown against the glass. The attack in Aenir'sford had been partly successful, though Whitlock wasn't dead, yet. He entertained a fleeting notion of somehow putting her in the cage she had destined for him, then shook it off as a dangerous fancy.

I have to be sure of her soon. Avritha had suggested strongly that he hire one of the really powerful witches in the city, never thinking that perhaps she should help with the ferocious expense that entailed. *The manrauq. Smoke and lies. Still, it might do* something. The Wizard was out of the city, therefore out of the question, leaving only two almost as powerful, Eyeless Sinka or the Blue Mage; one of whom might be persuaded to take part in a House war and kill for a price.

AENIR'SFORD
ELEVENTH IRON CYCLE, NINTH DAY

"Captain," Sova said.

Megan looked down at her. The ship that took the dead of Aenir'sford across to the east bank of the river was small, with an open well and a dozen oars a side; her party stood next to the tiller. The bodies were below, with her thoughts.

"Yes, Sovee?" Her brother was there; last night he had simply stopped breathing. Yvar was still alive and the Haian was optimistic that he would stay that way.

"What . . . what do you think happens to people when they die?"

The Zak glanced off over the backs of the rowers, to the waste of snow and dead reeds on the eastern shore. It was morning-dark and dank cold, just light enough to see the ragged clouds above and the wind blowing spume off the waves. Porridge sat uneasily in her stomach, and her eyes felt sandy.

"What were you taught, Sova?"

The girl did not look nearly so much a child these days; it was hard to see the cowering Thane-girl of Brahvniki in her now. Her cloak was drawn about her and thrown back over her right shoulder, and the edge swayed about her boots; the tight-drawn fabric showed the outline of her brother's shortsword at her hip.

"I was taught," she said slowly, "that Gothumml and His wife and Son and the company of the Saints lived beyond the cloud. A Thane man who lived by the Book and the Laws would go there to dwell forever in glory with them; and a good woman could serve her men there as on earth. Bad Thanes and foreigners went below to Fehuund in his cave of ice, where worms gnawed them until their souls were consumed."

She considered. "I don't believe it, any more. If Gothumml

made the world and sent down the Book and the Laws, in the Ves'landt where we Thanes came from, why doesn't everybody follow Him? The priests say that everyone else worships Fehuund, but that's just not true. I know that now." A frown. "I knew it before. I had a nurse, when I was young; a Yeoli woman, from Tinga-e. *She* didn't worship a devil; she said her people believed that everything returns to the spirit of life, and death is like sleep for ever."

Another frown, deeper. "She told me a lot of things that I didn't think I remembered, until now. That you should never be just yourself, but try to be other people in your head, so that you could understand them. About how she'd been a teacher and a sort-of monk, before the pirates captured her . . . But what do *you* think, Captain?"

Megan sighed. "We Zak think that there are two gods, two spirits that contend for us and the world. One is the Goddess, Who made the world. It's Her will that things have life, and bring forth more life in their turn, and return to Her when they die to give the life-stuff back to Her. That's why we give our dead back to the birds of the air; they're Her messengers. She gives without asking return, and receives beyond even Her giving. Her messengers take the dead back to them, and She takes their spirit to become part of Herself, so that our dead are alive in Her, and become part of all that lives."

Sova bit her lip. "Then . . . Captain, why did you say the Zak who . . . who killed Francosz and the others should be burned and buried in rock?"

Megan's mouth opened slightly, and her lips thinned. "Because there's another god. The Dark Lord, the one who sent the Phoenix to burn and break the earth. The Goddess raises mountains; He wears them down. She gives life, and death in due season; He takes life untimely, the babe in the cradle, the corn before it ripens. He is the Un-Shaper. If your life is spent in leveling more than building, destroying more than creating, making ugliness out of beauty, you go to Him and become . . . nothing. You destroy yourself, become un-real because you deny Her who's the source of existence itself.

The Dark Lord is like that: a hole in the universe, a hole that hungers to unmake everything." She paused. "There's an old story, I don't know if it's true, that by burning the body and locking the ashes in dead rock you can keep the soul away from Her."

Shkai'ra had turned back from the railing. Sova bent her head in the Kommanza's direction. *"Khyd-hird?"*

The tall woman pulled her hand from under her cloak; the orange wingcat was wrapped around it, her wings folded about the hand itself and her tail around the wrist; she was sucking energetically on Shkai'ra's thumb, until the cold wind hit her. Ears went back and her mouth opened in a resentful hiss. Shkai'ra shook her hand tentatively.

"Off! Off!" she muttered, then; "Ahi-a, all right," and stuck her hand back under her cloak. A hump scuttled to her shoulder and began to purr loudly.

"After death?" She ran a hand along her jaw; the sword-callus that ringed thumb and forefinger rasped on her skin.

"Well, my people have many gods: we don't think our gods rule other people, who have their own weaker spirits. When you die, your body should be burned (Megan turned like snow when I told her that) or buried in soil; then, your ghost lingers for a while. Especially if you're killed and lie unavenged; then you need hellwind to blow you into the afterworld, hellwind made by your comrades or relatives killing your slayers. Sacrifices help, too, and ancestor-shrines. Then you go over the Bridge of Judgment; if you've been a coward or a traitor, the weight of your sin pulls you off, demons eat you, and you get reborn as something low—a slave, a cow. If you fall but have enough in you to fight, you may get reborn as something better: a war-steed."

"Then, if you battle your way across the Bridge, you come before the gods; there all your deeds are judged. Everything is recorded, nothing is forgiven; you chose your own next life as your punishment. In the end, if you've had enough worthy lives, the gods make you part of their war-host, and also part of themselves, somehow; ask a shaman for what that really means. Then, when the world is broken and changed again, the way it was in the Godwar long ago, you fight at their side against the dark spirits of *zoweitzum*." She shrugged. "Rebirth seems sensible enough, I've met the belief often as I travelled. Don't know about the rest." Another shrug. "We're all going to find out someday, *nia*?"

The biers were brought up from below, and the volunteers from the crew of the *Vetri* took them up; the bodies were canvas-wrapped, and there was no smell after so little time in this cold. In the silence someone coughed, wood creaked beneath feet, an endless chill sighing of wind through acres of dead dry rushes in thin ice.

The east bank settlement was small, a few long houses and boat sheds for the shuttle ferries, mostly drawn up for the winter now. Churned dirt and snow coated the street, lay less soiled along the rough-made road that wound out through the frozen marsh. A single wagon waited, its two horses drooping their muzzles to the ground and snorting puffs of white breath.

The six bundles were laid out on the boards of the wagonbed, and Shkai'ra stepped up to add the smaller blanket-wrapped form of Ten-Knife-Foot.

The mourners were a dozen strong; some lit torches of wood and tar-soaked cord, others shouldered their spears or twofangs and fell in as the wagon creaked slowly into motion. The torches trailed streamers of orange flame and black smoke, the flicker cast shadows across hoods and caps. They trudged east, winding along sand-ridges or through low spots where ice and oozing black mud crackled up around the studded wheels of the wagon.

The Zak burial ground was visible over the snow long before they reached it, long poles topped with the platforms to hold the bodies. No burials had happened in a while and the older poles were canted in the wind; rags of cloth fluttered from them, but the snow hid the usual scattering of old bone about the bases. A fresh grave had been hacked into frozen ground nearby, with a marker in the Thanish style, plain but of cut stone.

Megan watched as the bodies were brought out of the

wagon, unwrapped and tied to the platforms. Overhead, the birds were circling already, like black kites in the wind, calling. The five poles grated into the deep-dug holes, swaying with the weight on top until rocks were mounded around them to hold them steady. The mourners who would not be speaking cut locks of their hair, let them fly away hair by hair in the wind.

Boryis the rower stepped forward and called Mara's name, a sob that stretched in the wind like the plumes of flames and smoke from the torches. Yuri spoke for Renar. Cerwyn, Vodolac's net-mate, called his name into the wind; their voices squeaked small and alone under the sky, answered by the birds hovering above. Megan called Mateus's name, and Nikola's; calling the Goddess's attention to the dead, freeing their souls.

I feel as if some weight I've been carrying is gone. The ravens circled, waiting. The living were tiny under the great leaden dome of the sky, but achingly visible.

Sova had stood back respectfully while the Zak bid farewell to their dead; the words the Captain had used for the ritual were beautiful, but she couldn't help a shudder at the sight of the circling birds. Four of the Zak helped her carry Francosz, lay him in the deep trench. She took the wooden shovel and cast the first load of earth; helped set the heavy granite marker with her own hands. The others stepped back when she knelt by the new-made grave mound and drew her sword that had been her brother's and laid it on the ground before her. She was conscious of Megan and the *khyd-hird* standing behind her, making their own good-byes in silence, but she felt alone with Francosz.

"Brother," she said softly. "I thought of burying this sword with you, because you were so proud of it. But that would be silly, and I don't . . . feel so silly, anymore. So I'll take it and use it, instead. I killed the one who killed you, and it was horrible, but I'm not sorry I did it."

She looked down at the metal: a plain tool of fine steel two feet long, with a simple crossguard and wooden hilt wrapped in hide. "I didn't have enough time to know you, Francosz. I loved you when we were little, and then they took you away to start making a man of you, and we were growing up strangers. Then it was us two together again, when we were so frightened and alone, and you did everything you could to help me.

"You were very brave, Francosz. I think you would have been a good man if you hadn't died, and I would have loved you always. I don't know if there's a heaven, or if we go back to the Goddess, or are reborn, or if it's only sleeping forever . . . I wouldn't want to serve you in Gothumml's house, like the priests said. I want to be your friend, Francosz, and I will. Always. Always."

The tears flowed, but her voice was steady, and her hands as she sheathed the sword and rose, dusting the gritty snow off her knees.

Ten-Knife had a small grave of his own. Megan and Shkai'ra paused by it.

"It's as if a little part of our lives was gone," the Zak murmured, leaning into Shkai'ra. "He was with us from our beginning together."

Shkai'ra nodded. "Killing everything small enough to catch, stealing anything he could eat, clawing the ratshit out of anything valuable or spraying it, making more kittens than any other ten toms. Never lost a catfight. Never lost any fight, until the last one." She took a pointed stick and thrust it into the half-frozen ground beside the little mound, and then a string of tufts of hair from beneath her cloak.

"Long time since I took a scalp," she muttered, tying it on firmly. There were five locks of dark hair. "Good-bye," Shkai'ra said, and pricked her thumb to smear a drop of blood on the stick.

Somehow it's impossible to believe someone's dead until now, Megan thought. *Not until you hear the wail of names and see the birds settle, or fill in the hole. Even then it's not enough because what you're burying isn't really them but empty copies of them. Somehow it's as if they are alive somewhere and one day you'll walk around the corner and this person or that person will look up and say "Ah, there you are." As if it were you who had gone away. Or the cat*

*will weave between your feet. As long as you can remember
them.*

"Heavy storm on its way," she said, turning away from the
graves. She put her arm around Shkai'ra's waist. The cart was
already trundling back to the river, followed by everyone
else, on foot.

Sova snuggled under Megan's free arm and the three of
them held to each other as they walked. Behind them a raven
dropped out of its circle, swooping low, settling. Another
followed.

AENIR'SFORD
ELEVENTH IRON CYCLE, TWELFTH DAY

The Aenir harbor engineer bent over the wetwell in the
center of the wrecking barge, peering. The rectangular hole
was walled to above water line and open below; four stout logs
went up from the corners to meet over the center of it, and a
block and tackle was suspended from the crown. A cable ran
down into the water, straight with the strain from the grapple
on the end, hooked into the bars of the sunken cage; it
swayed slowly, cutting long, dark streaks through the grey
slush-ice that formed and broke on the surface.

"I can't *see* anything wrong," the Aenir said in clumsy
trade-Zak.

Megan winced; Aenir'sford was theoretically a free merchant city-state, like most towns of any size on the Brezhan.
In practice the squires and cattlebarons of the east shore
hinterland had a good deal to say in its internal affairs, a say
that extended to finding well-paid posts for their relatives,
including some who thought a ship was steered from the
same end as a horse.

"Then let someone *competent* see to it," she snarled, ignoring the wounded look the Aenir threw at her. She turned and
looked out over the town. Since the storm had ended just this
morning, Aenir'sford was a mound of a white again, with
only the second-story walkways shovelled free.

The repair slips were just off to Megan's left. The work on

the *Vetri* was coming slowly. She hadn't pushed because the storm and the ice flows spinning down from further north were already too thick to sail in. The ice usually jammed the river just above the island, where the Vechaslaf and the Brezhan met, sending sheets of water flowing over ice that looked like crumpled lace, and froze north from there.

The Aenir had gotten the cable up again and recoiled. At least they knew how to handle *that*. With much arm-waving and shouting in Aeniri, they apparently managed to get the hook set and the other end of the rope snugged in the windlass. They'd been *that* far twice already.

SLAF HIKARME WAREHOUSE

The main warehouse of the Sleeping Dragon had been half-empty for a long time; when the original owner arrived to throw Habiku's hirelings out in the snow, there had been no objections. With the half-burnt *Zingas Vetri* still smoldering on the slipway, few were going to question the actions of the one who had saved the city in the last war; they remembered the Siege well here, and Megan Thane'sdoom. Nobles and merchant princes might have shorter memories and more concern with their F'talezonian trade, but the voice of the *n'rod*, the freefolk's assembly-in-arms, spoke loud in any Aenir town, and even the most arrogant lordling did not cross it too openly.

Offices and clerk's apartments made quarters for Megan, Shkai'ra, and the deck officers of the two ships. There were many among both crews who would keep to the feud, whether they travelled toward Habiku Smoothtongue by water, ice or over knives of fire; those who had their own reasons to hate, or others whose bond to the Captain was closer to a vassal's love of a good lord than that of a wage-servant for employer. Aenir had come volunteering, too, more than were needed. A full hundred men and women were bunking in the warehouses and sheds, using them for weapons practice and preparation otherwise. Just now three-score were sitting about the walls of the timber hall, watching the blonde foreigner from west-over-sea spar with Shyll teRyadn.

By Zaik Victory-Begetter, he's good, Shkai'ra thought. She was in full Kommanz kit, armored from pate to boots, circular shield up under her eyes and a curved wooden sword in hand. The man facing her wore only soft plainsboots, a running kilt and jerkin, a steel cap and small buckler for protection, and an eight-foot spear with a painted wooden head. It had been twenty minutes now, with no killing hit for either; the crowd around the walls was watching in tense silence broken only by a collective *hnnnuhh* of breath as they met, clashed, parted.

They circled, their feet *rutching* on the rough sandstone flags. Shkai'ra's vision focussed to the narrow world framed by the sides and nasal-bar of her helmet; within it, her opponent moved like a leopard, like a wolf, like a dancer. They were both sweating, even in the dry chill and dim light from the overhead shutters, but she was carrying half her body-weight again in war-harness . . . His spear darted out like the flickering tongue of an adder, eyes, neck, knee, waist, elbow, drawing sword and shield in a minimalist dance of response.

Enough. Shkai'ra attacked.

Great Dog, she's fast, the teRyadn thought.

His spear jarred on the shieldboss, glanced along the sword; the woman let another strike go through, moving a precise fraction of a centimeter so that it glanced from a flared shoulder-piece. Then she was moving forward again, moving like machined surfaces gliding in a bath of oil, the fanged mouth painted on the shield coming at him with relentless speed and the wooden point showing around the corner, held just *so*.

She's too *good*, ran through him. He was backpedalling almost as fast as she advanced, and then she was in sword reach. Point and edge, smashing shieldboss and steel-rimmed edge were everywhere. For a second they were toe to toe, the violence between them a flicker of movement far too swift for an untrained eye to follow. Then he locked the spearhaft against the guard of her sword, buckler against shield, set his feet and strained.

Too good. You could tell a lot about a people by seeing their wargear and training style; there were clues in the decoration, the shapes, the movements. Zak fought with cunning economy, the sneaky pragmatism of the small against the large; teRyadn fought with exuberance, a Thane tried to beat you down with smashing hammer blows. This woman had been trained in a school that aimed to produce living killing-machines . . . What had his Megan tied her life to?

They shifted, grunted, breast to breast in the momentary intimacy of combat. All that he could see between helmet and shieldrim was a glint of grey eye, but he could hear the controlled harshness of her breathing.

She isn't my Megan, he reminded himself, with a momentary flush of shame. She was a free woman, free to chose her own lifemate. *She never was mine*. All he had ever had were hopes that he scarcely dared admit to himself.

Her sword-arm was bending back; she was strong, but his bone and muscle were heavier, thicker. Not that it would win the bout; as soon as his hand went past the shieldrim it would be pinned for a punishing stroke with the metal edge. Anger flared in him against this rival who didn't even know she had beaten him. Against Sarngeld who had brutalized the child-Megan and left her too frozen for his gentle warmth to melt. Against Habiku, who had put her out of reach before time had its chance to heal. And against himself, wallowing in selfish misery when he should be wishing Megan joy in a lover who was strong, beautiful, loyal.

But only the rival was here. Anger fueled, fired, became something beyond itself. He leaned into her for a final surge, then *used* the solid springsteel pressure, leaped backward with all Shkai'ra's strength to boost; backflipped, landed on his hands and bounced into stance, ready. Shkai'ra was not her own momentum and the burdening weight of her armor pushed her forward three fatal steps before her legs could absorb the force.

The spear flashed out; not to strike, she could still have guarded against that, but between the ankles to trip. He sprang to the side and levered; the woman's greave struck the ashwood spear with a *crack* and she went forward in a clattering crash of lacquered leather and iron on stone. Shyll ran on the balls of his feet as she landed and curled herself beneath the shield; giving no chance for recovery, moving recklessly close. The long weapon twirled like a baton in his hands, striking, battering, booming on the shield with a thunder that filled the room louder than the cheers of the spectators as they surged to their feet.

A thrust rang off the forehead of her helmet as she struggled to one knee, with a sound like hammer on chisel, rocking her head back with a wrenching impact that must have dazed at least. He felt a moment's fear as he realized the blow could have snapped her neck. Then she was set again, weight resting on knee and shield, and sword ready with the point angled up to waist height.

"Peace!" she called hoarsely, the clicking guttural accent almost hidden under her panting. The sword flipped in her hand and she held it head-high by the "blade."

The glorious tide of anger died in Shyll, leaving a pool of soured resentment. Winning the practice bout would prove nothing, help nothing; it was even emptier than revenge. "Do you concede?" he said. The room was hushed again, with sharp interest; the little army was already as gossip-hungry as any small hamlet, and there were bets to consider.

"I concede we'd be absolute idiots to spend all morning battering each other into pulp when we've got real work to do," she said tartly, loud enough for the room to hear. A toss, and the sword was in her left hand, held against the outer grip of the shield in the tips of her fingers. Her right hand undid the chinstraps of her helmet and swung it free; sweat rivered down her face, flushed and calm. Nostrils flared as she controlled her breathing.

"I also concede," she continued, with a slight incline of the head, "that you've got the wind of me; I thought I was in good condition, but you could run that gods-abandoned *dog* of yours into the ground."

There was laughter from the spectators. Shkai'ra was a martinet and a batteringly severe arms-master. Eyes turned to Inu. He had been sitting in a corner with his Moryavska; flattened to the ground, with a slight bristle in his ruff. Shyll had not smelled *entirely* as if he was just playing with the strange pack-leader-bitch. But, "Stay" was one of the Words, and now everything was all right. His tail thumped the stones.

Shkai'ra extended her right hand. "Let's go wash down; I need to go over those duty rosters with you again."

It was a reminder; they were commanders, with responsibilities. *I have Megan's war to win before I can go,* he thought bleakly. He forced a smile and grasped the gauntlet, hauling Shkai'ra erect and accepting the slap on the shoulder she delivered.

"I wouldn't care to face a line of you teRyadn coming to me across the plain with those dogs," she said as they handed weapons to the practice-masters and headed for the door. "Not without a *fast* horse."

Sova had been watching the bout, but not as an idle spectator. She leaned back against a grainsack and swung the weights, stone disks set on either end of short hardwood handles. Out to the side, *hold* it, in until they met over her chest, *squeeze* as hard as she could. All the repetitions, but no more; then over her head, then Tze braced his back in front of her so she could do the leg-pushed against it.

The dust from the barley inside the coarse burlap made her sneeze. The warehouse smelled of grain, of an ancient cargo of brown sugar once shipped up from the Mitvald, now overlaid strongly and pleasantly with the sweat of healthy, well-fed bodies. Sternly, she made herself divide attention between the exercises and the fight between the *khyd-hird* and the tall handsome friend of the Captain's. It was difficult; they were glorious, like dancers or that big spotted cat in the cage at the fair.

They were all special, Shkai'ra, and the Captain, and Rilla, and Shyll and the others, and it was incredibly special that *she* could be a part of it. Like a band of well, not knights, but heroes fighting a tyrant, in those old stories that Francosz had—

She stopped, her eyes going wide and glassy; her body tensed and quivered. Instantly, Tze was up and kneeling by her, arms about her. Piatr was on her other side; hands and voices comforted, and others nearby looked away in respect that the two had enforced with words and fists. Sova came to herself, panting.

"Sorry, sorry," she murmured, ashamed, but relieved to feel them there.

Shkai'ra was the first thing she remembered after the barge, and Megan had been there. But they were often busy . . . Piatr had taken her to the Haian, Tze was there, but well enough to be up and helping with the other patients. The thick man had come to her, sat beside her, and Piatr had spoken for him. The gobbling sounds were strange to her, but his hands had shaped the air and given color to Piatr's words. How he had been the Captain's friend, second mate of her ship, and Habiku had had him kidnapped. Kidnapped, his tongue torn out, put in the quarry in Rand, and now he learned that his lifemate and two children had been turned out of their house and pension once Habiku took the House . . .

Tze had looked at Piatr then. Sova looked between them, dropped her eyes in sudden shame, would have fled if they had not held her with gently irresistable force. She *knew* Piatr's story; she remembered the sickly-sweet pleasure of tormenting him, when he was the only thing in her life weaker than she. His hand had forced her chin up. *How can he look at me, how can he do anything but hit me? How can be sorry for me, I threw things at him, Francosz . . . Francosz tried to drown him, we were bad to him like Habiku was, only not so much because we were smaller . . .*

"Wrongs done in ignorance can be forgiven, little Thane," he said. "Your brother acted no worse than he'd been taught; and when he got an opportunity to learn differently, he did. Wrongs done in full knowledge of the wrong, they can't be forgotten." The one-footed man nodded to his tongueless friend. "We *know*, Sova. We *understand*. He's taken things that can't be put back. You can talk to us, and *we understand*."

The Thane girl had looked between them in gathering

wonder before she spoke. "Let me tell you," she had said in a
voice choked with the first of the tears. "Let me tell you
about my brother. My brother was—"

She shook herself back to the present. It had only been a
few seconds; she squeezed her friends on the arms. *Friends*,
she thought. There was moisture on her lashes as she ran to
the entranceway to collect Shkai'ra's armor and help with
the unlacings. She worked quickly at the thongs and buckles
and straps, wrapping the pieces reverently and tucking them
in the armor bag; only since the burning of the ship had she
been allowed to handle them, and the *khyd-hird* was still
showing her how to clean and polish. It meant that she was
somehow a relative of Shkai'ra's now.

Shyll and Shkai'ra had been talking until she came, in low
tones. They stopped and were *too* quiet until she left; she
deposited the bag at the feet of her friends with careful
control, frowned and turned to Piatr.

"Piatr, there's something . . . something not friendly between Shkai'ra and the Captain's teRyadn friend. I . . . I
don't think I should ask either of them or the Captain about
it. What's *wrong?*"

Piatr sighed and rubbed his stump thoughtfully; the wooden
leg was off, and Tze was going over it critically. He looked up
from the carving and made an elaborate over-to-you gesture
to his friend. Piatr glanced around to make sure there was
nobody within earshot, and lowered his voice.

"Ah, Sova, you know about loving? The way spouses—
lifemates— do it?"

"Well, of course," she said, feeling suddenly uncomfortable, even with him. "I'm a woman now, and the Captain and
Shkai'ra explained everything to me." Sova colored at the
memory of the horrible embarrassment of that night. *I've got
to learn to think about it*, she thought doggedly. *Everyone
else does, and they don't get sick when they do. Sailors even
do it, right where everyone can watch if they don't have a
room. People will laugh at me if I get upset.*

Piatr sighed again. "Well, the Captain and Shkai'ra are
lovers. Have been for years, from what I've heard; I wouldn'

be surprised if they did get married and become lifemates—"
he stopped for a moment, looked down at her where she sat,
arms around knees. "You do know that people of the same
sex can be lovers?"

"Of course," she said, blinking innocently. "I mean, the
Captain and Shkai'ra are the first lovers I've seen, so I thought
so." A frown. "I don't know how the bit about making babies
and fertilizing eggs comes into it, though."

The Zak rolled his eyes. "That's the first time I've had
occasion to say anything good about how that bitch of a
wo—ah, your mother raised you. Kept you so Goddess-hating
ignorant that you couldn't even pick up the stranger Thane
prejudices." He sighed again. "Where was I? Oh, well, you
see, I think—it was obvious to everybody with half an eye,
except maybe the Captain—that Shyll wanted to be the Captain's lover. For always; he stayed with her for years, helped
build up the House, never settled with anyone else even
though those teRyadn are a pairing kind."

"The Captain didn't like him that way?" Sova said. This
was better than a story, but kind of sad as well. Shyll was *so*
pretty; it was really, really sad to imagine him wanting to be
close to the Captain all that time.

"Child, she didn't like *anyone* that way. When she was
very young, younger than you, she was raped—you know
about that too?"

Sova made a face. "Like that man in the storeroom the
other day?" One of the Aenir volunteers had come in while
she was looking for some tackle; he had tried to touch her
under the tunic, and refused to stop. She had yelled and
kicked him in the kneecap the way Shkai'ra had told her, the
others had come running, and of course Piatr and Tze had
believed her . . . they had taken him away, hitting him as
they went; she hoped they had hurt him, he deserved it.

"Worse, Sova, much worse." His face crinkled. "I was
there."

"And you didn't help her?" He winced at the indignation in
her voice, and at memories of his own.

"I couldn't. Neither of us could; the Arkan, Sarngeld we
called him, was master, the worst sort of bad master, he was

the Captain, he had the law behind him . . . Never mind,"
he said, watching her confusion. "It happens. It's bad, but it
does. She had a baby, and it was too big and she too young
and the healers had to cut; that's why she can't have more.
There, there, child; it's an old grief, long avenged. But that's
why she didn't want a lover then, she was hurt in her soul."

Sova put her chin on her knees again, brooded. "Shyll is
sad because the Captain picked somebody else while she was
away." She shook her head. "That's sad, it really is. Like a
song." Another long silence. "Piatr . . ." she looked down.

"Yes, Sova?" Tze touched her foot in reassurance.

"My . . . my father, he was Mother's only husband." She
used the Thanish words; the trade-Zak that every rivertown
or wealthy child learned had no equivalents with meanings
even roughly similar. "And she was his wife. But I heard her
say something once, she didn't know I was listening, about
him making babies with a, she said 'doxy!'." She frowned. "I
don't know what that word means, but is this mating thing
something you can only do with one person at a time? Because it's going to be very bad for Shyll, isn't it? I know it
would make me really, truly unhappy if somebody else were
to be the *khyd-hird*'s apprentice, if I couldn't be as well. Of
course," she added thoughtfully, "I don't know enough about
this lovers stuff yet, really. Maybe that's silly."

He hugged her close. "No, Sova; it's just more sensible
than adults can sometimes be." A sigh. "I don't know . . .
your people mate by pairs, or so their laws say they should.
Zak usually do, but not always. TeRyadn? I don't know,
really; and this isn't the steppe, anyway. I hope something
can be done, because otherwise Shyll may leave the House
once the fighting's done, and that would be a bad thing,
because he's a good man, brave and skilled and he's served
the House and all of us well. He's a good friend." Sternly,
"And you must *not* talk about this to *anybody*. Understand?"

She nodded. "Nobody except you and Tze?" They nodded
vigorously. "All right," she sighed, and shook her head again.
"It's all really sad, like I said." She made a face. "Numbers
practice next. Goodbye until dinner!"

*   *   *

In the steamy heat of the bathing room, alone, Shyll buried his face in his hands and wept, clenching the fingertips into his skin until the nails stood white with rage and frustration.

It was late afternoon when the cage rose our of the wetwell, streaming crystals of water and steaming in the cold air. Mud was caked all along the solid bottom and the bars of one side where its own weight had pushed it into the harbor muck. The other bars still gleamed like damp teeth in the grey afternoon. Megan's lips tightened as she gazed at it, slowly turning on the end of the cable, but the expression on her face could hardly be called a smile. "Leave it at the Slaf Hikarme dock," she said. "We'll look after it from there." *Rather have a loose Ri thrashing around my warehouse than this crew,* she thought. *Tze and Piatr will be able to polish up my Cage.* Then she checked herself. *No. His Cage. His Cage.*

The oxcart bore the Cage slowly through the winter streets. They were less crowded, now. Most sailors had dispersed to their cold-season jobs for the interval between ice float and freezeup. Woodcutting in the forests, or crafts, at their families' farmsteads or even in idleness if they could afford it, and the outcity merchants were gone. Aenir'sford had room enough within its walls now, with only the core population of full-time artisans, laborers and traders; even so there were enough for a crowd to gather and watch the Cage go by. It had acquired a mythic aura, already. Murmurs followed it; children were lifted for a better view.

Damnation if I'm going to leave it sitting out for every apprentice bard to moon over for inspiration, she thought. There were a particularly irritating note to the cheers that followed her, and she had to force herself to nod in curt politeness.

Dark Lord curse that harp-smacker who thought up 'Long she brooded on her wrong/In those black eyes Death's own song.' *Fta! So I don't have a smile for everyone who passes . . .* It was *her* revenge, but every living human in creation seemed determined to push into it, invited or no.

There were five guards at the warehouse courtyard gate; two

of her own Zak crewfolk, with twofangs and dart throwers, Moshulu leaning on his hammer, and a Rand with the long curved sword of her folk. The Rand saluted snappily, bringing the blade up before her face and down again; the others repeated the gesture more clumsily. They were in no sort of uniform, but wearing green and black headbands with the Sleeping Dragon embroidered; Shkai'ra had suggested it, and Megan had authorized an order with the sewing guild. Now it seemed pretentious, somehow.

She's playing general again, Megan thought. *If they ask for a password, I'm going to scream. Koru bless and Dark Lord curse, I'm a merchant skipper, not the leader of a warband!*

Instead, a group turned out to bring in the Cage. By the simple expedient of a dozen strong backs and pairs of hands they carried it in through the courtyard gate and into the barn door portals of the warehouse. The great structure echoed to the cheers of her followers as the emblem of the Slaf Hikarme's rebirth was carried the full circuit of the half-timbered building, then reverently placed on a low frame of logs. Piatr and Tze came up, hand in hand with Sova. They looked at each other over the girl's head, and smiled; it was not a pleasant expression. They brought out a bag of sand, oil and rags, brushes and buffing-leather and set to work.

Megan started as Sova cleared her throat. The Thane girl set down her stool, sat and held out the Y-shaped heel-grip; despite herself, the Zak felt a shiver of relief as the wet leather of her boots came off, to be replaced by felt slippers. She ran her eyes over the rest of the crew there in the warehouse. They had been split into squads of eight, with leaders and under-leaders, the size of the groups that could sleep comfortably in a single medium-sized tent. They had brought a good ten of the large sleds, fifteen-foot models; overhead she could hear and smell the work of reconditioning, glue and varnish and a grating sound as bone runners were sharpened. Harness was laid out on the lower floor, being oiled back into suppleness; a group was gathered around a sandtable map of F'talezon, and another was going over the frame of a knock-down iceboat that Rilla would use to reach

F'talezon first, with the letters that would damn Habiku in court.

The cheerful bustle grated on her nerves; even the off-duty crews felt like sandpaper on the prickly-itchy surface of her skin: some were asleep, some eating, or dicing, or making love. There were gaps, like missing teeth. Rowing Boryis was sitting next to one of his friends, staring at his hands. Megan felt a burst of anger at the sight of him, shame at the anger, then anger that she felt the shame . . . Obligation. She went over and put a hand on his shoulder. He looked up, tears on his face.

There were no more words to say to him, she could only squeeze his shoulder and go on. Mateus would have been *there*, probably sorting his kit, keeping a eye on the sparring to yell if it got too heated. *He was solid, like a tree,* she thought. *I return, and he was there to support.* The missing left holes that could not be filled, like an alteration in the familiar landscape that took years to seem natural.

I never lost this many I cared for, before, she thought. Not since Mother and Father, so long ago, back in the River Quarter. Then: *I never knew there were so many I* did *care for.*

She stopped, stared up into the dimness of the high, barn-like ceiling.

Outside again. The makeshift kitchen-corner had been enlarged, curtained off with canvas and board; she could hear the sound of the first shift cleaning cutlery and pots, talking and splashing in the hot water. Smoke rose, and cooking smells of hot oil and meat and frying onions. Somebody shouted behind the curtain, and there was answering laughter.

In a month you may be dead, she thought, and was glad she did not know their names.

She had set up an outline target of a man six feet tall in one corner. The pine boards were already chewed; her hands automatically checked her knives and she toed the farthest mark.

THUNK. The first knife quivered in the soft wood. *Left eye.* THUNK. THUNK. *Shoulders.* THUNK. *Throat.*

The puff of her breathing was inaudible to any except the kitchen staff, but the sound of the knives hitting the target carried to the sparring circle. THUNK. THUNK. THUNK. Like the hammering stroke of the Dark Lord's wings, or his laughter. Inu stuck his nose around the corner of the kitchen wall and whined.

Shyll ducked under his muzzle. "Megan!"

He smiled at her, and she felt the same unwilling lightening of her mood his smile had always brought. She scowled at him, and he smiled again, as if to say: *No, I'm not going to be polite and let you enjoy being miserable*. Irritation warred with her sense of the ridiculous, and lost for the moment. Her eyes returned the smile, if not her lips.

"I've talked Rilla into a game of cniffta, if you will," Shyll went on.

She started as if coming out of a dream, hand still raised from the last cast. "I'm out of practice, Shyll." Then she blinked and shrugged. "All right."

He grinned at her. "You two were among the best in the River Quarter."

She snorted. "*Among* the best? *The* best, then!" They ducked back into the warehouse, climbing to the second story, empty now but for the sleds stacked against the walls. It would be tempting fate to play in the open, with passers-by within knifecast.

Cniffta . . . She shucked down to just her breeks; you needed full agility for catching thrown knives. That was the whole point, and the reason it was the Zak sport above the others, the advantage of speed in a world of giants. The chill air of the warehouse raising gooseflesh all along her arms, making her nipples stand up. "I need to warm up first." His eyes flickered but his expression didn't change.

"*Megan!*" Rilla called from the main part of the hall. "Come on! We've got to show these slackers what *real* knife-work is!" Rilla winked at Shyll and opened the case of knives.

Megan looked at the rows of horn-hilted daggers in blue velvet, then at Rilla's grin. "You didn't have these commissioned, I hope."

"Honestly stolen, coz! Honestly stolen from Habiku Rat's

Ass." Rilla swept Megan a bow. *Maybe*, she thought. *Maybe with Megan having an akribhan, Shyll will look at me for a change*. "All ten?"

Megan put a mock-fearful hand to her brow. "True steel? Oh, dear. A whole matched set of knives? How difficult!" It was the old joke between them. They'd learned and played with all different weights and balance of blades, when they were children. A matched set of knives would be easy.

They took up stance in the sparring circle, in the open, Zemelya and Danake preparing to toss them the knives as necessary, rather than driving them into end walls, close at hand. Four knives began the pattern, thrown and caught between the cousins in a smooth arc. "Toss!" Megan called and the seconds both added in one knife. "Toss!" Rilla yelled a second later and they kept eight knives in the air. Megan laughed. "Trying . . . to . . . throw me . . . off, *fatrahm?*" using the affectionate term meaning father's sister's child. She twisted in place a full circle and never missed a knife.

"Ha! Watch . . . this!" Rilla caught four and dropped them one after the other, somersaulted in the air, keeping the other four going, then, stooping and throwing, brought them back up to eight blades. Megan snorted and changed the pattern of her throwing until a glittering waterfall of all eight spun over her. "Toss!" she called and caught the two thrown in, one from near, one from far, then spread the arc back out between the two of them. The patterns between them grew more and more complex, each of them trying harder and harder tumbling moves between the spinning steel, until with a skittering clatter Megan dropped a blade and the pattern fell apart.

She was smiling though, and breathing hard. "I told you I was rusty."

" 'Bout as rusty as Inu's fangs." Over the heads of the crew, Shyll could see Shkai'ra's head, the orange flitterkitten sitting on it.

Shkai'ra reached up, pulled the kitten loose. It promptly coiled its tail around her wrist. "Sheepshit, cat, you've got claws on you like . . ." She paused. "I know what to name you!" She grinned. "Megan, what do you think of . . .

ahm . . . *Poivrkin?* Fishhook?" By that time she was through
the crowd. She scratched the newly named Fishhook behind
the ears. The flitterkitten started to purr. "You know, you've
been doing all the stretching and so forth on board but your
wind is suffering. A long run might do you good." She looked
at Shyll over her head and grinned. "We could ask Shyll to
get Inu to chase you."

He only hesitated a second, then he grinned back. "Sure!
I'll tell him to lick your face!"

"I've had a good workout, courtesy of the doglord there,"
Shkai'ra nodded at Shyll. "And he as good as beat me; showed
me *my* wind needs more work. So, come on. This warehouse
has enough stairs and halls to run around, as well as outside."

Megan stood looking at them all, Rilla's flushed face, Shyll's
slightly pale one, Shkai'ra's smile. *There's more going on here
than just trying to cheer me up. That's what Shkai'ra's trying
to do. I do love her. Why am I so upset that Shyll doesn't
seem to like her?*

"Right then, *baba*," she said, more lightly than she felt.
"Let's see you keep up with me."

Rilla looked at Shyll as Megan and Shkai'ra started their
run. "You're jealous, aren't you?" He started and turned to
her.

"Is it that obvious?" He walked over to Inu and sat down,
throwing his arm over the dog's neck, burying his face in the
shaggy fur. Inu muttered, half whine, half growl and nudged
Shyll in the side with his nose. Behind them she could hear
quiet preparations for a feast. Shkai'ra had thought it would
help Megan to get her tired, bathed and massaged and drunk.
Everyone else thought a party, a wake, was a wonderful idea.

"How much can I bear?" he said almost to himself. "They're
a pair." She went over and sat down next to him, put her
hand on his shoulder.

He put his arm around her, comfortably. *He doesn't even
realize*, Rilla thought. *It's a comradely arm, not a lover's.*

"Yah. They're a pair."

Well, Rilla thought. *Womanizer or not, he's never looked
at me, even while Megan was busy shying away. I might as*

well try to be the sensible one. "By Zak law, if you can stand the Kommanza—is that the name?—and if Megan agrees, you could marry in a three."

"*Marry?*" His voice cracked and he stood up. "Marry that—" He broke off as the sound of a pair of running feet boomed on the boards overhead.

"Or," Rilla said, "you could try to make Megan jealous of *you.*" He looked down at her, sat down abruptly.

"Jealous? She's never been jealous of me being with anyone before." He looked down thoughtfully. "Who could she be jealous of?"

"Me," Rilla said quietly. Inu licked her ear.

"Rilla!" He looked at her, shocked.

"Never mind. Forget I mentioned it." She got up and stalked away to where the rest of the crew were quietly setting up trestle tables. *Rilla*, he thought. *Rilla*.

Chapter 18

They lay in the bath, steam still rising though it had cooled somewhat. Megan leaned her head back on Shkai'ra's arm, laid her hands delicately on her breasts, let herself float, trusting the Kommanza to hold her. "It's so nice to be able to lie in a hot bath. Especially since you were crazy enough to go out in the snow."

Shkai'ra snorted, then nibbled gently along the Zak's neck. "You paid me back, going over the roof."

"For the first time in days, I feel relaxed." Megan quivered as Shkai'ra's lips found one of her nipples. She closed her eyes and sighed. "Relaxed enough not to—ahhh . . . go through the roof when you did that."

Shkai'ra smiled and raised her head, looking down at her lover, running her free hand down in the water, around the Zak's navel, brushing lightly over the scar on her lower abdomen and the inky curls between her legs. Megan moaned, arched her hips as Shkai'ra gently slipped a finger past her outer labia and stopped.

"Shkai'ra!" It was almost a shriek of need. The Kommanza smiled again, kissed Megan on the lips, as she moved her hand.

Nothing to feel but her lips, her fingers . . . ahh. A time-

310

less time. Megan writhed and gave herself to her lover, her hands tensing open as color flared behind her eyes; violet and red and the one unseen. As the wave of orgasm faded she opened her eyes, looking up into the other's grey gaze. Shkai'ra paused a long second, then moved again, bringing the second and third waves of sensation rushing through her.

She floated, held only by Shkai'ra's arm under her neck, boneless and light. For the first time in days, light, the weight of all the things she'd carried washed away. She dozed, then opened her eyes.

"You'll have to get on the edge of the tub, Shkai'ra, for me to do you," she whispered. "If there's one thing I can't do with these claws, it's *that*." The red-haired woman hugged her close.

"Not tonight, kh'eeredo, tonight's just for you." She crinkled her face in a warm smile. "I'm going to dry you off, rub some oil into your back, and we can get something from the kitchen before bed." Megan's stomach rumbled and she buried her face in Shkai'ra's neck, feeling pampered and cherished.

"That sounds wonderful. You're so good to me."

"Only the best, kh'eeredo-mi, only the best."

"Remember how we met?" Shkai'ra said. Megan was facedown on the bench, bonelessly relaxed as the strong fingers kneaded warmed oil into the muscles along her spine. Her laugh was muffled by the long spread of her hair, spilling over her face and pooling on the floor.

"How could I forget? Still raw from the slaver and that damned swamp, I plump into the Weary Wayfarer's bath and there you were . . ." she sighed. "Next thing I know, we're eating together; I wake up in a nightmare during a thunderstorm, and you've broken in to see what was making me scream . . . Did you do that whenever you heard someone scream, back then?"

Shkai'ra laughed. "No, heart's delight, only if I'd wanted to be in their bedchamber anyway." Another laugh. "Say I was fascinated with the thought of fucking with somebody whose head only came up to my breasts." A final stroke along the length from the nape of the neck to thighs. "It's all worked in; let's dress and go eat."

"Mmmmmph," she replied.

"You sleepy?"

"No, just feeling good. And very, very hungry, all of a sudden. My appetite hasn't been of the best . . . what luck! I feel hungry too late for the last serving. Oh, well, they might have some stew on the hob."

"That they might." A pause, and the rustle of coarse paper wrappings. "You remember Milampo?"

"The merchant in Fehinna? The fat one with the terrible taste in everything? Of course. We made as much out of stripping his sanctum as the Sleeping Dragon did in any two years, before Habiku drugged me." She sighed. "It's three types of miracle that we managed to get the jewels back over the Lannic. I do regret we lost most of the bulkier things."

"Like those silk tunics?"

"Fishguts, yes. Not that I care much about clothes, I leave that to peacocks like Shyll, but it was a good day. Feeling safe after the fighting, and calling in the clothiers; Ten-Knife, playing with the silver and jewelled message-ball . . ."

Shkai'ra sighed, looked at the package in her hands, missing the old tomcat. Megan looked up from the bench. The Kommanza shook her head, raised her hands. She was standing in front of Megan, smiling a little sadly, and holding up a tunic. Knee length for the Zak, with a squared neck and short sleeves; everyday wear on the western shore of the Lannic ocean, in the south coast cities of Almerkun. Of heavy, dense-woven silk dyed creamy, bleached wheat yellow, bordered with figures of dolphins and seaweed picked out in lapis. The Zak sat, parted the damp mass of her hair, flung it back to trail behind her to the floor behind the bench. She studied the cloth more closely; it was not identical. Could not be, those chests had been lost when storm threw their ship on a reef in the Fire Isles. Yes, the color was a little darker, and the designs had been done by a hand that had never been born under the eye of Fehinna's God-King.

"Oh," she breathed softly, looking up. "Thank you."

"Wear it," Shkai'ra replied. Megan stood and tied on a

fresh loincloth, then raised her arms for her companion. The fabric slid down over skin still sensitive from the bath, the touch of the silk like the caress of thousandfold fingers.

"Ah," she said, then, startled: "Shkai'ra! Why now, to show the firewatch while we beg a bowl of leftover stew?"

Shkai'ra grinned, and dropped another tunic over her own head: dark blue, with bullion medallions along the hem. "This one *I* missed; ruined it getting down to the docks to catch the ship you were leaving on, that day in Illizbuah. As for the firewatch," she winked, "maybe we can do something about that. Here, comb your hair straight; don't bother to braid it back up—"

"Shkai'ra, what—" The Kommanza laid a finger across her lips.

"Shusss." Megan looked at her, puzzled, shrugged and carefully tugged the comb through her hair. "Done? Good. After you, Teik ClawPrince." Shkai'ra held the door open with a sweep of her hand. Megan gave her a strange look but went through.

The hall beyond was dark, but the door into the hall was open a crack, light streaming through it. She pushed it open, to a roar and a blast of warmth, cedar-resin smells from the braziers that glowed along the wall, spiced food.

Cries of, "Welcome home! To revenge! To the Cage! To Life!" crashed around her ears. Rows of trestle tables covered with steaming dishes of spiced rice and bowls of borscht with sour cream and platters of fingerling gar, stuffed and roasted, dishes of sturgeon caviar stretched down the hall. Almost everyone brandished a glass or a stein, wineskins or bottles of *wadiki*. Inu was barking like a peal of distant thunder, Shyll standing beside him, one hand on his ruff, a slightly shaky smile on his face. *Why is Rilla on the other side of the room from him?* Megan had time to wonder before she was swept into the crowd, a glass thrust into her hand and splashingly filled.

"Hey! Hey! Careful of the tunic!" she cried, holding the glass out at arm's length, sudden tears blurring her vision. *Of all the dumb things to do*, she thought. *Cry*. Someone thrust a linen kerchief into her other hand. "Don't worry, somebody'll stay sober and guard the place," Shkai'ra whispered and steered her to the head table.

Shouts of, "Dry Cup! Dry Cup!" greeted them. Megan turned, raised the tumbler of . . . *what?* she wondered, as she stepped up on a chair and raised it. A chai cup, but her eyes watered as she brought it to her lips.

It turned out to be *wadiki*, flavored with aniseed; a F'talezonian brand, distilled from amaranth. Fiery, cool, a little tart, the effect waiting as she leaned back with her Adam's apple working, until the last drop trickled past her teeth. *Then* it struck, on an empty stomach; she reeled in the seat, until Shkai'ra threw an arm around her to steady her. There was another roar; she looked down the long room, laughing faces, eyes full of . . .

Myths, she thought. *I took a ship from a fat pervert and kept it, though I was a child. I built a middling successful trading House, quickly because I knew the river and wasn't afraid to try something new. I was a good master, because I remembered what it was like to be on the bottom, with no rights and nothing to bargain with. Fought when I had to, won by wits and good luck and because I had good people with me.* A stubborn honesty interrupted. *Oh, well, breaking the Siege of Aenir'sford was a little spectacular, maybe. But the Thanes were badly commanded. And then I went away, and Rilla and Shyll kept the myth alive by fighting a man everyone loved to hate, and winning.*

Then I came back, did a few flashy touches . . . Yet the naked admiration did not bother her this time, as it had when she saw it previously. *Dark Lord take it, tonight's a night to be easy with myself.*

She leaned into Shkai'ra's steadying arm. Good-natured laughter pealed out, and a cry arose: "Give her a kiss! Give her a kiss!" Others took it up, until the room was chanting it; someone else thrust a stone flask forward to refill her cup, and even then her merchant's mind noted the broken wax seal: Dragon'sNest Cavern, Year of the Lead Phoenix. She coughed, spluttered.

"*Give her a kiss!*" vied with, "*Dry cup! Dry cup!*" She emptied the cup, and the hall swam again. She looked down at Shkai'ra and took her head between her hands—then leaped down from the chair and wrapped her legs about the Kommanza's hips, her arms around her neck in a long, flamboyantly passionate kiss. Shkai'ra set her down, and she staggered a little before steadying. Everything was magnificently clear; all the faces about her were suddenly transparent. She knew them, knew herself, knew the secrets of the earth.

I am not afraid. Now, nothing can make me afraid. As Shyll steadied her she turned into his arm, snaked a hand behind his head and kissed him. He went rigid with shock and she froze. *No. I can't.* His hand came up to touch her cheek and she pushed the cup into it instead, pulling away. *But part of me liked that very much.* She started the chant, "Dry cup!"

The cry was taken up and Megan sank into her chair, looking away from him; they were not sitting on cushions tonight, in deference to the naZak majority and the cold flagstones, she supposed. Shkai'ra settled at her left and Rilla at the right; after a moment's hesitation Shyll took the stool beyond Rilla's. Megan grabbed at a roll, dipped it into a bowl of salt caviar and began eating with a hand cupped under her chin to catch the drips.

"Got to sop up some of this *wadiki*," she muttered. The salted eggs tasted rich and spicy; her parents had served them on feast days, before her father lost his arm: they were the classic middleclass delicacy. "Dark Lord, you'd suppose I wa leading them to conquer F'talezon an' put Ranion's head on a pole. With Avritha's beside him. Which might not be such a bad idea . . ." The realization that she had spoken aloud made her clap a hand over her mouth; Rilla laughed.

"It *is* a good idea, even if it's impractical, coz." Rilla shook her head. "Not even a DragonLord as bad as Ranion is going to go against the inheritance kin-laws, not without some shadow of right; Avritha can only help Habiku hold on to the Sleeping Dragon as long as you're presumed dead. She can make the law look the other way while he tries to see that you *are* dead, before you can make claim before a magistrate, but these blades—" she nodded to the crowd of their followers "—will see to that."

"Urghf," Megan said: Shkai'ra had just picked up a mussel in its shell, dropped a dollop of spiced vinegar on it, and poured it into her mouth.

"No business tonight," Shkai'ra said. "Tonight, we drink!" The hot food was coming around, the fancy dishes Piatr had labored to create in close conspiracy with a dozen others. Pit-roasted pigs stuffed with nuts and bread and onions, half a dozen kinds of fish, hot breads, what winter vegetables were available. Not as refined as a noble's table, but this was their own effort. Megan had forbidden servants inside the encampment until Habiku was dead; they took turns serving each other, with only the officer's table exempt as a mark of respect freely given.

Megan picked up a piece of grilled pork, dipped it in chive-rich yoghurt and pushed it into Shkai'ra's mouth, repeated the process with Rilla and Shyll. "And eat," she said.

THE WAREHOUSE
LATE THAT NIGHT

Lanterns and braziers had guttered low. The feast was thinning; it was quiet enough for the amateur bards to make themselves heard. Some had been surprisingly good; Inu had an unfailing ear for the off key, of which he thoroughly approved. Megan felt herself giggle at at how *hurt* he looked when the artists he decided to accompany were shouted down in a hail of breadcrusts. *Thank you, Inu*, she thought. *A basket of beef bones for stopping that accursed 'Long she brooded on her wrong/In those black eyes Death's own song.'*

The chair had been upended, and Shkai'ra was using the back as a sloping rest; Megan reclined against her, head curled in the hollow of her neck. She refused the pipe with a smile.

"More, and I'd go to sleep. Not ready for that quite yet." *To our dead, farewell, in whatever world waits. The revenge is for you, but that's tomorrow's thought. Mateus. Vodolac.*

Mara. Nikola. Renar. Francosz. Goodbye. Koru, tomorrow I'll pray for Yvar who is in doubt. Ten-Knife. Peace. The overstrain was fading like the herb smoke out the windows. She had reached that rarest and most pleasant stage of intoxication; floating without being detached from sensation, languid without the over-the-edge plunge into unconsciousness. Movement was still possible, as long as it did not involve balance . . . Shkai'ra drew on the pipe; Megan looked up to see the quick glow of the ember outline the eagle profile.

"Thank you, my love," she said. "The winter river and F'talezon will be easier, with this to remember." She let her head roll back. "It's time to leave . . . Didn't I see Sova being carried out around an hour ago? Rilla and Shyll are gone, and Annike and . . ."

"If you think it's time to sleep, kh'eeredo," Shkai'ra said gently, with only a trace of slurring to her voice.

She had near twice the body mass to absorb it, after all, Megan thought. "No, lifemate mine. In a few hours. Right now I have a very strong desire to make you very happy—" she wiggled her shoulders against her companion "—and, luckily, I know a way."

Shkai'ra chuckled and touched her on the tip of the nose. "This was supposed to be your treat, kh'eeredo. And you usually get too sensitive to be touched after the first few."

"Tonight isn't usual. Tonight I'm going to do what I want, *everything* I want and nobody's going to stop me, even myself." She smiled openly, a slow grin like a wicked child's. "You can carry me upstairs, for starters."

Rilla wiped Shyll's mouth after the last racking heave and wiped his face with a wet cloth before she closed the pot.

"You know better—" she started to say. He turned away from her.

"Don't nag, Captain, it doesn't become you," he said bitterly, slumping back down on his bunk. She clenched the cloth in her hand, hiccuped and threw it at him.

"See if I try to help you and your beautiful behind. I'm ju' . . . jus' . . . almos-t 's drunk as you. Fuck you." She turned her back on him and lay down. They'd thought nothing of bunking together before all of this had started happening. *I'll move out of here tomorrow*, Rilla thought. *He hasn't said anything about what I said but if he does, I'll kick his teeth in*. A few envious tears gathered in her throat but she swallowed them.

Shyll took the wet cloth off his face and stared at her. *What's wrong with her . . . oh. Yah. This afternoon. The whole dunged world is falling on my head*. He blew out the candle, refusing to lie down, because that made the slow, portside spin of the room worse. He leaned his head back against the pillow and the wall, dozing, on the verge of fading out when he heard a giggle on the stairs outside. A muffled bump, two people laughing. Megan and *her*.

They made it up the stairs, laughing helplessly. *I never heard her laugh. I could never make her laugh like that*. Above their door clicked closed. A single set of footsteps wavered across the floor and a sharp creak as something was dropped on the bed. Someone yelped, giggled loudly; violent shushing followed, both of them whispering loudly to the other to be QUIET! He ground his teeth. *Damn old buildings*, he thought. *You can hear every sound*.

Above, the bed creaked again; rustle of blankets and clothing hitting the floor, whispers muffled by the feathertick and pillow. A gasp fading into a soft, passionate moan. His hand clenched tight on his mattress, pounded once. Drunken tears flowed down his face. *I love her. I love her*.

Damn them. He stared up at the ceiling. There was a rustle in the same room with him and Rilla sat down again on the edge of the bed, putting her hand out in the dark. "Poor Shyll," she whispered.

"No! Damn it! No! I don't need pity!" His whispered shout hurt. *Shit. Did* they *hear that?*

In the dark, Rilla touched his face. "Shyll." Her voice sounded surprisingly sober, intense as only drunken truth can be. "It isn't only pity for you. I'm tired of being second best. I like you, and I said so; so there. I won't be ashamed of that. I'm a friend. *You've said that*. I'm not going to say, come to my bed because Megan can't, you'll never see me say, take me if you can't get what you want; I'll do. I'm tired of being Shadows'Shade! I've wanted you and never had the guts to say it and I'm here as a friend." Her voice slurred a bit more. " 'B'sides. You're too drunk, so why don't you take a friend's comfort?"

"You're not second best, Rilla. Rillan, I never thought . . ." His tongue stumbled over itself. "I've always thought you were beautiful, but I'd never treat you like that . . ." They gathered each other into a hug that ended with his head on her shoulder. "Rilla, I'm mixed up, confused. I don't want to hurt you or her, or me, or anyone but it just dog-sucking *hurts so much!*" He cried on her and they fell asleep comforting each other.

Shkai'ra lay on her face and shivered slightly in the dark at the feel of the steel nails trickling down her back. It was warm under the tick, even if the room had gone unheated-chill; there was a childlike feeling of trust and helplessness in the sensation of razor-edged steel on her skin. "Ah, love, enough or I'll melt and trickle through the floorboard—"

"Oh, shit," she said in the middle of a yawn, turning and putting her face close to the other's ear.

"What, akribhan," Megan said.

"Shhh. I was too drunk to remember, we're right over Rilla n' Shyll's room."

Shkai'ra could feel the Zak woman stretch and yawn. "Hmmm?"

Shkai'ra sighed. "Was meaning to tell you, but I wanted to wait until later. Guess now is best; drunken counsel at night, sober counsel in the morning. We have a problem with your friend Shyll."

Megan exhaled wordlessly and curled close. "I . . . I think I know what you mean."

"Mm-hmm. Sparred with him this morning, and it nearly turned into a grudge fight. He's good, that one; very good indeed. We went twenty minutes—"

"How many breaks?"

"Not a one; haven't been so winded ever, outside real combat. Toward the end something happened in him; he went off like a furnace stoked with turpentine and pumped with a bellows. Kh'eeredo, if it'd been real, he might have killed me. Might; but then I'd have been in combat mode too.

"Kh'eeredo-mi. He loves you and has for a long time."

"Shyll? N—" She interrupted herself, thinking of the look on his face in the dance ring when he had his arms around her, the look on his face when she kissed him. All the bits and pieces she'd ignored in the years before she'd been drugged suddenly came back. "Koru," she breathed. "Fish-gutted fool that I am . . ." She looked down at Shkai'ra. "Akribhan, he'll be eating his heart out. Piss. What am I going to do? I've gotten as close as I can . . . tonight, and it scared the scales off me."

Shkai'ra was silent for a long moment. "Kh'eeredo, I've never known you to be ruled by a fear. First, tell me . . . what do you feel for him, really?"

"I . . . I've never thought about it. I don't know. I was scared enough of sex when you and I started . . . you know. You know, and you're a woman. With a man, any man—" She paused a long moment and Shkai'ra kept her silence. "In me somewhere there's a child terrified of being touched, the smell, the thought of him using me that way." Her voice thinned even more, took on a very rare note of panic. "I'm nobody's whore. I'm nobody's slut. I won't have him touch me. I won't . . ." Her eyes were wide as if she could see into the past, then they flicked closed and she shook herself. "*He* owned me for a long time, Shkai'ra. Five years. Five years.

"Shyll . . . I, I know he wouldn't hurt me but I'm so terrified . . . If he left . . . I trust him. But Habiku was the other one I trusted. I don't want him to leave—but I can't trust him. I don't know!"

"Shhh, shhh, it's all right, kh'eeredo, you're *not* that child any more. Nobody can make you do anything you don't want to do; if you don't want him, he can take it in his hand and walk to Fehinna . . ." Megan gave a snuffling laugh and relaxed again.

Shkai'ra's voice turned meditative. "You know, heart's delight, I've been raped too; starting as early as you, although it

was less of a shock to me, of course, my people don't think of
it as much more than a wound in combat. It's bad, but . . .
well, there's no sense in letting the kinless bastard who did it
rule your life from the grave." She paused. "Remember how
you hated to have anything inside you, when we were together at first? Just a second, don't be startled." Shkai'ra
eased a fingertip between her legs, into her. "Now it usually
doesn't bother you, unless you're startled; like being pinned.
Unlearning a habit; it took work, there were times when you
nearly clawed me, but it happened.

"This man Shyll; well, from what I've seen, he's wanted
you since he met you. And never a word, never a touch out
of line. That's a patient man, and a gentle one, too, I think.
You could unlearn other habits with him, *if* you want that."
She slid her arms about the Zak and cradled her, rocking.
"*T'Zoweitzum*, looking back on how you talked about him,
these two years, and the way your body speaks below your
hearing when he's near . . . I think you do, at least in part;
and I think you should have what you want and need. Also,
he's a proud man . . . and you know this people's customs;
we may be talking into the blizzard, perhaps he'd never
accept a place with us."

She stroked Megan's hair. "What's between us is as endur-
ing as the steppe grass and strong as the rivers; I've no fear
anything could damage it." A grin in the darkness. "And it
wouldn't be any hardship at all to throw my own legs around
him from time to time, either.

"*Kh'eeredo*, he's spent two years an outlaw for you, never
knowing if he would live to see sunset . . . and now we've
shattered his hopes. Well-a-day, the world goes as it will, not
as we'd have it, but we owe him either hope or a clean end to
his pain, don't you think?" A more practical note. "Seventh
and last, I'm not happy at the thought of going into battle
with a man suffering what he is. I don't doubt his skill or
courage or loyalty; he'll fight by my side for your sake, even if
he comes to hate me. But a tormented man makes mistakes;
mistakes could get you killed, or me, or him. Best we think
on a way to settle this, one way or another, before too many
weeks are past." A squeeze. "Together, *nia*?"

Megan nodded against her neck. "*Ia. Dah.* I was going to say I'd talk to him. I will. You're right, my heart. I don't want to hurt him."

The night was a snowy glow over the city, like a healing hand.

AENIR'SFORD ISLAND
NORTH SHORE
ELEVENTH IRON CYCLE, TWENTY-SIXTH DAY

Megan stood on the stub of a tower at the northern end of the main island, looking at acres of old, tumbled stone buried under mounds of snow, and the blackened timbers of what the Aenir had built on the foundations. Watching the two crews scramble under Shkai'ra and Shyll's direction, training.

The ruins were old-Zak; Theocrat Meywidova's reign, eleven hundred years ago, she thought. The Aenir had put a bastion here, timber and earth on the stone foundations, but that fortress had been one of the first things burned out during the siege and not yet repaired; the Aenir felt safe, and had concentrated on housing and reequipping the harbor.

There was a certain melancholy to the shattered stone. No novelty: there was old-Zak work all up and down the Brezhan; Brahvniki itself had been founded by her people. Cycle on cycle, and each tide seemed to ebb further for the people who had sprung from F'talezon's riverside mountain.

So long ago, she thought. *The Zaki empire stretched along the river to Brahvniki, east over the steppe, demanding tribute even of the Ryadn. West of the Moryavska tribes and north into the Salt Mountains.* Little was left, a ribbon of territory on either side of the river for a few days' journey south of the city, a scattering of half-forgotten settlements in the northern woods.

Now we live in enclaves all along the river we once ruled, subject to other laws, dependent on the DragonLord's waning power. We are still wanted for our skill but are feared for the manrauq. We dwindle; Zak are fallen as low as these stones.

She shook off the mood as Shkai'ra panted up, her quilted jacket opened with the heat of exercise.

"How are they shaping?" Megan asked.

"Not bad. In a standup fight of ranks in open country, drilled soldiers would slaughter them. But most of them're pretty fair individual fighters, some really good. Plenty of spirit, I've never seen a scratch warband with so little in the way of quarreling or discipline problems, and they're learning to work together. Good officers, too, even if they're new to the work on land; Shyll's got an eye for ground, and the blades will follow him with a smile, I think. For alley fighting or ambush work, they're very good indeed, and they'll be better still when we reach F'talezon in a month or so."

Megan nodded. "And I'm learning to handle a fight bigger than I can see," she said. Shkai'ra laughed, in the midst of rubbing a handful of snow over her flushed face.

"You're doing it a lot better than I could con a ship, kh'eeredo."

Shyll had come up while they were speaking. Shkai'ra raised her practice sword in casual salute and continued speaking to Megan:

"Well, I'll run them back to town and meet you on the canal for that skate practice you were threatening." She turned, leaped down six feet to the snow, waited a second while Sova scrambled down to follow, and trotted off into the ruins.

Shyll climbed up beside her, metal skate blades dangling from his left hand, ringing.

"Let the others finish, let's go test the ice," he grinned at her. *If I didn't know better*, she thought, *I wouldn't think anything was wrong*. She smiled back, sitting and patting the stone beside her.

"I haven't skated in so long, you'll be able to laugh at me stumbling," she said.

"Gods of the Dog, no!" He pretended to cringe. "Mock the Grrrreat Spit . . . ah, Whitlock?"

Inu panted up, spraying gouts of powdersnow into the air, scooping up mouthfuls of it, barking through them. Fishhook clung to his ruff, wings spread, ears back and eyes wide in a mixture of fear and excitement.

FRIENDYESGOODYESLICKPLAYRUNRUNRUN. The dog's thought was clear and sharp as ever; he braced its paws on the sides of the ruined tower and raised himself ten feet, almost enough to lick her foot with a reach of the washcloth tongue.

She had tried to summon the light on her hands the last night and found that the overstrain had knocked her powers back somewhat, it was more reddish than orange. Shyll settled beside her, and she tucked a hand into his arm and squeezed for a moment before taking the skate blades and running a leatherclad thumb over the edges.

"I remember the first metal pair I could afford, though wood and bone are almost as good."

"I remember you and Rilla teaching me." Shyll looked sideways at her. "She held me up from behind and you whirled around me. 'Showing me how it's done.' " He chuckled. "My seat has, at long last, forgiven you."

"Shyll." He turned and looked at her expectantly. She put her hand out to touch his arm. "I . . . I care for you, Shyll. I care for you too much to ask you to wait for my fear to ebb. I fight it, but to ask you to wait . . ."

"I'll wait." His face was somber. "Let me decide how long I'll wait. I'm too confused right now to make any decisions." A brief flash of smile. "Any sensible ones. I was thinking of leaving after everything was settled in F'talezon, but now I don't know. You—and Rilla too—are throwing a lot of things at me all at once. Don't worry, Megan, I won't do anything until I've thought about this a lot longer."

"All right, Shyll. I really haven't had time to talk to you alone. That's the problem with being the fishgutted 'hero.' Everyone wants to talk to you." Poivrkin fluttered up from Inu's neck, his disappointed whine trailing after her. He wanted to be up there, too. The wingcat landed half on Shyll's lap, half on Megan's, mewing and proud of herself. "Even the animals." She scratched behind the orange ears.

"Penalty of becoming famous, Meganmi." He stood up and offered her his arm. "Let's go skate and get you back in practice."

F'TALEZON
SLAF KIVNIY, INNER CHAMBER

The room was cool blue stone, carved out of the mountain near the Dragon'sNest, the original rock was left in its flowing, splashed shapes only somehow transformed from granite. In the center of the room, on a cushion covered in blue fox furs, a man in grey-striped black robes sat, staring into a mirror.

His hair and beard were salt-and-pepper grey; it was a friendly enough face, squint-lines around the calculating eyes that showed little of the ruthlessness he was capable of.

The gilt frame he stared into was set with pearls. In the center, where silvered glass would normally be, was a paper-thin sheet of a bone mosaic, ranging from the delicately sliced skulls of mice, through the long, wide slabs of ivory cut from thighbones. He breathed on the surface and it cleared, bringing sound and vision into his echoing room.

"—There's really no probl—" Shkai'ra's feet shot forward on the ice and she landed on her back, arms spread. "Sheepshit," she said. Inu scrambled by, paws flailing and skaters dodging in the narrow confines of the canal; plumped to his belly, slid to a stop near Shkai'ra and began to lick her face. Grimly, she struggled up with the dog as a handhold; he came helpfully to his feet, and she rested her hand on his shoulder to steady herself . . .

This is my quarry? he thought. *Habiku, you are a fool if you need to pay my fee for . . . ah.*

—In the crowd of Aenir's townsfolk, young couples skating hand in hand, weaving lines of craft pupils yelling as they snaked by, holding on to each other's belts, sedate families pulling infants on sleds in the torchlight, Megan glided up, turned around, linked hands with Shkai'ra as she wobbled. "Here, akribhan, both our right feet together."

There was light enough to see both women clearly, from the great bonfire in the center of the ice, from lanterns strung from slipways and the masts of ships in the dry docks, and from the huge, ten-foot iron firebasket slung between the mouths of the steel dragons over the harbor mouth.—

Still, the Blue Mage thought, *All this fuss over a minor-powered witch? Or is the half-Zak ClawPrince hiding something from me?*

He raised an eyebrow, watching the party on the ice. *How confident you must feel, Whitlock, to celebrate Shamballah's rising so openly in the midst of a House war. Perhaps you have the possibility of growing into my range of power, become a threat perhaps?* If there was such a prospect, she showed no signs of it. He watched Inu break up a game of stick, watched Megan's friends throw her into a snowdrift, watched the drift be torn apart for ammunition for snowballs.

Well, Habiku. You are willing to overcome your well-known despite for the manrauq to enlist its aid, and you, or rather Avritha, are paying my fee. Whitlock, we will see how well you like snow.

AENIR'SFORD
ELEVENTH IRON CYCLE, EVENING
TWENTY-SIXTH DAY

"I would never have thought only ten people could throw *Inu* into a snowdrift," Shkai'ra said, shaking the last of the snow out of her jacket and re-donning it.

"*I* would never have thought any *two* people would pull me out from under a pile of crewfolk and then throw me in a fresh patch," Megan said. Then, "Ah, Rilla. The moon's up."

The other nodded. Zak were coming together on the ice where the enclave touched the harbor, a growing crowd of small, dark-clad folk from ship's crews or the enclave, with a thin scattering of true-friends from other breeds. The moon was near full, huge and bright, floating over the horizon and showing its curve as if the far hills and plains were only another country across the valley. Shamballah shone silver and clear in the sky near it, off the darkened quarter. Megan tucked her arm in Shkai'ra's and Rilla took Shyll with her: with Sova between them they coasted to the edge of the crowd.

The teRyadn seemed to know what was going on, and dropped a hand on Sova's shoulder as they halted, bent to whisper in her ear:

"This will be strange, but very beautiful, Sovee. Only a few naZak are allowed to be here." She looked up at him and nodded, her eyes huge with fear and wonder.

"Try not to jump, heart'sdear," Megan whispered up to Shkai'ra. "I know you hate spook-pushing but this is a celebration." A pause. "It's been a very long time since I welcomed Shamballah with my own people." Shkai'ra nodded silently, her gaze on the moon.

The Zak were all within arm's reach of each other, several hundred strong, with solemn-faced children as young as six holding their parents by the hand. The wind rose, whistling around the harbor, bringing the smells of snow, cocoa, the fire and the city with it, then faded. The torches had burned down, and the firebasket slung from the dragons was a red glow of half-dead coals. In the dark, in the silence, someone, a woman, whispered:

"One such night was when the world died. We were out in the snow, and on the horizon, the Great Phoenix reached its beak out of the world and then even the snow burned."

"We live."

The answer was like the wind blowing through a grove of pines. Shkai'ra felt the hair rise on the back of her neck. It was as if the answer came from more Zak than could possibly be here on the ice or in the enclave, like a breath from further north.

"Once the Dark Lord decreed that all should starve, saying we were an evil empire, and a million deaths were nothing to him."

"We still live."

"Though the world died . . . " The lead voice died away and the answer came.

"We live."

A light bloomed among the Zak and spread, a steady unflickering yellow that came from everywhere and nowhere. Shkai'ra heard Shyll and Sova inhale sharply, like an echo of her wondering delight; it was as if they were at the center of a living flower, a flame without heat growing from the black ice, under the unwinking stars.

The light flowed out and up, growing more orange and red until finally Shkai'ra could see it being passed from hand to hand as if every Zak were holding a candle, but their hands were glowing with their own power; as each palm touched, the light flowed. Megan reached her hand to Rilla, whose color was a dim red. As their palms touched, the older Zak's flared bright red-orange. In the circle there were one or two who glowed yellow, one green. When every Zak's hands were flaming Rilla held her hands to Shyll, smiling. He put his hand on hers and her color rose enough to cover his fingers. Megan held out her hand to Shkai'ra and Sova.

The Thane girl hesitated, reached out, laid her palm on the woman's and breathed a slow sigh as the light lapped over her fingers, an impalpable tingling. Shkai'ra reached slowly, not from fear but in a calm exultation; the light seemed suddenly like the homelight seen through a storm, and yet a thing unbearably distant and remote. Her hand touched Megan's, felt the familiar callus and texture, yet changed and unique this moment.

For a dozen long breaths the light grew and shone under the paired eyes of Shamballah and the moon; then it died as gently as it had risen. Normal sound returned, but no voice was raised above a murmur as the Zak turned to one another, embraced their neighbors, wishing them another World's Birthday. The silence broke like an eggshell, hatching the season before the New Year, three iron cycles from now.

They linked arms, Megan, Shkai'ra, Rilla, Shyll and Sova; exchanged one long wordless look and turned to skate to their dwelling, moving in a slow dancer's rhythm.

Tomorrow, Megan thought. *Tomorrow I'll think of the Cage*.

F'TALEZON, THE DRAGON'SNEST
DRAGONLADY AVRITHA'S RECEPTION
CHAMBERS
TWELFTH IRON CYCLE, FIFTEENTH DAY

"Oh my, how careless of Habiku," Avritha murmured. "How very, very careless and foolish. A clever man, but he *will* do these things."

The woman who knelt on a cushion across from her was a vendor of tapestries. Her family had been deep enough in debt to see bankruptcy and the River Quarter beneath them; the Red Brotherhood held their notes and had emphatic means of collecting. The DragonLady had bought the paper, made a loan free of interest. The merchant had been in Avritha's service ever since, like many others, bought with money or gratitude or secrets known and shared. Information and orders moved with the tapestries now.

Avritha lifted the pot of chai from its rest; that was a platinum dragon, the mouth spouting a small oil-flame to keep the drink warm. She poured with a graceful turn of the wrist. "You are quite sure, Katrina?"

The merchant lifted the cup in the fingertips of both hands, waited for the ruler's lady to fill her own. "Well, you understand, ZingasSmiurg, the bird merely brought the rumours of the town. The ClawPrince Megan Whitlock was definitely attacked; servants of hers were killed, and her arrow-ship *Zingas Vetri* badly damaged."

Avritha nodded. So much was good; the Hand she had sent south on Smoothtongue's urging had acted competently, given the short notice.

"Her cousin, Rilla Shadows'Shade, met her shortly after the attack, and showed her the documents. They discussed them in public, and made no attempt at secrecy: direct communications with the Thanish Oligarchs. Information on F'talezonian naval dispositions and court politics, including—" she sipped at the tea "—ah, unflattering appraisals of the DragonLord himself."

Very unfortunate, Avritha thought. *The price of pampering you, my half-Zak love, has just risen somewhat above that which I am willing to pay.*

Ranion was not yet *quite* ready to ignore the united opinion of F'talezon's warrior nobility and merchant princes; the Thanes had been a thorn in F'talezon's side since their arrival on the Brezhan broke the hegemony of the Theocrats, eight hundred years before. Besides being the worst persecutors of Zak living outside the power of the DragonLords, they were commercial rivals in every market. The Mutton-Eaters' star had been rising, these last few generations, until the disasters of their latest war with the Aenir; and those defeats had been largely due to Zak assistance.

One of the few things that Zak and Thane shared was a long memory for an injury. The Thanes would be eager to recoup their position, preferably at Zak expense to make the gain lasting; the Aenir could afford defeats, they were a numerous people. F'talezon's ruling classes were equally eager to see the Thanish power further weakened; the city was living on its capital, hence needed strong leadership to avoid losses . . . which was one major reason the Upper City and the merchant ClawPrinces had accepted the DragonLords so long: at least an absolute monarchy maintained internal peace and kept outsiders from fishing in troubled Zak waters. They would *not* tolerate treason or weakness in the face of F'talezon's chief rivals; too much in the way of accumulated wealth and power was at stake.

Hence *Ranion* would not tolerate it. His power was absolute against any single magnate, but in jeopardy if they united to throw him off, and he was still sane enough to know it. He had been growing harder for her to control of late, even so.

And, to be sure, I must consider the city's interests as well. There would be no game if outlanders came to kick over the board, and however uncomfortable the Nest could be, penniless exile or a gibbet would be more unpleasant still. Katrina was a very minor ClawPrince indeed, but she was obviously expecting the DragonLady to do *something*. Mirrored several hundredfold, that expectation had power as real as the Dragon's.

"Thank you. You have served me well. I am grateful."

They bowed gravely, the agent's a trifle lower than the circumstances and respective ranks required.

"No thanks are needed, Woyvodaana. I remember, and my kin through me."

Avritha made a small gesture of dismissal. "Nevertheless, thanks are given . . . Do you admire the service?"

"Of course. A recent piece, but the workmanship is superb." Neither was crass enough to mention the value of the metal. "Vodywar II's reign? Mastersmith Bornovda? It reminds me of another by her."

"Your taste is impeccable as always, Katrin, my dear. Consider it yours. No, no protests! In your house, I know it will be appreciated as it ought, not lost in the clutter."

After the merchant-spy had left, Avritha sat for several minutes, making notes. On memory, not on paper: *that* had been darling Habiku's mistake. Then she rang a bell, summoned certain persons, gave orders.

"A pity," she sighed to the empty room when she was alone again. "Your lies were so convincing, my love, that it pleased me to believe them for a time." She shivered, drawing the costly, Rand-made jacket closer about her shoulders and clapping for more blackrock to be added to the brazier. There were two courtiers she knew, brothers, rivals for her. *Rivals if they know their own interests*, she added mentally. By now they hated each other, for the things she had forced each to do to the other to prove their devotion. It would be entertaining to invite them to her apartments together, and see how they competed in *that*.

As entertaining as anything. Her mind paused thoughtfully. *Or as entertaining as anything is likely to be until Megan Whitlock arrives*. Yes. There were definite possibilities in that; Ranion's interest might be aroused, which would be an added bonus. She would watch and wait; Habiku had probably taken her advice, and her money, to seek magical help, despite his fear-induced disbelief in the manrauq.

He might survive Whitlock yet, in which case it would be as well to begin distancing herself at once. If he did not . . . well, he would still serve her purpose one more time. His death would keep Ranion happy.

Chapter 19

Shkai'ra watched the shadow of a cloud racing down the blue-grey ice of the frozen Brezhan, turning the surface to a darker shade and then passing on upstream. There was very little snow on the river itself, a few hard thin rills, drifts along the banks where rock or an overhanging tree caught the wind. The sleds were backing and filing around the entrance to the harbor; they were drawn by shaggy little ponies, or teams of man-weight dogs—curl-tailed and sharp-nosed beasts like miniature versions of Inu. There had been time enough to work the draught animals and accustom them to each other, but formation work was still difficult.

The sleds themselves were heaped with neatly bundled supplies: grain and frozen fish for the stock, food for the humans, blankets, tents, spare rope, weapons, skates, tools, medicines, documents, money, maps . . . and the Cage, securely lashed to the center vehicle and burnished blinding bright. Most of the war party were squatting by their assigned sleds, bulky in their winter gear, loaded down with their packs and personal weapons; they would skate alongside and push, or haul on lines. Moshulu patted his hammer where it was lashed to the top of the sled. Shkai'ra tasted the feeling of the band, found it good, a tense, eager readiness, mixed with just enough apprehension to prevent sloppiness and boredom.

"A month to F'talezon," she said as she led her horse over to Megan. The roughened surface of its horseshoes made crick-crick sounds on the chipped ice of the harbor mouth.

There was a fair crowd gathered to see them off, waiting on the harbor ice; the last week had been frantic, last minute preparations once the central river froze hard, combined with just enough in the way of farewell feasting to avoid giving any important Aeniri irreparable offense. At that, they had had to be brusque to keep the city council from turning the departure into an all-day matter of toasts and speeches. Formally, Megan Whitlock was simply returning to her home city to take up her affairs; that made this open preparation possible. The Aenir would be glad enough to see a friendly ClawPrince in F'talezon, but they would not make an open breech with DragonLord Ranion to do it.

Megan glanced up. "If we're lucky," she said. "The days are short, and we can expect a bad storm once a week at least, this early after freezeup. It calms down after Dagde Vroi, usually, although the ones you do get then are longer." Shkai'ra nodded, led her horse to check the pony sled near her. Dagde Vroi, the Days of Fools, was the Zak midwinter festival, a month-long carnival famous for no-holds-barred practical joking and for the number of births nine months later—and also clandestine settling of scores.

Megan turned to Boryis, who stood next to Haian and Yvar, who was well enough to sit on a sled to see them off. Rowing Boryis. Mara's Boryis. He'd decided to stay behind in Aenir'sford for the winter, then head south. "Well, Boryis, there's still a space."

"No, Captain, respectfully, no." He looked down at his mitted hands. "It finishes here, for me." The eyes he raised to her were dry. "Mara wouldn't be dead, if we hadn't agreed to work for you and your House—" He held up one hand. "No, let me finish. We knew that we were getting involved in a blood feud, and took the risk. I thought the worst risk was dying, but it wasn't. Any more of this is going to twist me. I've been hurt but I can still heal; any more is going to cripple me. That's all. I don't want to carry your House quarrel with me the rest of my life."

She shook her head at him. *And let Habiku get away with what he's done? Never.* "I see. I didn't understand, Boryis, and I don't really know if I do now, but it's your choice."

"Captain, I understand that you have to clean up and get rid of him . . . He'll go on doing wickedness as long as he lives, it's his revenge on the world but . . . if you don't mind a bit of unasked advice . . . Please don't let it twist you too far."

"I won't, Boryis. Go well." She shrugged off what the man said and turned next to Feranden, the Haian physician. Yvar Monkeyfist was with him, his face still a ball of bandage; the healer was almost as thickly bundled, what showed of his brown skin looking a little grey with the cold. Megan smiled, remembering Haiu Menshir in the southern sea, forested slopes silver-green with olive trees or green-gold oranges, open-walled houses with windchimes ringing in the warm breezes. The wiry little man had come a long way from the Healer's Isle, but you found Haians in every town of consequence. *Except F'talezon. Because of Ranion.*

"Feranden, thank you for coming to see me off and bringing Yvar. Thank you for the care you've given my crewfolk."

He sniffed. "You hef come to veesit me often inough," he replied in the sing-song accent his people gave all the many tongues they learned. "Eet is no matter. End eef you wish to thenk me, stop cutting peepole up with those knives of yours."

She shook her head; Haians were absolute pacifists, whom no amount of experience could shake. Of course, they were protected by the World's Covenant, and would withdraw completely from any land where one of their kind was attacked. Still . . .

"I'm not going to waste time arguing self-defense with you again—" she began.

"You weel never stop keeling by keeling the keelers," he interjected.

"—but remember that lass, Hacia?"

He nodded. "It ees a shame, she would make a good helper and learns quick, but her family cannot spare her wages, and I cannot pay more than board."

Megan pulled a small pouch out of the pocket inside her cloak. "I was going to have this sent. It's enough for the first year or two, and by then the extra business you can handle should cover it."

He blinked, looked down at the money. She closed his hand over it. "Thenk you," he said, looking up at her again. "Eef you mainlandeers must have peepole telling you what to do, then they should be like you, Migen." A smile, hidden by the scarf but visible in his eyes. "Of course, most of thee lords ere not . . ."

"We 'insane mainlanders' need every Haian or Haian-trained we can get," she said, smiling, and knelt beside Yvar's sled. "Goodby, Yvar," she said clearly and distinctly. He reached up a slow hand and squeezed her mitten; wasn't speaking well, yet, and he would never be quick again. Not even as quick as most men who had lost both feet below the knee.

"When it's safe, I'll come back for you and take you back to your family in F'talezon. You'll always have a place with the House."

He nodded, made a sound. Sova looked around Megan, bit her lip, then came up on the other side of the sled. "Here, Yvar," she said, and laid down a huge complex knot. It was a trifle lopsided, and not as neat as he would have made it, but it was a Monkey's Fist knot beyond doubt. "See, I remembered. It's the first one I got to come right, so I thought you should have it."

The muffled sound he made might have been a thank you, or a laugh. Megan whistled and the first sled cracked itself loose and started forward, the hiss of bone and steel blades like a breeze rising. They turned their faces north. *Habiku, I'm coming home*.

The frozen river is different, Sova thought. *It's like a necklace*. A day's travel was only six hours this time of year, so far north, but it had taken them further than sailing would have. The wind pushed, mercifully at their backs, threading stinging fingers through cloth to scratch at their skin. The sun was setting along the western bank, behind black rocks slick with ice, behind green-black pines whose roots curled across their surface like the fingers of an arthritic old man. Grains of ice and powdersnow whipped past, a low, knee-high mist joined by occasional back-gusts from the higher banks.

Breath puffed through the scarves wound around faces, leaving a frozen rime of crystals scraping against cheeks and lips.

It's not really as alive, somehow, as it is in the summer. But it's still there, under my skates. My legs hurt. Cold really makes me tired. And she was hungry again.

The line of sleds were to her right, further out toward the center, where the wind would help them more; a sail flashed by further east yet, the skeletal form of the iceboat back from scouting. There was a continuous hard creak of ice under feet and hooves and runners, bitter whisper of the wind, a feeling of impending cold that overrode the sweat and effort of the long journey.

Inu trotted up, disdainfully ignoring the sidelong sniffs and occasional barks from the canine midgets toiling in their traces. Shyll was beside him, skating smoothly with a hand resting on the greathound's back. He was dressed in trousers and jacket of winter wolfskin with the mottled white fur outside, and ice goggles of white northern ivory; the spear moved smoothly in his outer hand with the swing of his stride.

"Hitch on," he called; he gave her a quick check, and she could see him ticking off the state of her padded jacket, and the woolen facemask that kept her cheeks from frostbite.

Sova leaned, glided over and slipped the weighted wooden bar she'd been carrying into a pocket before painfully digging her fingers into the dog's ruff. Shyll leaned over to look, then took her hand.

"How long have you been carrying those things?" he said.

"Well . . . all day."

"Was that on orders?" he asked crossly.

"Ah, no. No, sir." She removed the other bar. "Ah, the *khyd-hird* said do it as much as I could."

Shyll snorted. "Don't call me sir, it makes me feel old. Has she told you about pacing yourself?"

Sova yawned and leaned on Inu, looking down at the dog's

feet in their leather pouches with the garskin bottoms that gave him traction on the smooth surface. "Yes, sir. Said I should remember that there's a reason for hurting."

He sighed, as if unwillingly reassured. "And you're just at the point where you can ignore pain, and have to make a year's progress in a month."

"S-Shyll, we're going to be in F'talezon in a month."

And you're going to see as little fighting as I can arrange, he surprised himself by thinking. *Why do I . . . oh, Gods of the Dog, she's a good youngker and she tries hard, and she's lost her home and family. Inu likes her.*

"Draw your sword," he said for answer. She pushed herself away from Inu an arm's length for more room, and reached across herself with her right. The clench on the hilt was painful and light; she nearly dropped it before the point wobbled up to guard, and it was a struggle to resheath it while moving.

"What shape would you be in to fight now if you had to?" he scolded as she sheathed it. "Habiku aside, this is hungry country. Here," He whistled to Inu, and they stopped. Sova lurched, a sudden pain lancing through her legs. "Let me see . . ." He brought the greathound around to shelter them from the wind, and undid her gloves.

"Ri dung, you've been skating with your hands clenched around those things! Didn't anyone tell you that they'd freeze if they weren't worked regularly? You can thank good gloves there's no frostbite. You're carrying a spare pair of mittens inside your jacket? Switch to them until we make camp, it's only another half-hour. Wiggle your fingers and put them under your armpits."

Rilla swept by, circled back and braked to a sideways halt that sent ice chips scattering. "Something wrong?"

"Young stoic, driving herself into exhaustion, risking frostbite," he said lightly. She bent to look at Sova's hands.

"Hmmm. Better not try carrying your weights and so forth after today. It's going to get colder." She looked up, her light brown eyes serious over the red scarf. "Ever been on a long ice journey?" Sova shook her head. "Right," Rilla continued. "Listen to him." She jerked her swaddled chin in Shyll's direction. "He's an old hand at it. It fools you, lets you think, 'Oh, this is easy,' until you fall on your face. Cold leeches you like bone marrow sickness. So, take the next rest spot on the third sled down. Change off with Moshulu, hear?"

"Yes, ma'am." Rilla stopped, took a deliberate second look. Shyll broke in.

"She calls me 'sir.' "

"Oh, that must make you feel ancient." She twinkled at him. "Sova, just call me Rilla, all right? You can call him anything you like as long as you—"

"Don't call him late for dinner," he chimed in with her and Sova laughed at the old, old joke; her stomach rumbled.

"Come on," the Zak said. "I'll see you up."

As they sped to catch up with the third sled, he slid up to his place, Inu panting comfortably beside him. *She's right,* he thought. *It's going to get a lot colder if I read the signs right.* Then: *It's not a necessary chore, looking after the youngker. It's . . . enjoyable.* There hadn't been many children in his life, not since he left home, and then he had scarcely been more than a child himself. Since then, they were squalling bundles on their parents' backs, or shouting packs under a window . . . He snorted, and used the butt spike of his spear to pole himself faster.

Shkai'ra concentrated on the ice under her horse's hooves, trying not to think of another frozen river from a long time ago—*eight, nine years ago,* she thought. Then, *No, I've laid those ghosts to rest.* Although there had been a small, dark witch involved then, as well. That had been in her homeland . . . *It's just as well to be an exile,* went through her. *No obligations but the ones you chose yourself, no folk or kindred but the friends you chose along the way. That Zaik-eaten shaman who wanted to eat my heart said my fate would be to dwell with ghosts and witches; damned if he wasn't right.*

Megan was handing off her line to Stanver. *I don't think that this was what he meant.* Shkai'ra smiled behind her scarf as the Zak woman coasted over.

"Shaping well," Shakai'ra said. 'We've made over thirty

miles today; I'm surprised there isn't more trade this time of year. It's not comfortable, but it's fast."

Megan pulled the wool scarf down from below her eyes to speak more clearly. "Wait until a blizzard hits. The snowfall gets lighter as you go north, but the winds don't. They can pin you down for a week or more." She looked up at the sky: clear, with a fringe of blue haze about the risen moon. Hard cold tonight. No storms for the next twenty hours, at least. "Expensive to keep people or beasts fed in the open, too. And wait until we hit a drifted section in a bend, and have to dig our way through. Toward winter's end they can pile up ten times manheight in places."

Their followers waved or saluted as they passed; there were even a few cheers.

"They're in good heart," Shkai'ra said.

Megan shrugged cynically. "It's the first day. They've been telling each other lies about how great their leaders are, to keep up their spirits, and the lies get bigger and easier to believe each time they come round." Someone had been spreading the tale of the Karibal to Rilla's crew and the newcomers, and the challenge in Brahvniki had grown as the tale spread upriver.

"I want to check on Sova," Shkai'ra said. *You're still uneasy when people love you, love,* she thought. *Gods, though, it is a burden, all those expectations. Dreams in their eyes . . . Enough to frighten even a cold heart like me; lucky I am that I'll never have so many want to lay their lives on me.* "Most of the others are used to winter journeys, or they've got tentmates who are to watch them." *Wish I hadn't been so busy, all day. Left her here . . . Glitch, godlet of fuck-ups, take it! Oh . . . Over there where Shyll and Rilla and the greatpuppy are, Sled Four.*

ON THE ICE NORTH OF AENIR'SFORD EVENING, TWELFTH IRON CYCLE, THIRTEENTH DAY

Travelling on the ice of the upper Brezhan is easy for a day. Day after day becomes a hazy dream of whispering blades and wind and the ice is everywhere: underfoot, in your clothing, against your face, hanging on your lashes and tips of your hair, in the air you breathe. It becomes a personal enemy. The whole body is never warm, not hunched over a fire behind a windscreen, not tumbled together with ten others in a tent, under furs and blankets and all but your outer winterwear. The wind sucks heat, pushing through the glazing of even the best leather, down around the cracks of your facemask and up the tight-bound connection between gloves and sleeves.

Work is unending misery, a dragging at the limbs that doubles and redoubles the effort needed for the simplest task. Sweat is a mortal danger, for the layers of air trapped between dry garments are the best protection a traveller has. A wet foot means a stop, lighting a fire, drying skin and boot and changing the wrappings next the skin. Every breath leaches water into air dryer than the hottest desert, and there is no water except what you melt. Nose and throat and lungs are always tight and sore; lips crack and bleed and freeze and crack again. Survival means unending alertness when a single neglected detail can kill, but the cold numbs the mind first of all. The wood and leather and metal of tools turn brittle and lose strength. The body burns as much fuel as it can digest simply maintaining its warmth; effort draws down the last reserve against extremity.

Even for the most experienced and best-equipped, every day beyond the first is danger. The Zak say winter is the Dark Lord's breath; the fire of life offends it. Each sunset means more weakness. In the end, it will kill.

"What killed him?" Shkai'ra muttered to herself.

The rising wind fluttered the dead bandit's clothes, multiple layers of rag and felt and hide, good furs and thin burlap; she knew the stink would have been killing if it had not been so cold. It *was* cold, a lowering noon when it seemed the only colors in the world were dun-white and black. She shivered; a week of hard effort in this had drained even her reserves of strength. Her face had gone a little gaunter, bringing out the foundation of strong bones as the body struggled to keep the internal fires warm enough, and not even three heavy meals a day were enough. Fishhook mewed in her ear. The kitten was cuddled in under her jacket, tail wrapped around the back of her neck.

She bent again to examine the figure, feeling a stiffness in her bones that was a foretaste of age.

Little showed of the corpse's face apart from the crude birchwood snow-goggles and beard peeling with frostburn. He was hidden from the river below the low bluff by a cunning screen of snow and woven withes, and one dead hand gripped a woodchopper's axe; there was a hide bucket of javelins across his back, a long knife thrust sheathless through his scrap belt. The dead lips were pulled back from the lips, a stick of frozen jerky protruding in an eternal mid-chew.

Shkai'ra rose and shivered again. *I thought I'd seen the Black Crone all his faces,* she thought. *But there's one always ready to surprise you with a fresh ugliness.*

She turned, scrubbing at the breath-rime that threatened to block the slits of her snow-goggles, and took a slow careful breath through the icicle-fringed woolen mask. A too-quick gasp in weather like this could damage your wind with ice in your lungs, too many and you were courting lungfever and death. Below the low rise, the river turned east for a space; a giant drift had formed across the way, three times the height of the tallest among them. The sleds were halted in a row before it, and the doll-sized figures of men and women and horses toiled at breaking a path through a wall of snow thirty feet from edge to edge. Even across a quarter-mile she could sense the heart-deep weariness of them. The wind was from the northeast, blowing a long sheet-plume from the knife-edge of the drift, dipping like quick smoke down onto the workers below and settling into the fog their shovels raised.

She pulled the mask down and shouted, a long echoing call: "*Meeeeeggggaaaaann!*"

A knot of figures had been gathered around one of the fires, drinking their hot, honey-sweetened milk as they took their turn at rest. Four turned, saw her jerk both hands skyward in the "come here" signal, began to toil across the snow-packed ice, around the half-sunk boulders at the river's edge, up the slope. Shkai'ra stood with her hands thrust under her armpits; she was out of the wind. While motionless a thin layer of slightly warmer air formed around your skin, within the layers of your clothes. Her only movement was fingers and toes twitching, in thick gloves and boots.

Shyll was the first over the edge, using his spear as a prop up the steep path of scree and bush and treacherous patches of ice beneath snow. He was breathing with careful slowness, and the hooded mask of his face turned alertly as he walked toward her.

That is a hardy man, she thought ungrudgingly, and she had been bred by a land as bitter as this. *I've softened a little, living in the southlands these last years. Keeping up with him pushes me.*

She heard Megan curse and scramble below as a brush crumbled in her hand, then push herself over the lip; Sova followed, with Rilla behind her boosting. Shkai'ra removed a hand to wave at her, feeling a little glow of pride as the slight, dog-weary form straightened. The girl was showing what was in her on this trip; going to her limit and beyond, despite the constant draining misery. It was when the world tested you that you learned what you were made of; much trained-in weakness was melting off Sova with the puppyfat, revealing a core of pride that sustained her when many tougher reared would have broken.

"Look what our scouts didn't find," Shkai'ra said.

Shyll bent over the dead bandit, grunted. *"Graukalm,"* he said.

ONE DAY'S TRAVEL SOUTH

Cold. Hotblood kill. Taste screaming. Good. Redcoat. Run. Run. Coldwind. Open mouth, bare fangs. Hate. Hatewhistle. Sharp black claws dug into a snowdrift in a tangle of dead trees. *Lie waiting. Wait now. Run in snow coming. Redcoat near. Nofear near. Hotblood kill.*

*   *   *

Megan nodded as she examined the corpse. "*Graukalm*, grievouswind," she said, moving to stand near Shkai'ra and looking eastward, into the twisted wood of dwarf hemlocks. "It's rare, thank Koru, akribhan. It comes out of the east, out of Zibr, usually in a storm or with it. No warning, except a sudden stilling of the wind, then it *drops* on you, out of the upper air, weatherwitches say. It can freeze you in five heartbeats or less, no amount of clothing is any good. Freezes even white bear in their tracks; it only lasts a few seconds, but unless you're under some cover that's enough."

She looked at the man again. They were in debated lands, neither F'talezonian nor Aenir nor Thane. These harsh uplands had never been densely peopled, the soil thin and rocky even by northern standards; the original Zak inhabitants had been a thin scatter of woodsdwellers, living mainly by the hunt. Long ago war had passed over the marches hereabouts. Some had died, others had moved away, or intermarried with the trickle of strangers who wandered in, ready to endure the bitter earth for the sake of space and a home under no law. Now the folk were like the land, of no particular nationality and with an evil reputation for murder by stealth and longshore piracy.

"Shyll, check further along, will you? No, Sovee, I think you should go back and tell Annike that the ambush she and Shkai'ra were expecting isn't likely to happen." As many goods and beasts and vehicles as were with her was a standing temptation, and the wild folk would not know hers for a caravan of fighters.

She turned and looked northeast. The noon sun was a pale white glow through the overcast, and the wind was coming in fitful gusts; she sucked on the pebble under her tongue to moisten her mouth and slitted her eyes. *Are the clouds heavier there?* she asked herself.

"Rilla," she said. "Cerwyn's weatherwise, isn't he?"

Her cousin nodded; she had pulled a dart from the quiver on her shoulder and rapped sharply on the corpse's arm. There was a crack, and the fist gripping the axe broke off like an icicle; the iron head struck rock at the unmoving feet, and shattered like glass.

"He is . . . Coz, this happened fairly recently. Not more than two hours, and we've been here one at least. Longer, and the cold would have leached."

Shyll came back, tension in the set of his shoulders. "Twenty of them," he said huskily. "They had a covered fire and they were sitting around it. Like this, all around it, sitting there frozen in mid-motion."

"Come on," Megan said. "I feel itchy about this and we'd be better if we were together."

They made their way down the bank, careful to touch the earth as little as they could. The crews were working in shifts, half an hour at the drifts and half behind the leather windscreens strung out from the sleds; the cooks had the log platforms for the fires set up and the small, hot blazes were flickering beneath the ceramic pots in their beds of clay and sand. Shkai'ra passed one, took a cup and noticed sap freezing on the end of a stick as it melted and dripped out from the central portion that burned in orange-gold coals.

"Cerwyn!" Rilla called. There was a delay as the man came back from his place on the snow-face; his dark wool and bearskins were dusty white with the talc-fine crystals, and his steps dragged. No matter how fit, even a short spell of physical labor in this weather exhausted as a day spent breaking rock in summer would not.

"Yes, Captain?" he said to Rilla. They had all become adept at reading the set of shoulders beneath a hood and mask; his showed dull apathy kept moving only by will.

Slow, Rilla thought. *We're all slow*. It was as if thought were an oil, like the tallow used to grease machinery, that turned cold and thick and viscous and made the wheels grind more and more slowly, until all you wanted was to lie down and sleep . . .

"We found the ambush Annike and Megan's akribhan were expecting," she said.

"Good," he said. His home was not many days northwest of here. "Too many 'breed woodsrunners around this bend. They look at the bins and smokehouses and know they won't make it to first harvest . . ."

"They were dead. Better than twenty, outlaws by their

looks. Local folk, who knew the winter, they had full gear
and a covered fire. Grievouswind. Tap the weather, Cerwyn."

"Vilist, Teik," he said, with the slightly antique courtesy of
backcountry village-Zak. He leaned the long-handled wooden
shovel against a sled and turned in a slow circle with his
hands outstretched and his face turned upward to the sky.

"Hard to . . ." he murmured, then stopped as if frozen
himself, facing the northeast. "It's warmer around here. Only
a little, and the wind's dropping."

They all froze and looked at each other. "*Storm!* Teik,
storm out of *Zibr* coming fast. Worst I've ever felt, Teik, it's
the Dark Lord's own and it's *hungry.*" His voice was rising,
an expert's panic at a known terror that he meets with no
time to make preparation. "How could I not have felt it? It's
as if it was hiding. *Teik! There's a grievouswind riding in like
a mad Ryadn on her Ri.* Soon, soon!"

"Annike!" Rilla called sharply. "Temuchin! Call off the
digging."

Megan steadied Cerwyn. "Tents, pull the animals in!" She
shouted. "We need all the warmth we can get. Stake everything down to the ice, stake it hard. Half the tents, everyone
pile in on each other. Throw some snow over—no, the wind
will do it. Jump!" She wheeled and started yanking at the
lashings on the nearest sled. "Shyll, we'll use the lee of the
drift."

Shkai'ra shook her head as if clearing it. "I'll get the woodcutters," she shouted, already running back toward the bank
and south, to where a team was chopping at fallen timber.
"Sova! Pull in the ice-fishers, over there behind the curve of
the drift. Run, girl, run!" A horn began to sound, urgent flat,
blatting sounds.

The leather screens were pulled down, people moving as
fast as the cold allowed, staked down between snow and
close-hauled sleds. Shouts and neighing and barking were
lost in a rising whistle; frantic arms shovelled snow on the
loose edges of the leather windshields and the tents, darkening the long rectangle along the edge of the drift where the
ponies and dogs were made to lie down, crowding it close.
Sledges ran on steel spikes, as the hook-ends were dinned

down over the runners of the sleds to nail them to the surface.

"Hurry!" Cerwyn called. "Hurry!" Hands made brutal by necessity threw the ponies down, hobbled them and tossed their horse blankets across. Wiser, the sled dogs were burrowing under snow or anything else available, whining, huddling together in masses of fur and fear-snarled teeth, burying noses under tails in circles of protection.

"Inside. Leave the fires! Everyone in!" Megan and Rilla yelled, listening to be sure that everyone answered, slapping at arms and shoulders as they ran past. Even then the cousins had time to feel a brief surge of pride at how little panic there was, no heedless flailing. Northeast, the light had vanished; low cloud and a white-roiling ground haze of fallen snow pushed before the wind hid what was coming, but the eyes of the mind could see it, like a great wall toppling with ponderous acceleration. The woodcutters came gasping up, streams of white pluming through their scarves, and crawled into already crowded tents.

The wind was rising again as the edge of the blizzard came closer, and suddenly snow was flicking at them like a thousand, thousand miniature knives, the tiny crystals of a deep-winter storm. The light faded, as if a dark blanket had been thrown on top of the clouds to dim the sun. Then the wind struck with force enough to throw everyone left standing to their knees; the circle of visibility shrank like a puddle of water in the bottom of a sink when the plug was pulled. The roar of the storm sucked in every other sound; a woven bullhide rope parted noiselessly in the deathbird shrieking, the plucked-string note vibrating through the ice under their feet.

"Sova!" Shkai'ra called, running back in the woodcutters' wake. A bison pelt blew into her, the thirty pounds of leather and hair flicked along like a paper scrap, and almost knocked her down once more; she gripped the weight of it.

I didn't see her come back with the fishers. Twenty seconds more and she's dead . . . Glitch, is that the tents? "Sova, answer!"

"Shkai'ra!" Megan, blocked by the press of people getting

into the tent, saw her disappear in the swirl of snow as the wind hit, shouted over their heads, gasping at the knife-like pain in her lungs from cold. "No . . ." But the Kommanza was already gone.

Shkai'ra stumbled to the edge of the drift—*too Glitch-taken cold—the fishers and Sova must have gotten back*— She turned around. The air went still as glass. *Cold falling.* She half-heard Megan, frantic, calling her. The shelter was a hundred yards away. *I've been very stupid,* she thought. The visibility had dropped to arm's length, and the wind sang in her skull, she could feel it sucking warmth through the layered thickness of her clothes. *Sova's either under cover or she's going to die, and so may I.*

The drift was near, an almost vertical wall with the wind keening along it. Then there was a moment's silence, with the snow coming straight down, drifting. The killer was above her, dropping with the inevitability of age. She wrapped the bison cloak around herself and dove into the side of the snow, burrowing desperately and heedless of the danger of smothering. It was light-packed for all its size, each tiny bubble of trapped air another ounce of insulation. The *graukalm* was like a hammer pounding darkness into her eyes and ears. *Dark.*

Rilla caught Megan just as she was about to go after Shkai'ra. "No, coz, no, no." Megan squirmed, freed a hand to claw and froze as the cold fell.

"Shkai'ra," she whispered. The darkness in the tent was barely more tolerable then outside, a huddled clot of warmth knotted tight against the *graukalm*.

Shyll and Rilla wrapped their arms around her and she clutched at them as if they were storm anchors. They were lying crouched together in the dark, across other legs and bodies. She couldn't go out there physically. One deep, even breath in the cold darkness. Another. She reached for the *manrauq*, plunged into power like a swimmer into cold water. *Shkai'ra.* Behind her eyes the world burned brilliant orange, flickered to yellow for a second, steadied. *Yellow? Where's my familiar red?* She dismissed the thought. *Shkai'ra.*

Her mind reached out for the familiar shape nonshape of the Kommanza's mind.

The knot of minds curled warmly around her. The pattern of winds and pressures of the storm curled around them. The shape of the mind curled around the storm, spiderweb through the half-living, natural energy-web, holding it hunkered down over them like a vulture tearing at a half-living victim.

A blue-violet haze of a mind. Cold. Cultured. Intent to kill. Not the Wizard but someone almost as powerful. The Blue Mage.

As she recognized the mind forcing the storm down on them, he found her. In the sea of the manrauq, a whirlwind swept around her, eddied to catch four minds near, and dragged them all down; falling, falling . . . Megan strained against the mental hand cramming her down into herself, felt edges peel away as she was forced back into what she had been . . . *Nightmare.*

She opened her eyes in the half-gloom of the old River Lady's cabin, knew that he was coming. His heavy tread made the board outside the door crack, like it always did. Thunder rumbled. She was twelve.

Rilla hung onto Megan and Shyll, felt the leather bow over their heads from the wind, felt a crackle like the edge of lightning bolt and . . . *Nightmare.*

Mam's due home soon. She took Megan away. Rilla huddled by the drug-still, listening to it bubble. *I didn't steal anything today and she won't have anything to drink. She'll be sober enough to hit me.* The front door creaked. *I've got to hide.* "Rillan!" Mam's voice from the front room. Rilla scrambled under the bed, watched the door open and Mam's muddy shoes cross the floor.

Shkai'ra tried to shake her head as she woke up. The snow pressed around her from all sides. It was dark and the wind howled like a snowtiger, clawing away at her hiding place. Dark and close . . . *Nightmare.*

Zoweitzum, the little crawlers are right behind me. Zaik damn these walls . . . She was in the sewers under Fehinna.

Megan had been here a moment ago, had wiggled around on her back and down into the water. *I'm alone with all the weight of the city on me, pressing down in the dark—the walls shift, smear me into the dark, close, close and it's coming behind me. One thing, no. Hundreds, the sewer crawlers following the blood trail, green eyes . . .* There was a shivering rumble and the walls moved closer.

Shyll pulled the soaking wet scarf away from his face, put his arm around Megan, felt her tremble . . . *Nightmare. I can't fail. I might die if I fail. If I succeed I'll be a Ryadn, riding the most splendid of creatures. Not teRyadn, outcast. My Ri. Terrifying. Beautiful. It was out there, somewhere. His Ri. To bond with him, or kill him.*

It reared up from the spring grass, struck out at him, not bonding, refusing him. It nipped his arm, drove him staggering to the right.—In the tent, under his parka, a crescent-shaped bruise sprang up, started seeping blood.—*It's playing with me.* Mad green eyes glittering. *It'll play with me, tear me apart.* He ran.

Rilla looked up at Marte's face, at the smile. "I'm not going to beat you dear." *She's drunk already.* "I got rid of an ungrateful brat. Megan isn't going to bother you any more dear." She hiccuped, fell onto the bed and laughed and laughed. "I sold her bond to a River Captain. He'll take good care of the little fiend, devil me with my brother's shade, will she!"

I'm alone. My bigger cousin gone. I'm alone with her. I'm . . . I'm . . . This can't be true.

Something about that sounded right. Little girl Rilla opened her mouth to cry, to wail loss and loneliness, stopped. *This can't be true.* The nightmare froze. *Megan. Megan's gone. No. Megan's . . . Megan's b—* It was like lifting a boulder, granite ridges gouging into her . . . *Megan's BACK.* The dream broke, sending her tumbling into another. She was on the deck of a ship, holystoning the deck, preparing to finish because of the thunderstorm brewing. She cringed aside as the Captain, the Arkan Sarngeld, stamped by.

*   *   *

The walls were closing in. Shkai'ra whimpered, turned her head, bit into the leather of her sleeve and bruised the arm underneath, slammed a fist across six inches of space into the rock of the wall. The water stank, and the walls were barely more than chest-width apart. The multiple click of claws and hungry jaws behind. Darkness ahead, the small spaces, crushing, confining. *Control. It's coming. No, control. Move. Move now. . . . It's coming.* Fear welled up to clot in her throat. *Mad green eyes. This isn't. Real.* A dream. It was a dream.

She was dicing on deck as the Captain came aboard. She looked up, then away as he went below, going to play with his new toy. She shrugged. Poor kid, glad it's not me.

Shyll ran. His lungs were burning. *Run. Run.* The Ri was right behind him, nip marks burned all across his back. It bit him again to make him turn. He tripped, fell in the dirt, rolling. It reared over him ready to stamp him into bloody slush.

No. Inu howled. *Inu. Inu.* The dog leaped over him with snow scattering. *Snow? This isn't spring.* Inu hit the Ri neck-high, and both of them vanished.

He got up from the deck, grabbed the burlap bag of roots and hoisted it to his shoulder to take it down to Piatr. A thunderstorm brewing. Rilla putting the stone away, Shkai'ra dicing with Tze . . . Captain going below to ride the F'talezonian girl. *Poor little brat.* She was too young, too small.

Run in snow. Hotblood kill fear. Run. Close Redcoat. Close. Tastebite fear.

Sarngeld pulled the door open. Twelve-year-old Megan cringed back on the bunk. *"Come here, my little one,"* he said in Arkan. She stared, wide-eyed, and didn't move. *"You understand well enough. Come here, or I'll have to get you."* He walked over, sat down on the edge of the bunk, pulled off his boots and breeches. She tried to get past him, running for the door. His hand shot out, clamped around her upper arm, whirled her around. *"That's my girl, that's my good little slut."* He clamped his legs around her, let her struggle while he pulled his shirt off, rubbing himself against her. *No. No. Don't. Papa, Mama, Rilla, Shkai'ra . . .*

The dream wavered and a blue thread pulled her back in the Arkan's hands. He picked her up like a doll, held her down on the bunk with his weight, letting her struggles excite him. When he pulled her tunic off, she started to scream.

At the first scream everyone on deck jumped. Shyll put down the bag of roots.

"Cold," he said.

Shkai'ra dropped the dice. "Megan," she murmured. "I know that sound, she's having the dream again."

Rilla stood up from where she knelt. Tze and Piatr came up on deck, blinking.

"I can't speak," Tze said. "I'm doing something I should have this time before."

A yellow flare lit the sky as the thunderstorm broke, drowning another scream. A yellow of magic.

Piatr, in the real world, in the tent, warm, with the storm outside, remembered Sova's whisper. "Why didn't you help her?"

Inu was barking, howling in the storm, Fishhook hissing at something that most of the other Zak couldn't see.

They broke the door down. Sarngeld was laughing, rising between the opened knees of the child on the bed; her feet kicked in futile protest. He turned a startled indignant face to his crew as they interrupted his pleasure, opened his mouth. They pulled him off, hurled him against the wall, driving their fists into him. Little Megan, on the bunk, rolled over, looked at them wide-eyed. Then they stopped, held the huge blubbery man against the boards of the cabin, sweat shining through the thinning blond hair on his scalp, blood and tears on his face.

Megan, white lock of hair gleaming yellow in the light from

her eyes, steel claws glinting, stepped through the door. She walked over to Sarngeld, *his real name is Atzathratzas*, put up a hand, hooked her claws into his throat. He choked, dying, shrivelled into nothing and blew away. Megan turned to her younger self on the bunk, gathered her in her arms, rocking her. *"This can't be real,"* young Megan whispered, looking up into her own eyes. *"I'm dreaming."*

"I'm dreaming," she whispered in the real world. The storm hammered at the shelter, at the snowdrift, at the tiny shape running up the river in the wind, fangs bared.

Shkai'ra saw the rage pull her away from the nightmare; it shredded like old wet felt as her fists beat gleefully Sarngeld's ugly Arkan face, crumbling of bones and teeth . . . *Daydream, this I've daydreamed, no time, not now.*

Reality. She had been lying in the snowdrift, dreaming. (*Why?*) The wind had scoured away most of the snow around her. She could hear the hiss as the ice crystals whirled away, dragging precious protection. The grievouswind was gone, over, but her body had begun to shake uncontrollably, and the blizzard was almost as bad. A few minutes exposed to the violence of it would suck the life heat away, the crucial areas around heart and lungs chilled past the point where they could recover.

A scream. At first she thought it was part of the storm, then a clawed paw broke through the crust by her face. It vanished as the Ri reared, letting an icy blast of air into her face. The beast from Aenir'sford, the hallucination . . . no, real. It was here.

Redcoat sister. Hotblood kill for you. Who kill?

No one. A communication without knowing how or why; not words, but the meaning that words were made of. It snorted, then lay down next to her, snow piling on both of them. *Redcoat sister warm. Hot. Stay.* She burrowed close, pulled the bisonskin robe over them both, laid her cheek on its lowered neck, feeling the warm pulse of the vein. It was hotter than a horse, big, smelling carnivore-rank, but warm, warm; she curled up against its belly and their weight sank them deeper. A rumble, and the undercut drift slid down on them again. Pain in hands and feet, stinging welcome pain, overwhelming drowsiness. The Ri began to purr.

They slept.

Megan gathered her will, felt her friends and followers break free, add their strength to hers, raised her sight to the vaguely outlined blue eyes in the storm. "You've lost. Cease."

"Yellow witch," a cool voice answered her. "You cannot defeat me."

"I already have." She drew on the strength around her, hurled it into the netting holding the storm on them. It whirled out yellow, trailing the wills of those who would help her, grew, grew and cracked the blue web of power across. Faintly, in F'talezon, she felt/heard a cry of pain. (*A gilded mirror began to bleed.*) The manrauq shifted and the storm ceased to be the unnatural monster. Wind still struck the felt-lined leather with buffeting fists, a roar of white noise too much for ears to bear; the cold still drew. But it was simply a storm now, the thread of purpose withdrawn from the fabric of it, the living will to harm.

Enough. I was paid to kill, not suffer. I will remember. He withdrew, leaving only the threat of future revenge behind.

She shivered, opened her eyes, sensing more than seeing Rilla on one side, Shyll on the other, close in the chill vibrating darkness. Pain between her ears, but no sign of overstrain. She embraced them both, shakily, opened her mouth to try and say something, shook her head, fighting to stay awake. "Shkai'ra's still alive out there somewhere," she whispered, pulling them close. Hurt and weariness were good; they tasted of victory. Somewhere deep in her mind, scar-tissue had pulled open, and that hurt too, an ache that seeped across memory and will, but the pus beneath was draining, she could feel it trickle away.

Chapter 20

ONE WEEK NORTH OF AENIR'SFORD
TWELFTH IRON CYCLE, SEVENTEENTH DAY

Megan woke hungry. For a moment the sensation overwhelmed her; hunger for sweets, a human's reaction to extreme cold. Another hunger, this time for meat. Raw, red, torn from still-moving bones; bolting gulping lumps down a muzzle thrown back and working, working, blood running into her fur (*fur?*) . . .

She sat up, bumping her head on the taut leather above, shaking off the alien sensation. *Must be a dream.* The others were waking around her; she could feel them in the close darkness of the crowded tent. A flicker that was closer than touch, sealed off, locked away, forgotten. The hunger, from some creature, was coming from a little further away.

Megan clamped down, the touches fading to the background of her mind; time enough to explore them later. They *did* seem permanent . . . and they *had* all experienced the dream . . . her attention shied away from that, became aware enough to hear a sound conspicuous by its absence.

"The wind!" she said. There was a muttering stir, and Shyll knelt up to press his ear against the tent-roof above.

"It's gone," he said. "Gone, not just muffled."

For a moment they all whooped and babbled. *Five days*, Megan thought. *Four days. Now we can find her.* She unlashed the bottom thongs of the flap, where it had been tied to ensure an opening to give them air. One broke with a crackle. The weight of snow on top pushed it down, spilling snow; brilliant sun filtered through it into the darkness. People behind her were laughing.

She pulled down the snow-goggles, tightened the fastening of her mittens, squatted and drove herself arms-first into the snowpack, clambered out. It was colder than the tent, but warm enough not to hurt much on the tender skin of her cheekbones. Behind her the tent was a black hole and a lump in the north-tending slope of the drift . . .

Megan blinked and looked around for the permanent landmarks. The bluff where they had found the dead bandit was still there, but the slope beneath it was buried; the snowbank they had been digging through had marched right over them in the course of the storm. It had almost doubled in size, as well; her mind adjusted distances and identified the line of sleds, the tents by their sides, the lumpy heaving area that would be where the draught-stock had been thrown beneath the leather sheets of the windshelters.

Looking northeast, she squinted and raised her right mitten to shield against the fierce low disk of the morning sun. The river was bare, the ice burnished and smoothed by the scouring winds. Noise was growing about her as Shyll and Rilla went from tent to tent. The under officers and bosuns were shaking themselves free; she heard a whistle, saw her followers wading to break out shovels and scrapers.

Here and there, small mounds shifted, struggled to standing and shook themselves, barking. A greater heave near her tent, and Inu arose, flailed snow in all directions with a vigorous twitch and trotted off after the teRyadn, bringing his platter-sized paws up chin-high to step through the four-foot depth of the snow. Everything was blue-white, clear, bright, sight stretching enormous distances under the cloudless dome of sky.

"SSSSHHHKKAI'RRRRRRAAAA!" There was no answer. Sova came up behind her, pulled her scarf down.

"Captain, where *is* she?"

Megan forced herself to calm in her reply. "I don't know, Sovee. No one's seen her since the storm hit." A blast of

worry leaked past her shields. "No, she's alive, I'm sure."
She's alive, but not in any of the other tents as I thought.
Shyll and Rilla and Cerwyn came up. *How has she survived
four days without food or shelter? I can't feel any pain* . . .
But frostbitten limbs did not start paining until full consciousness returned. For a moment she had an intolerable mental
image of Shkai'ra gangrenous, limb-lopped—

"We'll organize a search party with probing poles," Rilla
said.

"She's got to be under the snow somewhere," Shyll added.
"It's the only way she could have made it. We—"

"Maybe Fishhook could find her," Sova said, tugging at
Megan's sleeve. Megan looked down at the kitten, who was
chewing on Sova's fingers. "She was with you all this time?"

"Yes, Captain." A scowl. "And she peed all over my jacket!
If it weren't so cold, it would smell *awful*." She plucked at
the garment, breaking yellowish ice off the surface.

HUNGRYFOODNOWFLY! Feelings of a teat between her
lips and *sweetwarmdeliciouslove* flowing into her mouth; tastes
of cooked gar swooped off a diner's plate, pigeon breast, rare
roast beef in lovely boneless chunks from Shkai'ra's fingers. . .

The kitten's thoughts were easy to direct. Megan reached a
finger and scratched along the folds of her wings and her
head, laid a finger between the folded ears.

FLYNOWFINDFRIEND, she sent. The flittercat looked
at her, blinked, mewed and hopped over to Megan's shoulder, shaking herself. She leaped, flapping hard and nearly
touching surface before she lifted; they were mostly swoopers
from ambush, poor flyers at best.

Fishhook circled once, twice, dived for a spot near where
the old cut had been.

The snow erupted as if exploded out from within. A fanged
head broke free, a head horse-shaped in outline but with an
enormous carnivore gape, mad green eyes staring as the
fangs snapped at the flitterkitten in a striking-snake lunge.

"*Gods of the Dog, it's a Ri!*" Shyll yelled, bounding back
and diving for his spear; Inu bounded at his side, fur standing
up to swell his bulk, a thunderous growl building.

Fishhook back-winged, yeowling, slid sideways and labored

for height, coasting back to Sova and landing with a thump on the back of her jacket. The flitterkitten clung, squeaking panic; the skin webbing of one wing had been torn by the Ri's tusks. Behind her, Megan heard the racheting click of a crossbow being wound, and the clack of a dart being loaded into a casting-stick.

A hand reached up out of the snow and slapped the Ri.

Megan stood frozen, blinking, mind struggling to cope with the information her eyes sent it. The Ri wavered to standing, head low. Shkai'ra dragged herself out of the hole in the snow beside it, pulling herself up by the creature's legs.

"Shkai'ra," she called, heard her voice break in a tremulo and disguised it with a cough. "Do we need to shoot that thing?"

"No." The Kommanza's voice was hoarse and raw. She took a step, staggered, steadied herself on the Ri's whithers. The animal swayed, as if that weight was too much for it; skin hung in folds from its neck and flanks, and the ribs showed like hoops. Lids drooped over the burning grey-flecked emerald of its gaze, as if the burst of energy had drained the last reserve against extremity, as if it would lie down and sleep forever soon.

Megan found herself walking forward, numbly. The Kommanza looked weak, with skin peeling from cheeks and nose and forehead, but standing, standing, her hands stripping her face clear of goggles and mask.

"It's a friend of mine. Is there anything to eat? We're starving. Nuts and honey. Water, I ice-burned my tongue melting snow. Stew. Meat, meant for whatever it is here, whatever it is, it's warm, and I'd be dead or worse without it."

Megan reached her; the Ri slunk its head sideways, back when Shkai'ra's hand pushed it.

"Akribhan," the Zak whispered. "My love, it's a Ri, it can have anything it wants for the rest of its life, it can feast on veal and milk and beef loin." Their hands met.

Shkai'ra smiled, ignoring the pain and cracking and blood from her lips. "Heart's delight, I . . . dreamed." Shyll caught Shkai'ra by the elbow as she swayed.

"Inu, down!" Shyll shouted. "Down!" He had to shout twice more before Inu's ruff flattened; the greathound backed without taking its eyes from the Ri and flattened to the ground. It was crazy not to kill a weakened Ri, but orders were orders or the pack was nothing. He would watch.

Megan chuckled, from under Shkai'ra's arm. "We have to have a talk. A *long* talk, but first there's work to do."

Between them Shyll and she supported most of the Kommanza's weight; Rilla followed well to one side with their equipment. The Ri staggered after.

"Half-frozen horse meat is going to have to do for it, love," Megan said, and Shkai'ra mumbled half-conscious agreement. The Zak commander looked around at the bustle of digging out, at fires already going in a circle of wind-shields. "The Blue Mage did us a favor. We don't have to dig through *that*."

Cerwyn came up, anxiety and relief on his face as he caught the last remark. "I was thinking I'd turned mindblind, to have missed that storm coming, but if it was the Blue—"

He stopped, looking at the Ri. It opened one eye, snarled weasel-shrill deep in its throat, bared its teeth at him.

"What in the Dark Lord's name do I do with *that*, Captain?" he asked.

Megan looked back over Shkai'ra's limp arm.

"Feed him, of course."

EVENING

"A good thing we didn't lose any people," Megan said.

"We needed the rest," Rilla was saying. "And the meat."

They were sitting in one of the tents still buried in the snow, the warmth inside welcome. Megan spooned up the last of the horsemeat stew, nodding. Lamps gave heat and guttering light, picking out their faces as they sat around the remains of the meal; Sova snored in one corner, ignoring their soft voices.

"We'll have to cut supplies. We lost a few dogs as well and can't haul all that stuff. All the food though; that's a self-correcting problem."

There was a murmur of agreement. Everyone was busily looking everywhere but at each other. Megan "listened" to her family, heard and felt the unease, the tension, the embarrassment. *My family?* she thought suddenly. *Mind, are you trying to tell me something again?* She looked at each of them in turn. *We'll have to talk about it* after *I get Habiku*. The hate was a familiar friend. Her eyes darkened and she turned away, alone again.

TWO DAYS LATER

"You're sure?" Megan said.

Cerwyn nodded. "It was like having something in your eye that you don't notice until it's gone," the first mate said. "*Now* I can see the weather; nothing coming for three days at least. Steady south winds, clear, about as cold as this. Worse at night, of course."

They were standing around the cairn of supplies they could no longer carry; two days had served to rest and refit, pile the surplus foodstuffs and cover them with canvas, throw water and rock over the pile to make a fortress of ice and stone. Four less sleds, but with the extra humans on each, the speed should be about equal, she decided. The four frostbite cases were safely bundled up on the rest-sled, everything was tight and ship-shape . . . A middling-grey day, half cloud covered, but thinning to clear. Metallic blue ice stretched down before them, like a road forged of swordblades.

Rilla walked over from the iceboat. That had been recovered and repaired; it quivered behind her, a twelve-foot, oval shell of smoothly curved planks, crouching on the three long legs of its outriggers. The forward runner was pivoted, and there was a stubby mast with a triangular shell. The crew stood by their places, waiting.

"All ready, coz," she said. "Four days and a night to F'talezon, saving dead calms and storms." An iceboat was the fastest form of transport on the river, but unstable and fragile. "Between those documents and the money, I should be able to get *somebody* to listen . . . Keep him off your back until you get there, at least."

"Be *careful*," Megan began, then shrugged ruefully. "Ah, coz, it's all been said and I trust you. See you by High Festival Day." A slight smile of the eyes. "Koru knows, it's appropriate enough that we'll get there and have it out with Habiku 'round about the *Dagde Vroi*."

Shyll trotted up at his tireless lope, skates clattering about his neck on their thongs and Inu at his side. Sova was draped over the greathound's back, squealing with delight and thumping out a drum-beat on his ribs with the flats of her mittened hands. The dog's ears were back slightly; they flattened and the look of resignation in his eyes deepened to misery as Shkai'ra approached on her Ri.

The wolverine-horse had spent most of the past two days lying up on a pile of dead ponies, eating and sleeping. Its condition was visibly better, and so, unfortunately, were its spirits. The Kommanza swung down out of the saddle; it had been struggle enough to get the animal to accept that, and reins or bit were out of the question, and unneeded in this case.

It danced beside her, clawed feet scritching on the ice, looking at the other humans. *killtear breakbone bloodspurt hotwetsalt screamfunfunfun?* it thought hopefully.

Shkai'ra sighed, walked around to the black muzzle and gripped it by a lock of the platinum mane that was not coarse like a horse's. It flowed between her fingers like watered silk, or her own red-blonde locks.

"No," she said firmly. It wasn't necessary to speak, Megan had told her that the Ri sensed meaning below the level where words were formed, and speaking could tempt her to use concepts beyond its limited comprehension, but habit told.

"No. Stay. No kill, no fight. Eat later."

sulk. deadmeat. sulksulksulk.

A moving patch humped itself up Shkai'ra's back under her jacket, stuck its head out beside her neck. Fishook laid her ears back and hissed at the Ri. The Ri stretched out its long whippy neck and hissed back, a sound like an iron kettle.

Megan hugged Rilla as close as she could through the layers of bulky clothing. "Be careful, coz."

"I will."

Shkai'ra stood, took her hand, then they pulled each other into an awkward hug. "You have a good wind."

"*Dah*." She turned to Shyll. He was gripping his spear with both hands. He jammed it into the ice, took her in his arms and lifted her to face level, kissed her. "We'll be right behind you. Distract him enough and we'll ride right down his throat."

"*Dah*." For a second she buried her face in his collar, then they pulled away. She walked to her place.

The crew rocked the iceboat to crack the runners loose, tightened the ropes to bring the sail into the steady wind. They pushed, running beside it, to jump into their seats, lacing themselves in as the iceboat picked up speed.

The iceboat swept past the caravan's line, already faster than a galloping horse. Waves and cheers from the crews in their traces, hands waving from the boat; Sova jumped up and down, flourishing her sword. The spot of sail receded, tilting and dipping as the sprung outriggers bent under the wind's thrust, sending long, shining-white sprays of chips from the runners. Just before it was completely out of sight, Inu howled after it, a long hollow call echoing along the ice. Shkai'ra swung up onto her Ri.

chase? it thought.

Megan skated further out toward the center of the river, where the whole train could see her, waved an arm about her head and chopped it down to the north.

Avritha looked at the beautiful ivorywork on the bowl, breathed in the delicate scent of dried flower petals in it.

A nice try, darling Habiku. Not good enough though.

"Take a note, please, Aylix." Her secretary took up her pen. "Teik ClawPrince, I received your lovely gift. How nice of you to think of me in this festival season. Unfortunately, I will be somewhat busy in the next few days and will be unable to thank you personally . . ."

Chapter 21

ON THE RIVER
BETWEEN ICE-CARAVAN AND F'TALEZON
TWELFTH IRON CYCLE, NINETEEENTH DAY

The wind was steady, the weather clear. They only had to stop once to dig through a drift in a bend of the river. Rilla smiled to herself as they rounded Bayag Isle, thinking of the fight with the *Kettle Belly*, then the smile faded. *Too many people died there.* Blood feuds between Houses were an old Zak tradition, but this one was a monstrosity, it had left a trail of bodies and wrecked lives along the whole length of the Brezhan.

ON THE RIVER
TWELFTH IRON CYCLE, TWENTY-THIRD DAY

"Your papers are in order, Teik." The guard at F'trovanmeni folded them shut, slid the seal ribbon around them. *Good thing it doesn't mention my name*, Rilla thought. *Some here might resent it.*

"Thank you. I haven't been home in a while," she said. "Anything interesting going on, Teik Toll Guard?"

She had been past here only once in the past two years, and that in the dark of a moonless overcast night. The towers and booms of the outpost rose about her, docks with stone bollards and massive curtain-walls down to the carven rock of the isle itself. Those would stand regardless, but there were missing slates on the roof of the custom house, broken windows patched with board; the guards' uniforms showed signs of neglect.

She ground her teeth. *Ranion, this is F'talezon's protection. Where is tax money going?* A rhetorical question, to anyone who had been listening to the rumors. Not one safe to speak aloud. *And I have to appeal to the DragonLord's justice?*

"Ah, Teik courier." The guard was eager to talk. Not many came up or down the river in winter. "There's a great House feud going on, the Sleeping Dragon."

"I've heard of it, yes."

"Well, it's getting so that the Woyvode is taking an interest, which is bad."

"Hmmm. I had been thinking to deal with the Sleeping Dragon, spices and gems. Perhaps I shouldn't . . ."

"Wait until things settle. There was a battle south of here just this fall."

"Oh?"

"Aye, Rilla Riverwolf you know, the pirate who has a demon-dog, was involved. Megan Thane'sdoom's cousin, near as fierce. Sent four of ours back, in their bare skins and lucky to have them."

"I see." Inside, Rilla smiled. "I heard about that, going through Brahvniki. I saw the Cage myself, coming upriver, but kept my distance, you may be sure."

He whistled. "Not for the likes of us to stick our snouts in, 'less we want to get them kicked," he agreed, rolling the engraved wooden seal on the inkstone and again on her *laissez-passer*. A shake of the head. "Don't know what things are coming to."

They'll be through here in a few days, Teik Guard. Well, I shouldn't waste more time, and my crew is getting cold . . . Good day, and the blessing of the Goddess on you."

F'TALEZON, THE UNSEEN GUILD
MASTER YARISHK'S OFFICE
TWENTY-FIFTH DAY

Her master's chamber hadn't changed much. It was still un-
fashionably cluttered, packed full with bits and pieces. He always
said he knew where everything was, always seemed to know
which pile of paper had what information amidst the red and
black cushions, white rug, blue wall hangings, redwood lapdesk.
A comfortable clutter. *One of the places I first felt safe. He
taught me how to read as well as steal.* A F'talezonian smell,
burning blackrock and incense, with the underlying tang of rock.

Master Yarishk looked much older than he should have.
The Guildwars must be very bad, Rilla thought. *Those Red
Brotherhood upstarts.* The Thieves Guild was a F'talezonian
institution; outsiders seemed unable to grasp that the only
real way to control crime was to organize it. Otherwise the
city would be overrun with amateurs and freelancers, you
wouldn't be able to buy reliable protection or get stolen
goods back undamaged at reasonable prices.

"You need to see the Tyrant himself, hmmm?" her
Guildmaster said, thumbing through the documents she had
brought and making *tsk-tsk* noises. "No one lower will do?
Why not the Woyvodaana?"

She shook her head emphatically. "She's supporting Habiku."

"Ah. Well. There might be someone we could bribe to get
you into an audience, but I can't guarantee she won't know."
A pause. "On the other hand, our sources say she's been
denying Habiku audience. Possibly a lover's quarrel, but she
always did have a good sense of political timing."

Rilla looked down at the sealed packet. "I have to risk it."
She tugged at the fringe on the cushion. "Master, how bad
is he now?"

He rubbed his wrinkled, deft old hands together, ran them
through his thin, steel-grey hair. "Bad. Paying for blood. The
court is becoming a very mad place, literally. They're playing
insanity to stay below Ranion's notice and too many of them
are starting to believe their pretence."

"I'll have to appeal to his craziness, then."

"Carefully, child, carefully. If you must, well, I won't stop you, but I'd hate to lose one of our best journeymen." A smile, crooked teeth. "Even if you and your cousin are neglecting your first Guild for the Rivermaster's."

Ranion lounged in his cushions and whitefox furs, petting one of the snow leopards. The audience chamber was white this week. White hangings, white furs, white pets, white clothing; it amused the DragonLord to violate the Zak tradition of formality. The courtiers rustled and whispered in white linen and silk. Fresh roses lighter than cream stood in alabaster vases. The only black spot in the room was Ranion's hair and clothing and his two guardian greathounds; even the enamel armor of the guards who stood motionless along the walls had been redone.

Rilla lay on her face just in from the door, waiting permission to crawl forward and rise.

He is *crazy*, she thought, fear clenching her stomach tight, remembering the guided tour that had taken her past the pits where the *sirrush-lau* were feeding. No DragonLord before him had demanded more than the bow of respect, or sinking to one knee on state occasions. *His eyes are mad*.

"Come here," he drawled languidly. Then, "Rise. I am informed you had something amusing to tell me."

She rose carefully to her knees, keeping her eyes down after one horrified glance at the flame-eagle picked out in black and crimson on the wall behind the five dragon heads of the throne. The Dark Lord's symbol. Ranion lounged beneath it, his face still the too-white pastiness she remembered, but the slim lines of his body were thickened by a small potbelly, obscene on a man of only twenty-five years.

Goddess, forgive, protect, she thought, skimming rapidly through her plan and the new court etiquette. "Yes, Dread Lord." *He must be starting to imagine he's the Dark Lord himself. May he meet the real thing and be disabused.* "If I have your permission?" A nod.

She broke the seals of the package in her hand. "This is the text of a message in the hand of Habiku called Smoothtongue, self-claimed ClawPrince and junior master of the Rivermaster's and Merchanter's guilds. It is addressed to Schlem Valdersson, Senior Executor for the Council of Three of Thanelandt."

Ranion's face took on a petulant frown. "Why should he be writing to them?"

Rilla speeded her words. "It is in code, Dread Lord, but the cypher is known to me and your officers, who can authenticate. It concerns you." His brows rose, and she cleared her throat. "Please, Dread Lord, these are Habiku's words; otherwise I would rather—"

"Yes, yes. Proceed."

". . . as to Ranion, his madness proceeds apace. The city as a whole has lost all respect for him, and it is only a matter of time before their anger at his stupidities, gross mismanagement of the city's finances and defenses, and inattention to anything but his own perverted amusements renders anger greater than fea—"

"Cease! Be silent!" Ranion was on his feet, face purple, hands clenched. The greathounds were up, their basso snarling echoing from the stone of the walls behind the hangings. The ranked courtiers murmured in horror.

A very dangerous child to have a tantrum, she thought and bowed her head lower. "You!" He gestured to one of the guards. "Bring that here."

Ranion scanned it quickly once it was in his hands, dropped it and called for cloths to clean his hands with. "I'll feed him to my—"

"Ranion, dear, sweet love." Avritha's voice purred. He wheeled on her and visibly calmed.

"Yes, my beauty?" He sank back down on his cushions, held out a hand to her. She rose from her cushion with the courtier Uen's hand to help her up. Her skirts rustled like paper, creamy roses woven into blue-white, her raven hair shimmering under a white fall of lace, red lips smiling at the Woyvode.

"Why not let the ClawPrince put him in her Cage, my love? Wouldn't that be amusing?" She ran a hand down his arm, raised his hand to her cheek. "You could see her do it." Her voice was warm as white velvet. "Then, perhaps, you could go and view the Cage at times, and see how he's altered. So boring, corpses."

Ranion leaned back, stroking the lace on her hair as ab-

sently as he stroked the snow leopard. "Megan Whitlock."
His eyelids drooped, dark eyes glittering through his lashes.
"That *would* be interesting. Wouldn't it? Amusing?" The
court obediently murmured agreement, tittering. "Yes. I've
heard so much of this Cage." His eyes took on a musing look.
"Really, it's quite clever to bring it closer, and closer, and
closer . . ."

"ClawPrince." He directed his gaze on her. "I find that the
usurper Habiku has wrongfully stolen your birthright. And
your cousin's, of course." He waved a hand negligently. "This
judgment holds if—if your cousin brings him to my little
mezem, alive, and punishes him there."

He raised one finger. "As long as I *don't* have to find
against *you* or your House, for property damage in the city. I
do have my beloved people to care for. Do I not?"

The question was addressed to the court. "Oh, *yes*, Dread
Lord." The answer came very quickly, not too loud, a rippling murmur.

"Dread Lord, pardon my ignorance, unused to following
the lightning-swift play of your wisdom. Am I to understand
that we, that is my cousin and I and our followers, are to
defeat Habiku, seize the House and its assets, and bring him
and the, ah, the Cage here to the Nest?"

"Yes! Yes!" Ranion was bouncing on the cushions. "It's so
Arkan!" He must have seen her bewilderment; what did a
House feud have to do with the Empire? "I'm very much
taken with Arkan ways, lately. Aren't we?" he asked the
court. There was a murmur of agreement. There were murmurs of, "*kellin, kellin,*" the cry the spectators in the arena of
Arko gave when the gladiator struck the killing blow. "I've
got my own little, umm, *mezem*—" Suddenly Rilla understood it was the horribly mispronounced Arkan word for
"arena" the DragonLord used. "—here in the Nest, that's
where we'll have it. But the whole *city* will be my *mezem*." A
frown. "You may go now. Clerk, send a transcript of this
audience to Habiku Smooth—to Habiku Cagedweller. Those
very words."

". . . dweller." Habiku looked up from the sealed transcript.

"I am to understand that the DragonLord is placing me under arrest?"

"No." The armored hand extended for the document, which was to be read once and returned. There was no nonsense of a single trooper this time; a full hand of hands, under the banner of House Skydragon, the ruler's personal sign.

"These are the words of the Dread Lord, let all hear and obey. The dispute between yourself and Megan Whitlock is declared private. She may enter the city but not leave, nor any of hers, until the affair is finished. Neither may you leave, ClawPrince, nor any of yours; the gates are barred. Any damage to persons or property outside the House of the Sleeping Dragon will be punished under the usual laws. All other actions taken by servants of the House will be considered outside the law for the duration of the feud; only the principal who is brought to judgment at the Nest will be held accountable." He paused. "Clear?"

Habiku nodded. "And if I win?"

The officer examined the tips of his gauntlet. "If we are to deal in the hypothetical . . . I am instructed to say that, in that event, there will be a *personal* settling of crimes and accounts."

Habiku knew what that meant; execution for him personally, or possibly even the chance to commit suicide, pardon for his followers and the House assets to go to whatever collateral heirs could be found. Only Ranion's word, but the pattern was whimsical enough for him; this would mean that Habiku's personal followers were assured that they would not fall under the Nest's proscription if they fought for him. Actually, a threat of displeasure if they *did* desert him, and deprived Ranion of his long-distance gladitorial contest.

And Mother, he thought. No way out of the city for her; the secret lower ways would be barred to him, and the main gate was the strongest single fortress in the known world, nothing passed it without official approval. Not that she could survive a winter journey now, in any case. This was a promise of pardon for her, as well.

Habiku nodded curtly and waited for the troops to withdraw from his entrance hall.

"He's *insane!*" Habiku yelled, throwing a jug against the wall and wheeling on his steward. Lixa stood behind him, smiling, smiling. "You won't survive me, bitch," the tall man snarled. "You, steward. You're not at personal risk, and nobody will employ you if you run now. Send word to the River Quarter that a pound of dreamdust is offered as wage to any who'll fight for me. I'll win yet. Offer twice the usual wage and the promise of permanent employment to any freeblade—"

Chapter 22

"He's insane! The man is stark, raving, mad!" Megan said with genuine horror as her cousin relayed the DragonLord's message.

"You don't know the half of it, coz," Rilla replied, remembering the atmosphere of the Nest. "And it's catching."

Megan leaped to her feet and began pacing. She and her chief officers were housed in the Guildhall; *not* the conventional major complex of Guild buildings on a main Middle City street. Even in F'talezon, there were limits to how openly an organization of thieves, assassins, fences, protection-sellers, smugglers, ganglords and jailbreakers could operate. Consequently, the main chambers of the Hall were scattered over half an acre of the city's north slope; the connecting passages might be secret, aboveground or both, the rooms themselves sealed-off portions of ostensibly legitimate buildings. Some *were* legitimate; the thieves had long had a working relationship with the Rivermaster's Guild, and cooperated often.

This room looked like a counting house basement; the grilled windows were at street level. It had been a record room in her apprentice days; there were still a few racks of scrolls against the walls. Shkai'ra fluffed up a cushion and leaned back on one elbow, watching Sova across the room as she industriously burnished her helmet.

"It's crazy enough," she agreed. "Why so angry, kh'eeredo? Clears the decks for us. Not as neat as having Ranion scrag him, of course."

Megan halted and laughed bitterly. "Patriotism," she said. "I've been away two years, and it's like seeing a friend after that long, one who has a wasting illness. Day to day you don't notice it. Bad enough the city services are run down the way they are, raw sewage spilling into the water and so forth even during the good years, but Ranion's allowing a private war within the walls!" She paused, silent and brooding, continued in a slower tone:

"I can remember, when I was a little girl, only the nobles had household troopers, and they were more like police than soldiers. Only people down in the River Quarter went armed with more than a single knife, and even there an open fight was gossip for the whole town for a month. It's been getting worse . . . the Red Brotherhood going around opening eggs with maces, House feuds, Guildwars . . . Goddess, it's been getting worse since long before I was born. So my parents said, at least, and the chronicles."

Shkai'ra thought back to the road up from the harbor, switching back and forth along the slope, with forts at each turn. The cyclopean works down at the cavern, towers and battlements carved from the rock, springsteels, dartcasting wheels, rock- and flame-throwing engines, endless rows of slips for warships. Then the main gate into the city, a broad smooth tunnel right through the ridge into the valley, with a hulking castle atop it and portal after portal. Even greater fortifications on the other side of the little river that divided the town, and mountains everywhere else around, burrowed and tunneled with diggings, slits for ambushes, secret roads. Street after street, paved and walled and roofed with slate of grey and black, unburnable.

"You're right," she said. "This is the strongest city I've ever seen, stronger even than Rand or Illizbuah, smaller but stronger. The only enemies you've got here are the ones you let in yourselves." A pause. "Ourselves," she corrected.

Megan nodded, and Rilla echoed her. "Habiku's a boil we have to lance," she said. "After that, cure the disease."

The Zak commander knelt and her subordinates gathered around the map. "We have to take the House." She looked up at Shkai'ra, a few others of the naZak.

"That means more than my home, the building, although that's the heart of it. My manor . . ." She blinked, thinking. "Can be turned into a fortress and I can't count on him not having found my private ways in. Then there's the warehouses down on the docks, repair yards, workshops . . . a lot of the capital is tied up in materials put out to private artisans, but they don't count, they're independent contractors, not House servants. Furthermore, we have to take everything without damaging the bystanders."

The junior Master representing the Guild spoke. "Master Varik said to warn you that the Red Brotherhood will be intervening . . . We will not, although we wish you well." He sniffed; it had been barely a century since the Red Brotherhood split from the Guild, and the older organization's members still despised its parvenu greed and crudity. "Against policy. However, he *does* say that any Brotherhood bravos you kill will be credited to you. Unfortunately, you will be fighting mostly dreamdust addicts. Over a hundred, and several score gangblades from unaffiliated or Brotherhood packs."

"Fishguts." Megan turned her back. "Numerous, and completely indifferent to death."

Shkai'ra shrugged. "Rabble, and I doubt if they're well-armed."

Megan turned back to the guildsman. "My thanks," she said. It would be unfair to expect the Guild as a whole to do more for her; it was an umbrella organization of independent entrepreneurs, after all, each with their own interests.

"It is nothing," the guildsman said, rising. "Oh, one more thing, Master Whitlock. From Master Varik, in his personal capacity. It seems, with so much time to prepare, Habiku has made an elaborate plan, involving a reserve to be committed against you when your main attack is made." A thin smile. "In Master Varik's opinion, this simplistic plan is perhaps due to listening to too many stories of kingly heroism. In any case, here it is, as of this morning's updating.

"There are a number of 'troops' he's stationing in these tunnels, here," he pointed. "Around the manor."

"You mean that once we're committed and all of us are in the tunnels, they'll take us in the back," Shkai'ra said.

"In effect, yes." The guildsman barely nodded to her.

"We'll take the warehouses first. He's waiting for us in the House, isn't he?" Megan looked to the junior master who nodded. "Right. Let him sweat. We'll take it back a bite at a time and since it's *Dagde Vroi*, we can use the masking and costumes, and so forth, to our advantage."

She tapped one claw against her front teeth, looked at Shyll and Shkai'ra. "You two and the Ri are going to be one big festival trick and everyone is going to be looking for the witch casting the illusion." She smiled. "No one is going to know that you're real until it's too late, especially dusters."

The Stairs were the nearest thing F'talezon had to a main street: stairs indeed, from the River Quarter in the southwest to the main gate, then a road smooth and broad enough for carts in the same direction after that to the main market square; stairs once more past the Lady Shrine and up to the Dragon'sNest. Tonight was the first of *Dagde Vroi*, and the whole length was thronged with the folk of F'talezon lit by the erie glow of *kraumak* light, and the red of torches. A light snow sifting down out of a night sky glowing with the reflection, flakes falling slow and fluff-huge into the bowl of light. Carnival in a city of witches, Zak in costumes real or magical, depending on the strength of their talent or the depth of their pouches. The festival days when nothing was forbidden . . .

A woman dressed in her best felt coat and boots, light brown braids falling to her waist, attended by three flying ribbons that chased each other around her, fluttering in the wind.

A man with translucent wings, butterfly gossamer with hints of pastel colors.

A child dancing with an animated wooden puppet of a dog, its wooden paws clicking in time to his shoes.

Glowing eyes and hair wreathed in hot orange flames, a girl followed by a six-foot lizard with the head of a man.

Three boys stood on one of the steps of the street, between a clothier's shop and a silversmith's, with intense concentration on their faces. Above their heads, suspended in mid-air, a girl dressed in red feathers shrieked at them and swore and scrambled at nothing, trying to get down. She stopped yelling, started concentrating, and one of the boy's eyes opened very wide. They let her down.

And up the center of the street, two of the finest illusions seen that night: tableaux, group presentations; there were artisan clubs who saved and slaved for most of a year to fit themselves out for such. First, two teRyadn trotting on either side of a greathound, pursued by a Ryadn mounted on her Ri; all surrounded by the illusion of the rippling, knee-high feathergrass of the Ryadn steppe. The noise of festival died down about them, *ahhhs* of admiration going up, passers-by following to point and exclaim. All Zak had some access to the manrauq, the magical talent, but the skill needed to build so complete a moving scene, to transform the sight and sound and even smell of three ordinary Zak, a pony and a mongrel hound into this. It was quite out of the ordinary.

Of course, it was not faultless. The figures' feet dipped below the surface of the "grass," and there was a wavering indistinctness to some outlines that a sharp eye could detect . . . and the flitterkitten on the Ryadn's shoulder was a failure in research, they were uncommon anywhere outside the Brezhan valley, but all in all, though, a lovely piece of work.

"Shit," Shkai'ra muttered under her breath, looking ahead to Shyll and Sova, trotting by Inu's side, back to the second "tableaux." Her Ri, Hotblood, took the opportunity to stretch that impossibly flexible neck out toward Inu's hindquarters.

no, Shkai'ra thought firmly.

A complex concept came in return, elements of *youredcoatliestillnofun* and *hungrythirstydogtastegood*.

"First time in my life I've been called a killjoy by a long-legged weasel," the Kommanza muttered to herself. She could feel the armor on her back, the movements of the gear slung around her saddle; it was disconcerting to see nothing but skintight leathers on a body not hers. To the Ri: *don't you ever think about anything besides killing and eating?*

A wordless image of a bucking sheri gripped between his forelegs, squealing as he thrust.

goodwettightslidesmellpushpushpush, too

She sighed. *kill soon. kill walk-up twolegs.*

fun. funfunfun

Behind them came a group more complex, but less magical; a representation of the great conqueror Vekslaf naZak's Bane. The general and his followers were in modern Zak war-gear, with a few antique flourishes; behind the general came a cart with a trophy of weapons, and a string of figures in "chains" of silver paper marching between the warriors. They were the touch of illusion, representative types of half a dozen naZak peoples. Not *real* naZak, of course; of the hundred fifty thousand folk within the walls, nine-tenths were pureblood at this time of year. Elsewhere on the Brezhan, outside the area still under F'talezon's grip, Zak might be persecuted for showing their talent. Here wise naZak reflected on the realities of power, and stayed strictly indoors during *Dagde Vroi.*

From Inu's side, Sova fought not to goggle at the passing multitudes. Wonderment warred with fear, an atavistic stirring at childhood tales. This was Fehuund's own city, the Witch Queen of the icelands . . . *No*, she shook her head. *They're just people, who can do things others can't. Good ones and bad ones.*

Shkai'ra looked back again, at her half of the warband. It seemed unnatural, somehow, to be hiding it by parading it in plain sight, armed to the teeth. Her own teeth were on edge, felt less of the quasi-sexual rush of approaching combat than she usually experienced before a fight. *Too many years since so much turned on the bow and the blade*, she thought. Too much was at risk; she looked forward at Sova, and envied her the story-bred confidence of romantic youth. The Ri stirred beneath her, and she focused her mind on images of pain and dying; reassured, Hotblood bent his head to sniff curiously at the "grass" that had no smell or feel.

In the Market square the throng spread out to watch. Watch the cniffta games between the card-painter's booth and the cutler's, join the raucous crowds betting on the spider-fights, or watch the shadow puppets of the *wayang* nearby. Food sellers shouted their wares, or used their art to make sure that the smells attracted patrons: roast beef, beef pies, spiced meatballs, maranthe sugar-cakes, hot kahfe. Shkai'ra put up a hand to steady Fishook on her shoulder as the orange tabby head swiveled sharply. Perfume sellers were offering their scents in crystal vials that glowed with colors suggesting the flowers of their origin.

The dance circle was busy as was the challenge ring, though one had to look twice to be sure that the people in both were real and not dreams. The best witches' illusions were so real that one could not tell until the figures bowed and vanished.

They made a full circuit of the square, next paraded through the worn slate sidewalks that fringed the houses. Three-story buildings of dark stone, tiny shuttered stores below, dwelling places and workshops above. *Gloomy city*, Shkai'ra thought. Tension touched the base of her stomach with a touch like cold jelly as Shyll turned and lead the procession off on a side street, south toward the valley wall. Natural enough; this type of travelling exhibit was done for *zight*, and that required exposure. But round about now someone might ask themselves why the two groups were sticking so close together, particularly since the second was not in the same league as the first.

Sidestreets, quieter and narrow, dark except where a house could afford to keep a *kraumak* in an iron-net holder over the door. An occasional reeling party, drunks slumped in the even narrower alleys that dove like tunnels between the big, stone-shuttered houses; upper story windows opened to take in the sight. There was laughter, cheers, an occasional thrown sweetmeat or coin; many here in the Middle Quarter were holding private revel.

The street ran level along the valleyside, but the alleys

were steep, upslope and down. Shkai'ra looked to one side, noticed the smooth U of wear in the central stone of a laneway. *Old*, she thought. Then she noticed the poor fit with the less-worn blocks on either side; the middle had been replaced more often than the flankers, several times, and had a chance to wear down once more . . .

No time to think. Hotblood caught the contagion and began to dance sidelong after Inu.

killdognow?

"No," Shkai'ra sighed. The animal's us-and-edible division of the world could grow wearisome.

The street was twice arm's width, overhung by eaves above. Then it flared out into a space perhaps three times as wide for ten times manheight, making a sharp turn upslope, to the south. The dosshouse Habiku's drug-bought followers were in was there, a good house sold for want of heirs and cut up into cubbyholes. The tunnel from the basement went three streets over, to emerge in a structure across from the House of the Sleeping Dragon; Habiku was expecting Megan to break her teeth on the strong walls of the manor, while his blades crept up behind. There would be some sane ones with them, just enough to control and guide them, and dole out the drug.

"Shyll," she called softly. Her hands were drawing her wheelbow from its sheath, the first shaft from the quiver on the other side.

"Yes?" Tense, elaborately casual walk.

"Just in case . . . good luck."

"And to you."

Shkai'ra took a last deep breath. *Freeze*, she commanded the Ri.

Now for the subtle strategy, she thought. The ones in the broad doorway were a score or more, thin and gaunt and mad-looking, ragged but carrying new arms. Lamplight spilled past them; there must be a hundred or more in there. Forty with her, all told.

"We'll each just have to kill two and a half," she muttered. Fishook fluttered up into the night sky. Then, pitched to carry: "CHARGE!"

Her first arrow pinned a man with a twofang to the door post, her second nailed two together before they realized that the tableaux wasn't playing any more. Fighters dashed past her, darts and twofangs and the naZak weapons snatched from the cart of "trophies." General Vekslaf howled in Annike's voice and bounced forward with a long knife in either hand.

The illusion broke as they poured across the square. Hotblood crossed the stone in two leaps, screaming. *funfunkill-killNOW!* shrieked in his mind as he bowled through the doorway a step in Inu's wake, his shrilling mingling with the dog's thunder-bellow. The Ri trampling with claws and tearing with his tusks. *good killnow run!*

Megan had checked the entrances to her secret ways into the house. One had been pulled down, one showed signs of recent use, one was barred and guarded (*the one into my own office*) and one was deep in two years of dust. When night fell, Rilla and ten others waited in the dark. Time stretched, until she felt the sudden flare of excitement with Shkai'ra's taste to it.

Fishook skittered out of the sky onto Rilla's shoulder. She jumped.

"That's the beginning. Let's go." The door of the unused secret passage that Megan had found swung open under her hand. She thought of Megan, touched her shape of mind, thought, *NOW, coz!* and dimly felt her acknowledge.

Above, on Flutterwing Lane, twenty people tried the wall around the Manor of the Sleeping Dragon. As they reached the top, witchlight sprang up all around and the low, sinister *thupthupthup* of darts hailed through the dazzle above. The figures wavered and vanished. The dartcasters blinked as their rounds struck, met no resistance. Another alarm, around the corner, off New Cheapstreet. Again and again, at every wall. Megan sagged against the wall, pulling what power she had. Again.

This time there was no answering flare and only a dart or two. "Hsst!" She scrambled up, using climbing claws as well as her own in the cracks in the mortar, fighting off the headache growing behind her eyes. Grapnels swung; the others followed, avoiding the broken glass set in the top. No witchlight, no darts, good. They dropped down and were in the gardens.

Megan crouched and ran along the low line of snow-covered bushes that marked the young maze, around the white mounded rose trees. *Rilla should break out in the small dining room, next the fireplace. We'll break in on the Tower side. We'll have him between us, then.*

Sova plastered herself against the entranceway as the Ri went by, a black streak through the black night, the platinum flare of its mane and tail incandescent white. The smell was all around her for a moment, sharp musk and blood. Shkai'ra rolled out of the saddle, rolled again to avoid being trampled, bounced to her feet.

"Down!" she yelled to the beast, pointing to a narrow stair. "Down, kill, *stay. Eat!*" Hotblood was more than intelligent enough to understand blocking a bolt-hole while the rest of the pack drove prey to the killing ground. It poured itself down the cellar stair, into a space that a horse would have found impossible. Paws flexed and gripped stone treads, spine twisted, and the Ri flowed down into the cellars of the house.

"Sova." The Kommanza barked it. "Follow me. *And stay behind.*"

She pounded up the stairs, worn wooden risers in a central well that extended up the full four stories of the house. Inu's bellow echoed again, shaking the thin pine boards beneath their feet. Sova followed, shortsword out and buckler in hand, eyes wide with an excitement that slowed everything around her, the splintery bannister at their right, the worn, skewed doors off their hinges, even the scents of ancient pickled fish and urine. Landing, landing, landing; the treads glowing and slippery under her feet, the reason plain when they found a *Vryka* crewman sprawled dead, the knife that killed him still in his throat.

It was dim enough for the light to be black; her nerves chilled suddenly at the blind gape of eyes and mouth and ragged cut neck, windpipe still fluttering.

"Right," Shkai'ra muttered, plunging in that direction. "Work our way down." Sova could hear no panting in her voice, despite the sixty pounds of armor and weapons. The Thane girl had merely a steel cap and steerhide jerkin, but they weighed on her already.

Into the corridor. A single oil lamp down at the end of a line of doors. Shkai'ra wheeling, booting open the first on her left. Flinging herself in; a brief ugly crunching sound, and coming out with the bottom of her round shield dripping. Sova forced her eyes away. There were no others until the last door. Those must have been alerted, because they jerked the thin planks open just before her bootsole would have struck.

The tall Kommanza jerked forward into the room, pulled by her momentum and the weight of the armor; she catapulted back out with her shield tucked into her chest, struck by the end of a bench with four sets of hands running it forward from the other side of the room. She struck the opposite wall with a crash that shook the floor and cracked half a dozen boards weakened by dry rot. The dreamdust addicts followed, half a dozen strong.

Shkai'ra was coming to her feet before she was fully conscious, staggering to one knee; the leather and metal and fiberglass of armor and shield dinned under their cheap, stone-headed maces. Sova had time to see one drive himself onto the point of Shkai'ra's saber and crawl up it hand over hand before the sixth was upon her.

It was a woman, skeletal gaunt, her ulcerated face oozing through thin burlap bandages. She was laughing or sobbing as she attacked, impossible to see which; just possible to see that her pupils had swallowed the iris of her eyes. Zak, just under Sova's height; the smooth round globe of her macehead swept up over her right shoulder, came down with a blur of motion. Sova managed to jerk her buckler up to block the shaft behind the stone, but the impact jarred her down to the muscles in the small of her back; she skipped back, but the scarecrow figure followed, its rags flapping. The blow came again, again, again, like a nightmare where she blocked an identical stroke as she backed down a corridor without end.

Watch for patterns, a voice in her mind said. The *khyd-hird's* voice. It *was* the same blow, just very fast. She set teeth and leg, thrust. The point of the shortsword punched through rag, into a body no heavier than a child's. Sova swallowed acid and withdrew, twisting, as she had been taught, ignored the falling body to go to Shkai'ra's aid.

A hand clamped her belt, threw her down; fingers settled about her throat and squeezed like a cage of wire. Dreamdust is a very specific nerve poison; it speeds the firing of the neurons, redirects pain signals to the pleasure center, even as it suppresses appetite and the immune system. Addicts die, but until they do they are as immune to pain and shock as a berserker. The world swam grey at the edges of Sova's vision.

Rilla trotted down the dark corridor. The others were single file behind her, Moshulu scraping along, swearing in a whispered mix of Moryavska and Zak. The passage was just wide enough for his shoulders. In the glow of the *kraumak* she held, she could see the thick fuzz of dirt shaken down from the street above and the streaks of greenish-brown scum and rust crusting the stone. The stairs.

Wooden, spiral stairs that lead up to the floor below Megan's old apartments. The little dining room. *The last time I saw it, it was dark, lit with a few candles, Megan showing me how the secret door by the fireplace opened.*

The dust sifted down as quiet feet padded up after her. *Four more flights. Three flights. Two. One. Here's the door.* She raised her hand, pulled the latch—nothing happened. She yanked harder. The door shifted a fingernail's breadth, and stopped. She pried at it and it grated wider to show the mortar of a new brick wall. She gaped at it. *Bricked in? Bricked shut? Oh shit. Ohfishguts, ohshitohshit ohshit*

Pain. An echo, not her pain; pain in her head, her arm. Thick salt rage, reinforcing the chill determination. "Moshulu!" she called. He was right behind her, and she was startled to see tears running down the thick bearded cheeks. *Goddess, don't let him collapse now!* The Moryavska was speaking softly, something that sounded like names, hauntingly on the edge of understanding. The same ones over and over.

"What's wrong with him?" She asked Jakov beside him; quicker witted, he had picked up trade-Zak quickly.

"Nothing wrong, Captain", the man whispered. "Now realizing we where evil men come from. Ones who burn village. He say names; names of wifes, child, sister, brothers, all die, all be sold before you rescue. Moshulu say he see them soon; to rest quiet, he love them, now he come."

Rilla Shadows'Shade swallowed and stepped aside. "Tell him we have to break down this door," she said.

The woman Sova had stabbed sat on top of her, giggling, a red-grey bulge oozing out of the hole in her. Strangling, strangling. Sova hammered at the elbows with the edge of her shield, felt one crunch, the fingers loosened. She heaved and the woman fell sideways, her head hitting a cracked board in the wall, driving her temple onto a protruding nail head. She stopped moving, grip falling away, stopped sliding down the wall, held by the nail. Sova struggled to breathe, but there was something in her throat. Choking.

Shkai'ra sheathed her dagger in a man's belly just above the public bone and ripped upward. He tumbled against her, laughing and gnawing along the line of her jaw above the gorget, rotten splintered teeth sinking in and ripping. With a grunt she threw him back into the arms of his companions and skipped back. Three of them on their feet now. Coming forward, smiling, one smiling past the purple growth that had eaten half her face. Body at her feet; another. Sova . . . back arching, face purple, eyes turning up into her head. The maceheads were rising, blood running down under her armor from the teeth wounds along her jaw.

They laughed, soft, merry sounds. Ignoring her knife; they must have been given a gram apiece at least. Sova was dying. Shkai'ra flipped the long fighting-knife in her hand forward, blood-slippery hilt sending it into a thigh instead of a throat. She went down on one knee, tearing the gauntlet off her right hand with her teeth, salt taste in her mouth.

"*Down Habiku! To me, to me!*" she shrieked, as she spat it

out and raised the shield above her, sheltering. The dreamdusters skittered forward smiling, and their weapons glinted dark, sweeping in full-armed arcs. She checked. Sova's tongue had fallen back into her throat. *Flip her over facedown, can she breathe . . . ?* Her other hand moved the shield, heard the frame cracking as the hirelings bought with their own death attacked it like peasants threshing grain.

Ah! Block the pain. Too many blows, mad-eyed dwarves beating on her like an anvil. One landed on her arm above the shieldrim. Strength left her with an impact that sent ugly vibrations down through ribs and spine; the lower rim of the shield sagged until it touched the ground. She snatched at the haft of another with her sword-hand, too far, too much swing before she could intercept, something broke in her palm and it was slippery and she gripped, gripped, her mind judging angles for the kick as the other two lifted.

In the passage, someone whispered, "I hope no one notices . . ." A reply, equally hushed: "Not notice a forging hammer beating through a brick wall?"

Moshulu braced his feet at the top of the worm-eaten stairs, swung the hammer back to touch the wall behind him, swung . . .

THUWHAM! The mortar crumbled around the twelve-pound head. THUWHAM! Bricks bulged. Shouts from through the wall, distant, feet running up stairs.

THUWHAM! One brick slid forward a knuckle deep. Good-quality mortar, some distant portion of Rilla's mind noted, as she coughed with the lime-dust. THUWHAM! Mortar powdered down on heads below. THUWHAM! The first brick fell out on the other side, muffled on a cushion below. THUWHAM! Three more bricks. Someone threw open the door of the room, started to run across, armor clashing.

THUWHAM! Bricks fell from above the hole, pulled by their own weight and the vanished support beneath. Bricks and mortar fell back into the passage, bouncing on the stairs and off shields with dull floorboard thumps, on a helmet with a dull clang; somebody swore in Aeniri.

Rilla blinked her eyes clear and looked up, shielding them with the fingers of one hand, dust on her lashes and white against the thin black leather of her glove. The hole was open to chest-height now; a twofang probed through and the Moryavska snapped it with a sideways twist of his hammer. More, half a dozen; she could feel the first ram into the big man's leather breastplate over the stomach, penetrate a finger's width with an impact that shook through his body and the wood of the stair, down to her.

"Quickly, Moshulu, quickly!" she shouted, uselessly; the peasant hadn't learned more than a half a dozen words of any language she could speak, and they could be bringing up fire or vitriol or *anything*, Megan could be lying dead under the walls, they were caught here like meat in a sausage-grinder . . .

Moshulu roared the names he had been muttering under his breath, raised the sledge overhead and smashed it down into the remaining section of brick wall. It crumbled, fell; the sledge dropped from his hands.

Not enough, not enough, Rilla knew, as he stumbled and the edged steel probed for his life. If Habiku's followers could hold the entranceway it would be one against one until the end of time, with all the advantage to Habiku. Moshulu roared again, coughed blood in the middle of it; the twofangs were flickering at him now, he was above her head, there was no *room*. As his knees buckled he surged forward, and the bear-thick arms swept out, clutching the thicket of ashwood poles, drawing them to his breast, immobilizing them with his deathgrip as the blood and sweat poured down into his beard and his body shook with the yanking efforts of the ones who had killed him to withdraw their weapons.

Rilla screeched and bounded straight up; the knives were in each hand as she vaulted the dying man's body, out into the midst of the slayers.

Megan killed the last dog as it leaped on her, tumble under slash whirl *kick*. Habiku had bought heavy, wolf-hunting dogs to run in the gardens, but at least the bigger beasts tend not to sound as they attack.

An absurd thought; a thief's thought. Yappy little dogs that

*stay out of reach, yelling, are the worst. At least the big ones
attack you and you can keep them quiet.*

The others with her made a line of shadows that rushed
across an open space, across the snow. From the roof someone yelled, a white-burning ball of metal fell to hiss and sizzle
in the snow, lighting them clear as day, pinned in the open.

A cry of pain, someone, Piatr, down. Megan rolled, as
darts and arrows hissed around them, scooped a double handful of dirt and snow, felt the sharp jerk as a dart caught her on
the back, clatter off a bone-plaque, doused the light. *Run for
the house wall.* "Go! Go!"

The first-floor windows shuttered with metal-bound wood.
*Plaster dust in my teeth—Rilla; pain in my arm, hand, head,
worry, desperation—Shkai'ra; fighting, urgency—Shyll . . .*
She scrambled straight up the Tower wall, stone scratching
under her claws, the climbing claws on her felt boots. *Second
story, third, window, guarded. Image of an open window,
push!*

The guard swore, pulled out a key and, believing he was
locking it, unlocked it. Megan, above it, grabbed the cornice
over the window, kicked with both feet, swung in on top of
the guard. They went down in a tangle of arms and legs and
too-long weapons. She dropped the knife, slashed his throat
with her claws, hooked the grapple, dropped a rope.

Rilla'll be on the second floor. Other guards were running
down the corridor, from the other windows. Splintering crash
as an unguarded one broke in down the way. She crouched,
seized the twofang, leaping across the corridor to put her
back to the wall, raised it just in time to block another fang.

Shyll lunged up the steps, heard Shkai'ra yell. Saw Sova
down, the Kommanza going down, two maceheads raised.
They were getting in each other's way. He leaped over the
body of a woman, threw the spear, saw one stagger back as it
went through his throat. The other mace came down once,
crunching on Shkai'ra's armor; she slid down on top of Sova.
The addict raised the mace again and Shyll slammed into
him, dagger half drawn, stumbling over the two on the floor,
landing on top. The macehead rang on the wall, rolled away.

Pain in his arm and hand and back, burning along his face—no not his, her's. Inu scrambled up snarling, hopping forward with one paw hugged up against his chest.

His hands were locked on the addict's throat, who was smiling. The duster clawed at Shyll's eyes under the helmet, he jerked his head back as the man bucked, threw him off balance.

Shyll rolled with it, dragged the duster with him, slammed him into the wall. He *heaved*, threw the addict back over Shkai'ra and Sova. The duster rolled, started to get up. Inu grabbed him and shook him in half.

Shkai'ra crawled to her knees. Shyll looked up at her, saw the eagle features gone chalk-white, blue around the lips. Her left arm was dangling, moving with the sway of her shield; the other was held cradled against her chest, already swelling like a tight glove overstuffed with water. She grunted with every movement, deep in her chest, pulling in breath by main strength.

"Why?" he wheezed.

"Had to. Sova down choking, blue, didn't know how long. Shit, shitshitshit—"

He moved to her side, his knees making ripples through scumming liquid that drained through the warped flooring; paused to check the Thane girl, found her breathing hoarsely but steadily. Shkai'ra shuddered once and went very still as he removed her shield.

"Broken couple places, shit *no* don't take the armor off, the plates spring back into place 'less they're cracked, splint it well enough for now. Strap it across me . . . shit, *ah*, shit I'm not going to be worth *shit* for six months, Megan needs me *now*, some sheepfucking general *I* turned out to be, I underestimated them, only dusters' I've seen were dying in gutters—"

"We all did," he mumbled around a thong as he fastened her right arm securely; imagining the pain from fractures grating unsecured, he shuddered. A long gouge went from his nose to the corner of his right eye. "Turds of the Dog, they won't *stop* when they're juiced up."

"Finished," he said. He bent, swore again as he took Sova's

slight form over one shoulder. "Cracked two ribs, c'n I lean on you?" They made speed toward the staircase, and Shkai'ra's fever-bright eyes noticed the greathound. He looked a different breed, save for the size; the armored forequarters were dark and slick from muzzle to haunch, and one ear was gone.

"Dog?" she rasped.

"Fell through fuckin' rotten floor, just his legs, ones below sliced his foot before we could break the rest out. Last ones went out the windows 're down into the cellar to the tunnel, we heard the Ri get them, other's 're running for the River Quarter."

They reached the ground floor, and the teRyadn laid Sova out in a line of wounded; nearly half the forty who had entered the dosshouse were there, and ten of those were unmoving.

"Thanks," Shkai'ra muttered as they turned toward the cellar.

"Thank you," Shyll replied, clutching at his side; the other hand held a light hook-axe.

"What for?" Somebody had brought a *kraumak*, and hung it on a thong around the Kommanza's neck. Another Ri-scream echoed up the narrow stairwell, and a moan of obscene pleasure.

"Know Megan's got a good one, now," he said. "Besides, like Sova 's if she were m'own." They were both panting, leaning against each other as their breathing came back under control. Behind them, the survivors, the hale and the walking wounded, gathered. It was important to strike before the impact of their losses sank in, before wounds stiffened.

"She could die because I waited," Shkai'ra said, her boot on the first step. Shyll was beside and behind her, gripping her belt; it would do little good if she went into the cellar face-first. Something was dripping on her head, something warm from above.

"Still better to have someone who'd save the child," Shyll said.

me, Shkai'ra thought to the animal below. *redcoat. i come.* The shrilling below continued. A blast of:

*welcomeeateateat*fun, came to her, with: *gratitude warmgood oooh tastefunny*.

They stepped into the arched cellar, and saw the Ri. He was standing over the last of the dusters, holding him down with one paw and extending his neck toward the man's face. Gripping it with delicate lips, almost a caress; the duster gurgled as the fangs set. Without transition the Ri was rearing, shaking the man like a rag, shaking, screaming, the duster screaming with either agony or pleasure beyond human knowledge, and then the face came away with a sound like the tearing of heavy canvas. The man was back on his hands and knees, the front of his skull red and pink and pink-white of bone, the eyes still staring, naked jaws clamping as he shook his head back, forth, back. The Ri tossed its muzzle to swallow, came to him again on dancing feet, bent daintily for the next bite:

fun! he sent. *fun! oooooo, tastefunnyooooo*. The man was near dead now, and Hotblood moving in a circle.

funnygoodtastetaste Staggering, lying down with a contented sigh and a purr like a huge cat's, tucking the long muzzle by its side and protectively over the twitching, faceless body.

sleepsleepdrowseeyesclosedwarmsummerbeescubsoooooooh. The green eyes closed, and Shkai'ra descended to kick it in the side. One eye opened on her again, blinked, closed.

"Now we know what secondhand dreamdust does to Ri," Shyll muttered. He had never been so close to one, not since his choosing-day when *his* had tried to kill him. *So glad it did*, he thought.

The others were boiling down the stairs behind them, ready to race heedless into the tunnel whose door clanked rhythmically in the draught, a black mouth.

"No, no!" Shkai'ra shouted. "Shields first, polearms next. Get a dart in your casters, third rank. Now. *Move.*"

Where in Halya are the Dark-Lord-taken reinforcements? Habiku thought, slamming away from the fight on the second floor, up past the slaughter on the third, *hasn't reached the stairs here, yet.*

*   *   *

They came through the basement tunnel with no resistance, emerged in an empty wine cellar, up into the atrium garden. Rilla leaned over the ballustrade on the second floor, shouted down:

"Here! It's still going on higher!" And disappeared. Shyll shuddered at the thought of all those stairs. *No, climbing up's a Halya of a lot easier than going down. Rilla, Megan, wait for me.*

They climbed, seemingly forever, one step at a time, hearing bootnails grind on stone steps, hearing the fighting get closer. Third floor.

The windows were broken in, shutters swinging, snow and bitter cold blowing in. Shyll and Shkai'ra, leaning on each other, gasping, Inu whimpering, fangs bared. Rilla on both knees, hands clutched around her middle —The Kommanza looked up. Rilla and Shyll's eyes met Shkai'ra's and the linkage set by the magic on the ice snapped free and—

—*Megan's back shielding the young Rilla while Marte staggered about mouthing threats against her daughter, and the wood whistling down—*

—*Megan dancing in the circle, seen by Shyll, the movements together warm as love, music taking them beyond themselves as they made beauty as transient as a snowflake and he must hide desire for true friendship's sake—*

—*Megan kneeling beside the fire on a beach under palms, nightwind fluttering the black hair that was her only garment, reaching out to Shkai'ra with small hands whose nails glinted as bright as her eyes—*

—*Megan seen frowning over a lantern-lit desk, pen clenched between her teeth as she puzzled over the ancient text—*

—*Megan turning with a sweeping gesture to present the* Lady Grey Wolf *to Rilla, her face calm with confidence—*

Then the images and their auras of emotion blurred: Megan's face, again and again, laughing, frowning, set with anger, soft with passion, yelling with battle-rage. Love, need, fear, resentment, friendship, a final image—

—*Shyll weeping, with his face pressed to Rilla's breast, her arms rocking him, anger and despair—*

"Gods of the Dog," Shyll whispered. "What happened?" They were joined, all of them felt Rilla's exhaustion, Shkai'ra and Shyll's pain, Megan's rage—just winded, from her—

Megan, a twofang slash across her face and left hand, leaned on a twofang in a body, too tired to pull it out. She shook her head. "No . . . time . . ." she gasped. "Think about it later . . ." She had fifteen or sixteen left out of thirty, perhaps some in the garden were only wounded . . . Rilla, seven. Shyll and Shkai'ra, twenty-one.

"He's in the Tower," she wheezed, then straightened. *My hate is warm. Ride it. Cherish it.*

"Gods of the Dog, more stairs," Shyll muttered. Megan turned, yanked at the twofang, almost falling as it came free, used it to lean on, heedless of the damage the bottom blade did to the floor.

She paused at the door into the Tower and her office, saw the faint blue line around it. A red witch would never have noticed it. She pointed the fang at the door and jammed the steel head into the center of it, yellow flaring through her headache. The warding snapped with a crackle and a drift of woodsmoke as it burned the door.

It swung open. Silence. She mounted the steps, hearing her own breathing. *Habiku, you son-of-two-brothers, I'm home. I'm here and I'm going to drag you to the Nest and put you in a steel Cage for the rest of your Goddess forsaken life.*

The door at the top was open. She prodded it with the fang, expecting a hiss of dart. Something. Nothing. Everyone was behind her. She gathered herself, burst through the door, rolling, lunged to her feet, stopped.

"Rather dramatic way to make an entrance, wouldn't you say?" Habiku sat at the east window, Lixa held across his lap, a knife at her throat. She lay very still, held in his arms, his legs. "You know, this one is a distant relative of yours?" he asked conversationally, pushed enough with the edge to raise a line of blood. "You're overly fond of your own kin, Meganmi. I propose a little contest. You and I. Just you and I. Right here."

"Habiku, you always could talk your way out of almost

everything." She leaned on the twofang, shifting her weight wearily, looking down.

I've got her, he thought gleefully. The knife in his hand turned into a yellow viper, twisting to bite his hand. With a yell, he threw it away.

As it left his hand, a knife flickered from Megan's, turned once in midair, struck with a solid "thock" hilt first in the middle of his forehead. She followed its flight across the room. He relaxed a second, stunned; Lixa squirmed out of his hands. He wobbled, shook his head and Megan kicked him carefully in the temple.

"Almost everything," she said, panting, looking down at his unconscious body. "Almost."

"And then?" Ranion said, leaning forward eagerly on the edge of his cushions. The private *mezem* was an alien growth deep in the Dragon'sNest, a round circle of sand, surrounded by ditches, with two bridges, and gates for the fighters. The Imperator's box, on the north side, and the seats all around. A glass arch above, with F'talezonian snow and cold beyond it; below, air heated to the Arkan warmth, and a circle of courtiers about the lord of the city. Courtiers, court wizards, generals, dragged from their beds late this morning of the second day of *Dagde Vroi*; Avritha cool and distant in black nightrobes, her jeweled nails and gold finger chains resting on Ranion's arm.

Megan completed her account, conscious of the flat exhaustion in her delivery, a bone-deep distaste at the sight of this master of all her people hanging on her words. She glanced around at the white marble, the gilding and indigo-dyed silk. Her survivors stood behind her, and behind them, the Cage, gleaming in the lavish illumination of the great yellow *kraumaks* set around the skylight above.

The DragonLord was a little disappointed with the brief terseness of their stories, but there was enough else to keep him edgy with delight. The scattering of pictures about that the court artists had made on the scene of the action; he was particularly taken with a sketch of the Moryavska, Moshulu, dead on his knees with the twofangs clutched to his breast. The ever-helpful Uen held it for him, to catch the best angle of the light.

For the first time in more than twenty iron cycles Ranion had left the Nest himself, on a elaborately guarded and guided tour; the battle with the dusters had been enough to leave him silent and trembling with sheer excitement. Luckily, he had accepted their tale of the Ri Hotblood dying of tainted flesh . . .

He pointed at Shkai'ra. "And is this the barbarian from over the Lannic?" he said. Nobody in F'talezon had seen a human from across the fabled outer ocean in living memory.

She stepped forward, bowed low despite the pain of her arms, spoke a long sentence in a liquid, flowing tongue.

"What was that?" The Woyvode asked.

"Dread Lord," she said, in her gutturally accented Zak, "so do they address the God-King in the greatest realm of far Almerkun, my home."

Megan felt her mood swing crazily from black despair to a wild exhilaration. She recognized the language; it was the first she and Shkai'ra had had in common, though native to neither one. Fehinnan, the street-argot of Illizbuah: *"Why don't you try eating the peanuts out of my shit, sonny?"* Warmth flowed to her, under the pain. Shyll and Rilla were at her back, the teRyadn's weight supported across the Zak's shoulders, and half his face concealed by a bandage. The coldness, the hate she'd cultivated jarred like a knife against bone. *I* . . . They were *there*, and she relaxed control to let their presence grow.

"You have the most *interesting* servants, ClawPrince," Ranion said. "And now . . . my promise! Habiku Cagedweller, all for you." He leaned forward, hands on knees. "Once you've put him in the Cage there, I'll have it delivered to your House as soon as it's repaired. Then, you *wouldn't* mind me visiting, sometimes, would you. No, no, don't protest at the honor. Even your DragonLord deserves some relaxation, some amusement." He winked. "I'm sure we'll find *many* ways for him to amuse us together."

Megan set her teeth, turned. *Like you?* she thought. Somewhere a herald cried in Arkan: she caught the words for
"victory" and "chain". Habiku was led in between two guards,
their hands on his arms. His eyes sought hers, and he smiled
broadly.

"Meganmi," he said. "Did they tell you my mother killed
herself? There's just the two of us, now. As I always wanted
it."

Ranion laughed behind her, and the court followed. She
could hear them, hear Avritha's clear chuckle among them. A
guard prodded the door of the Cage open, and another pressed
a silver hammer into her hand, for the blows that would seal
it forever. She walked forward, toward him, a rustling at her
back as the others followed. Close enough to have to crane up
to meet his honey-brown eyes, lock of hair on his forehead,
smiling down at her as he had before, this time with a
purpled bruise on his face. She caught the faint scent of
violets he had always used.

"Together forever," he said. "As I always wanted. As you
always wanted." The face twisted, slowly, the expression
seeming to crack and shift like an egg about to hatch, hatch
something . . . *"But you can't keep me alive forever! And
when I'm gone, your life will be as empty without me as mine
was without you!"*

She stopped, the hammer weighing in her hand. *Habiku.
Dark Twin. Hate/love/love/hate I've been as taken with you,
as you with me.* In her mind she remembered her own
hoarse shriek and the smash of furniture under hands. Boryis's
voice, "Please don't let it twist you too far." She thought of an
empty cage swinging in the atrium of her house, herself
standing below it. *I'd be weeping, raising my claws and
cursing you for being dead.*

*My life would be empty. In that vision I'm alone but for the
Cage. But I'm not alone, here,* the warmth of the other three
around her like cradling arms. *I've beaten you. In my office,
I beat you. If I put you in that Cage I'll be like you until the
day I die.*

She drew a deep breath, reached up to stroke the lock of
hair out of his eyes, as she'd always been to afraid to do. He

jerked in shock. "Habiku. Had you or I been any different, we could have been friends. Even lovers. But I won't lock myself in that cage with you. I forgive you."

Megan turned away, handing the hammer to Lixa, who stood behind her. "Woyvode, you have graciously given me my sweet revenge. I will not answer for anyone else, but it finishes here, for me." She bowed very low, and felt Shkai'ra and Shyll and Rilla in her mind, understanding why.

Habiku unfroze, wrenching at the guards, screaming, "No! No! It had to be you! You, Megan! You! No!" He twisted one arm loose, whirled one guard into the other. Then he was free, staggering toward her back. Ranion was on his feet, mouth open. She turned, and saw a guard's twofang catch him in the back, once, twice. Habiku coughed, fell to his knees, drooling blood, stretched a hand toward her. "You . . . " he whispered and collapsed.

Epilogue/Epithalamion

THE PLATEAU
WINDWITNESS PLACE OF VOWS
FOURTH IRON CYCLE, FIRST DAY
YEAR OF THE PEWTER RI
(Spring, 4974 A.D.*)*

"Oh, sheepshit," Shkai'ra said. "Is this a stain? Megan?
Rilla? Shyll?"

The tent was large and square, empty save for their dressing tables and racks; the gaily colored canvas boomed and
rattled in the eternal winds of the high flat area above F'talezon.
Vows taken in this mountain-ringed place were more sacred,
carried to the Goddess on Her winds.

The others came to Shkai'ra, and Megan rose on tiptoe to
solemnly examine the breast of her tunic. They were dressed
alike, in the formal, knee-length, belted robes, trousers and
low shoes, their hair garlanded with the first tiny flowers of
the northern spring. Shkai'ra's hung unbraided, silk-smooth
and red-gold, halfway to her waist. It emphasized the sudden
chalk-pale color of her skin as she sat abruptly on the stool.

"What is it?" Rilla asked with sharp concern. "Is it the arms?"

The casts had only been off for a month. The Kommanza
shook her head, flexed her arms; the left was almost as good
as new, and even the sword-hand would recover its strength,
with exercise.

"I'm . . . I'm fucking terrified," she said, and turned her head to bury it against Megan's chest. The steel-nailed hand stroked her hair as the tall woman's harsh features flushed red in turn.

"Why, what is it, love?" Megan said softly. Her own skin glowed, making the fresh-healed twofang scar seem like an adornment. "All the way through those interminable lawspeaker papers you were as attentive as a judge, even when it was giving you headaches." Converting the House of the Sleeping Dragon from its rare status as a sole proprietorship to a more conventional clan corporation had not been quick or easy.

The reply was muffled. "That was simple. Don't want our descendants knifing each other over portions three generations from now. But . . ." She hesitated. *"I've never been married before!"*

"Neither have I," Shyll said, resting a hand on her shoulder and drawing Rilla close. "Not even once, much less to three . . . I'm nervous too, but damned if I'm going to show it. I had my fits before I let Rilla talk me into it."

A head popped in the doorway: Sova, in her best also. "The priestess says she's ready," she said. "She means it's getting kind of cold in that thin robe and she's sixty, and she wants to get down the hill to the feast. Inu's going to start barking soon, Fishook is chewing on his ruff."

The Kommanza took a deep breath and rose. They linked hands and walked through the tent flap into the early sunlight, through the avenue of their guests, cheers and laughter. Sova walked importantly before them, and the young grass and thrown flowers were soft beneath their feet. The city was a multicolored wrinkle in the blanket of the world behind them, silver thread of the river edging it. The priestess waited in blue robes, by a table set with a loaf, salt-bowl, knife, cup.

"Gods, I could use a drink," Shkai'ra muttered without moving her lips. Megan and Rilla squeezed her hands reprovingly as a silence fell; she could hear Shyll's choke turning to a light clearing of the throat.

They halted, knelt on the spread cloth, the outer pair turning inward so that they formed a U. The priestess stood at the open end, raised her hands and faced the four corners of the world. Lined-faced, white-haired, she smiled at the two Zak, even kneeling the others were nearly as tall as she.

"Winds witness! Winds witness! Winds witness!"

A murmur of response from the onlookers. Afterward, Shkai'ra was aware mainly of fragments:

"—love in honor—"

"—all children of one blood—"

The loaf was cut and they reached together to sprinkle the salt, each taking one bite of bitter amarantha bread.

Megan: "So I swear." She reached her hand to Shkai'ra, yellow light glowing around the fingers.

Shkai'ra: "So I swear." She said and took it, reaching with her free one to Shyll.

Shyll: "So I swear." He took her hand and linked it with Rilla's, whose fingers were glowing red.

Rilla: "So I swear."

The cup passed, and the priestess upended it to show it empty. "Goddess witness!"

She handed it to Sova, who returned it to the table and knelt between them and bowed her head, flush and white succeeding themselves across the pale freckled skin. The priestess bent slightly, spoke to her:

'Sova, do you consent to be the child of these, as of their blood?"

"Yes. Oh, yes."

"Do you, in union, consent to take Sova as yours, child of the blood?"

"We do." All four of them answered.

The priestess of the Goddess stepped back, motioning them to their feet. "Then as Her witness, I call to the winds that this union is made. Give joy to Her who made it!"

The crowd's silence broke, and they rushed forward to lift the newly wedded four on their shoulders for the journey back to the city, wineskins already being passed hand to hand.

The End

Appendix I: GLOSSARY

akribhan—a Zak endearment
Almerkun—continent across the Lannic Ocean
Amam—Tor Enchian title of nobility
amaranth—type of grain, like barley
anschal—Zak, excuse me
Arko—empire west of Yeola-e
Baiwun Thunderer—a Kommanz god of war
bayag—witch/devil figure
bayishka—marriage negotiator, matchmaker
Benai Saekrberk—Abbey of Saekrberk across the river from
    Brahvniki
Benaiat—Abbot
Brahvniki—freeport on the north shore of the Svartzee
celik kiskardas—Zak, lit. "steel kin"
chiliois—one thousand strides, approx. equivalent to a kilo-
    meter
ClawPrince—merchant prince
cormorenc—spearbills, giant cormorants
cytokenska—Zak animal healer
DragonLady—the DragonLord's wife; aka the Woyvodaana
DragonLord—ruler of F'talezon; aka the Woyvode
dreamdust—Zak drug, ferociously addictive; reroutes pain
    through the pleasure centers, causes an AIDS-like break-
    down of the immune system
F'talezon—Zak capital at navigation head of Brezhan River
F'trovanemi Isle—major Zak base south of F'talezon
fatrahm—Zak, blood relation on the father's side

398

Fehinnan—the Tectate of Fehinna, a nation on the east coast of Almerkun

Fehuund—the Thanish devil

flahmbrug—Zak, volcano

forus—Brahnikian, foreigner

Fraosra—lit. siblings, brethren of the Abbey, monks

frehmat—Zak, lit. "one who is not directly related to me who I trust like kin."

gar—predatory fish of the Brezhan, averaging seven meters long

Glitch—Kommanz god of misfortune

Gods'Tears—Zak drug that causes unconsciousness

Gothumml—head god in the Thanish pantheon

graukalm—killing cold out of the steppe, the so-called grevious, or monster, wind

Haian—native of Haiu Menshir, the Healer's Isles

Halya—Zak, hell

Hoparu-ho—group of tribes living in the far east

Hriis—migratory, monotheistic desert tribe

Illizbuah—capital city of Fehinna

iron cycle—thirty days

Iyesi—first empire after the Fire

Jaiwun Allmate—a Kommanz fertility goddess

Kaila—Yeoli curved sword

Karibal—tribe living within Hanged Man's Rock

Kchnotet Vurm—"The Knotted Worm," a tavern in Brahvniki

kh'eeredo—a Kommanz endearment

Khyd-hird—Kommanz, teacher, guru

kraumak—glowing stone created by Zak magic, used in locations where torches are dangerous

Kreml, The—keep in the center of Bravniki

Leyshi—Aenir horse goddess

manraug—Zak magical energy

Mar—Tor Enchian, mother

Mitvald Zee—Zak name for greater ocean, of which Svartzee is a part

Mogh-iur—tributary kingdom of Arko, near the Moryavska tribe

Moryavska—tribe north of Arko

Nardimoot—annual meeting of the Praetranu where public debate is allowed

naZak—lit. not Zak, foreigner

night-siren—genetically engineered plant, considered dangerous

Oestschpaz—tributary west of the Brezhan

patrischana—Zak, father's sister's child

poivrkin—Zak, fishhook

Praetanu—council of ClawPrinces in Brahvniki

Raku—wandering desert tribe

Rand—native of the Kingdom of Rand

rokatzk—Zak curse

Schvait—a northern federation of kingdoms

Shamballah—bright, stationary star visible in the northern hemisphere; also, Zak name for paradise

shirrush-lau—dragon-like creatures, carnivores

Slaf Hikarme—(House of the) Sleeping Dragon

Stroemfiar—clan of barge owners on the lower Brezhan

Svartzee—so called for the dark-blue color of the water

Tchernebog—Aenir, hell

Teik—honorific, medium rank, equivalent of "sir" for both male and female

teRyadn—agricultural people of the Steppe

Vechaslaf River—large river joining the Brezhan at Aenir'sford

vetri—Zak, winter

Vra—monk

vryka—Zak, grey wolf

wayang—shadow puppet theater

yangbohtgh—Zak, young squire

Yeola-e—nation southwest of Brahvniki

Zak—the witch-folk

Zar—title of the Benai of Saekrberk

Zibr—southeastern steppe country

Zingas—Zak title, equivalent of Lord or Lady

ZingasSmiurg—DragonLady, aka Woyvodaana

Zinghut Muth'a—Kommanza name for death, lit. "The Black Crone"

zoweitzum—Kommanz curse

zteafakaz—Kommanz curse

Appendix II: CREW LIST

Crew of the *Zingas Vryka* (*Lady Grey Wolf*)

Rilla Shadows'Shade—Captain
Annike—second mate
Ochen—ship's carpenter
Temuchin—bosun
Dannake—supercargo
Iczak—ship's healer
Shenka and Jakov—Inu's attendants
Piashk—able crew
Yahn—able crew
Boryis—able crew
Deigjuburg—a Moryavska
Moshulu—a Moryavska

Crew of the *Zingas Vetri* (*Lady Winter*)

Megan Whitlock—Captain
Piatr—cook and quartermaster
Mateus—first mate
Cerwyn—second mate
Zemelya—supercargo
Yannet—able crew
Stanver—able crew
Agniya—bosun
Ilge—able crew
Alexa—able crew

Mikail—able crew
Norvanak—able crew
Jimha—able crew
Yuri—able crew
Vodolac—able crew
Osman—able crew
Bocina—cabin-kid
Mara—able crew
Rowing Boryis—able crew
Nikola—able crew
Renar—third mate.
Yvar Monkeyfist—able crew

ELIZABETH MOON

THE DEED OF PAKSENARRION

Anne McCaffrey on Elizabeth Moon:

"She's a damn fine writer. The Deed of Paksenarrion is fascinating. I'd use her book for research if I ever need a woman warrior. I know how they train now. We need more like this."

By the Compton Crook Award winning author of the Best First Novel of the Year

Sheepfarmer's Daughter
65416-0 • 512 pages • $3.95 _____

Divided Allegiance
69786-2 • 528 pages • $3.95 _____

Oath of Gold
69798-6 • 512 pages • $3.95 _____

ENTER A NEW WORLD OF FANTASY . . .

Sometimes an author grows in stature so steadily that it seems as if he has always been a master. Such a one is David Drake, whose rise to fame has been driven equally by his archetypal creation, Colonel Alois Hammer's armored brigade of future mercenaries, and his non-series science fiction novels such as **Ranks of Bronze**, and **Fortress**.

Now Drake commences a new literary Quest, this time in the universe of fantasy. Just as he has become the acknowledged peer of such authors as Jerry Pournelle and Gordon R. Dickson in military and historically oriented science fiction, he will now take his place as a leading proponent of fantasy adventure. So enter now . . .

AUGUST 1988 65424-1 352 PP. $3.95

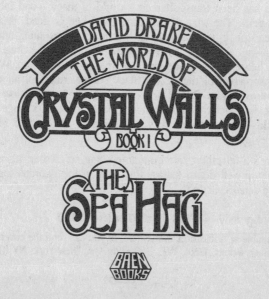

DAVID DRAKE
THE WORLD OF
CRYSTAL WALLS
BOOK 1

THE SEA HAG

BAEN BOOKS

MAGIC AND *COMPUTERS* DON'T MIX!

RICK COOK

Or . . . do they? That's what Walter "Wiz" Zumwalt is wondering. Just a short time ago, he was a master hacker in a Silicon Valley office, a very ordinary fellow in a very mundane world. But magic spells, it seems, are a lot like computer programs: they're both formulas, recipes for getting things done. Unfortunately, just like those computer programs, they can be full of bugs. Now, thanks to a *particularly* buggy spell, Wiz has been transported to a world of magic—and incredible peril. The wizard who summoned him is dead, Wiz has fallen for a red-headed witch who despises him, and no one—not the elves, not the dwarves, not even the dragons—can figure out why he's here, or what to do with him. Worse: the sorcerers of the deadly Black League, rulers of an entire continent, want Wiz dead—and he doesn't even know why! Wiz had better figure out the rules of this strange new world—and fast—or he's not going to live to see Silicon Valley again.

Here's a refreshing tale from an exciting new writer. It's also a rarity: a well drawn fantasy told with all the rigorous logic of hard science fiction.

February 1989 • 69803-6 • 320 pages • $3.50

Available at bookstores everywhere, or you can send the cover price to Baen Books, Dept. WZ, 260 Fifth Ave., New York, NY 10001.